Born For Silk

A Dark Love Story

The Cradled Common

Nicci Harris

THE CRADLE

ALSO BY NICCI HARRIS

The Kids of The District

Facing Us

Our Thing

Cosa Nostra

Her Way

His Pretty Little Burden

His Pretty Little Queen

Their Broken Legend

His Perfect Little Heirs

Black Label Nicci Harris

CurVy 13

CurVy Forever

ISBN ebook: 978-1-922492-33-3

ISBN print: 978-1-922492-34-0

Edited by Margot Swan

Internal graphics by Nicci Harris

Cover design by Nicci Harris

Map Design by Ed Napoleao

Character illustration: Athena Bliss

I COULD TOTALLY WRITE

—for the dark romance girlies who want a huge, genetically modified king with an unnaturally large...

But instead I am going to dedicate this to my husband who has supported me from the first time I hit publish in 2018, through broke times, when I was absent, when he had to pick up the slack, when it seemed I was more invested in fictional love stories than my own.

I love you, babe.

Our story is the best.

Foreword

*A thousand years of climate change, genetic engineering, and war
destroyed civilisation as it was.*

*From the remains came the age of The Trade and The Crown. In return
for resources, security, and a meaningful purpose, citizens accepted a life
of service to the new world.*

GLOSSARY

The Cradle: A dystopian land governed by a socialist-inspired regime called The Trade. It comprises of three separate land masses, Horizon, The Mainland, and Aquilla.

Horizon: The desert to the North and West of The Mainland Cradle. The Horizon has no mapped landscape. It is thought to be completely uninhabitable.

The Mainland: The largest land mass of The Cradle.

Aquilla: The island south of The Mainland Cradle.

The Strait: A hectic stretch of ocean between The Mainland Cradle and the island Aquilla.

Redwind: A thick, fierce, sand-laden gale that blasts The Cradle in its entirety. The desert soil is red in The Cradle; hence, the colour of the wind turns the atmosphere to a haze of crimson — a red wind.

Red Decline: A sweeping desert landscape situated in the centre of Aquilla. It is extremely dangerous and isolated.

The Trade: A socialist-type government that appoints Trades to citizens at birth. These Trades are, typically but not exclusively, inherited from a birth person.

Trade Man/Woman: A citizen of The Cradle who accepts a life of service to The Trade and The Cradle.

Meaningful Purpose: A spiritual state of enlightenment achieved by a Trade man or woman when they accomplish an act of service predetermined by The Trade.

Tower: A city governed by The Trade.

Ruins E, S, N: Derelict cities/towers.

The Neck: A long, narrow stretch of land that must be taken to reach the southernmost part of Aquilla.

The Estate: Situated in Aquilla. It is the most lavish Tower that houses The King and The Queen and can only be accessed by travelling The Neck.

Gene Age: A historical period characterised by the mass-genetic engineering of humankind. During this time, there was a rapid shift from a natural human conception to an engineered one. In the early years, it was to better improve physical attractiveness or dissolve undesirable traits before birth. Hundreds of years later, technology was used to progress human evolution by engineering animal traits into the human genus that would aid in surviving harsh environmental changes. From this age of engineering came two different classes of humankind—Xin De and Common.

Xin De: The genetically engineered human.

Common: A human without any obvious Xin De genus.

Gene War: The civil war between the two species of human, Xin De and Common, that eventually destroyed the old-world and civilisation as it was.

Nictitating Membrane: A third eyelid not found in Common humans. An engineered design in the Xin De genus. It is a thin membrane at the inner angle or beneath the lower lid of the eye. It can extend across the eyeball. The membrane's purpose is to clean dust and debris and is organically found in many beasts, including but not limited to, felines and birds.

Xin De Maternal Death: A death during pregnancy or birth due to the Xin De gene producing an oversized baby or incompatible DNA strain with the mother.

The King: A man born the heir to The Cradle. His duty is to support The Trade and give the citizens a figurehead leader and enforcer.

The Queen: Typically, the sister of the king. Her duty involves abstinence from intimacy and personal relations. Her role is to mother The Cradle and offer them a Goddess-like figurehead to adore and worship. Humans, by nature, seek someone to worship.

The Trade Master: A man who matches the power and influence of the king, however, he is appointed by the reigning monarch and the lords of The Cradle to uphold The Trade's Law and Traditions. He is given the key to all Trade secrets and power over the Shadows (secret agents). Once appointed, his title cannot be taken away, even as new monarchs rise.

Shadows: A Trade. A secret, elite group of individuals who are nameless and faceless assassins for The Trade.

Lords: Men who govern or manage a catchment of The Cradle within The Trade regime.

Catchment: A geographical area.

Silk Girl: A Trade. A breeding girl. A girl born of a Silk Girl with no previous miscarriages. She is protected and raised in peace and tranquillity. She is to have no negative experiences in her life in order to prevent the spread of epigenetics—generational trauma.

Silk Aviar(y(ies): A large bird enclosure made from glass that contains a boarding school for the young women Born For Silk—the Silk Girls.

Common Communit(y(ies): Minor cities for Common who do not serve The Trade and live with their own free will. With this comes minimal support or protection from The Trade, often resulting in a poor quality of life.

Endigo: A cannibalistic human-type being. Their modifications are not part of the engineered Xin De genus, but undesirable and unplanned mutations. A byproduct of hundreds of years of corrupted human genetics.

Old-world (colloquial term): The world before The Cradle and The Trade.

Rite: A Trade person's ceremony or inauguration.

The Revive: A Trade Initiative to bridge the gap between the two species of human—Xin De and Common—by breeding Common with Xin De.

Sandules: A genetically engineered powder.

First-light: An estimated period of time in the morning—the sun first lightens the hazy sky.

Crown-light: An estimated period of time at the middle of the day—the sun has the least amount of Redwind to penetrate, and its heat can be felt on the top of your head.

Last-light: An estimated period of time in the evening—the sun disappears for the night.

Missing Moon: The moon has not been seen in hundreds of years, though citizens are taught of its power and influence over the land and sea.

The Crust: Literally: the soil/dirt. Spiritually: a kind of afterlife/paradise/nirvana.

Collective: A group of individuals that work as one unit for a Trade.

Sired Mother: A Trade. Women who protect and raise The Cradle's babies. In other terms, a child-care Trade. They are retired Silk Girls who have achieved Meaningful Purpose.

Medi-deck: A small holding space where the Silk Girls get their medical scans and vitamin shots.

The Circle: A hexagonal shaped foyer with five room on each angle. One for each Silk Girl.

Aquilla Cats: A previously extinct, large cat that now runs rampant through The Cradle. It can be identified from other cats by its larger size and stripes along its back.

The Queen's Army: A group of Trade women who protect and accompany The Queen everywhere she goes.

Watcher (Born For Parchment): A Trade. A woman or man born to watch, convey, and report back to The Trade, Lord, or Warden responsible for the individual being watched.

Guardian: A Trade. A man pledged to protect a Lord.

Marshall Blue: A Trade. A public law enforcer.

Guard: A Trade. Military-trained personnel who guard, defend, and fight for The Trade.

House Girl: A Trade. A woman/girl used for entertainment and/or acts of a sexual nature.

The Common Relations Guard (CR Guard): A Trade. A Guard who follows the king on campaigns to record and relay events for the citizens of The Cradle to watch once a week on the singular scheduled hour of Trade Updates.

Windmill Farms: Windmill farms cover over 30% of the inhabitable parts of The Cradle. They are the land's primary source of energy.

Windmill Forest (colloquial term): The stretches of Windmill Farms that feel never-ending, stretching for hundreds of miles.

Black Matter Mines: A line of mines on the northern most part of The Cradle just before the Horizon where toxic minerals are excavated, and batteries are broken down and recycled.

La Mu: A genetically engineered plant that has varying medicinal purposes. The leaf: a sedative and muscle relaxant. The seeds: a powerful contraceptive. The root: in small doses, acts as an anti-inflammatory, but in larger doses is highly lethal.

Opi (colloquial term) Opi Lava: can be applied topically or taken orally. A genetically modified version of the old-world opioid—morphine—used for extreme pain and as a mild sedative.

The Trade Connect Building: A building in every tower that has a network of underground copper lines for communication across The Cradle. It's use is centralised and controlled entirely by The Trade.

Modistes Girl: A Trade. A girl responsible for designing, creating, and fitting apparel.

HORIZON HORIZON

HORIZON

HORIZON

...MINES......

RUINS H

BLACK
MATTER
TOWER

MINES

MINES

UPPER
TOWER
LOWER M

SICK AVIARY

THE STRAIT

COMMON R

THE BITE

SEE AQUILLA MAP 2

HALF-TOWER

THE KING'S SEA

THE CRADLE

The Cradle map —56 The Mainland, Horizon, Aquilla.
Southern Hemisphere.
Ocean: The Strait, The Kings Sea.

M. catro

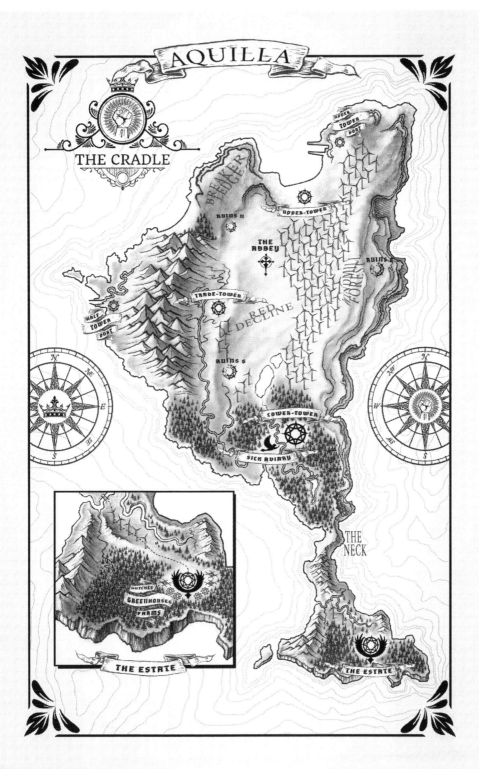

PART ONE
TO BE A KING

CHAPTER ONE

ROME

Aged Eighteen

Vows of a king:
    To be a king is to master one's passions and rule with the sole purpose of uniting The Cradle. Each new citizen needs the opportunity to have a Meaningful Purpose.

A Common Community.

That's the first one I have ever seen.

Pressing my eye to the periscope in the king's military tank, I watch as the fractured abbey emerges like a wraith through the red haze.

Nature throws her fierce body around the looming old-world compound, but it withstands the Redwind and sand.

It is indestructible.

Just like me.

We plough across the Red Decline toward the isolated community, tank tracks chewing the unsealed road, machinery humming, gunner braced and ready.

My pulse hammers.

Hundreds of tiny Common men and women flock to the tower edges, arms shielding their eyes from the wind that lashes like exploding glass.

The gate to their desert community opens, dragging along sand and debris.

The tank presses in through twin stone walls, and I wait for collision, but the driver is masterful at his Trade.

We pass through unscathed.

"Rome." Turin's voice booms in my ears with even his whispers.

I lift my head, painfully aware of my thunderous pulse, and align myself with the clarity inside this metal fortress. My eyes meet Turin; attention is my response.

"Not a word," is all he says.

I clench my teeth, caging hundreds of objections. Words won't make him treat me like his heir, like a man. Like a king.

As he moves toward the front of the vehicle, his bulk brushes the metal edges. Our container is cramped, but he is *enormous*. Thick across the shoulders, long arms, and hands the size of a Common human's head.

He is a monster.

And I will be, too.

Soon.

I am not a child.

My Guardian, Kong, watches me with amusement as my mind reels, the words hanging on my tongue but flaring in my eyes.

I crack my neck from side to side. I want to make decisions. I am ready. Ready to be the successor in The Cradle.

What I was born for, built for.

"I know that look. You're only eighteen. What would you have to say to the Common anyway?" Kong asks, reading me.

I look at him. "Eighteen is a man."

"No." He shakes his head against a single laugh. "Your father is ninety-three and still has the appearance of a fifty-year-old. That's pure Xin De genetics. You are no man. That is a man."

Disdain climbs into my voice. "I know his age."

He nods toward Turin—my father. "Look at him, boy."

Boy... My lips curl into a snarl. He is the only being I can stand calling me that.

"Why?" I argue. He is also the only one I argue with because our respect is mutual.

Despite my age, he listens to me.

"Because"—he moves closer, care for my wellbeing unhidden in his frustration— "it's my damn job to keep you alive. And it's not the fucking Common or Endigos that will get you killed. It'll be at the hands of your own father if you let that slip through your mouth."

I lift a brow. "Let what through?"

"What you're thinking. I would die for you, boy. I would fight your father for you. Have him rip my head straight off my shoulders. Don't put me in that position. Your father might be one of the last pure Xin De before The Trade introduced The Revive. Your mother was only half. You won't be as massive as him."

I frown at Kong. "I'll be bigger than him."

"Do you have the prince?" A Guard calls from the front where four others prepare—pulling on leather armour and loading their automatic rifles—to exit through the hatches as the vehicle chews along the dirt floor, slowing and easing into place.

"My mother is two-thirds Xin De," I whisper as the Guards bustle ahead of us, heated conversations and readiness in the air. "Turin saw to it. He told me he wouldn't allow The Trade to mix my blood too much."

Kong folds his thick arms over his chest. "Still not pure, boy."

Fucker.

Sneering, I look through the scope.

The Common duck from the giant tank tracks. Murmuring

their awe, they circle the two colossal military vehicles, creating a crowd around them. They gape, their eyes the size of saucers set into semi-translucent flesh, blue veins snaking beneath pale skin.

Common men and women have always reminded me of fish. *I wonder what their skin feels like. Soft? Hot or cold? Or both? So fragile the world dictates the temperature?*

Nothing like mine; my skin is always warm, engineered for the world. A thick sheath with compact molecules to combat the wind, endure the heat, deter the cold, block the sand—survive. My skin is designed to *survive.*

I glance at Kong. He grins at me, before fisting my leather chest plates, reminding me I need them even with my engineered genes. People want me dead, and a bullet will still pierce my skin.

"Do I?" he asks. "Do I have the prince?"

I relent. "My mouth is sealed."

"Will you keep it that way?"

"Ready," a Guard calls, and the rest hustle through the hatches. They quickly create a protective ring around Turin as he climbs into view.

I listen. Even from in here, I swear I hear the entire community gasp. Kong is right—Turin is a single-man army. Designed for battle. A warlord.

Twenty bullets already float deep within his tissue, and he is twenty-five percent metal after several wars and surgical enhancements.

I begin climbing from the tank, watching the interaction outside as I go.

"Bless you." A tiny Common man steps forward to shake Turin's hand, finding his own disappear into the massive mitt. He tries to steel himself, but Turin of The Strait shadows him.

He visibly trembles, dried blood on his forehead cutting through caked dirt and sweat.

The pulse in my throat builds to a beat between my ears. *Is it excitement?*

No. As my feet hit the dirt and all eyes land on *the prince* for the first time, it becomes clear-as fucking crown-light that my charged heart has nothing to do with excitement.

I am *nervous* to disappoint *him.*

Him. My father—Turin.

The man is basically a stranger, and until a few days ago, I wasn't even certain I was his heir… Though, I had my suspicions. I am bigger than the others born from his Collective. I am stronger, and the eagles like me more. I felt his blood inside me but had to wait. Anonymity is sacred until the heir turns eighteen. Old enough to defend himself—myself. Then, the great reveal. That is now—this day, *this campaign.*

I walk to stand beside him, and Kong halts at my left flank— my shadow and shield.

The wind is trapped outside the abbey fortress, but it creeps the perimeter walls, whistling and warning us. It is still there.

"We are indebted that you came," the Common man says, stepping backward once, craning his neck to peer up at his towering Xin De King. "I am Colt."

"We do what we can," Turin states, apathetic, his voice a thundering note capable of trembling rocks below his feet.

I envy him.

He is without emotion.

Will I ever be like that?

As if to answer me, the vision of my sweet sister flashes in my mind, and I feel *everything.*

Cairo, The Trade Master, approaches from the rear vehicle— never sit the king and The Trade Master in the same tank. At least one must survive an attack. I know this from my studies.

He takes his position at my father's right hand. "How many Endigos came through?" he asks, dropping his cloak to his shoulders, displaying flawless, unscathed features. A manicured beard and neat, short, dark hair—the man is pretty.

Too pretty.

I glare at him.

It's almost an insult to a war-stricken land. He's never seen a battlefield, but spurs hundreds of men onto them. He must be in his thirties but appears only slightly older than me—his Xin De Genus is strong.

But so is mine.

Colt takes a large breath. "Fifty. Maybe."

"Armed?" Cairo asks.

Colt nods stiffly, a sad memory glossing his eyes. "Yes. They scaled the walls. Opened the gates from the inside. We lost men and women—" He swallows over a lump. "My wife. That is, the mother of my children."

"We know what a wife is," Cairo offers. "We are not ignorant of the old-world *traditions*."

"Marriage is part of our religion," Colt says, then presses on. "They took supplies. They stayed all night. They raped our women. Made us watch. They gutted our priest and cooked his intestines on that fire." His voice breaks. "They feasted on him."

Turning his gaze to the compound surroundings, Turin seems to analyse the raid.

I follow his line of sight.

To the right, a smoking fire hisses of the cannibalistic event. Across the square, rugs outside each door are stained with splashes of blood, a pattern that comes from energetic hacking and slicing.

The men and women look exhausted.

Dirty and bloody.

My mind reaches and imagines—women and men being dragged from their homes last night. Raped. Murdered. Their screams touched the walls, the haunting energy still clawing at the brickwork as we stand here.

A growl sits in my chest.

I'm not sure how I feel at this moment. Not remorse for Common I don't know. The only truth that flows like molten steel through me is Tuscany, my sister, will never leave The Estate. I will lock her in my wing when I'm The Cradle's Monarch and

Protector if it means sheltering her from all this… This Common savagery.

"They destroyed the mill." Colt's voice cuts into my thoughts. Clearing his throat, he appears on the brink of tears.

He wipes his face.

Tries to stifle his emotions.

"That was the only one we had," he manages to say. "It powered the entire community."

"You operate outside The Trade," Cairo points out. "You know this is a choice. Your lifestyle here is your choice. The isolation is your choice."

"Freedom is our choice," a man from the community calls from inside the sea of small, exhausted Common.

In The Estate, that is treason.

Darting my eyes between the crowd and Turin, I wait for his reaction. For retribution. I want to see how Turin manages The Greater Cradle.

But no consequence comes.

He is unmoved—almost robotic.

"*Yes,*" Cairo finally addresses the phantom voice. "And this is what you get for your freedom. Lucky for you, we are not so selfish."

"He understands," Turin states, back to business. "What else should we know? Can you describe the Endigos?"

Colt shuffles. "It was dark. They wore hoods. They kidnapped ten women. Two men." Suddenly, his eyes veer around as he notices several of our Guards fielding out into the compound, some carrying equipment and others checking the Common over for wounds. "W- what are they doing?"

"Doctors. Nurses." Cairo gestures toward a man with a crew following him, all heaving pieces of machinery. "This man works for the Windmill Trade. He is the best we have. He will build you a new mill, and these men will help repair your homes and treat your wounded. They are all healthy Trade men. You'll feed them.

You'll do as they ask. You'll respect them. *They* have Meaningful Purpose."

Colt squeezes his eyes shut, regret weighing them down. "I understand." With a sigh, he looks at Turin. "Thank you, my king. Thank you."

"*Sire*," Turin corrects.

"The invitation is open to your young." Cairo clasps his fingers together in front of his long purple tunic. "Children under five are acceptable," he says in a drone, almost bored voice. "Any older, and it's problematic. The need for Meaningful Purpose should start in the womb, you see." He nods in the direction of the rebellious voice from earlier. "Or radical perspectives fester. Weeds knit together."

"The women that were taken..." A young girl steps forward, hesitant but brave. She is younger than me. Pale, but pretty, and when she sees me, she blushes, a scarlet hue touching each cheek.

I fight a grin.

I wonder if she'll pinken all the way down to her slim thighs if I approach her. Had my fair share of Xin De girls, but never fucked a Common girl with rosy cheeks.

"They left babies," she continues, despite the heat from my gaze.

Kong mutters to my side, "You're too damn handsome, Rome."

"You're not my type," I offer in jest.

Turin looks down on her, and her blush sinks to a fearful white. "And you want me to take them?" he asks pointedly.

"Sire." She bows, collecting her thoughts, before returning her gaze. "For a better life?" She breathes, uncertain, looking at Colt, pleading through a shaking voice.

"A *meaningful* one," Cairo corrects.

"Yes. And comfort and food. Shelter. *Protection*. Not like this..." The young girl turns, gesturing to the faces of the Common who outwardly despise The Trade, who refuse our system. Who want to live in their own communities. "*Please*. I do not think we can care for orphans."

Cairo smiles, but it is snake-like. Wider than needed, with no alliance from his eyes. "Each and every Trade citizen is protected."

"My sweet Odette." Colt, her father, touches a small bruise marring her jaw, and she closes her eyes on a deep sigh filled with meaning.

"You won't take any of the older girls?" Colt finally asks turning back to us. The traumatic night of carnage creates an obvious desperation in him. One that goes against his own beliefs. "We have two boys and three girls under twelve—"

"We cannot," Cairo dismisses.

Ahead of me, there is suddenly movement and murmurs, the dishevelled Common parting to allow four young girls through. Small, slim, wiry girls. Vulnerable as they already are, they also carry babies, two each, one in each arm.

Seven Guards set their weapons down, ammunition rattling and clinking, metal on metal. The unnerving sound widens the girls' eyes and slows their small feet.

"Give the babes to the Guards," Cairo orders with an unaffected tone that pacifies others but bothers me.

Sobs dissect the air, the women protesting this exchange. Each babe begins to mewl as they are given to the huge Xin De Guards. Direct and businesslike, the men scan the babes for sickness, running a warm laser across each plump cheek.

The babes cry louder.

"Wha- What is that?" Colt stares, eyes widening. It is likely he has never seen this level of technology before.

"It doesn't hurt," a Guard confirms.

"Anything we should know?" Turin asks, and I hear indifferent due-diligence in his tone.

Defeated, Colt shakes his head. "Thank you for taking them, Sire. We cannot care for them."

An assembly line of Guards passes the infants along and up the tank before handing them through the hatch. The sound of mewling disappears within the metal fortress, but the moment of quiet soon twists into wails and sobs from the watching Common girls.

"We are lucky," Colt says to his people. "They will be safe. We cannot care for them here. Can you? No. Settle yourselves down now."

"There is no *God* across The Strait," Odette says. "She will need me. Can I go with them? Protect my sister."

"They do not believe. And will not allow you to practise." Her father holds her hands between them as the last infant is loaded into the tank.

"Well then." Odette turns to Turin. "Sire, you must know the little black-haired one is allergic to Opi Latex. She is my baby sister."

"That is a genetic burden." Cairo looks the girl up and down as if she is to blame. "A weak woman produces a weak child."

Lifting her chin, she says, "She is strong in all other ways. She fought through a fever without intervention. Strong things survive because they are strong. Fragile things survive despite it."

Turin almost smiles at her. "Very well."

"You will look after her." Her eyes hit mine like a hammer to a skull, and I frown. She asked me—directly. I should say no; it doesn't concern me, but I don't. I want to be their saviour—*her* saviour.

The Cradle's Monarch and Protector.

And the teenage boy in me is idiotically envisioning the rosy skin between her thighs. To see if she feels the same as a Xin De girl. Her eyes are so... telling. Watery. Red. Wide. *Vulnerable.* I want to see them pop open when I sink inside her.

"I will," I say like a fool, and the silence that precedes could shatter glass.

Kong clears his throat behind me.

I feel Cairo's eyes slicing parts of my flesh from bone, but I gaze straight at *Odette*—such a Common name.

She interests me.

What could this God have over her... This fairytale that some

Common still cling to. Didn't we prove there is no God when we altered his apparent creations? When we enhanced and fast-tracked evolution with genetic engineering? We changed the entire damn homosapien species as it was, improved it, and birthed the genus Xin De.

Ignorant Common.

She looks at her father again. "God is in her heart, Daddy." Her violet eyes well up. It is weak, but endearing, nonetheless. "That will not change."

~

Further discussions fill the air between our circle, but I am not listening anymore.

Less than an hour passes, and we are once again on the road, parting the chaotic wind, tank tracks grinding southwards down the Red Decline.

Sitting back in the tank, my skin prickles against the corruption in the air.

We offered the Common community Trade men and supplies for the coming months. The aid, exchange, supplies... It seems all too philanthropic to me. Not the image of Turin I've had all these years growing up.

Then again, he gains a far superior prize for his visit to the raided community—fresh-faced babies for The Trade.

We are travelling through last-light toward The Neck when the tank stops abruptly—again.

Frowning, I peer through the periscope, the infrared light activating against the dim, to find we have parked within the skeletons of a city from long ago—Ruins S, I would wager. The echoes of civilisation fade into the desert winds.

Across from us is a once-white truck adorned with scars, windows painted with messy black strokes, and a bonnet showcasing a grill not unlike the mouth of a rabid dog. A true manifestation of the life lived in the desert.

13

"The fuck are we doing here?" I ask as Turin readies himself to climb through the hatch. I don't know why I ask. I don't expect an answer, so I press my eyes to the scope and search the outside, right and then left.

We are alone.

Can't see the other tank.

Then I see *them.*

Movement through the Redwind catches my eye. I feel the unsettling crawl of eyes before I make out the shady figures of hooded men as they appear from behind the truck. Their bodies part the thick sand-filled air, wind waving their cloaks.

Endigos.

If Xin De became part beast during the Gene Age, then Endigos are the vultures. They'll feed on anything without remorse. Teeth thin and flexible for filleting, and nails long and sheer, but there isn't a great deal to feast on out here—except Common.

Turin approaches the truck, and one of the Endigos flings back the canopy, exposing the tray, the wind aiding, blasting the fabric backward.

On the metal bed, bodies are stacked in careless piles. I squint at the bloody mounds. Slim torsos. Short legs. A small arm swings free, flapping in the wind by the tyre. A female arm. Branded on her wrist is a purple flower-womb sigil.

A Silk Girl...

Turin leans over the tray, inspecting the bodies. Uncertainty builds inside my gut, too many questions firing at once, churning my blood.

Why is the king meeting with Endigos?

To what end?

Turin finally notices the woman at the bottom of the heavy stack of flesh and reaches for her arm. He inspects the tattoo. Showing no sign of emotion, as is the way of a king, he drops the arm and returns to the tank.

I frown at the truck.

"Boy?" Kong's tone is deep with warning.

I sit back and stare blankly at him. "We knew about the raid." My mind swims with thoughts. "Maybe even organised it. For her? Who was she?" It is a statement, but still implores an answer.

He deadpans. "I don't get involved."

"Or was it for the babies?"

"I don't get involved in politics, boy. You'll know soon enough, I am sure. Your father wanted you to see or else you wouldn't be here. Must admit, one hell of a lesson for your first campaign as the heir."

Chapter Two

Vows of a king:

To be a king is to suffer alone under the burden of decisions and the weight of necessary evils and truths.

To enter The Estate, we travel the length of The Neck, a windy, thin stretch of land flanked by cliffs and lapped by rough seas.

It is the only way in and out. For this reason, The Estate is the safest place in The Cradle.

The tank roars forward between soaring limestone walls. Hundreds of Common and Xin De are on the streets today to mark my arrival, but more likely to celebrate my sister. It is not just my reveal as the heir—my little sister is taking her place as the future Queen of The Cradle.

Trade residents crowd the entrance. Large Martials monitor the gathering; Common men and women from other Trades dress in their most elegant clothes, eager to shake Tuscany's hand; small boys blush at her beauty; tiny girls raise flowers in offering to their queen; men enjoy a day off from their Purpose; women smile.

I grow bored of looking at them, too many to take in, so I slump back into the tank as we stop at the foot of the stairwell to the piazza.

I climb out, overdue for a moment of sanctuary and truth, alone with my sister. I smile when I see her.

Tuscany is standing on the stone steps in a white gown. Stunning. Skin like mine, tanned, but unlike mine, hers is flawless and smooth. And her hair, only a few shades darker than her skin, falls over her chest and to the dip at her back.

She looks like a goddess.

In this moment, I understand. Understand why the Common and Xin De alike will fall in love with her. The idea of her is a conditioned response. Someone to worship. She is their future mother. The mother of The Cradle. Pure. Elegant. Feminine. It's a spectacle they willingly soak in.

I frown and turn to watch the Guards, the Xin De men, and the crowds of Common also staring. My muscles twitch. I don't care for the kind of attention she has—she is only ten.

They look at her as though they— The Cradle and all its people—own her. All of her.

All the parts inside and out.

Trying to hide the darkness stirring in my stomach, I walk to my sister and see her face light up as it always does whenever she notices me.

Her smile helps…

"Rome!" She darts down the steps to greet me, her hair is a pretty golden-brown river trailing behind her. She is sheer sunlight in this hazy land.

We knew we were related before they told us. Tuscany bothered me all through my childhood. Only a sister could be that annoying and adorable at once. And, of course, the eagles like her as much as I do, although everyone likes Tuscany.

The product of a Common Silk Girl, my half-sister is tiny and sweet to behold. I suspect she was chosen from my other siblings to be queen due to her relatable physique—so the Common will find comfort in her.

Fear in me.

Comfort in her.

The king and queen.

"It's only been a week," I dismiss, while every part of me softens to not cut her purity to pieces. Even at this age, I feel hard and sharp, like a well-carved blade. Not gentle, not kind, like her.

"And you have been with Turin. I knew you were my brother. I knew it all along." She wraps her arms around my middle, and we walk half-embraced up the steps. "Will you tell me everything you saw? The Red Decline. The dessert. The mill farms. Oh, how I dream of seeing the endless forest of sky-scraping windmills."

I nod curtly.

I am not ready to lie.

I feel Turin and the Guards close behind me. Cairo, too. Their presence is a torch at my back, the heat forcing my arms to tighten around my sister for reasons I can't explain.

In the piazza, we are welcomed by Turin's Collective and their Common. Women flock to see Tuscany, praising her beauty and offering her sacred heirlooms—gifts, flowers, and fine jewellery.

Children cuddle her legs.

I step aside and watch her bathe in the fuss and adoration. She deserved it. I want it for her. She vows to love The Cradle, to lay with no man and to bear no children so no individual is ever favoured by her. For this, she deserves the adoration for the life-long sacrifice she will make for her Meaningful Purpose.

I watch on as a woman gifts her a ghastly diamond ring. But Tuscany wears a face of pure appreciation and takes it, sliding it on her finger as if she cannot wait to display it. "Thank you. Yes, I will wear it for you."

I laugh, and she flicks me a playful frown that warms my cruel heart. I am smiling at her. I only smile for her; she is the only person I love.

She seems to have fun.

What young girl wouldn't have?

I try to relax, but a haunting presence stirs around me.

On the far side of the piazza, eating from the banquet table, are six of the fourteen born from Turin's Collective in the same decade as me; boys who want to be the heir, and the girls who dream of being queen.

Only now do they know who they bow to. The Cradle will be mine *one day.* And I will choose my Collective, the lords who govern The Trade lands, from them.

I already know who I will choose: Bled, Darwin, Medan, and my half-brother Turin Two. The rest will be given Meaningful Purpose as lords and ladies in minor towers across The Mainland if they are deemed worthy. Or sent to warden other Trades, if they are not. If they irritate me.

But Tuscany, she will be queen soon.

She is a mere ten years old but Turin's sister—the late queen—died this past summer. Everyone has been waiting for a new goddess to worship.

And worship her they will.

"She'll need you," Kong says, joining my side and standing to watch the exuberant scene as I am. I don't know what he means. She will always have me.

His words unsettle me.

I turn from my sister, but he is walking away, past a Common girl with her face painted in all gold, disappearing between double doors toward his wing.

As we move through the night, the Missing Moon surely perched high, my sister grows lethargic from canapes—sweets with every kind of chocolate imaginable.

I grow bored of all but her.

Yet, I let her have her moment.

She appears at my side, a smear of brown on her lip and a half-eaten truffle waving in her hand. My sister is high on sugar. "When I am queen," she laughs, "I am going to travel to every

Common community in The Cradle and give them all chocolates. I hear they don't get to eat chocolate."

She is endlessly sweet.

Naïve. Innocent. Trusting...

I lift my hand and wipe the truffle from her lip, half smiling, faking bemusement. "You will never visit a Common community when I am king, Tuscany. They are far too wild and savage for you, sweet sister. Besides, I think chocolate is the last thing on their minds."

She looks at the treat in her hand. "That's so sad."

Dammit, I am a bastard.

"You will do great things. You will have your Meaningful Purpose and mother The Cradle like no queen ever has. I am sure," I offer.

She brightens. "Will you walk me to my room, dear brother?" She spins and dances toward her chamber. I slowly follow. "I am so full now, and it's nearly time for my rite. My last night as just me. I think I take vows or something. I hope whatever it is involves rubbing my feet while I have a huge sugar crash and fall asleep like a big, overfed house cat." She giggles, glancing over her shoulder at me.

I can't quell my smile.

We reach her door. "I'm going in now. Do you think something weird will happen? Like chanting and candles. I hope I don't laugh and give myself away."

I tap her nose. "I hope you do."

The large oak door opens at her back. I survey the plush room, finding candles glowing on the sills and a marble table with ointments and towels. There are two women in white and coral colours—Trade Nurses. And—

I frown, my fists curling in tight at my sides, when Cairo appears from the corner of the room, his fingers making a pyramid at his waist.

My pulse thrashes.

He smiles at Tuscany. "I do hope you enjoyed yourself tonight," he says. "You must be elated. You're so close to Meaningful Purpose, my princess."

"What is this?" I ask, nodding at the room, the candles, the ointment, the women. *And you!*

Why are you in my sister's room?

"Rome." He offers me his attention. "I was checking to ensure everything is prepared for her and up to my standards. I will take my leave now. You both need to sleep."

He strides toward me, but I refuse to budge, forcing him to fit through the space between my shoulder and the door frame. He does and says nothing.

It feels very wrong.

I glare at Cairo's back, scorching him, wanting answers to my suspicious mind. My guts twist and turn as he walks down the hall.

Tuscany's finger touches my frown, smoothing the crease. "Go to bed, Rome. I think you need rest as much as I." I return my gaze to her, a place it likes to be. "Come to me in the first-light. Early? As soon as the fire turns orange. I will tell you about the chanting and foot massages, and you can tell me about The Cradle. Deal?"

I sigh. "Deal."

Doing a little dance in place, she closes the door. I hover outside for a moment, feet not wanting to move.

Noise from Turin's Collective and guests still whistles through the hallway. Their gathering, the drinking and feasting, continues.

Staring at the door, I shake the discomfort away. Tension pours through my veins as I turn to leave, the weight of my first campaign stacking rocks on my shoulders.

What would have happened if Tuscany saw the outskirts of The Cradle today? The babies being taken and the dead woman with the Silk Girl tattoo? What if she smelt the cooked flesh in the old abbey and felt the phantom of carnage still crawling along the walls after the raid?

I can't allow her to see the truth.

I storm into my room, reeling over the message. The lesson

from Turin. To be the king means keeping secrets from the one person I love. To keep her pure and innocent means my emotional isolation.

And that is Turin's first lesson.

I lie down and look at the ceiling. Glare.

I spend the night memorising it, unable to sleep and less able to relax. Eighteen, and I feel the weight of a hundred tonight.

I toss and turn.

My body suffers, open and raw, like holding the truth inside is akin to capturing a wild animal within me. It shreds at its enclosure.

It burns and rips.

I don't know when it happens, but first-light crawls along the floor and up the walls. It is barely time to rise, and my eyes have had no rest, but I stand, pull my pants on, throw a robe around my shoulders, and wander down the dim hallway.

Paranoia twists inside me.

At the end of the long passage, I see my sister's door is open. The artificial light from inside shines, making shapes on the dark hallway wall opposite. Suddenly, a shadow blocks the light. Turin leaves the room with a glass vase in his hand, and I- I-

I stop in my tracks. My muscles refuse to move, not an inch, too tight like a coiled band.

Then they snap.

I take off down the hall.

Something is wrong.

I need to get to her.

Two Guards attempt to slow me, stepping in my path. "My prince, wai—"

I throw them both into the walls, crack the age-old brick under the force, and knock them both out cold.

Dead, maybe.

I don't care.

I round her bedroom door and enter her room. The light hits me in harsh brilliance.

I scan the space as though possessed; the bed is empty, sheets bunched; a woman in the corner stuffs bloody rags into a purple canvas bag; the washroom is illuminated by a glowing gap bordering the door.

What have they done?

Letting my rage burn through me, I stride toward the door against the tension of shuddering limbs. I reach for the handle and pull it open.

Then I see her.

My sweet sister is naked, being helped by two women into her claw-footed bathtub. Her slim legs tremble to hold her weight, her skin is pale and clammy, a blood-filled drain skewers her stomach, and crimson fluid seeps through a white adhesive bandage at her lower abdomen.

She gazes up at me, all sunshine gone from her eyes. "They took it all." Her voice breaks. "All the parts I won't need now that I am to be Queen of The Cradle."

PART TWO
WELCOME TO THE CRADLE

CHAPTER ONE

Aster

Nineteen Years Later

Buzzing fills the air, the electric notes twisting my spine tight.

This is a big day.

The *biggest*, actually.

Through the cracked window to the tower promenade, men and women brave the red gale to watch. Their grasping eyes move from girl to girl, keen to witness the ceremonial moment take place.

"I'm so proud of all my girls," the Silk Wardeness says, circling us slowly. "You have studied hard and shown true dedication. This mark will seal your Trade. Meaningful Purpose"—she smiles— "is in your future."

The girls squeal once.

I drop my gaze to my worn hide boots and the seam of my mauve dress, avoiding the sight of Iris's arm laying perfectly still for the tattoo gun.

I don't hear her respond to the needles' penetration, but I know they are in her flesh as the buzzing tones deepen.

Behind me, the other girls shuffle in line, anticipation crawling inside their feet. They hide excited chatter in their breath. I, on the other hand, am wary of the pain.

The wind outside the parlour suddenly howls. A moment later, Iris lifts her slim arm to display the brand. She smiles with pride.

"It's official," she breathes in awe. Her green eyes land on me, cruel in an instant. "But not even a brand will make you any more than Fur Born," she says with a snarl.

I clench my teeth and hold her sharp gaze as she saunters to join the line with the other marked girls.

"Next," the tattoo man calls, and a girl behind me bumps me forward.

Time slows.

The gap between me and the buzzing is empty, ready to be filled. The gun is suddenly louder. The man's patience wanes as he stares at me. The girls' shuffling is riotous in my ears, though I am quite certain they are not moving at all.

I am the one moving.

Carelessly, my heels slide backward, recoiling from the tattoo gun when a monstrous form eclipses me, and two huge hands grip my shoulders.

Someone holds me in line.

Someone enormous.

A gasp, a pin drops. Now there is no noise at all, and I wonder where all the breathing has gone… It's too still.

The man with the tattoo gun is staring above my head at the towering figure behind me. His startled expression snaps to submission, and he bows his chin.

It can't be…

As a statue held captive in big hands, I twist my chin and peer up. Up. Up.

To his face.

His face.

Even with his cloak pulled up and shadows dancing the outline of his strong brow, I recognise him. I'd know his face through the dense Redwind.

He is stunning.

His face is a masterpiece. Chiselled yet smooth. Square jawline. Scars that only enhance his virile features. Blue eyes that glow as he stares intensely down on me, penetrating my soul. The colour blue should be peaceful, *calm*, but his eyes are anything but.

They whisper of cruelty.

They demand obedience.

My king.

I turn in his grip.

Everyone in the parlour drops to their knees, but I remain standing, unable to bow with his massive hands wrapped so powerfully around my upper arms.

"My king," I offer, lowering my gaze.

"Why do you hesitate?" he asks, his voice a deep timbre that presses on my chest, making my lungs and heart strain to work.

"I—" I stammer and force my eyes to hold the ground respectfully. *Hesitate? To get the tattoo? To bow? To speak? What?*

I cannot answer.

"Don't you want my mark?"

I blink my confusion, blood draining from my cheeks. *Of course, I want his mark.*

And finally, I look up at him.

This cannot be real.

I've seen him on the big screen in the Silk Aviary—the one for Trade Updates. At least once a month, they show moving pictures of him on campaigns in The Cradle, visiting Trade men at the windmill farms, or shaking hands with lords from Trade towers.

This is *so* much better.

Seeing him in the flesh. Smelling him.

Stunned, I nod my head. "Yes, of course."

His gaze holds me arrested. "Then"—he stretches the word with no mirth— "why hesitate, little creature?"

29

I swallow the lump in my throat. "It'll hurt."

"Have you not been given any Opi?"

It is like the others in the room have faded away, leaving only him and me. Captured in a time apart from all others.

"The others have applied it topically, but— But I'm allergic," I say softly.

His brows draw in as though he is recalling a painful moment or reliving a feeling, then— "I see," he states, calm resurfacing. "Hereditary, I imagine. From your mother's side?"

"I'm sorry."

"Your name?"

I look at his hands, still warming my arms. *Why are they still there? I like it. But why?*

"Aster." I breathe. "Like a flower." I look up at him again. "We are all just flowers, not like you, my king. You're a city from the old-world. Everyone important is named after a city from the old-world."

I don't know why I said that.

He doesn't need a history lesson.

My head feels as if I inhaled a cloud and now my thoughts are surrounded by white and confusion.

"Just a little flower?" He frowns, the question so curt it stirs the energy around us.

I simply nod, enraptured. "Yes."

His palms slide down the length of my arms, leaving one to circle the column of my wrist. He could squeeze it to dust, his grip so encompassing.

"Would you like me to hold your hand, little Silk Girl?"

I think I nod.

The next few moments I meander through in a dream state. He presses my wrist to the tattoo table, and I anchor myself to his gaze—almost feline. Lots of Xin De have glowing irises.

Unbinding my wrist from his grip, he moves his hand to blanket mine, pinning me to the counter.

"Gentle with my property or you'll discover the true meaning of pain," he orders the man, though his eyes haven't wavered from me.

He holds my hand.

I hold my breath.

Heat from his palm radiates into my skin.

The buzzing starts, his eyes anchor me, pain from the needle fires, dark intent rolls through his gaze, and I practically moan against my conflicting senses. Warm discomfort pools in my bellybutton. Blue eyes pierce through me to my bones deeper than any needle.

Everything is hot.

Painful and pleasant.

And his eyes.

Oh my, his eyes.

"It's all over now," he states smoothly, releasing my hand, a cool absence sweeping across the grieving flesh.

I blink up at him, the loud fantasy of him and me and whatever strange painful, pleasure that was slips away.

Heat flares through my wrist, so I look down to see the tattoo's burning presence. It is pretty. A purple womb created from flowers and stems. The same smile I saw on Iris's face slides across my lips.

I am officially a Silk Girl.

Too soon, he is striding away. I am flooded with desperation that I'll never see him again, that he'll forget about me, that Iris and the girls are right about me being Fur Born, so I reach for him before I can think.

Gasps expel.

Eyes widen.

My fingers clutch at a piece of his velvety shroud.

"Take me with you, my king." The words tumbling from my lips like apples from a barrel.

Shit.

He turns, a creature more predator than man, but his

expression becomes one of amusement. I'm not sure I like it. It's playful in the way an eagle might play with a mouse.

Looking down at my small hand, clinging to the fibres of his jacket, he says, "Not today."

"I'm ready," I blurt out, ignoring the girls who gape and the Silk Wardeness who shakes her head, scolding me silently. She doesn't dare speak in his presence. It's a vow. *Speak only when spoken to. Never touch the king without permission...*

Yet here I am...

He studies me, dark eyes drilling through my confidence. "How many years have you bled?"

I swallow. "Five. I can live Meaningful Purpose, my king. I'm stronger than I look."

"You're small."

"I'll eat more," I counter.

"What was stopping you before?" His lips twitch with a smile when I have no answer for him. "You have an answer for everything? But not this."

"I know what I want, my king."

"And that is?"

To prove them wrong.

"Meaningful Purpose."

A pause thickens the air.

He steps toward me again, his gait graceful, contradictory to such a large, menacing man.

He cups my face in both big hands, his fingers cradling the back of my head. He could crush my skull. Pop it.

Gone.

I wonder whether he has. I'm sure he has crushed bones within these warm hands, turned them to powder.

Looking down at me, he drinks in the sight, the intensity in which he maps each feature, in which his gaze slices across my cheeks, eyes of violet, my parted mouth, peels me back to bone and breath.

"You're pretty." The words are licks of warmth, and my knees buckle with each letter. "I bet the other girls *despise* you."

Shit.

I glance quickly at the girls, at Iris and Lavender. "We have no jealousy, my king," I lie. It's one of our vows: no jealousy between Silk Girls.

Meaningful Purpose is what matters.

"*Lies,*" he purrs, and all the hairs on my neck rise. "Do you know what I do to people who despise me?" He lifts my chin with his thumb, a silent demand to answer him.

I shake my head. "No."

"I give them more reasons to."

Then his hands drop from my face, and disappointment hits my stomach as he strides away.

The press in my chest gives way when he disappears into the streets, closely tracked by two men who might well be his shadows. But I know they are his Guards. *The Guard.* One of them is *Kong*. His Guardian.

I have studied him. That is surely him. He is large, tanned-skin, and has long dark hair that he pulls away from his face and into a knot at the back of his head.

The quiet stretches to a low, frantic musing between the girls and the Silk Wardeness. "Did he come to see us?" "Perhaps, Ivy." "To check on his property?" "Why would he be in the Lower-tower?" "Visiting Lord Bled, perhaps." "I don't know, girls. Quieten down."

The questioning continues, and the tattoo man calls, "Next," but I'm still staring at the door to the parlour.

Outside, the Redwind now swallows any sight or sound, but for the unmistakable screech from above, piercing and fierce, parting the atmosphere to warn us *he* is here.

His great eagle—Odio.

How I wish to see him. His wingspan must be larger than my outstretched arms to coast the deadly gale.

33

I exhale hard, finding plenty of room in my chest now that he isn't close. He's an enigma like his eagle, present but too high to ever reach.

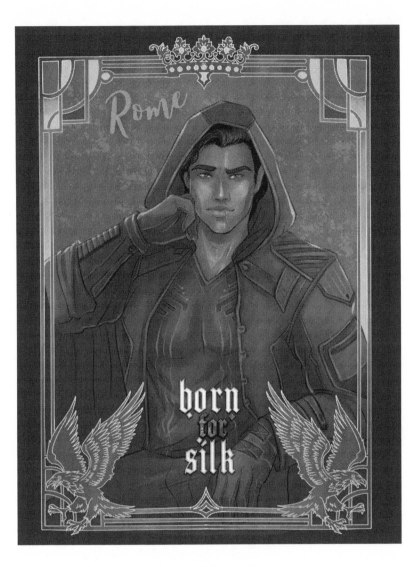

Rome of the Strait,
The Cradle's Monarch and Protector

CHAPTER TWO

ASTER

I wander down toward my favourite place.

It's the setting of my earliest memory, from when I was too small to talk fluently, but too fast on my feet for the Silk Wardeness to keep me in her sights.

I had wandered off the pretty pebbled path and into the depths of the aviary, following a scent that I couldn't quite place. Like mushrooms with floral notes. Wet, yet fresh.

I walked with flowers in my fist, birds rattling trees overhead, and ladders in my forever-ruined stockings, in a direction without supervision—with freedom.

That was when I saw it.

A body of water that boasted more colours than possible, a light reflecting yellows and oranges in an endless green abyss.

A pond.

It was the first one I had ever seen, and I couldn't swim for the life of me, but I needed to touch it.

I knelt on the grass bedding by the bank and placed the flowers down on the greenery. I skimmed my fingertips across the moving colours along the water when an odd shape caught my eye.

Blinking at it, I reached across and plucked the strange thing up. It was a baby bird floating on the water. Belly up. Legs awkward. Feet curled over as though they were wilted petals.

"Bird," I whispered, the feathers tickling my young palm. I remember that it felt so small. Even to me. So wildly insignificant —even to me.

I didn't know this at the time, but that young bird had hit the glass boundary of the aviary and broken its little neck.

I was too small to understand empathy, but I had a feeling inside my chest that pulled and pulled and pulled. I felt like the bird, all upside-down and tense.

Alone.

It was my earliest memory, but it would become a tradition that lasted for many ages. I would soon spend many days collecting broken-necked birds for my friend.

For my friend to eat.

I reach the bank and wait.

A big raptor-bird appears from the bushes. Its wing is perpetually broken, and its beak is already covered in blood from a first-light of cannibalistic hunting.

It's not pretty like the other birds, possessing the beastly mutations so many animals have since the Gene Age. Like birds don't usually have teeth, but this one does. Rows and rows. Thin ones to filter. I sometimes imagine that he is a dinosaur, not just a flightless mutant.

"It's a big day," I say to him, because it is nice to speak aloud and be heard. I sometimes forget I have a voice if not. If not for this bird.

I cross my arms over my chest, and he approaches slowly. "You come when they are distracted. Only then. You're afraid of them but not me. I take offence. I'm terrifying."

I sit down, and he pokes around at my hand. "I have no birds for you today, but I met the king. He spoke to me." I look down at my tattoo. "He touched me."

As though to remind me it's muck-up day, an evil laugh echoes within the aviary; its shrilling chords cause birds to take to the air.

I stand and watch, wait, scoring overhead for that one little bird too frightened to stop in time before meeting the sheer glass walls that keep us safe from the Redwind.

"They are all celebrating," I whisper to the air. My black hair and white dress flat down my body as though weighed, reminding me of the lifeless atmosphere. "Do you birds get stronger in here? Or weaker? Because you don't have any wind to help you glide. You must do all the work yourselves."

I hear Raptor squark and croon in anticipation of his meal. If the birds drop dead into the water, they will float. I learnt that fat floats and so do birds because they are full of air. And my friend doesn't know how to fly or swim, so without me, he'll miss out on lunch. If it's close enough, I will dive in and retrieve the bird for him. I'm not sure why I started doing this... Maybe because the little bird from my memories reminded me of myself, and food, horrific as the premise is, is still a purpose. I wanted the little bird to have Meaningful Purpose. "They don't have the vast to discover either," I muse. "To stretch, to fight for survival. They stay small. I'm a different kind of caged bird, aren't I?"

"There she is!"

Hiding Raptor, I whirl around to find Iris and Ivy appearing through the foliage, powdered entirely in purple sandules. I don't hear my friend disappear into the reeds, though I know he does.

"You don't want to celebrate with us, Fur Girl?" Iris circles me slowly, her fingers curled, cradling something within them. Sandules, probably.

I step away from the pond, drawing their eyes with me. "Muck-up doesn't appeal to me."

"You don't ever want to play with us," Iris mock-moans, flicking her red hair over her shoulder. It's wild, like flames, and her skin is pale, like snow.

39

The two together are a rare beauty.

Or so I am told—often.

"What do you do out here all alone?" Ivy asks, blocking the passage through the trees to the Silk House. She is tall, which is desirable in The Cradle, and she knows it. "Talking to the trees again? Trying to connect with your Fur people?"

"You're not pure. You're Common, too," I spit out, and she throws a handful of purple dust at me. The pretty colour powders my dress. As though that is supposed to upset me. It's *his* colour. It's a symbol.

"Not purple," Iris hisses. "Not for her." She squats behind me, but I refuse to give her more than my side profile as I listen to her movements. "She needs something browner. Darker. Like her dirty Fur blood."

My senses prickle when her fingers dig into The Cradle's rich crust. I play the scene in my head for a second; she throws the soil at me, they laugh, and then leave.

I don't care. "It's muck-up. Do your worst."

As another girl, Lavender, pushes through the pendulous limbs ahead, stepping around Ivy, a small ball of dirt bursts at my spine.

As I presumed; now leave.

The three girls circle me, slashed and marked in purple dust, proud and wild. Their eyes are arrowed, wicked intent sparking.

I feign calm, but my heart thrashes. I hope they cannot see my pulse drumming in my neck. I feel eyes on me from every direction, then heated laughter that seems to collect and tangle together.

"Iris, let's get this over with," Lavender says with an intensity that makes my pulse harder to control. "I just want her out. She makes me break my vows. The way he held her today in the parlour." She huffs. "*Jealousy* isn't allowed between Silk Girls."

Want me out?

"Jealousy?" Iris shoots her heated gaze across the ring to her friend. "You might be *jealous.* I'm not. I've got the nictitating membrane. See?" She bats her lashes and shows the sliding lids.

"And my line has never lost a baby. Not once. I'm the prize in this house."

"Of course," Lavender agrees tentatively, but Iris isn't happy with the accusation.

"You." Iris points at her, and I turn my head to keep up, but their circling makes me dizzy. "You do it, and I'll make sure he chooses you as well. We can live together as Sired Mothers. I know you're strong, Lavender. You'll have Meaningful Purpose."

Do it... do what?

Just breathe.

I want to run, but that seems even more frightening than staying still. It'll be over soon. They'll beat me, maybe? Humiliate me. I can take it.

I'm watching them closely, whipping my head around to keep all three in my sights, when the ground becomes a blur. I stumble, and they lunge for me. Kicking at them isn't enough.

Ivy grabs my hands and pins them over my head. She leans over me, a smile like a mean rat etched to her lips.

Lavender pins one of my legs, but the other jolts around.

"Hold her down," Iris orders.

"I'm trying!" Lavender whines.

Ivy kneels on my forearms so she can slap my cheeks, disorientating me enough for Lavender to pin my calves down.

Her weight shoots pain through my bones.

More birds flock from the trees around us, not wanting to watch any more than I want to be here on the ground.

Frantically, I fight them, but they are bigger than me. Taller. Heavier. "Stop it. Stop it."

"Ugh!" Iris gets annoyed with Lavender's attempts to control me. "I'll do it then!"

"What are you going to do?" Ivy asks Iris as she drops down over me, eyes cutting me to bare bones.

"We're going to ruin her seal of purity. We are going to open her."

He words crush my bravery.

41

Blinking heat from my eyes, I refuse to cry. I turn to look at the pond, pleading with every inch of need for my raptor to rear up and protect me.

Be my *friend.*

He has disappeared. The pond is motionless. A mirror that reflects the swaying branches overhead. *Is he real?* Maybe I imagined him all this time. Imagined a broken creature in my mind to ward off the loneliness.

"She'll tell," Ivy hesitates.

"No, she won't." Iris smiles. "Then she'll be cast out. Wardeness will think she has touched herself and broken her seal. And she will be disgraced."

I'm shaking so hard it's impossible to see anything when Iris shoves my dress up and tugs my knickers down. I'm stiff with pathetic fear as she pushes a wooden twig between my legs. The sharp end scrapes along my thighs.

"Get off me!" I scream. I want to gyrate harder, but I'm afraid. Afraid she'll do more damage. I twist gently to make it harder for her to get inside me.

Between the feeling of sharp stabs at my thighs and the look of pure hatred in Iris's eyes, I cannot breathe.

Or think.

A squawk from overhead startles the girls enough to loosens their hold. Iris and Ivy stumble back, leaving Lavender alone and holding me. So, I pull my legs free and kick upward, connecting with her chin.

"Oh!" she cries out, and the others gather her from the dirt. They look no worse than expected from today—muck-up day wild. It is normal for the girls to get dirty after our ceremony. They pull Lavender away, and all three disappear into the foliage like wraiths that never were.

Just breathe.

On my back, I blink ahead at the branches reaching in and out of the sky like green fingers scratching a cloudy, grey canvas. We are everything we aren't meant to be, full of jealousy and bitterness.

Is this life?

I don't want to look down, though I can feel the wetness between my legs, which means Iris broke skin. The sickening sensation makes my throat burn.

I hear my bird screech; the scent of my blood probably bothers him. No longer alone, I brave the sight. I push to a sitting position; fire explodes along my thighs, snatching a defiant whine from my throat.

I'm hurt.

Stabbed.

My white dress is destroyed, crimson-stained fabric muddied with dirt and purple sandules.

I push off the ground.

Absently, I toe the pond, a snake of blood rushing to meet the water, spreading out like dye. I blink at the water as though he can see the tiny molecules approaching him. "I have to get out of here."

Without a second thought, I pin drop into the pond, instantly enveloped by watery arms. And it's so quiet and still, for a moment I consider death. What it must feel like. Cold. Quiet. Weightless. Where do we go? To The Crust? What is The Crust? Is it a place or state of mind? Or are we just sown back into the dirt, food for the flowers. What about my thoughts? Where do they go?

My dress floats around me, dancing on the wings of fluid. I blink, focusing underwater—no stinging. No salt; it's fresh water. I search but cannot see far, rocks and trees blocking the distant body of the pond.

What will you do?

I resurface with a gasp, and the warm air hisses along my skin. "I will say I fell in," I chant the plan to an empty bank. "The wound will heal. I'll pretend it never happened."

You must go through it, *Aster.*

Go right through the adversities to the other side.

Meaningful Purpose awaits you.

~

Walking back into the quadrangle, dress and hair stuck to my body, dripping like a drowned beast, I keep my head high as the other girls turn and stare.

Their clothes are covered in purple. Their hair is tousled by excitement. Smiles are wide, then fall when they look at me.

While I'm an unusual sight, sure, that's not the reason for the hostility. It's muck-up day and no one likes me. So, being pushed into the pond is a reasonable assumption for my drenched state.

Low conversing suddenly invades me like buzzing bees, but I stride right through the chattering girls, straight toward my housing.

Vines strangle the sandstone buildings that surround the courtyard, thick green snakes that hunt for something long lost. Something natural. Air. Sun. Wind. Nothing is real in the Silk Aviary. The glass dome shields us from the Redwind, but the vines get so confused. Twisting themselves into knots in search of something more.

At the entrance to my personal chamber, I push inside. Leaning on the beautifully carved oak door, I decide quickly and quietly that today never happened. Nothing good can come from drawing attention to myself in here.

Moving fast, I hide the stained dress and my knickers in the mattress until I have time to clean them in the washroom. I bury the sensation of raw flesh, walking through the ache until I can bear each step.

I pace in the room, flexing my hands.

It's fine.

I will be fine.

A single tear slides down my cheek.

CHAPTER THREE

ASTER

Anyone around bullies enough, starts to develop a kind of harm gauge. A protective measure.

What will it be today?

Snide comments? A fistful of food thrown at my dress? A foot that slides out at the perfect moment and brings me to the floor? An elbow to the face?

What today, Iris?

In the weeks that followed that day at the pond, four Silk Girls from the house, including Lavender, were sent to placements across The Cradle to start their Meaningful Purpose.

It's not meant to be sad, but they just leave.

And it makes me wonder...

What's it like?

On the other side?

I may see them again when—or rather, if—we become Sired Mothers one day. We'll be older then. Maybe time will change them. Maybe some of them will want to be friends.

And I'll forgive them.

Feeling heat slide along my left cheek, I scan the quadrangle's ancient brick and stone boundary walls to find Iris's gaze setting my skin ablaze.

She is standing beside the Silk Wardeness.

Why does she hate me? Because she believes that I'm truly Fur Born? Is she that much of an elitist?

I stare back at her, reading the intent today.

My gauge shudders beneath the telling leer, until our Wardeness grabs her elbow and walks her... straight toward me?

I step backward a few paces before finding my spine, locking it into a defensive rod.

I stand still.

"Aster." Wardeness stops in front of me, her fingers still clutching Iris's elbow. "Show her what you have, Iris."

I blink at Iris, and she pulls out my stained knickers from her satchel.

What the f-word?

"I don't know what that is," I say far too quickly. Most of the blood washed out in the pond, but the white fabric has splotches of pink, evident staining from something red.

"I think you do," Wardeness presses.

"They are not mine," I lie.

"They are. I would know. I got them for you."

"I bled. I had my bleed. I was embarrassed. It was weeks ago. I forgot all about—"

"You two take me for a fool," she spits out. "I have seen the way you both behave toward each other."

It's really one-sided...

She purses her lips as though a lemon seeps juice below her tongue. "Like children," she says. "Not like Silk Girls. You both have His mark. You will go to a lord or a member of The Guard. Maybe even to Kong if he ever decides it's time. Iris, you're the senior girl in this house until that happens. And Aster, you have such promise. Don't let all that talent go to waste. And I will not be made a fool of. Do you hear me?"

46

"I don't have any ill feelings toward—" Iris begins, but Wardeness isn't accepting any lies today.

"Don't fib to me." She grabs the knickers from Iris. "Now. I don't know why you hid your blood or why Iris was showing it off like a flagship to the other girls, but I know you two are at odds. Trade will, I hope you aren't chosen for the same placement, but if you are, then you need to remember your vows. I will lock you both up and have you repeat them from first-light to last-light if I must."

Fury bubbles inside me. "I don't have a problem with Iris, Miss." I stare at Iris, bored. "I couldn't care less about her."

Iris's teeth clench behind her fake smile.

Wardeness pinches her brow between her fingertips. "*Trade Help Me*. Okay." She lowers her hand, resolute, and stares at us; a strange expression moves across her aging face. "Tonight. Gosh, I have only ever done this once before. But you are both very desirable Silk Girls. I cannot have your foolish ways stop you from achieving Meaningful Purpose. It is too important. I care too much for you both. Tonight," she begins, her voice lowering. "I will collect you from your rooms, and we will go for a night ride in the van. It will be only the three of us. And you must not tell the other girls."

"Of course, Miss," Iris coos. I can hear the bullshit in her voice, but so many believe her to be sweet.

Around us, girls drag their feet to eavesdrop. I don't like the idea of going anywhere in the middle of the night with Iris, but foolish interest whispers between my ears.

"That will be all for now, girls." The Silk Wardeness looks between us expectantly. "Go back to your independent studies. I will see you tonight."

I keep my composure, nod stiffly, and walk to the study hall, not looking up or around until I'm certain that I'm away from Iris and her groupies.

An entire night with Iris.

Oh joy.

I push open the heavy wooden door and am greeted by empty desks, a quiet room, and a single girl, Cherry, kneeling at the platform, probably asking The Cradle for two sons and one daughter in her future.

Ahead of me, high and proud, the magnificent portrait of our king hangs, framed by stained-glass windows.

Ambient light from outside filters through the glass, casting the mural in colours, bringing the images to life. His eagle, a black and orange figure like an umbrella over the portrait. The tides of The Strait below, navy and black waves, and white foam. The Redwind, depicted in red and orange fragments, creates a fishbowl effect around the piece.

I tilt my head as I study it, feeling warmth pool low inside me, taking in the regal sight and artistry before me. It doesn't do him justice. Not now that I have seen him in the flesh. Felt his hands on me.

Swallowing the reverie, I move toward one of the desks. The Silk Wardeness' outing sits in the front of my mind.

A team exercise, maybe?

Some kind of bonding?

It doesn't matter.

Whatever she has to show us won't change Iris. And I need to win by excelling. In ballet. In poise and manners. In being a Silk Girl. So I can leave this glass container and see more of...

Anything.

I open my desk and retrieve the text, *Anatomy of a Silk Girl.* I flip to chapter seventeen, Perineal Tears, and start reading.

At the end of the day, after studying and ballet, I wash the sweat from dancing off my skin with scolding water.

It's always extra hot.

The wooden shower mat beneath my feet is warm, too, almost too warm. Floating around in the puddles are fresh petals, the scent of which mingles with the tree leaves, cedar, and tar used to heat the room year-round. Heat in the showers aids to cleanse us.

Cleanliness is a virtue.

Especially for a Silk Girl.

I wash, thinking about what I read, about the Xin De Maternal Deaths and why my Trade is so important to The Cradle. *And...* why being Fur Born means I'm at risk.

Am I strong enough to carry a baby with Xin De genes? When they grow so large, so strong, so quick.

I was assured years ago that my mother was Silk Born. That she was kidnapped by an outlawed Common man and that is why I was first marked as Fur. My blood is Silk, though. The story goes that The Guard found my mother dead in a pile of ash and bodies. I was found later.

That is the story I was told.

I am not really a Fur Girl.

I turn off the shower.

I'm wandering from the stall absentmindedly, my thoughts reeling and rolling over, when I bump into someone.

And it all happens so fast.

Iris shoves me against the wall, knocking breath from my lips. "You say nothing tonight, got it!"

I quickly search behind her to check for her followers, but she's alone, which seems strange. I frown. "I have nothing to say. You tried to hurt me, tear me, but you failed."

"They'll know you're Fur." She sneers. "See scratches all over your skin. It's important to live a delicate life. It says so in the books. Peaceful. Stress and trauma get into the cells and infect the babies. I have the Xin De DNA. I have the strength. I am perfectly at peace!"

"*Yeah,* you're the picture of tranquillity right now."

Red builds beneath her cheeks. "My seal will be a perfect shield and Sire will choose me because of it. Not you. He can't. He won't choose you!"

Gosh. She *is* jealous of me...

Power slides across my lips, resting into a smile. "You're really jealous of me, aren't you? You're not disgusted because I was Fur Born. It has nothing to do with me. You're *jealous.*"

"Filthy little Fur Girl!" She lifts her hand to slap me, but I catch her wrist. It vibrates with her rage.

"No." I shake my head, glaring at her. "I'm not scared of you. Jealousy is not a virtue, Iris. You're imperfect, too."

"I'll ruin your face next."

She is losing it. I lean closer. "Do you know how to swim, Iris? I do. I jump in the pond and swim all around to catch birds. If you touch me again, I'm going to drag you into the deep and hold your head under until your lungs fill with water, and don't worry, I won't be punished. A creature lives near that pond, and he likes to eat birds. Pretty red birds like you. They won't find your body. He'll pluck you to bones, red feather by red feather."

A moment of hesitation flitters through her angry stare before she tugs her wrist from my hand. She backs away slowly, grasping at a cruel smile. "The creature isn't real, Aster. Your only friend is make-believe. You still have an imaginary friend. It's pathetic."

I blink at her.

"I've heard you talking to it," she goes on. "It doesn't talk back. It isn't real. They'll see that you're not fit to be a Silk Girl. They'll see that you're odd and not want your genes tainting their legacy."

Chapter Four

Aster

The van comes to a stop.

We exit the vehicle under the cloak of night. I cannot see much through the face mask, but follow the lamp held ahead by the Wardeness. Whistles from the gale dance around me until we are declining steep steps away from the fingers of the night and into a dimly lit concrete underground space.

My heart races knowing this is an unusual practice; sneaking away at night, just the three of us—the Silk Wardeness, Iris, and I —accompanied by two Guard: one ahead of us and one behind.

My body vibrates with nerves and something else entirely. Something strange and as lovely as it is alarming—excitement. I like the idea of sneaking around, like the idea of secrets and journeys.

I shouldn't want such things.

Curiosity isn't a virtue.

I look at Iris as she clings to the Wardeness's cloak—*granted, the company could be better down here...*

When the tunnel creates a sanctuary from the wind and sand, I pull my mask down and sling back my hood, which bunches at my shoulders.

I look around but see only steep concrete bathed in a low white hue from flickering tracks of lighting hugging the cracked grey ceiling.

"Will you note the lighting issue for when you come back tomorrow for your deliveries?" The Wardeness asks the Guard ahead. "There must be a windmill down."

"Noted, Ma'am."

The grey walls seem to disappear into the dead straight distance and my imagination takes over as the mundane trek continues for many minutes.

I picture the land above this tunnel. An unknown city or plane or farm. No glass walls of isolation. The aviary is all I know—I have only ever visited the Lower-tower a handful of times for special occasions, and even so, we are rushed from shop to shop, hidden and surrounded by Guards.

A few minutes pass, and I almost miss the steel door that the Wardeness stops beside.

She knocks twice and steps backward. The gasp of air escaping the door gives homage to its age and tight seal.

"Mother Rose and her sister are awake," another Wardeness says through the door. "Bring the girls inside but don't touch a single surface. You've not been tested or checked for ailments."

"This will never be spoken of." The Silk Wardeness turns to us, her cheeks flushed from the walk. "We travelled far because I trust these Mothers with our secrets, not all would allow such a visit. Or I would have taken you to a nursery closer to home. If anyone was to find out we let you in here with the babes, Trade be merciful, they'll only have my head. The king himself doesn't know the location of each nursery. Only a handful of people in all The Cradle know where we keep the precious babes."

"Why risk it then?" I ask.

"Listen to me." She cups my cheeks. "I care for all my girls. I care deeply. I can see the path you will take, and it is pitted with pain." She wraps one arm around Iris' waist and holds the arch of my neck with the other. "My girls." She squeezes with affection. "This is your future should you choose to overcome your corrupt feelings of jealousy and hate for each other."

We enter.

My breath catches as the warm, softly lit lounging area comes into view like a flower opening, revealing soft pinks, reds, and a scent unlike I have ever known. I sniff the air.

"Baby powder," the Wardeness says to me, sweeping her hand to the side. My eyes follow. Along the wall are babies in rope hammocks, some stirring, cooing, and others mouthing in their sleep. I know they are babies because I have seen pictures of them, but they are even more beautiful in the flesh. They have such big heads for the size of their bodies, short limbs with rolls of plump skin bunching at every crease. They look like dough. Nothing like the little bird I found. Nothing so tight and frail. They are round. Chubby, even. Delightful.

"Welcome, Silk Girls," a woman in an apron says, rocking a hammock with her hand to a baby's chest. It mewls gently. Her voice is husky and deep but somehow soothing. "I'm Mother Rose, and this is what it looks like to be on the night shift with the babes. The light-hours are far wilder and fun, but nothing beats the nights when we cuddle and sing."

"They are lovely." Iris's voice unsettles me, gentle and kind, and I turn to stare at her.

She slowly returns my gaze and doesn't harden her expression. Every nerve in my body pricks up. I barely recognise her features like this. "Aren't they, Aster? Just so peaceful."

Startled by her, by some magical baby force that has her melting into someone capable of kindness, I gaze back at the source of her affection. The baby squeezes Mother Rose's finger. My heart feels like it might pop.

"These are the babies of The Cradle," the Wardeness says quietly with a sigh. "*Trade willing*, I wasn't a Silk Girl, so I never had a chance to be a Sired Mother, but you girls do, and the most coveted Trade for women is to care for these little ones. No studies. No eyes on you. All the food you wish, the clothes you choose, and peace. It's guaranteed."

I look at Iris again, my lips forming a tight line. She is right.

This is the offering: a place away from the Guards, away from the Redwind, from the eyes that track us, the militant rules. This is the promised retirement for a Silk Girl. *If* we give The Cradle two boys and a girl.

"One may be a lord," I murmur. "Imagine that."

"One shouldn't *imagine* anything," Iris states, straight from her textbook, the dangers of speculations.

"*Hosh-posh*, we are all women here." Mother Rose waves her hand. "Just a couple of old hens living out our lives in peace and tranquillity. Meaningful Purpose. Meaningful duties. We can talk in here."

My ears basically grow. "About anything?"

"Anything." She leans in, a playful smile teasing the corner of her mouth. "We are old. We're done. What are they going to do with us if we natter? The babies can't understand us." She winks at me, and I giggle once.

Iris squares her shoulders. "But I have nothing to talk about. My mind is too fixed on my Meaningful Purpose."

"Oh, *lies*." Mother Rose dismisses, and I gape. "I can see the attitude all over this one's face. You look like someone twisted your nose. You have thoughts. I am certain. You're having them right now. Probably about me."

Iris takes a step back, lifting her chin in defence. "What about the other..." she trails off before finishing with, "girls, *erm*, women? They might *misinterpret?*"

"There is a thought. Good for you, dear." She looks between us. "Don't you trust each other? You don't trust your Collective with your thoughts? My dear sweet, Silk Girl, you are not perfect, and your imperfections will be blemishes your flock must hide for you. Hide from The Trade and your lords. You will succeed together not alone. The only confidant you truly have is your fellow Silk Girls. You wear the pregnancy and the birth together. It is not easy. Your pregnancy is hard on your body and the birth is harder still. And one Silk Girl will not supply The Trade. There is no *I* in Trade."

I blink at her. "Pardon?"

"Such younglings. It's an old saying, from the old-world. There is no *I* in Trade. Achievements come when we act together. Such is The Trade's way; failure usually happens alone. History shows us this."

On the journey home I feel a shift between Iris and me. She sits close and yet, quiet.

My bully gauge is silent, too.

The chaotic winds outside howl, but through the tinted windows, it's merely an abyss of black swirls. It's early—first-light perhaps, but no direct light will come until the sun is high enough to cut through the thick Redwind. And to think, there are people out there. In the waste. In the wind. Merely surviving.

And by choice.

I could have been a Fur Girl.

I'd be out in the Redwind, skin peeling from the gale, eyes red raw, running for my life, hunted, killed, raped, and eaten. If I were lucky, it would be in that order.

Fur Borns are free but not protected. That is the life I was saved from when they brought me home—to the Aquilla Silk Aviary.

I look at Iris who bats her eyelids softly, slumber's heavy presence weighing on her. I am yawning, sleep clinging to my lashes also, when there is a loud bang.

The car flips, throws us forward, and then— I scream as we become weightless, gravity drawing me in all directions.

My vision blurs. I can hear the van bashing as it rolls and slams, rolls and slams, my body hitting the roof, the side, thumping, smashing, shattering glass, and the sound of screams rattle the space.

Fear and adrenaline course through me when the van ends the

perpetual revolving and slides on its side, the crying of metal on rock twisting my spine into coils.

The vehicle stops completely, the air is thick with silence, and my own breath is a staccato beat in my ears.

I blink around and groan from pain, a warning my body is bruised and twisted. To the side, Wardeness lies unconscious. In front of me, Iris moans, a small snake of blood trickling down her forehead. "Iris? Iris?"

Suddenly, a big, bloodied hand reaches through the shattered window behind her head and fists her hair.

My blood runs cold.

Her screams echo through the car as she is dragged backward through the glass, her arms and legs flailing around.

I find the strength to sob. Pathetic attempt to react, really. Paralysed, I watch in horror as her feet disappear into the ominous dark.

The screaming stops, the wind howls, and my breath shakes from between my lips.

A minute or more. I don't move. That is all it takes, though, before the life I know changes forever. The pretty glass house that protected me shatters.

"Hello, sweet bread." A man drags me from the car by my hair. He is cast in shadows, but the stench of blood and oils seep through the air like long fingers violating my nostrils.

I am being shoved forward between multiple bodies, the wind slicing at my legs and face, lashing me with the sand it breathes.

As I am pushed through an opening, I lose my footing and fall to the floor. The wind is suffocated when a heavy door shuts.

It's cold. Still.

"Well, well, what a catch." A man laughs. "Those crazy motherfuckers were right. Got ourselves a couple of Silk Girls."

I spin to my bum and squint through the dark. Five men in tatty clothes, soaking wet from something sticky, stand over me.

Fur Born men.

"*Aster…*" A female voice finds me as I stare at them. I turn to see the Wardeness and Iris beside me on the floor. Shadows move across their faces, but both are awake and waiting. Scared.

"The Guards?" I mutter.

"Do you know what you're doing?" Wardeness warns the men, her voice a tremoring mess. "These girls are the property of The Cradle, and I am their—"

"Shut up, woman!" the biggest one, with a bald head and square jaw, snarls before reaching for her and pulling her to her feet. She stumbles as he leans in, "You'll keep for weeks with all that blubber." Her eyes lock in on mine. She doesn't speak, but the terror she feels screams from her gaze. "Take the fat one to the basement."

While three Endigo keep watch, two drag our Wardeness into a hallway, and I slide my hand along the floor, looking for a piece of glass or debris.

My stomach churns.

I can smell burning flesh and hair. The air is electrified. I find myself inhaling a putrid smell and nearly gag as the body of air seems to roll down my throat.

"That's something aint it?" the same one says to me, grabbing a hold of my elbow and pulling me to my feet. "The smell of contaminated flesh. See," he pulls me further into the room, toward a fire in a barrel. "We cut his leg off and cooked it when it was fresh. Nice. Not as sweet as your legs will be." He licks his lips. "Don't worry. Usually, we keep the live meat clean, but the water stopped running when the mill went down last week, so we couldn't." He pushes me down onto a bloody bed; the cushions are stained, brown and red.

I take in my surrounding through side eyes: old mattresses, sofas, and barrels. So many different barrels, and one is on fire, the light illuminating a ring around us.

Then I see the man—the live meat.

My eyes hollow. My heart rings in my ears like an alarm. He is missing a forearm, sliced off at the elbow, and a shin; the kneecap is an avocado colour and oozes with yellow puss.

I cover my mouth to stop from vomiting.

Should I run?

Scream for help?

"No. No!" I hear a woman scream from somewhere inside the building. I snap my head toward the sound. I don't need to see anything. I can imagine what they are doing. Like my raptor's teeth—slicing into flesh, sucking muscles from tiny bones.

Screaming won't help.

The woman's guttural cries wind up, building and building until they cut off. Right in the middle. Like her voice box was severed in half, or perhaps she just passed out.

Hunted, killed, raped, eaten.

If you're lucky, it'll be in that order.

She wasn't lucky.

Across from me on another soiled sofa, Iris has her eyes squeezed shut, her hair is dishevelled, and her dress is stained and ripped. I sit upright and still, watchful.

"Can I touch that one?" A younger one bares his teeth, thin like sewing needles, and rubs at the swell between his thighs, staring at Iris. "I like that one."

"Not now, you fool," the largest one says.

Iris sways. Her body gives way and flops to the side on the filthy sofa.

"Iris," I whisper-shout. I won't be able to carry her out if we get a chance to escape. I need her to run. Fight. Survive. *"Iris."* But she's out cold. His words were too much for her to handle.

As I sit stiff like an obedient doll, my eyes veer around the room to watch the men as they go about their routines. The young one plops down on a stained pink sofa and picks his teeth with a rusty knife, angry eyes never leaving Iris's unconscious body.

The big one, the leader, moves over to a bench and lifts a barrel onto it; it must weigh a ton. He's strong.

Can't overpower him, not even with Iris.

A skinny one lays down on a tatty bed and rests his forearm

over his eyes; a large automatic weapon is thread into his belt. The gun could fill us with holes in seconds if we tried to run away from them.

Can't run.

The *live meat*, twitching and disorientated, stares at a puddle of piss on the concrete by his feet. He's given up. A man twice my size with far more muscles didn't escape…

Fighting back isn't possible.

I think about the dead baby bird, belly up and stiff. Like me now. It broke its neck on the glass dome. I always thought it was an accident, but maybe it would rather die than be trapped and taunted by the other birds. Maybe it was being chased. Hunted. Maybe it was courageous and resilient, not insignificant. Determined. It tried to break free instead of cowering in a corner of the aviary.

I'll be the upside-down bird.

I think through the dusky first-light as the Endigos take turns sleeping. I won't go huddled in a corner. There is a way out… I scan the cavernous space. It's an old factory of sorts.

I pay attention to details; the floor is cracked and so are the bricks, so maybe there is a hole somewhere small enough for me to fit through…

I keep looking. Strip drains run in tracks down the centre, maybe there is a well I could hide inside. Seven beds, but only five men.

Where are the other two?

Three sofas, and old tables are squeezed close together, probably for warmth at night. The echo of each slight noise denotes a larger area swallowed by the dark. The stench of death climbs along my tongue.

No clean water…

With that, I remember the closest mill is down, which means Trade men will be coming to fix it.

Alert, I mull the next few days or weeks over in all their horror. When I heard stories of Endigos and feral Fur men, I presumed they would capture and kill their prey. It never occurred to me that they would keep them alive, live with them, clean them, cutting pieces off day by day until they bid them farewell with a final slash.

I'm staring at the drains, thanking the pond for teaching me to swim and wondering where they may lead, when the young one stands. I hide my interest but track him subtly as he checks the other men are asleep.

With the others out cold, he turns to Iris.

I swallow as he approaches her. Placing a hand on either side of her body, he looks engrossed in her every feature. His eyes flick to her forehead, where the blood from the crash has dried to a crusty river. He leans over and his tongue lashes out, lapping at the bloody trail.

I gasp, and his eyes snap across.

He rises, staring at me.

My heart thrashes inside my ribcage, the fearful organ is desperate to leap free from the snare of his gaze. I shuffle backward on the mattress.

"Pretty, pretty, little girl. Pretty, pretty, little girls," he says, a taunting lullaby. He would only be a few years older than me, perhaps newly a man. *Is he mad?* I know nothing of the behaviours of men. The anatomy, yes, I'm quite versed in that area from my Silk Girl training, but not the manners.

I track him with my eyes as he sits back on his pink sofa, but now he's fixated on me. "I've never had a Silk Girl before."

"We belong to The Trade. To the king."

I don't know why I say it.

Such a redundant attempt to rattle him.

"*Ooo,*" he mocks, as I knew he would. "Where is he now? Have you met him? I'm sure you have if you're his Silk Girls." His face contorts with thoughts of anger and bitterness as he continues, "They say King Rome is the closest thing left to a pure Xin De." He leans into the barrel at his side and pulls out a strip of cooked, pink flesh, a seam of fat around the edge. All the while looking at me, he plucks pieces of the loin apart and plops them into his mouth. "They say he's full of metal and eight foot tall." The fire licks upward from the barrel between us. "I saw a pure Xin De once. The Trade left me and my family—*starving*. This bitch was dead when I found her in an abandoned basement. There was half a baby hanging from inside her. Still fresh. Both of them. Maternal deaths are so common that even at the age of nine, I knew what had happened. Xin De are too big for their own mothers. Without Trade help, women die. Just another way they control us."

He hates The Trade.

He talks around a chewy piece of meat. "I tried to cut the baby free so I could put it on salt for later, but the woman's skin was like hide. I'm part Xin De, got some of the undesirable mutilations, but I don't have skin like that..." Then he smiles at me, and my stomach turns. I roll my lips together to mask the revulsion I feel. "Not like you," he adds. "I'll go into you like a knife into that baby that hung from her. You're soft. Your skin is thin. They made you so fragile and made themselves so indestructible. It's no wonder the Trade has been trying to backpedal this fucking Gene Age disaster. Mix us. Blend Common and Xin De. So tell me, little Silk Girl, tell me all the tales of King Rome. Your saviour."

I know we are sheltered in the Silk Aviary, but Silk Girls are well read, so I don't allow him to frighten me.

Instead of detesting him for his vulgar story, I stare at this young man, unable to overlook the despair hidden beneath his layers of resentment. What must he have seen and done in his young life? Would I be any different if I had walked in his shoes? I hope I would still be *decent* even as I fought to survive.

It seems fruitless, but time is my friend, so I humour his request while I consider what to do.

"King Rome has a giant eagle named Odio," I begin, playing along. "He is as big as I am. Wings twice the span of my arms outstretched. They say he flies into each battle first and rips the head of the opposing leader right off his shoulders with his talons. Carries the head to King Rome and places it in his hands to symbolise the beginning of each battle."

The man leans forward onto his knees, murky brown eyes narrowing. He is dirty, yes, but youthful in a way that saddens me. "You're not what I expected from a Silk Girl. I've jerked off to the idea of the perfect little breeding girls you are. Pure. Unopened by a man. Adore, pleasure, provide, am I right? Nothing in your pretty heads except that." He hums in thought. "But you're... talking about beheadings, sitting there all stiff and alert, like you're going to try to take us all on. Is that it, little girl? You're not even that squeamish. Your friend couldn't stand the sight or smell, but you..." He studies me harder. "What are you?"

"I'm different."

"How different?" he poses, a challenge skittering along each syllable. "How different are you, little girl?"

"I'm just like you. Surviving." I look at his leader—at least I think he is— and remember the way he belittled him. He snores on his mattress. Quickly returning my gaze, I say, "With people ordering me around. Like the Wardeness. Those who think they know better than me. Or are smarter. Prettier"—I flash a look at Iris— "I'm just trying to survive in The Cradle. It's made for them, not us."

Fuck. I feel sick. I want Meaningful Purpose as much as any Trade citizen, and my words are profane.

We are staring at each other, and I feign intimacy, push it into the length and depth of our eye contact, using every inch of strength to not recoil or grimace.

His eyes drops to my throat.

I swallow as he leers, dipping his heated gaze lower to my chest and then my lap, where his vile thoughts are almost tangible fingers removing my clothes.

"Her red hair distracted me," he offers, as if I really care, as if I'm jealous he chose her first. "You're by far the prettiest girl I have ever seen. Ever."

I blink at him. "Thank you. You've been surviving for a long time. Since you were ten?" I steady my breath, stay calm. *I'm not afraid.* "How old are you now? Have you got a House Girl?" I know the answer, but I need him to say it, for the conversation to continue as I plan.

He finishes the meat in his hand. "Twenty-two, I think. It's hard to tell when the sun decides not to shine and the moon sleeps for too long. But I believe I'm twenty-two."

"And girls?"

"Women don't survive in this lifestyle. No. They don't live long enough for me to keep."

I stare straight into his eyes. "I could. I would."

"You think?" Hesitant, he stares at the other men stirring on their mattresses. "You want to survive with me?"

I hold my panic inside.

What am I doing?

With his blade in his hand, he stands up and crosses the flaming barrel to get to me. He reaches down for my wrist, and I try not to flinch. He gazes at The Silk Girl Sigil in disdain, growling, "You want this thing on you? A womb. That is all you are to them. A womb."

"I had no choice."

"Prove it."

I look at the drain.

Where does it lead...

They'll be looking for us. Near the broken van? Near the mill? When we are announced missing, will the Mothers tell them of our secret visit? Will they track the broken glass? Will they find evidence? Will it be too late? There'll be little pieces of me missing, digested and then waste in that drain.

The drains are manned by Trade workers.

"I'll cut it off for you."

His words land a hard blow. "Pardon?" My voice strains with the thought of removing *his* mark. *No.* No, I can't. I won't. Will he eat it?

63

He sneers. "So, you're a liar, then?"

I panic. "No. You just have to prove you don't think of me as live meat and dispose of it. Do not eat it. Do not eat me. Put it down the drain or," I swallow, "something."

A smile moves across his lips. "When Shank told me our Snakes saw a Trade van on the road, I thought he was crazy. Trade vans don't travel 'ere."

My pulse hammers. "What's a snake?"

"Men that live in the desert for weeks—scouts. They rotate the sand around our Ruins. Our territories. Tell us what's happening on the roads. They told us about *you*. Shank said to blow out the tyres, and I thought he was out of his fucking mind. Not a Trade vehicle. Askin' for trouble."

"Shank isn't very smart. We could have had more Guards," I mutter, keeping soft eye contact. He likes it. The way I am looking at him.

"Worth it; I have you now."

"Lucky, sure, but not smart," I confirm.

He sits beside me. I can see the bulge between his legs bunch upward. Yep, he likes my attention a lot.

He pulls my wrist to his lap, his dirty fingers and split nails curling around to hold tight. Drawing the knife up, I look at the rust and blood painting the shiny surface. I force bile back down my throat.

"Don't eat it," I say, head heavy.

"You're nothing like I expected."

"You're not what I expected."

"Come with me." He is suddenly dragging me into the shadows, away from the others. I cannot breathe.

I try not to panic. A girl who likes him wouldn't panic over being alone in the dark with him.

"You want to be mine?" he asks. "I'll keep you." I can smell the death on him, his unclean flesh and putrid breath rolling down my skin.

His hands come up to my chest, my body jerking when they both paw softly at my breasts.

"Small. They are small."

"I'm sorry."

"No, no, I like them." He opens my cloak to expose my dress. It's a dusty lilac colour, the king's hue, but he cannot see any colours in the dark. "I've never been with a girl who wanted it before or was alive."

Shit. My throat burns with bile.

Even as I try to remain calm, my body shakes violently. I've never been touched by a man before. My hands won't move, but I think I am supposed to do something.

To touch him.

All I can do is steel my spine and let him fondle, but when his breathing becomes rough and his hands too firm, I blurt out, "I've never been with a man."

I hope that he will slow down, but his hands continue to work on removing my dress; I block out the feeling. Bare, rough fingers slide along my skin; I concentrate on breathing.

Disgusting lips move to mine, *meet* mine. A tongue pushes in, and I twist my cringe of disgust into a moan of false enjoyment. But when the hard length between his legs presses against me, I stumble backward and hit a wall.

"Wait," I pant, exhaling his horrid breath from my mouth and inhaling clean air to replace it.

"Okay!" He huffs. "I'll cut it off first."

"Cut into the fat, too," the words spit out, "make sure it's all gone. Then put it down the drain."

"You're a wild girl."

I sob. "Then we can be free."

"I *am* free."

My hands shake. "We can be free *together*."

This might keep me alive, might make him defend me against the others, might… give me time.

Or that piece of me might float down the drain. I don't know what I'm doing. I grab my forearm, displaying the tattoo, twist my head away, and close my eyes.

A cold blade presses in and slides under my skin, curling the flesh and fat from my muscles, burning a trail so intense it sends violent noises up my throat.

I try to keep quiet, but it hurts, and a real groan crawls along my tongue before I can stop it.

I quickly mutter, "I'm sorry."

But it is too late.

"Wait. What the fuck?" One of the men is awake, but we are still hidden in the shadows of the large room. "Where is she, you damn fool!"

On a mission, I grab the slice of flesh, perfectly removed—a strip branded by The Trade—and move to the drain. I squat, shoving it between the grates. It disappears under the building and out of sight.

Fat is less dense than water… It might float. *It has to float.* Float all the way to the dam or irrigate yards that are managed by Trade men. They will see the sigil; they'll alert someone. It is a wildly arbitrary plan, but it is all I have.

I look down at my wrist, a shiny strip missing, the raw, bloody flesh screaming in the exposed air. My head spins. I lose my fight against the nausea. It swoops in, my muscles loosen, knees buckle, and I drop straight to the floor.

"Your tongue can't be trusted, little girl. Let's take it off for you. It gets you in so much trouble."

His threat rattles between my ears moments before a black silence swallows my world.

CHAPTER FIVE

ROME

Odio screeches above me.

Blood mists the air. On my right shoulder, orange first-light filters through the dark skies.

I stride across the dry range littered with twitching bodies, using my steel-capped boot to push them from my path.

My hood flaps in the wind.

Arid, hot air cuts across the sea from the north, carrying the scent of death, decay, and victory. Air that travelled The Strait, picking up the sharp notes of fish and boat oil. The invaders made it to the shore at Breaker Ledge, such a remarkable feat. They should be proud.

Only to be killed on the desert sand.

Holding my automatic rifle, I stride up the hill wanting the epic view of carnage. My thigh muscles burn, my lungs rattle. It's been a long night.

"Spare me," a weak voice says, and I stop halfway up the rock. The tip of my boot dusts the side of a Common man's face. Eyes wide with terror, blood flowing like a fountain around a bullet in his throat, but still very much alive.

I hover, giving him a final breath before I step onto his head, popping his skull against the hard red crust of The Cradle. "Meaningful Purpose starts in the womb."

I reach the top of the desert plateau, the wind threatening me, but I am too fucking big to be swept over. To be thrown backward. To be controlled.

I look out over the desert range, through the sand-mixed gale, and distinguish the grey shapes that represent bodies. Hundreds of them. And further in the distance, their cargo ship wedged on the shore, cutting the red sand open. Everything is red in the waste.

Moments ago, screams of pain, automatic rifles running and rattling, and wails for aid pierced the atmosphere. A continuous thunderstorm of chaotic noise.

Now, silence rides the wind.

Only the phantom of war stirs.

"You're wounded, Sire."

I touch my shoulder, feed my fingers through the leathers to a warm, wet spot and poke it. I barely feel the bullet hole, not above all the other senses sparking with action.

I smile coldly. Perhaps, I'll leave it there. Like my father did, claiming all the silvery lead inside his body like trophies for his tissue.

"I am fine."

"But it may fest—"

He stops midsentence when I turn to face him. Him—a random member of my Guard wearing a full mask to help him breathe through the gale. The sand would fill his lungs like an hourglass.

Staring directly at him, I breathe deep, the thin films of skin in my nostrils vibrating, filtering the sand and air. I was designed for this world. "Did you speak?"

"My apologies, Sire. I only wish to serve you." He salutes me, and ducks away with his rifle clutched to his chest.

Alone again, I take another moment but feel the presence of an old friend quickly approaching.

Odio's wings flick sand and debris around us, further clouding the atmosphere. His talons hit the red crust, and his left wing touches my thigh. A greeting.

Giant creature.

His beak drips with blood, slithers of flesh dangling, slapping his face in the wind.

"Beautiful," I say to him.

"You'll need that seen to, boy."

Kong.

My brows pinch.

At least my Guardian respects me enough to only call me boy when we are alone, though, I do not care for it under any circumstances. "Did we lose many to these rogues from Ruins H?"

"A few," Kong answers, staring at my back, his gaze tangible. "They will keep coming. They are starving up there."

"And I will keep killing them."

He faces the wind, staring out over the desert face. "I know your father kept his bullets inside, but your father was—"

"The king," I utter, but the message is clear.

"Yes." I hear his frustrated sigh even through the whipping wind and the sound of Odio aggressively plucking at his feathers, cleaning the blood from his majestic onyx coat.

"I care to travel to The Estate alone," I say, striding back down the rock, not wanting to continue this conversation given the direction I know it is going.

"Before you were born, your father nearly ran out of time!" He spits out, and I anticipated he wasn't fucking finished. "He waited too long. Focused on the war. Fucked the House Girls. Lost two heirs before you! He eventually stayed in The Estate and focused on his Collective and his legacy. And he made heirs." He chuckles, but it's mirthless. "*You* refuse to wear a protective mask. You refuse a Guard circle. You want to walk around, a great ominous force, and see them tremble and drop, but you don't have a damn legacy, Rome! Dammit, boy. I am here to help you!"

I spin to face him. "Then help me."

"Cairo came to me, Rome," he states, hesitant, and I frown. "He's tired of waiting, too. I didn't like it when he came to me, but he's right."

Is he tired? Is he here?

Fucking, Cairo.

"Is now really the time?" I sweep my arms wide, the bloodshed surrounding me, the whispers of final breaths still coasting the Redwind. *My* wind. *My* shore. The final breaths still plead with *my* name.

"While you're bleeding two inches from your heart?" he punches out. "Yes! I'd say now is the time, unless you want Tuscany in danger when you die. You must give your pairing heirs. You will do this for her, and, dammit, you will do this for me, Rome!"

He rarely speaks of my sister so when he does the intent holds weight. I don't speak of my sister either; she is a wound that never closed. But his affections for her have never been quiet, though never uttered aloud. They need not be. They are in his every motivation. Drive his every action.

I study him. "You speak of the queen out of turn, Kong. She isn't yours to defend. She is mine."

What little control he had leaves him in that moment. His face burns with anger. "Who are you punishing now, Rome? Always punishing someone so they hurt as much as you do. I am protecting your legacy! And your sister needs your sons to protect her when your rashness gets you killed. Without them, she will be taken from us. She is fragile. You know this."

"Sire." A member of my Guard pants, struggling up the hill, dropping to his knee in apology for the disrespectful approach. "Forgive my interruption, Sire, but Master Cairo has been informed that two Silk Girls are missing from the Aquilla Silk Aviary. We received a radio message from a Guard with reports of a crash. A Mill Trade worker found the van flipped over near Ruins N, outside an abandoned abattoir. He has sent Marshall Blues from the Trade-tower, but we are closer. Shall we go?"

"Rome," Kong warns. "*No.*"

"Yes," I say, thrilled at the premise of more blood on my hands and kills in my mental ledger.

"Send men from here," Kong implores. "You don't need to be rescuing Silk Girls. You have Trade men for such jobs."

"I don't take kindly to others playing with my property, Kong. You should know this about me." I smirk. "I am somewhat of a possessive man."

"Haven't you killed enough men today, Rome?" he calls out as I stride down the hill. "You are possessive, but you're not a man. You're the damn King of The Strait, and you're avoidin—" His words are swallowed by the wind as I descend, space stretching his voice to join the howling.

Chapter Six

Rome

A copper-coloured haze sets the scene.

It's fucking early.

"Remember there are Silk Girls in there," a Guard says to the men who surround the entrance to the old abattoir.

They brace themselves at each entrance, before signalling with their fingers, one, two, three. They open the old bovine hatches and throw the gas in. It is a clear, heavy gas that will creep along the floors, nearly undetected before it knocks everyone inside out.

I pick my entrance. A double door, clearly the main passage in and out. I want to be seen first. It is something Kong hates about me. I arrive first and leave last. The Guard like to praise this—my motivations being driven by loyalty and leadership. When, in fact, my motivations are selfish and singular. I am the king. I want the first flare of fear to fall on me.

Rome of The Strait.

There is a beat of wings and then a thud from behind us; I know it is Odio landing on the top of the tank, so I don't turn like the rest of the Guards do.

We wait for several minutes, until enough gas has leaked inside, like an eel through reeds.

Then I push open the doors. The Guards pull their masks down, but Kong and I walk straight in. One of the supreme Xin De evolutionary traits—thin films inside my nostrils that filter sand, debris, and heavy gases.

The red haze bleeds into a clammy and dark warehouse full of unconscious Endigos.

I stride forward, finding a young man on the floor. I step on his hand and roll my heel, grinding his bones to dust, mashing his flesh to red puddles. The boy groans but doesn't come to.

How utterly boring...

The gas collects around their beds and sofas, but—

I stop; a few meters away, on the floor a man crushes a small girl with black hair. Hair like onyx melted and swirled with blackberries—streaks of colour that are too dark to note, but add to the lush density, highlight and deepen.

I didn't imagine caring about this campaign, but her little hand in mine is still a warm memory.

I forget about the Endigo, the ecstasy of their fear, the kill. While I stare at her, my men move in and begin to seize the unconscious. The Cradle Relations Guard records the moment with a camera hidden in his mask. He'll use this footage for the weekly Trade Update. We will take the Endigos back to The Estate, showcase our success, promote the protection we offer to The Trade aligned Common and Xin De.

I wanted to kill a few first, but—

I stride over to the two collapsed bodies. Seething, I reach down and grab the fucker's skull, lift him from the tiny creature, and toss him to the side. The body hits a barrel, spilling the contents over the grey concrete floor.

It *is* her. I squat at her side.

Fuck me, she's pretty.

Even when unresponsive, she's striking. Her lips are flushed, eyes closed, long, dark lashes fan over pale cheeks. She is white, black, and red—a stunning contrast of bold hues.

I click my fingers at a Guard, impatient, and a mask is placed in my hand.

I'm scooping her into my arms before I can consider what has come over me. Call it interest. Call it boredom. A moment of psychosis, but it's not compassion or sympathy as I have neither, nor do I wish to.

I slide the mask over her face. "Breathe deep, little creature." She flops as though boneless. I nearly expect her to crumble to dust she is so slight. "Aster," I say her name as though I've said it a million times before. "Little Aster."

She inhales the reversing gas. It awakens her slowly. Her eyes move beneath their lids, then they open, her red lips parting on a small exhale as she gazes up at me.

"My king." She smiles. She fucking smiles at me… "You can see me. You are *here*."

I stare at her inebriated expression; the gas has hit her hard. Discomfort crawls along my fingertips, taking hold of my veins and coiling them in tight knots.

"I thought you said you would eat more."

She swallows when her face comes within an inch of mine. "I-I think that I forgot to."

Fuck. "You're weak," I say to her. I expect a wince or a tear, any kind of response, but I get an immediate acceptance of the truth in a sad nod.

"I tried to be strong. I tried to survive."

So close to her violet-coloured eyes, staring at her, staring at me, it is in this moment that words carve through my cranium. Words I tried to forget from a time that fades each year with my humanity. 'Strong things survive because they are strong. Fragile things survive despite it.'

It can't be.

The baby we took from the Common community? It must be.

An Opi allergy is rare. Her violet eyes, black hair, the age sits right... *Fuck.*

"You will look after her." Her eyes hit mine like a hammer to a skull. She asked me—directly. I should say no; it doesn't concern me, but I don't. I want to be their saviour— her saviour.

"I will."

It was an ignorant declaration from a time long before I painted my soul with the blood of hundreds and let it dry to a dark crust. Perhaps it was my last selfless moment.

My last slither of humanity.

Her hair falls like an ink-black river over my hand, my fingers, unbidden, moving through the thin, silky strands. "Do you still want to come with me?"

"Yes." In a daze, her gaze losing constancy, she lifts a hand to touch my face as though to check I am real. "You are here." I clench my jaw as her soft fingertips caress the rough surface. "You're so hard."

My heart squeezes.

I often forget the organ exists outside of firing my pulse for violence. It is too buried in layers of Xin De skin and muscles, lead and bullets, indiscriminate deaths and welcomed evil. My heart isn't often reached, no, *affected* by anything.

Forcing my eyes from her, I survey the warehouse; one Guard is taking evidence for Cairo; three are hauling unconscious Endigos outside; Kong is staring at me.

Fucker.

"What's happened here?" Kong asks, approaching me while I cradle this tiny creature in my arms. A Common Silk Girl with the audacity to touch me—*stroke* me—without permission.

I can barely look at him.

Scowling, I shake her hand from my face, and it drops. "I'll have the doctors look her over when we return to The Estate."

He stops. "We are bringing them back with us?"

Them? I look across at the other one being carried by a Guard. A redhead with a full body—perfect proportions for a Silk Girl.

"Cairo wants heirs. Yes?" I stare at Kong again. "We have two Silk Girls here. That's a complete set for my Collective. Why return them to the aviary when we already have them."

It wasn't a question; I don't know what bullshit it was.

"What a successful campaign, then?" Kong mentions. "It couldn't have gone any better if Cairo had planned it himself."

I hiss, "I thought you wanted a damn heir."

"I do. If this is how it happens then good. I only want to make sure you see the big picture every time. Not just the pieces but the player, too. What do you know about this Silk Girl?" Suspicious, Kong gets inches closer, but instinct forces my hand out, stopping him before he gets anywhere near the fragile girl in my arms.

He lifts his hands. *"Easy"*—his cunning gaze measures my expression— "I was going to take her to the other tank for you, Sire."

"I'm quite capable." I don't like the idea of handing her over for reasons I do not know, and don't care to dissect at present. It's simple. Surely. She's *my* property, and her current condition is *unacceptable.*

The CR Guard follows me, focused on capturing such a moment of pure altruism from their king. Yeah, I hate every fucking second. I stride to the tank, using my body to shield her from the winds.

I stare straight ahead, but feel her eyes mapping my face, hear her heart's rhythm race, fearful or anxious, so I hold her tighter.

"Close your eyes," I demand, and she does.

Needing to focus, I climb the outside of my tank with her scooped to my chest. The wind blows her black hair around, whipping it through the red gale.

Talons scrape on metal.

On top of the tank, Odio opens his enormous wings to hit the desert skies, but stops. Intrigued by the creature in my arms, he hovers on the current.

She has her eyes squeezed shut as he looks her over, head cocking, beady gaze shuffling. He blocks the wind to get a better view.

I climb inside and shut the hatch.

CHAPTER SEVEN

ROME

She opens her eyes just as the hatch closes. Her head rolls with the gas, seemingly heavier than her neck can handle.

I set her down on the green cushioned bench and ignore the backward glances from the Gunner at the front. This is foolishness. Bringing her into my space. She has already occupied too much of my interest and now I am practically alone with her. This isn't good.

The first time I saw her at the parlour, she walked backward into me. I thought she was pathetic in that second, a small, insignificant little Common girl who would never be selected for my Collective...

Then she looked up at me.

Those eyes...

She didn't drop to her knees; she leaned into me, spoke out of turn, and touched me without asking. She rambled about flowers and cities, too many damn spare thoughts, and I wasn't bored at all, a rare state for me, especially in the company of silly, little girls.

So, intrigued as I was, I felt the need to thank her for that, for making me feel *something*.

And now I know.

She is bound to the fibres of my last human cells, the parts of me that dwindle from nearly two decades ago when I was an idiotic boy who wanted to be a saviour.

She stares at me as though keen to map my bone structure. Blinking the cloud of gases and dust from the warehouse, my nictitating membrane slides across my cornea. She follows the sweep of the eyelid, seemingly fascinated.

I clench my teeth. Hate it. A shiver rushes the length of my body. The intimacy she presses without knowing is utterly torturous.

"Have you been inside a tank before?" I ask, sliding down the bench, adding space between us. Space that adds a much-needed reprieve from the intoxicating way her scent rouses my cock.

She is slumped backward against the inner wall, barely propped up, and I notice she holds her wrist protectively. "No, my king. Never."

I frown. "Were you not taught to address me as Sire?"

"Sire." She swallows, her tongue moving around her mouth in an odd way. "I'm sorry."

I prefer my king from her lips.

"My king will do." My forehead tightens further. "Why are you holding your wrist? And your mouth, why are you working your jaw? Are you hurt?"

"I'm sorry." She closes her eyes and shakes her head over and over. "It was naïve. I thought about taking off my clothes and pushing them down the drain for The Trade to find but I didn't want to take them off. The boy... He seemed to hate the tattoo. I let him. It's my fault. I didn't fight him."

"The fuck did he do?"

She smiles at me. "Are you real, Sire?"

She is out of her damn mind.

The tank roars and moves, and she shuffles around, nervous to feel the motion as it speeds up.

"My king," I correct, somehow cementing a unique relationship with this girl, one that bothers me, but I keep engaging in. She is like a kitten, erratic and endearing. Her energy is odd and entertaining—innocent.

Why do I care?

I can accept this interest as akin to one between an owner and a pet—nothing more. I owe her nothing. She is safe now.

I kept a foolish boy's word.

Though... Cairo would hate anything outside of the approved sequence of Trade interactions. I smirk. He would hate the conversations we have already had and the way she addresses me so informally.

I like that.

"You don't think I'm real?" I close the gap between us, inhaling as I catch her scent again. Maybe I should make her moan; she would know how real I am then. Does vulnerability have a damn scent? Well, if it does. This is it—*Aster.*

I reach out and grab her little wrist to inspect the place she is cradling so carefully. She winces. *Fuck.* I loosen my hold on her bony wrist, never knowing my strength nor usually caring.

I feel her pulse racing beneath her skin.

A frown tightens my forehead. My mark has been skinned from her, a smooth valley down to the weeping muscles. The raw area pools with white and pink fluids, and tiny beads of blood.

Anger spreads a red mist over my eyes.

"I may be dreaming," she repeats.

I grip her chin and tilt it upward. "Open your mouth."

She blinks but does as she is told.

Hesitantly, she spreads her pretty lips, revealing a pink centre but then... Her tongue flashes at me. The middle crease has a long gash, as though she has been sliced with a knife.

"Which one did this to you?"

I release her, but she doesn't move her chin, still peering up at me like the little kitten Tuscany was gifted the day after her rite. It was an offering to comfort her and bring her back to life. Tuscany was too gentle for this world...

I should have stopped him.

Could have saved her.

The kitten was her sanity manifested.

It was desperate for attention, but Tuscany had nothing left. She ignored it.

It starved to death over the three weeks that she refused to move from her mattress. The little thing gnawed at the tips of Tuscany's fingers while she was catatonic. My sister still has tiny scars on each digit from the desperate teething of her sanity.

Fuck. Why am I going there?

Aster pulls me from my dark recall, when she says, "After I convinced the Endigo boy that I was just like him—"

Clever girl... "How did you do that?"

"I told him that I would survive The Cradle... with him," she confirms, and I don't like where this is heading. My muscles tense, and my spine steels in agonising preparation. "I kissed him, and let him touch me and—"

"You what?"

"The leader said my tongue can't be trusted anymore, and he started to cut it with a knife, but then, I don't know..." Her eyelids bat, heavy. "His hand slipped. We both fell. I hit my head. I cannot feel my body right now, my king. Am I dreaming? I feel strange. Can I touch you again so that I know you're real? Can you touch me again so that I know I am?"

The gas...

Shock, too.

I stare at her, hard. "You're not afraid of me."

"Yes, but not for my life."

"Why?" I ask, thinking about the men I have just killed, their blood still drying on my leather armour and their pleas for mercy still echoing in the dark chamber of my soul. "I could strangle you with one hand."

"You have no reason to."

I measure her up, noting the scarlet hue rising beneath her cheeks. I make her blush. "Perhaps I'd enjoy seeing your life leave your eyes, little creature."

Matching me, she looks *through* me. I stiffen as her gaze pokes around inside my mind. I fucking hate it. "I don't think you're really like that. Deep down."

"And how would you know what I'm like?"

"I felt it." A bead of sweat forms on her brow, but it's not from nerves. "When you held my hand, you didn't want to hurt me then. Or did you?"

No, I didn't want to hurt her.

She is right.

"You may touch me," I say smoothly. "But don't get misguided thoughts about me and kindness. We do not exist together. You're the property of The Cradle— my property. Your body, your womb, is what matters to me."

"I understand, my king."

"More reversing gas, Sire?" the gunner asks, passing the mask back to me.

As she sways with the movement of the tank, I pull her to my lap. I cradle her entire body to my chest. Her little legs dangle over my thighs and her head nests in the crook of my arm on a pillow of her onyx hair.

She is flawless, pure—life.

And I am bloody, bruised—death.

"You're hurt, my king." She reaches up and presses her hand above my heart where my armour weeps with blood and a bullet hides deep in my flesh. "You're bleeding."

My chest tightens.

I hold the mask over her mouth and nose. My hand covers most of her face, so I part my fingers and watch her eyes flicker as she inhales.

A cruel smile moves across my face. "You let him kiss you, little creature?" Her eyes widen, but she nods into the mask. "And touch you?" I don't know what those words make me feel, but it burns a path in my muscles. "Where?"

Her eyes close on the answer.

"Show me with your hands, which parts of my property were played with," I order. "Do it now."

I gaze down as her arm lifts, her finger touching just below her ribcage, a supple spot. I track her finger as it moves upward, over her expressed ribs to the crease between her breasts. She cups a small, pert mound in her hand, her eyes never leaving mine, and squeezes it. I hiss.

I want to trace each place he touched. Follow her finger. Want to lick it. Want to mark it. Heat expands in my veins. Needing to ease some tension, I crack my neck to the side, then to the other.

So... This is the Silk Girl's prowess. A potent balance of innocence and interest; that boy didn't stand a chance to refuse her. This creature in my arms was conditioned from a babe to be what a man wants, as, what is the point of having a breeding vessel who cannot keep a man hard. She wouldn't even know how subtle the messages in her teachings are or how they consume a man's mind.

Like now...

With her slow movements.

Touching herself for me.

Slow. Behaved. Sweet.

But unknowingly seductive.

"He touched you there?" I growl, fighting against the pulsing need in my cock. I flex my hard-on against her underside but wish I could squeeze it inside her. Fuck, she'd be tight. Too tight, we'd both be in agony. "Did you like it?"

Slowly, her brows draw in and she shakes her head, trying to shake the mask away. I lower it, revealing her plump red lips. Red lips... too red. Blood has rushed to them...

Her eyes roll backward.

Fuck.

"Aster," I shake her lightly.

Not now. I look her over again, place the back of my hand on her forehead. Her skin radiates heat; she is burning up. Her perspiration is slick against my knuckles. Clammy. She's fucked. I part her lips to open her mouth and look at her tongue... Then it dawns on me. Bacteria.

Tetanus.

PART THREE
TO BE A SILK GIRL

CHAPTER ONE

ASTER

Silk Girl Vows:
Adore. Pleasure. Provide.

"What temperature do you want your shower?" Someone with an elegant accent asks from across the large room. I lift my wrist to see the smooth surface, skin grafted to the place my tattoo used to be—healing.

How can that be?

I must be dreaming...

I was only just in the tank with my king...

Or was I?

Why would I be alone with him in the first place? Confusion rolls through me. Maybe I'm still in that dank space—the Endigos are eating me slowly, and I have checked out like the live meat. Pieces of me being licked and chewed...

I blink at the new skin; I don't feel real. I have to be asleep. Fur Girls dream more than Silk Girls.

We aren't at peace.

Sitting on the edge of a giant bed, I swing my legs to and fro as though I were on an enormous cliff face. The carpeted floor is hundreds of miles from my toes, like a descent to the depths of The Cradle. Into The Crust I dive...

"I'm sorry," I say to the space below my feet, "What did you say?

"Oh!" She sounds excited. "You're coherent. The fever has let you go. That is wonderful. I have some questions for you. You can pick the temperature of your shower in The Estate. How would you like it?"

I wiggle my toes. I *am* dreaming. What an odd one this is. Everyone knows we have it hot. "We usually have it—"

"Scolding, I know," the kind voice says. "That is what all the Silk Girls say. But what do *you* want? Now that you have a choice of what you want?"

"Scolding," I repeat plainly. Not an answer or agreement, just a word that works and she used. Easy to pull out of my mind.

"Excellent choice," she praises, and I smile, proud. "And your sheet? You can choose the colour of your main sheet, but the rest of your bedding will be purple."

"Um." The complementary opposite of purple is yellow—we learn that when we arrange flowers. So I say, "Yellow is the best colour to match purple."

"Gold then?"

Why is this bed so high? "Sure."

"What flowers do you want? I'll bring you Silk Wisteria, but you can pick another species?"

"Flowers," I say, smiling. We are all little flowers growing through the crust of The Cradle. Suddenly, as the *f* sound makes my tongue flap, I remember I'm wounded. I stick it out and look down, trying to see the cut but my tongue isn't long enough.

"Don't do that," she says, poking my tongue back inside my mouth. "Tongues heal fast. It is mostly fine. It is a muscle after all.

It's your temperature that has been bothersome the past three days."

"Three days?"

"Yes, you've had a terrible fever."

Fever...

"You can pick whichever flower you want," she says, back to the same question. "I'll make sure you always have fresh ones in your room."

"Pick a flower," I repeat. "Pick the petals, one by one. He loves me, he loves me not, he loves me. Who will he choose? Um. Aster. I pick Aster."

"Most Silk Girls pick their own name."

"Aster is foreign, though." I wiggle my toes again, little beans waving. *A three-day fever?* "Aster isn't from around here. It's not like the rest."

"No, but that's okay. They produced seeds when you were named. And we started growing Aster ourselves. They turned out beautifully."

I laugh at the silly dream. "Really?"

"Of course. And your pills." She is suddenly in front of me, looking like a stunning Xin De Goddess. So tall and strong. She has brown hair and skin, long dark lashes, and a birthmark on her left cheek shaped like a star.

"Woah," I mutter, gazing up at her. Then I look down at the pills lying on her palm. Two tiny pills. One white. One blue.

"Do the other girls get these, too?"

"No. These are just for you. You were poisoned, Aster. You got tetanus and have been sedated and on IV treatment for the past three days. To help you heal. These are a low dose. Soon, you should be mostly better." She smiles. "Take them."

I swallow the pills.

"And finally, Sire would like to know what 'meal you will not forget to eat.'"

I blink at her.

"His exact words. So…" She nods to encourage me to answer. "What will it be?"

"I've always liked warm oatmeal and honey, but it's hard to get. They are both so rare. Just like Asters."

CHAPTER TWO

ROME

"What temperature did Aster choose?"

My ears twitch to the sound of her name, and I find myself detouring from the double doors that lead outside to the hunting grounds. Instead, I follow Cairo's voice toward his rooms. I wonder what he makes of her.

At the far end of the hall, the door to his chamber is open and a Watcher stands in the gap.

He doesn't allow anyone to enter his space except for me. Had he a choice, he might object to that, too. He does not.

"Scolding, Master," she answers.

Cairo nods. "And the flower?"

"Aster, Master."

"And the sheet?"

I continue down the corridor, the hard rap of my boots on the concrete draws The Watcher's attention. Noticing my approach, she swallows and bows, her chin to her chest, her eyes cast downward as I pass her.

"Sire."

"The sheet?" I press, strolling into Cairo's pristine quarters. Wall-to-wall bookcases carved from the rich, red flesh of ancient trees surround a matching single desk and leather studded chair.

Cairo doesn't look away from the three-dimensional screen across from him—a giant vision that covers the wall. He swipes his finger and pinches to move through the depth of the screen. Documenting the finer details hidden in each answer and filing them accordingly.

The Watcher clears her throat. "Yellow, erm, gold." She cannot read, though her eyes follow the holographic numbers and lines as though a secret may be revealed.

She is fascinated.

Outside Trade-approved buildings, there is minimal tech available. A single, large vision screen is in every tower to broadcast a weekly update and weather cautions. The Trade Connect Building has centralised computer networks to store data, and communication between other TC buildings is done through underground copper wiring. This is used strictly for security and intel purposes. We uncovered an old disc a few years back and are working on locating a satellite from the old-world, but throwing signals out into a hazy-cloaked abyss is the same as wishing on a star.

That is it.

Besides the Trade medical laboratories, all other tech has been banned since the Gene Age, when everyone had a device and the ability to communicate, create their own propaganda, influence… Dangerous times.

The Trade resurrected the land with the peaceful notion of returning to our roots, to Meaningful Purpose.

No entertainment. No confusion.

Basically, we don't fucking trust Common with tech anymore, nor do we think they are capable of peace and sustainability when they have access to it.

History proved this.

Cairo hums approvingly. "She is very agreeable."

Conditioned. He means conditioned. Compliant. I must admit, I am somewhat surprised she didn't choose a different colour or flower and give her individuality away.

It's there.

Cairo finally offers the girl his attention. "Isn't she." Then he looks at me. "Paisley," he adds, "Why do we have different Trades?"

She straightens, thinking it's a test. "So we all contribute to The Cradle, Master. So we all serve The Cradle."

"Yes, of course, sweet girl," he muses, "But why just one each? They link in some cases. Blend. For instance," —he leans backward in his chair— "why not have you dress Aster, too? Or bathe her?"

Her breaths become shallow, feeling an ulterior motive to his conversation. She is right, but not in the way she suspects. It is for me. Not her. "I was born for parchment. I'm to guide, watch, and convey."

"Yes," he keeps his face impartial, "but why can't you do more if it relates to your current role and placement?"

She presses her hand to her frantic heart. "I suppose that I could do more—"

"Don't panic yourself," he offers, leaning forward again, and she exhales hard. "I'm not asking you to do anything outside of your Trade, Paisley. I never will."

"Thank you, Master."

"That was scary? Wasn't it? The unexpected? My expectations? Not knowing what I needed. Overwhelming. I am sure you would prefer the comfort of the boundaries given by The Trade. And something always has to give—if we try to be too much. It's why a Silk Girl must not revel in grand ideas. She is to be singularly focused on producing. One can't be available to their lord, focused on his needs, if they dream of adventures. Their true Meaningful Purpose would suffer. Wouldn't it?"

"Yes, Master. Have I done something wrong?"

He smiles smoothly. "No, Paisley. Good girl. You may go back to your Purpose."

With a quick curtsy, she scurries away.

"Wonderful speech," I note. "Who was it for?"

I stop in front of The Trade Master, and he stands, offering me the slightest bow before sitting again. Ever the traditionalist, nothing stops him from his sequence of interactions and customs.

"Rome. You cannot execute a Wardeness without a trial," he states as he returns to his screen.

"I don't intend to."

"Good. I have booked it in two first-lights. We will travel together when you wake tomorrow. The Wardeness was born in the Lower-tower and so she will be trialled there, and this will give us an opportunity to meet with the Trade men at the weir, it is on the way, and they need to see your interest in their Purpose." He looks at me, intrigue well-hidden on his face. Not well enough. *I know you, fucker.* "What was the Wardeness' crime?"

I deadpan. "She was careless with my property."

"The little Silk Girls. Iris and Aster. She took them on an outing, correct? Without permission."

He knows the answer.

I nod, curt. "Yes."

He returns to his screen. "I watched the young Silk Girls leave the tank. The redhead seemed perfectly formed. Were there any issues with her that you noticed?"

"I didn't."

I didn't notice her at all.

"But you travelled with the other? Aster? Am I right? To what purpose did you need to accompany her?" he says, not asking the question he actually wants. "She must have needed something to warrant your attention?"

Does he know she was one of the babies taken from the Common community during my first campaign? Would he remember? We have harvested hundreds of babes since that day, so I wouldn't know how deep his recall goes.

I wouldn't put it past him to remember each baby.

"I met her at the parlour weeks ago," I state, withholding that piece of detail. "She was wounded when I arrived, and the CR Guard was having a field day with the campaign. I played along, for once."

He clicks his tongue, dubious. "I see. She seemed perfectly formed. Clean. Pretty. Is she well in all other senses?"

Clean. Pretty. "Her sigil was cut off and her tongue was lacerated," I say plainly.

"But she has been with the doctor for four days, yes?" He reads his answer on the screen. "The tongue is healing nicely, and so is the skin graft. We can brand her again once it's fully taken. But I have not been able to see either girl, as I've been occupied by the lords' imminent visit. Either way, we don't need her tongue or her voice, but trauma is generational. Epigenetics can change the path of DNA forever. Transfers from babe to babe. Are you certain you want her Meaningful Purpose carried out with a member of your Collective? There are other Silk Girls from other Silk Aviaries to choose from. If this Wardeness is as careless as you have seen, perhaps these girls need to be placed with lower value Trade men — a Guard perhaps."

Like fuck they will.

The past week I have spent balls deep inside most of my House Girls trying to fuck out the thought of her. I've been out of my mind, fierce, and hurt one of them badly.

And forgetting her?

It didn't work.

I widen my stance, making the mass of my body even larger. "You visited Kong and pressed me for an heir. I now have two new Silk Girls. A random selection. I don't seek anything outside of an heir. They will do fine."

He lifts his gaze once more, eyes hitting me hard. "You will choose one, then, Sire?"

He wanted this. He's desperate for the entire set of five to have Meaningful Purpose, a complete house. But I've never been a willing part of The Trade's chessboard, a piece placed just so. The king. The queen. The pawns.

"Who has the most power in the game of chess?" Kong asks me the day before my eighteenth birthday.

"The king," I answer, moving the pawn ahead of my favourite piece to give him an opening. I like moving the king around the board. He is the largest piece and that is my misguided priority.

"Why?" Kong moves his pawn.

"The entire game is about him."

"So he is important," he agrees, "certainly. But is he the most powerful? What about the queen?" He slides his queen out on a diagonal to target my king. "Why not her? She can move as many squares as she wishes, in all directions."

Annoyed at the thought, I look at the girl who I am sure is my little sister, sitting cross-legged a few feet away and playing porcelain dolls with her Sired Mother. "She is not being chased. That's why she's got more freedom to move. Nah. Not the queen. The game continues without her."

"True. But you're still wrong. Try again."

"I don't know, Kong. This is stupid."

"The player, boy. The player has the power."

I suppose—I flick my tongue—I didn't want my Silk Girl to be too compliant. It would amuse me to have her ruffle his feathers while carrying my heir—untouchable based on his own policies and practices.

"I will choose one. Perhaps the redhead."

"Perfect. Tell me when the union is made, so the others can begin. They have been waiting rather patiently. Well, all except one."

I turn from him and head back down the corridor toward the outdoor, thinking about her compliance.

Aster isn't compliant with me, she addresses me incorrectly, she speaks her mind, she dances sweetly on the line of appropriate behaviour and bats her lashes in nativity, but... She chose scolding, Aster, and gold. A conditioned response. Perfectly obedient.

A clone.

A boring little Silk Girl.

Doing as she is told to do.

Obeying the player.

Lost in thought and sentiment, annoyingly so, I freeze at the outdoor, and stare down the adjoining long passage that forks from this one.

To Tuscany's old room—the room we both died in—before she moved into the Queen's wing. The night she was carved open, I remember the agony in my abdomen, remember how sleep spun me, hurt me, tossed me around. I should have woken up. I should have known... She was calling to me. To make my way to her. To save her.

I scowl at the patched bricks several meters before it, from when I crushed the skulls of two Guards trying to stop me from getting to her.

Nevertheless, I was too late...

I open the door and head outside.

99

CHAPTER THREE

Silk Girl Vows:

For The Cradle, I shall adore all its children equally and with quiet humility. I have no claim over what I provide for The Cradle.

I stare at my feet, watching my toes disappear into rich, clean soil. I'm not sure I have ever walked outside with bare feet before.

Where are you?

What is this place?

I must have noticed the weather shift, cooling. Must have walked down the giant manicured hill, the one surrounded by castle-like buildings made of granite, veined with grey and white marble.

I must have smelt the fresh-cut flowers and sniffed the lemon and vinegar cleaning tonics through the open windows, must have walked these gardens more than once already, but I cannot recall the specifics.

I only remember eyes tracking me. For days now, between one

shadowy memory to the next, I recall several eyes on me—one from above, keener than the rest.

On my tippy-toes, I pluck a red rose from a tall perimeter hedge. Looking at it, I inhale. There is a breeze. My hair moves on my shoulders, the ends brushing my waist. Surely, I noticed such an odd sensation, a perfectly controlled gust from the south.

I must be at the very bottom of The Estate. I look down the green landscaped garden hill to a high wall in the distance, and beyond, to the tops of woven tree canopies. The branches move with life, but the limbs strangle together, unwelcoming and defensive.

I wonder how deep the woods are...

I know that to the north, an architectural masterpiece makes the Redwind behave—a fort of protection, with just enough vents to allow a conditioned atmosphere within the keep. I only know this from my studies. I have seen pictures of The Estate. It houses over fifty-thousand citizens and is entirely shielded by a rolling limestone wall shaped like the open wings of an eagle.

Foliage moves beside me.

"Are you ready for some lunch?" someone calls from my right.

A grumbling in my stomach suddenly answers for me. That's good. I'm present. I know what happened. The Endigos cut my tongue and sliced my mark right off like a strip of meat. Though, all the things that happened to me are jumbled together now. I am still not convinced I didn't bite my tongue while eating an apple or maybe Iris cut me in my sleep.

All possible.

Iris... is she alive?

And the Wardeness?

With the fever I've had... was it three days? I've been gliding through one strange land to another, stepping from cloudy plain to cloudy plain, never knowing which is real and which is a construct of my mind.

"Aster?" Someone touches my shoulder.

I look over at Paisley. I like her. She wears the cutest dress shirts, in all colours, and trousers that are pleated down the centre. I wonder if she presses them each day.

She has the strangest expression, and I realise I have the rose to my mouth as though I am going to eat it. I cannot have her believe that I'm not better, because I am.

"Are you ready for some supper?" she repeats.

"Yes." I drop the rose. "I'm ready."

"Are you sure? I can't eat with you today. Sire returns from the trial, and so you'll be eating with the other Silk Girls for the first time. I need to meet with him and Master Cairo."

"What needs to be done?" I ask. "Can I help?"

"That's not your Purpose." Taking my hand in hers, she says, "Come with me. We can just stand outside, and you can decide if you're ready to sit with the other Silk Girls. If you are, then I will leave you with them. If you don't want to, then you can eat in your room just this once."

I want to be ready.

To prove this, I straighten and keep her pace as we stroll toward their wing on the opposite side of The Estate.

"As you were a little foggy, I didn't get a chance to give you a tour of The Estate," she starts as we stride onward. "But you are welcome to enjoy the gardens, and every unlocked door you come to. Stay away from the forest line to the south, there are wild animals in the trees, but don't be frightened. Sire and his hunters cull them back into the mountains. It's what we eat most days. There are three new greenhouses, best not to go in there or you'll get in the way of production. The majority of The Estate dates back nearly two thousand years." As we pass under a stunning archway, she gestures toward it. "The original structure was renewed with unbreakable marble stone, but the integrity of the buildings still shows respect to the old-world. All except the piazza. The late, Turin of The Strait, The Cradle's longest standing Monarch and Protector, desired a more elaborate piazza, so fifty years ago he completely recreated it with crystal mosaic tiles and water fountains."

We walk between grand double doors and into the Silk Girl Wing, the scent of lemon growing with each step.

Entering a cloakroom, I remember I've not worn a coat. It was imperative whenever we visited the Lower-tower. The wind is sharp there. But here, the breeze swirls my hair and skirting all around my body, rising hairs on my legs and arms, and I quite enjoyed the subtle and playful sensation.

She continues her tour. "You'll find a library with appropriate reading material in your wing, as well as a room to dance, paint, and do puzzles. And, of course, the birthing suite with the finest luxuries and equipment for your safe delivery."

We stop outside double wooden doors fitted with square glass peepholes. Perhaps so the house personnel can peer in and see who is eating before entering.

I test it out, squinting through the square window and see a cute dining room painted in dark purple with trimmings and patterns etched into the walls and a large window that shows a long courtyard. Inside, four girls dressed in Paisley's pleated trousers stand in a corner conversing while four Silk Girls sit around a circular wooden table.

Straight away, I spot Iris, and remember... Like a flickering flame, the hours we spent captured by the Endigos. The blood, the live meat, and her head injury.

I blink, refreshing the sight of her.

She looks different. Softer. Or am I endlessly hopeful she will come around... I gaze between the other girls. Quite the most beautiful girls I have ever seen, and so round in all the right places. Unlike me.

"Enchanting, aren't they?" Paisley says humbly. "A full set including yourself. *Trade be kind*, each will have at least three babies. A girl, a boy, and a spare."

I cover my mouth when I see a lovely, dark girl is already pregnant, her beautiful round stomach stretches her silken dress, and crumbs dust the area in a playful way.

I've never seen a pregnant Silk Girl in real life. She *does* look as though she is glowing but then it is very luminous in that room with the large window offering crown-light, the hazy yellows bathing them and the table.

"She has Meaningful Purpose." My voice is breathy with awe. "Is that baby the king's?" I don't know why I ask, but my stomach tugs as I do.

"I'm sorry, what did you say?" Paisley whispers.

I look up at her. "I don't know. Is that wrong to ask?"

"I thought that was in your studies?"

"What was in my studies?" My eyes widen. There is something I don't know. "I didn't finish. Is it important?" She looks shocked, so I continue, "Please don't tell anyone that I asked. Just pretend I didn't."

"It's okay." She touches my shoulder. "I'll tell you, so don't ask that question again and give yourself away." She looks through a different square hole at the girls eating around the wooden table. "The four Silk Girls in there are for *his* Collective, four plus Sire."

"I don't understand." I swallow. "They share?"

"Share your womb? No, that would be messy." She laughs a little. "How would they know which one is the heir if they all put their seed inside every girl? They share the sight of you, but they do not share your womb."

I blink at her. "I still don't understand."

"All the Silk Girls are treated the same. All the babes are raised the same. To protect the heir, he is only revealed when he turns eighteen. A child is a frightfully fragile creature. No one can be trusted. No need to put a target on one."

"So, who knows?"

She keeps her voice low. "Only The Trade Master knows all, and the lord knows which child is his, as he picks his Silk Girl, but they do not know of each other's babe."

I nod my understanding. "And the Silk Girl."

"She will never know. That is utterly important."

"I'm sorry." I stare at her, confused. That can't be right. "I must be hearing you wrong. How is that possible?"

She pulls me to the side, away from the wooden door, lowering her voice further. "How do you not know what happens when he comes to you at night?"

"We learn of the night in the last six months of training. It is private until then. And I didn't finish. I was in the crash and now I am here, and my head is fuzzy."

She touches my cheek, drawing me back to her. "I like you, Aster. It's going to be okay. Don't ask questions as a rule. It's best that way. You'll wear a beautiful solid, silk veil, Aster. When a lord visits you at night and gives you Meaningful Purpose, you won't know who he is. This way, there is no jealousy or favouritism, and the heir's safety is kept to the highest degree. When you give birth, the child will be taken to a Sired Mother to raise and nurse, and you will return to your Meaningful Purpose until you have given your lord at least two boys and one girl. If he likes you, maybe more."

I nod slowly. I knew that last bit. That I wouldn't raise the child, but I thought I would know the lineage. But then, it is not mine. It's The Cradle's. It's all of ours.

I look at my hands, remembering why I have to get well. Why I have to be sane and clear. Because once I have fulfilled my Purpose, and if I am very good and lucky, I will be a Sired Mother and look after the babies of The Cradle until I am old.

"Are you ready to enter and meet the girls?" Paisley asks, walking back to the door.

I wonder what Iris will think...

"It's okay," she says straightaway, thankfully, because I don't know how to answer her. If they are anything like Iris, Lavender, or Ivy, then I am *not* ready to meet them.

She guides me back to the door. "I will see you after your meal and take you to your forever room."

I force myself to nod, and she opens the door for me.

The girls look up as I slowly walk in.

"I've seen you in the garden!" the pregnant one says, bouncing to her feet as though she isn't carrying a boulder under her silk dress. "You're feeling better then?"

I stare at Iris as she pales to behold me. *"That's* your ghost girl?" Iris startles. "That's the girl you keep seeing?"

"Yes," she agrees. Taking my hand, she says, "Come with me," guiding me to sit at the table beside her. "A full set. I am so excited. I've waited for this day. *My* lord, whoever he is, could not stop himself from starting early. I wonder who has that kind of hubris to just initiate my rite before a full set is even in The Estate." She lifts an eyebrow, her message clear—she believes she carries the heir.

I believe so, too.

She is the most beautiful girl in here.

Even compared to Iris.

I try to hide my face as a sinking feeling in my stomach takes over. Our moment—the king's and mine—in the tank comes to me in strange, curt images; his hand on my face, covering the mask; his eyes drilling me in place, intense to a tangible level; his desire for me, pressing at my backside—

"I thought you were locked away," Iris blurts out, before shovelling a spoonful of oatmeal into her mouth. "Finally gone completely mad. She has imaginary friends, you know."

Ignoring her, I look around the table, and a few of the others smile softly, wary but kind, each saying a little hello.

"Locked away…" A blonde girl says. "For what exactly?"

I look at her.

"She is very petite," a curvier girl adds quickly. "Sorry, I don't mean to be rude. Only it is rare now to see a girl under five-foot-five. How tall are you? What are you measurements?"

Umm.

"Do you not speak?" the blonde presses before I can answer either of them.

"I speak," I finally get in. "My tongue is healing, and it takes a bit of effort to speak." I withhold the truth about not having many

friends or knowing how to chitchat. Except with a mutated bird...
I am a witty conversationalist with him.

The blonde stares. "What is wrong with it?"

Uncertain, I sit down, and they all follow me with their eyes—
all four beautiful creatures.

I blink at them, reading. My bully gauge is broken, I can't tell
whether she is taunting me or merely asking a question.

I pick up the spoon beside the oatmeal, steamy ribbons carry
exotic spices and honey up my nostrils. I wonder how they came
to find such rich fragrances.

"I have a small, erm—" I look at Iris. She is staring at her meal
as though her appetite has vanished. "My tongue has a small
wound, and it feels a little awkward to speak at the moment. The
more I talk, the easier it becomes."

The curvier one, with lovely rosy cheeks and auburn hair that
matches, straightens. "*Oooh*, can I see your tongue?"

"You can't just ask her that," Iris deflects.

"No, that's okay." I stick out my tongue, and they take a big
breath in.

"*Cool,*" the curvy girl says. "I'm Blossom. You're lucky, we were
served honey and oatmeal today. Usually, it's fruit, toast, and eggs.
Sometimes soup. I don't really like eggs, especially because I know
where they come from, but they are good for us, so I do eat them."

The blonde smiles. "I'm Daisy. I'm so glad we are a complete
set now, and all so different. That is by design."

The pregnant one puts her brown hand on my knee, tapping
softly. "I'm Lantana, but you can call me Ana. You are the most
interesting thing to me. Seriously. I have seen you in the garden,
like a wraith. Half doped-up. White skin. Black hair. And you are
so lovely, I wanted to stare at you all day. I wasn't sure that you
were real. But my lord whispered to me at night, that you have
been through quite an ordeal."

"Maybe I'm not real."

They all laugh—except for Iris. I didn't mean to be funny, but their smiles become contagious. I think my bully gauge is in a state of sleeping.

Maybe this is what being a Silk Girl is meant to be? I wouldn't mind that at all.

~

"That was a successful meal," Paisley says as we walk through the Silk Girl Wing, under arches of wooden rafters adorned with gold and purple licks of metallic. "Follow me. I think it's time you settle into your forever room in The Circle."

Forever room.

That means it's going to happen. A lord will choose me. I'll grow babies, eat the most glorious food, and dance ballet. My entire life has been leading to this moment.

Floral wallpaper seems to move with us and stop— When we pause, it is outside a guarded door.

"Hello," Paisley greets, and the man at the door nods. He is dressed in full black, tactical leather armour, his head high, eyes level.

He steps aside, allowing us to enter.

This new room seems to be a kind of holding space with two painted footprints in the centre of the floor. There is another door, and it's made from an aged wood; I can tell by the veins and burns. Carved into the centre are flowers of all kinds and bird feathers woven through the foliage. Small birds—not eagle feathers.

"I'll show you what to do." Paisley walks to the spot, stepping onto the prints. "Stand by the wall."

Leaning against the wall, I watch as a white beam glides down her body, before beeping.

"What is that?"

"It is to check that I am well. And you, too. The Silk Girls sleep in here. No one enters besides the lords and the Watchers. You each have one. I'm yours. You will need to do that each time you enter and leave The Circle, or the door will not open for you."

She waves me over. "Your turn."

"Does it hurt?"

"You won't feel anything."

I step up to the prints and place a foot on each. The beam begins to slide down my body, and I feel nothing at all. Can it read my mind? My mind isn't entirely well. Can it tell I am nervous? My heart is a vigorous little thing in my chest.

It beeps, and I exhale hard.

"One final thing." She points at a dot on the wall. "Press your upper arm to the dot."

Breathing shallowly, I walk over and press my arm to the black dot, imagining it might measure me. My weight activates something mechanical inside the wall.

"It will beep twice," she advises, coming up to me. "Then it gives you a little pin prick." She holds me still. "Ready?"

Pardon?

Beep.

Beep.

I wince at the little prick.

"See, easy." She steps aside, giving me space. "Every first-light when you start your day, you must have your shot, or the door will not open for you. It's a special serum, with a concentration of vitamins and minerals. Formulated specifically for a Silk Girl."

I rub my upper arm, repeating the tasks in my mind; beam every time I enter or leave; arm prick each first-light when I leave to start my day. I understand. "You don't get one?"

"I don't get one. Let's go." She guides me through the pretty door, and I brush the wood with my fingertips wondering if the old tree has memories in its splinters. Tales of the sun, heavy winds, and giant birds of prey.

We enter an empty room shaped like a hexagon, with six walls, forming perfect angles. No furniture or décor but for a mural on the floor depicting a colourful garden, reminiscent of the ones outside. It's peaceful, quiet, and pretty—and without much character.

Is that what I'm to be?

On each angled wall is a closed door. "Six doors," I breathe softly, scanning the space. "Five Silk Girls and the exit."

"Yes," Paisley confirms, walking to what I presume is *my* bedroom door. "This is called The Circle. I have set your room up already. With your gold sheet, Aster flowers, and the temperature of your shower is set to hot. I'll leave you to get comfortable." She looks around, even though we are alone. "I also put a little light reading in your drawer... I know you can read. Lucky girl. This one comes with an illustration."

I nod, but then she is gone, back through the sixth door and out of sight. I look at the closed door to my room. Blink.

A *forever room*. But forever isn't *forever*, only until I stop producing babes, but it *is* many years.

I reach for the doorknob and— *'Why do you hesitate? Don't you want my mark.'* I push open the lovely wooden door, immediately swept up in the scent of flowers.

The room seems to open up as I walk inside. Tapestries adorn the walls, all depicting scenes from the gardens outside. An artificial fire hearth burns low flames around logs. In the corner, a sofa and a side table with a statue and a lamp.

I wander around.

How many girls have slept in here before me? Was the Silk Girl who birthed the king once in this room?

In the centre, is a grand bed carved from the same ancient wood as the doors. It is too high to sit on, one must use the stool fastened to the side.

That's for *a Xin De man...*

He can sit on this bed; I must climb onto it.

In a small closet, I find modest dresses in white and a few in various hues of purple. There is a pair of brown leather pants and hide boots—to protect our skin in the Redwind. And three pairs of sandals, one with flowers on the straps, one with vines, one with rope twined laces. They're not the exact styles as in the Silk Aviary, but similar. All Silk Girls wear alike dresses but for slight differences depending on the girl's shape. In the Silk Aviary, the Modistes Girl, a girl who has The Trade responsible for designing, creating, and fitting apparel, would choose a modest style for me, whereas she would dress Iris in lower cuts with shorter sleeves.

I shut the closet.

I take the small steps up the side of the bed and crawl on. The mattress beneath my knees is like nothing I have ever felt before. Soft, yet forming.

Rolling to my back in the centre, I stare at the ceiling. A sensation unsettles my stomach, a flutter of anticipation and nerves.

Will a lord visit me tonight?

Or tomorrow?

Will I know beforehand?

The veil.

I turn to my knees and crawl to the bedside drawers. I hold my breath as I pull it open. Like I thought, the veil sits just inside.

I slide it on. It is a solid black silk piece that cups the top of my crown, curtaining my eyes and nose, ending at my upper lip, leaving my mouth mostly exposed. Available. Open.

Staring through the lush fabric, I see dots of light, blurry shadows that could be furniture, but no further detail. I remove the veil and place it back inside the drawer.

Do I wear this each night?

Will it hurt when he...

When he opens me?

I flop backward and cover my face with my palms, taking a big breath. Suddenly feeling hot and bothered despite the curated temperature of the room. I wish I had someone to ask questions—about the... *act.* Maybe one of the other Silk Girls will be kind. I'll test her friendship by making minor mistakes, and then if she passes, I could ask her about the six months I have missed.

The details I should know.

Iris already knows them…

She is a summer older than me.

'I also put a little light reading in your drawer… with diagrams.'

My eyes widen on the ceiling.

Slowly, I sit up and look across at the drawer again. Stare. I go to it—again—and open it, now noticing other things inside: a brush, a small towel, folded white pages. *Right.*

Taking a big breath, I retrieve them before laying on my stomach and opening the pages up on the pillow.

My cheeks flush as I read the scene, a first-person account of being with a man.

I squirm on the mattress.

I wasn't entirely sure I could take him inside me. I was afraid to be in the dark, but he slipped two fingers through my folds. "You're ready," he murmured.

He pressed my thighs down and worked himself into me, making loud noises that rumbled from deep within his chest.

And I took him.

All of him.

I was shuddering with pleasure at each pump, at each thrust. Having the special places inside me rubbed, soothed, and massaged, every inch previously untouched, now pressed, and caressed. I exploded.

Hesitantly, I turn the page to see the drawing of a wonderfully curvaceous woman wearing a Silk Girl Veil. She is throwing her head back, her body arching upward, and he… A massive Xin De man is fully sheathed inside her. Veins pop along his arms as he pins her down, muscles on his abdomen crunch together—

I start to pant, feeling strange. So strange that I flip the page over, unable to look any longer. Shower, I need to shower— Or pee. I want to pee so badly.

I stand up and rush to the bathroom, sit on the toilet and feel a tingle when I wee into the bowl.

What the hell is wrong with me?

What the hell is happening?

CHAPTER FOUR

ASTER

Silk Girl Vows:

For The Cradle, I vow to live free of jealousy. It is a disease that does not leave space inside the heart for Meaningful Purpose.

"*Hmm,*" a girl named Island, The Estate's Modistes Girl, makes a drawn-out sound of contemplation as she circles my naked body. "Small."

I wrap my arms around my middle, darting my gaze to Paisley, who sits in the corner watching us. I know I'm small; it's literally been thrown in my face every day of my life.

Most Silk Girls have Xin De in them... But not all. In the past, only Xin De girls qualified to be Silk Girls, but since The Revive, the criteria are simply three generations of successful pregnancies and births. Sounds easy, but one miscarriage and you're out. *Forever.* But Xin De mixed girls carry and birth the babies well. Better, in truth. They can carry the babes for longer, some, all the

way to term. Which is not usual now given the massive size of a
Xin De fetus.

I follow Island with my eyes. Her face is entirely covered in
chalky white paint; her top lip is a bright red puckering arrow.

"Very sweet figure," she notes, "but you could be a tad fuller in
certain areas."

She stops moving around me. "To add volume, I'm going to go
with a heart-shaped neckline, really try to showcase those sweet
little things to the lords."

It's been two days since I moved into my forever room. I've
been told that there is a carnival in The Estate tonight. It is a word
I didn't know until today. It means party, of sorts. All the lords
from every tower will be there, giving the five in his Collective a
chance to view us amongst others. "I've never been dressed
before."

She finds a white, long-sleeve leotard with a heart-shaped
neckline—like she advised—on the gold-gilded clothing rack. "Put
this on first, then this long purple slip shirt. I will do your hair up
high, show that long neck and décolletage. You're the perfect
ballerina."

"So, you don't think I'm too small?"

"Look, it's old practise that the larger girls carry better. But I have
seen tiny things like you birth just fine. Your hips will do what they
will whether you have extra meat on them or not, and if the babe has
a high Xin De genus, you will not be expected to carry it to term
anyway. It will be incubated when it grows too large for your womb.
The Revive was meant to balance the differences between our kinds
and stop the species conflict, which is why more Silk Girls like you
are arising. The Xin De genes are recessive; you must have read this
in your studies. But—" She takes a big breath. "Some are opposed to
The Revive. They want purity. After all, Xin De were masterfully
designed to survive. It's in a Xin De Lord's best interest to pick a girl
who has some traits, height, strength, flesh armour, the nictitating
membrane, the film in the nostrils. Do you have any of these?"

I shake my head.

"I didn't think so. But you're a sight, Aster." She smiles widely. "Really, really, lovely to look at. You'll be picked quickly because they won't be able to take their eyes off you."

She's just being nice.

"I agree," Paisley says from the corner.

"What if no one wants me?" I ask Island as I dress, sliding my leg into the fabric holes. "What happens?"

"There are five lords and five Silk Girls."

And that is her answer. One of them will get stuck with me, whether they want me or not. She starts to fuss around with my clothing, a mother duck plucking duckling feathers.

A few moments later, I am dressed.

Dressed but not at all prepared.

"Don't worry, Aster. I've seen you move. You're lovely. Slow. Sultry. That's the ballerina training." Paisley looks at Island. "And her eye contact—"

"*Yes,*" Island agrees, "her eye contact is some of the best I have seen in a new Silk Girl."

I bounce my gaze between them, utterly overwhelmed by the subject.

"Remember," she purrs, "you have other body parts, too."

Island steps to my back and starts on my hair. "Far more interesting than big breasts and round hips."

I blink ahead. "Like what?"

A corner of Paisley's mouth curves. "Like your *lips.*"

"Eat fruit," Island adds quickly.

I cannot keep up. "Are you sure?" I look up, and Island leans to make eye contact with me while she pins my hair into a soft, loose bun on the back of my crown.

She looks like my Rapport after a feed, all teeth and cunning excitement. "Eat fruit while you look at the lords. Fruit is juicy. It'll slide down your lips."

My face flushes.

"*Oooh,* yes," Paisley gushes softly. "Don't wipe it off straight away, make sure they see."

"You cannot speak unless spoken to"—Island moves to stand before me. She lifts my chin and begins to paint my lips with a soft red blush while she says, "You cannot approach them or touch them, and you must be appropriately dressed, but you *can* eat and gaze at them."

"I can't," I begin.

"It's in your Trade to seduce, Aster. Make one of them want you. This is for The Cradle. You remember your vows?" Paisley approaches me, smoothing a piece of my hair into place. "That part about your irresistibility? And erm, staying in his…"

"His mind's eye," I finish, all this sinking, pressing down, like a weighted boulder of expectation.

Dammit. This is a lot.

I close my eyes and see the erotic image of the girl with the Xin De man thrusting into her. I place my face over hers; a shiver rushes through me. Then the man's face becomes my king's; I know it so well. Each piece: the scar on his lip, the predatorial blue gaze. He is every inch Xin De.

I wonder whether the other girls imagine it's him each time they spread their legs. That's the design, right? To have us all obsessed with him. It's why his picture hangs in the Silk House, why we know every inch of his face.

Despite never knowing whether we are the one he chooses or not, we care for him, in turn, for The Cradle.

I shouldn't think like this… Shouldn't question the reasons or speculate. It's a horrid habit.

All of this is. Well, it's to keep us without jealousy, to keep the peace, and to protect the heir at all costs. I know this.

But I do feel jealousy, jealousy toward Ana's pregnancy, Iris's Xin De genes, and Blossom's curves. And I am sure if I knew Daisy better, I would find something to envy about her also.

I'm a terrible Silk Girl.

CHAPTER FIVE

ASTER

Silk Girl Vows:

For The Cradle, I will be irresistible to my lord. I must be unmatched in my sweetness, a stunning landscape for his gaze, and a constant in his mind's eye. His indifference toward me would be my greatest failure.

I exhale hard and stroll toward the crowded Estate piazza beside the other new Silk Girls selected for *His* Collective of lords; Ana cradles her belly unaffected and content; Daisy strokes her collarbone, drawing every gaze to her lush chest; Blossom moves with a sway that creates a pendulum with her ample hips; and Iris flicks the red tendrils of her hair as often as she can, showcasing the heart-stopping colours.

I gaze back at Paisley and Island, who wave me onward and mouth, "Go." I turn to face forward again as a line from my vows beats between my ears: 'his indifference toward me would be my greatest failure.'

A glassy pond, lined with tiny blue and white stones, separates us from the entrance, but large rectangular platforms, arranged strategically, create a route over the water.

We step over them and then pass through an arch, gushing with vibrant pink and purple vines that crawl across the ceiling and frame the wide entrance.

And I gasp, as the piazza opens up, a space that blurs the line between reality and fantasy.

At my feet, a scene is depicted in mosaic tiles, it's The Cradle, from the mysterious Horizon across The Strait to Aquilla, where at the southernmost point, The Estate resides.

As I move, the land shifts as the plates have moved over time. I get dizzy and level my eyes, instantly awe-struck by the strange people, dressed in costumes, painted in gold and bronze, drinks sparkling like diamonds, waiters and acrobats and musicians. Wow. Too much to take in; it is truly a test in overstimulation.

It's peculiar how so many people can be in one place, so rowdy and occupied with the festivities, yet the presence of attention on us is undoubtable.

I feel him before I see him. He is far away, atop an elevated platform, sitting on a deep purple throne made from leather with studded accentuations.

He hasn't seen me yet.

The vision of effortless power, Rome of The Strait wears black, from his shirt, fixed with leather and metal plates at the chest and shoulders, to his lush cloak and metal-capped boots. He appears as gorgeous and unaffected as he does in all of his portraits.

Sighing, I acknowledge it's a different demeanour to the one I remember in the parlour and in the military vehicle. So much that I feel I may have made up the regard I saw in the dark depths of his blue eyes.

"*Trade be*, he is handsome," Blossom sighs, her eyes glued ahead, just like mine.

"Too handsome," I point out, then frown at the empty seat to his side. That's the queen's seat, I'm certain. I search the festival, wanting more than anything to see her in the flesh. A bespoken beauty, I have been told, age-defying, too.

I turn to Ana. "The queen?"

Ana shakes her head. "She is so often unwell."

"What do we do now?" Daisy asks, fidgeting with the long ends of her blonde hair.

"We could play a game," Blossom offers.

"We are on display," Iris spits out.

"So what? We can still play." Ana waves at the bright red lights of a game called One Heartbeat.

We wander over to it and watch the people before us play.

It appears the point is to grab the heart at the bottom of a dark, black velvet hole before the machine grabs hold of your hand.

"You're not meant to actually get the heart," Ana states. "It's just a little test of courage."

"I don't like this game," Daisy says, her cheeks paling. "I think I will just watch."

Some people before us are afraid to reach in, others try but then retract their hands with a squeal when the hole closes, and more get their hands stuck in the tight grasp of the machine. It is a game of speed and timing.

I place my hand over my chest and feel my heart beating inside.

Budum.

Budum.

When it's my turn, I watch the gap closely for a few moments, counting my heartbeat in my ears, focused. I brace my hand at the entrance—wait. I dive in. Snatch the heart and whisk it out, still beating in my palm.

I hold it up.

The blood from the organ begins to spill over my fingers, and the girls gasp as it appears to be real. A real heart still very active, thrashing between my fingers.

"Drop it," Iris cries, but I barely hear her.

I'm staring at it so hard, the thing still thrashing, oozing fluid, that I don't notice everyone has gone quiet.

Then I hear a long, drawn-out screech from the skies above me. A shadow moves over the festival, darting, then darkening the ground that circles the place where I stand.

Everyone except Ana cowers away from the ominous shadow, retreating to the safety of the lit areas of the piazza.

The shadow tunnels in, a dark entity homing in on me. I look up and inhale a sharp breath.

The underside of Odio quickly descending through the haze is a sight that snatches air from inside my lungs. His wings are black and brown, but for a silvery sheen that appears to almost sparkle.

His massive talons pound the ground as he lands, his body low to take the impact until he straightens, standing at my height. Eye to eye.

He stares at me.

I still hold the heart in my hand, but it has stopped beating, while my own heart races in my ears to replace the rhythmic countdown.

"Get her out of there," I hear someone mutter, but I am not afraid of Odio... Should I be?

"Aster," Ana whispers from close to my side, and time appears to slow as I sweep my arm back, tucking her behind me so that I stand between Odio and my pregnant friend.

Against my nerves, I step toward the great winged deity, presenting the heart for him to take. "I had a friend like you," I say, soothing, "in the Aquilla Silk Aviary."

I inch closer, and everyone gasps again.

"He was a vicious thing, not at all royal like you are." I take another step, my fingers and the heart a mere nail's length away from his razor-sharp beak. "You're such a handsome boy." Odio cocks his head from side to side, eyes piercing like the perfect predator he is.

My hand shakes violently, so I steady my breath again, and

control the tremors of adrenaline. I know he could take my hand off in a heartbeat—one heartbeat.

I turn my face slightly, gaze at him sideways, and then blink to let him know I'm relaxed.

Budum.

He plucks the heart from my grasp without even touching my fingers and pushes off the ground, wings whooshing the air around me.

I pant with excitement and relief, euphoria riding my exhale. I beam up as the beautiful creature coasts over the heads of The Estate guests, blood from the heart dripping a long crimson trail through the air like a pretty ribbon. My world is spinning, and the thrill makes me dizzy.

Finally, my mind aligns with my surroundings when I level my gaze and notice no one else shares my expression of awe and delight. I blink at the sudden change in mood. The festival and the other guests are all startled, gaping at me.

Dammit. I circle around to face the platform and freeze.

He has noticed me now…

Targeted me.

Rome has risen from his throne, scowling across the crowded piazza with a rifle perfectly ready to take me down.

I swallow.

I gape at the nose of the weapon, only now feeling fear dripping through my veins like a poison that burns in the wake of its travels. I hold my breath, and he lowers his aim slowly. I exhale hard.

Would he have shot me?

For feeding his eagle?

For the disturbance?

He continues to stare across the space at me. My pulse vibrates in my throat, and time stretches… Then he sits down and turns his head as a woman whispers something in his ear.

A beat of noise shocks me as the festival returns to full activity, musicians making music again, the rides whirling around, people chattering and moving.

"Aster." Ana grabs my arm and turns me around. "What were you thinking? Why didn't you drop the heart?"

"Was I meant to?" I ask, confused, as she starts wiping my bloody fingers with the underside of her skirt.

"See"—Iris huffs, throwing her arms in the air— "she is so weird. She nearly got us all killed by that beast, and now everyone thinks that *I* am with her."

Ana studies me quietly.

"I didn't want to be placed with her at all," Iris continues, and I look at the ground, wishing I'd just dropped the heart or not played at all. He was willing to shoot me—My king was going to shoot me down in front of everyone! All my elation over seeing Odio fizzles to shame.

"I didn't want to be anywhere near her," Iris continues to drive her message home. "The king saw! I was next to her. I am mortified. She is odd, and she ruins—"

"Let's get something to eat," Blossom offers, stopping Iris mid-break-down by rubbing her back. "Yeah? I can smell warm chocolate and butter. That means cakes or brownies. Ever eaten those before?"

Into the last-light, we stand at the side of a high, granite banquet table in a smaller dining room lit from above with lights strung together by twisted gold satin garlands. The table is chest height. For them. For the Xin De that make us feel like a different species altogether.

It is much quieter in here, but the vibrant activities still flitter through the open double doors.

I chew on a brownie, absentminded. He was going to shoot at me. That is how little I mean, we all mean, until we have Meaningful Purpose. Would he have raised the gun if I'd been pregnant? I know the answer. Very few are as precious as a pregnant Silk Girl.

He cared in the tank.

He *seemed* to care.

He doesn't care...

My king... Lies. His eyes lie. My heart twists. I remember what Island and Paisley said about the fruit, so as silly as I feel, I reach across and grab some strawberries.

We all felt the heat of attention when we first arrived, the lords' taking us in as they might a flock of birds, but it isn't until this moment that I actually see them.

They are hard to miss.

Down the length of the table, three men with the purple Trade sigil pinned to their cloaks, watch us and speak quietly amongst themselves. Each has a high Xin De genus; being well over six-foot-five inches, eyes like glowing beacons, and muscles that any Common man would cower from.

I have memorised them from my studies; Lord Medan, white skin and dark hair, the shortest and smallest, from the Upper-tower; Lord Bled with warm, brown skin and striking amber eyes, from the Lower-tower; And Lord Darwin, being the oldest by far, showing hints of true aging, greying and fine lines that often remain hidden until a Xin De reaches sixty or so, from the Half-tower on The Mainland.

The only one missing is Lord Turin Two, the king's half-brother, spare heir for The Cradle and Warden of The Estate.

Be irresistible.

Feeding a bloody heart to Odio wasn't quite what I wanted to be the everlasting image in his, I mean, *their* mind's eye. I bury the thought of the king, ram it down because I will have Meaningful Purpose with or without his affections.

So, I lift a strawberry and bite into it, the juices sliding over my lips. I can feel the liquid trailing down my chin just as keenly as I feel the heat of their eyes tracking its path.

"Allow me."

My heart pounds in my ears as I spin around and peer up, met by the smooth smile of Lord Darwin. He manages the southernmost Fishing Trade, though the Half-tower is notoriously corrupt and often dangerous.

Getting all too close, he lifts his thumb to my lip. "You've made a mess. What is it about you, then? That has the king rescuing you himself, I wonder."

I blink fast and shuffle from foot to foot, immediately uncomfortable, realising I'm in no way prepared to be touched by a man I do not know.

How can that be?

Iris was right—I *am* odd. I was more content with blood dripping down my fingers than with this man's thumb on my lower lip. Closing my eyes, I inhale steadily to not offend him by flinching under his attention.

He's wiping the juices, moving my lip beneath his thumb as he does when the curt voice of a nearby Guard booms. "Do not touch the Silk Girls."

My pulse races as *His* gaze hits me like lightning cracking through a dark tunnel.

I search for him, feeling him acutely in every cell, but don't find him. My hands immediately start to sweat, unsettled by the feeling of being watched.

"Everyone out while I eat," Rome suddenly orders, a slow but thundering timbre to match the storm his presence brews around me.

Everyone heads quickly for the door.

I drop the strawberries and trail them.

"Not you," he states, and I look up to find him sauntering toward me with his dark leather armour partly open, exposing a long triangle valley of tattoos down his hard, carved chest.

I grip the table to steady myself.

There is no fuss from the guests. The other Silk Girls leave; Ana glances over her shoulder; Daisy and Blossom duck away quietly; Iris smirks, enjoying that I am in trouble.

Lord Bled holds the door open as all other guests pass through the frame, and then he closes it behind him.

The door clicks, and within a second, Rome is hovering over me. One of his huge hands is gripping my hip and spinning me to face the banquet table.

He slides a hand between my thighs and lifts me from my core. Slinging me over the table, he presses my torso down, my cheek stamping the glossy top, heavy exhale misting the surface.

My legs dangle.

Toes try to find the ground.

"You'll learn that some attention is not good for little girls," he hisses.

I gasp, squirming under the weight of his large palm, only my backside moving while I don't stand a chance to wriggle free. He's so large, even larger now that he is angry with me for disturbing his party.

"I'm sorry about Odio," I whimper.

"Always answering back."

Holding me still, he slides his hand down to my thigh, then runs his fingers to lift my skirting up until my backside is bare. He spanks the flesh.

I cry out. "I said I was sorry!"

"Always speaking out of turn. Did I give you permission to speak? Did I give you permission to touch my pet or share your lips or smile with other men?"

I'm so confused but too scared to think straight. "No, my king. You didn't."

Reckless. Reckless girl.

I squeeze my eyes shut, and he spanks me again, harder this time, a sting racing through my flesh and jolting me.

"Not so clever now, are you?" He slaps me again. I can only imagine his true strength could break bones.

My pelvis pulses against the table as he rains down slap after slap to my flesh. Warmth radiates across my backside, and though I want the sudden shock of it to stop, I don't want any distance from him. I want this. His hand. His honest reactions that aren't ritualistic or Updates for The Cradle. The stolen moments, I live for them with him.

I whimper on the table as he shifts to stand right behind me. He presses his hips to my backside, blanketing me in the heat from his body.

My eyes flash open when the hard, long muscle protruding his hips presses to the crease between my cheeks.

That is *not* the size I have seen in my *Anatomy of Man* textbook.

I start to pant.

His sprawling hands map my spine and the sides of my body, touching, taking me in, inch by inch, as he thrusts against me through our clothes.

I moan. The way he touches me, grips me with force and possession, stirs my insides, wringing and coiling a bundle of nerves, low and demanding.

"Fuck, you're making me do dangerous things. Do you have any idea what men like me do to little things like you? You shouldn't be so eager to get attention. The only thing that protects you from being destroyed by me is your precious womb, do you understand? I could break you in two."

I nod fast with my cheek flush against the marble. The strange tight, aggressive feeling of need inundating me, hissing to be heard and tended to. My body flushes hotter than I've ever felt before. Feverish. Frightening.

"I feel strange, my king. Sick. Hot. Please, stop." Reeling, I push my backside into him, then roll forward to the edge of the table to ebb the pressure between my thighs. Moisture gathers in my knickers, hot and wet.

He lets out a long groan, savage. "That's not what you think it is, Silk Girl. You're not sick. You're ovulating." I feel his words in my bones. He strokes the new blemish on my backside, the span of his hand a blanket of rough, warm skin.

He grinds into me one more time, then stops. His hands leave my body, and my skin prickles—mourns—the heat from his palms. I blink, trying to centre my thoughts.

"I have him," a man says from outside the room.

"Very good." Rome breathes rough and rolls me on the table to face him.

Through my daze, I peer up at him but am immediately slung over his shoulder. He strides to his chair at the end of the room, carrying me like an inanimate object.

He sets me on the floor in front of it.

Blinking, I think about what to do. I know, adore, pleasure... I have been told what men like; I am not innocent to the mechanics of it. Just inexperienced.

I try desperately to ignore the warm, wet sensation between my legs.

His hand meets the top of my crown, petting me as he sits on the chair with his legs spread wide and my place between them. Shuffling closer, I find myself almost purring into his leg and thigh as I settle.

I am always on edge.

Guessing what people think.

Judging my own presence.

My bully gauge activated.

But the stroke of his fingers through my crown somehow spreads calm through my entire being, my shoulders lowering, my spine relaxing, a resting smile forming. I'm not sure I've ever had a *resting* smile before... I feel it in my chest like air. It's different to a lively one. It's so perfectly content; some merely surviving life may never wear one.

All rationale tells me to stay still and not speak, but I risk a glance up at him. Up his legs, two pillars of muscles, to the hard plane of his torso. I look at his face, expression focused ahead on the door. His jaw is clenching and unclenching, his blue eyes shadowed by fierce brows. The threat in his face flicks inside me, my nipples tightening.

I wrap my arms around them.

"Ovulating..." I whisper to myself, the word trailing to a pause. It's time. Tonight or tomorrow. That is why I am at this party. Why the lords have travelled to The Estate.

We begin breeding soon.

CHAPTER SIX

ROME

Though keenly aware of Kong at the door with my captive, my body struggles to not consume her whole. To not sink my teeth into her shoulder, thrust my cock through her seal, split her open to take me.

I can still feel her warm arse on my palm. I had to restrain myself, holding back so I didn't belt her to a swollen mess. Bruises are merely an expectation when I fuck a woman, hurting them even when I try not to.

"I will give you a few moments to settle after that punishment." I draw circles with my fingers in her silky black hair, calming myself down as much as her.

I lost my temper.

Furious about the scene with Odio.

Maddened by the eyes on her.

And then she swept Ana behind her, protecting the potential heir as though she were born to do it—*conditioned* to place that unnamed, untitled fetus above all else.

I sigh hard.

My hand smooths down her hair, fingers lazily dipping to her jaw before digging into her chin. I force her to look up at me.

Big, violet-coloured eyes peer up, eclipsed by long black lashes. "Time to get to know each other, little creature. I know you Silk Girls protect your seal, but do you also protect your lips? Has anyone else besides that fucker Endigo been on these?" I ask, swiping my thumb over the plump flesh of her rosy lower lip. She has been around the Guard, doctors, and other Trade men, most of her life. My tone deepens with warning. The answer better fucking be no. "Anyone licked them? Has anyone thrust between them so deep you couldn't breathe, but you revelled in every moment of that sweet suffocation?"

Her breaths became shallow, eyes wide, blinking faster. My little blinker. Swallowing, she can only shake her head.

The correct answer curves my lips up in one corner.

"On your knees and open your mouth. You want attention—" I smirk and begin to undo my belt. "Let's see if you like it. Everything has a consequence."

I know this is fucked, but it won't be the first time a Silk Girl was played with before she was claimed. Or even after. Only the womb is sacred, not the mouth. I didn't—don't— intend on claiming her to carry my heir. I will hurt her. I know this. I'll stretch her too wide; I'll bruise her... *Fuck.* And for fucking reasons I do not appreciate, I despise the thought of destroying her more than I want her wet pussy clenching around me.

But *fuck*...

Only slightly more.

She tries not to touch me, her little hands held by her sides, hesitant to do anything. A soft breath leaves her as she lifts to her knees between my thighs, staring at the leather of my belt open at the buckle. "Let's see if you can handle the kind of attention you are recklessly seeking." I lift my hips and lean backward. "Take out my cock."

Shaky fingers reach up to work the zipper down, and that

sweet nervous energy is all it takes to harden my cock, fill it with blood in front of her as she unwraps it.

By the time she gets the zipper down, I'm so fucking hard that my cock jerks into the air, so heavy and thick it feels like a solid tungsten rod.

Her eyes widen.

"Now, my sweet little creature" —I reach for the base, grab a hold, and squeeze upward to the tip, shuddering with the need to explode across her inexperienced pink lips— "Lick."

She leans down and at the first little lick, I groan and start to tug my length. I pump hard, jerking my cock to its full angry potential, veins rising with blood, while she licks the tip like a kitten lapping at fucking milk. "More. Open your mouth. You'll only be able to suck the head, but I need to see you try for more. Try your hardest, sweet creature, to pleasure your king."

A look of consideration flitters in her eyes as though my words were a true challenge to her soul. I like her even more in this moment.

I am mindful of the men waiting outside the door, but I don't give a fuck. They can wait.

She opens her mouth and rolls the swollen head between her lips and *fuck...* She suddenly moves, positions herself ready to go to war with my cock, hands meeting my tight thighs, and, as I jerk myself up and down, she bobs to suck my blood-filled crown.

My head drops back to the seat as I groan, heat hitting my temples and coiling around the base of my spine.

With my bicep burning as I work my cock, I roar, "Enter!" to the closed door. I'm about ready to explode over my little creature's pink lips, and I need him to witness this. To see who she belongs to. "The next time you think about drawing attention to yourself, I want you to remember this." I growl to her. "Hmm? Remember all the ways you'll be punished."

Kong strides in, shoving Lord Darwin forward until he falls to his hands and knees. He is gagged and already beaten.

Kong stands behind him. Darwin's eyes widen on me before darting to the Silk Girl sucking me dry.

Mine. My hard stare snarls the claim before I even admit it to myself. I will have her. I will keep her. If not to carry my heirs, then to sit like a pet at my feet. I *will* keep her.

So we need one less lord.

"Concentrate on me, little creature. Don't stop sucking your king, no matter what you hear." I stare at Kong. "Spill him."

Kong reaches around Darwin's throat and drags a slivery blade across the column, carving a scarlet seam into his flesh. A man I have known my entire life. A man who fought battles beside me, drank whiskey with me, grew up with me. His carotid arteries gush as my balls begin to squeeze to the same thundering tempo.

My snarl is savage as I grab black hair and shove her warm, wet mouth down my cock, stretching her throat, hearing gags and gargles and splutters of blood to my climax. It's a symphony— a damn work of art; the pulse of my cock flooding her mouth; the beat of his heart spurting blood over the banquet hall; my little creature's eyes watering as she nearly drowns on the cum I unload into her virgin mouth.

And that is what you get.

When you touch my property.

I shudder as I finish. I drop my head backward and loosen my hold on her hair, allowing her to lift her head, the end of my cock sliding from her throat.

She gasps for air.

Fuck me, she's pretty.

Still holding her close, I keep her angled away from the sight of Kong dragging Darwin's body through a seeping bloody puddle and out of the dining room.

I tuck my cock into my pants.

After a few deep breaths, feeling less tight and territorial, I peer down at her.

Violet eyes, black hair, rosy lips, and a flush of arousal that burns a trail down her neck and across her chest. She is lovely and needy, but she doesn't know what for. She has no idea that the past two first-lights in the Medi-deck before The Circle to her room, she was shot with an ovum-triggering serum along with a cocktail of prenatal vitamins.

I smooth her hair down from where I tangled the strands, petting her softly. "That's a girl. No need to draw attention to yourself anymore."

Wincing, she tries to hide the roll of her jaw as it seemingly cramps. I frown and reach between my thighs to massage her cheeks. "Does your jaw hurt? You may speak."

"Yes, my king."

"Now, we can't have that." I roll my fingers and thumb over her jaw. "You'll need to practise more."

"So… This will happen again?"

"Adore. Pleasure. I'm quite enamoured with you, can't you tell? But don't test me. I'm not a knight in shining armour. Nothing shining about me. Every inch of my soul is tarnished and calloused. I have been through wars, started them, not just dressed for them. Understand?"

"Yes, my king."

My hand falls from her face. I nod to the door, needing her gone before she finds a new tunnel in my mind to dig into. "You may return to the carnival. Be quiet and well-behaved."

Her shoulders sag, and my lips twitch with a smile. "You said it was time to get to know each other."

I raise a brow, peer down. "Excuse me?"

"You said it was time to get to know *each other*." She hesitates and shuffles. My eyes follow her little wiggle of nerves. "So, do I get a question, too?"

Well fuck. "Very well."

"Actually, my king." She sits back on her heels. A little pet at my feet, shoulders lower than my knees, face the same size as my palm. "May I have two questions? One isn't about you. So, it's not a get-to-know-you question."

"Intrigued. Go ahead."

"What happened behind me just now? I heard… choking noises."

I frown at her. Blood. Death. My orgasm rushing out at the same time as my old friend's blood… I can't say it.

Were she any other girl, I would explain in detail what I just watched while she licked my cock, but I can't seem to bring myself to utter the words. *Why the fuck not?* And this restriction, this *consideration*, reminds me of Tuscany. All the lies I've spoken in honour of her purity. The truths I keep from her, to keep her innocent.

"I can handle it," she presses.

Reaching between my thighs, I hold her cheek and stroke my thumb over the soft, blushing skin. "My Trade is brutal and violent, yours never will be again."

Fuck knows where that came from.

I clear my throat and lean back. "And the other question? Make it quick."

"Are you pure Xin De?"

My eyes narrow at her audacity. Not a single person has asked me that, not since I ripped my own father's head off. I ram the memory away.

But I answer her. "I am mostly, but no. Not pure."

"Can I see your enhancements?" She straightens, lifting to her knees. "I have seen Iris'. But not up close. Can I see yours? Up close?"

"You're quite a charming little creature."

My half-smile turns into a tight line when she climbs onto my lap and sits that perfect little arse over my cock. Warmth from her needy pussy radiates on my lap.

I frown but restrain myself.

Her black hair falls forward, twin curtains covering her small, perky breasts, but unable to hide the tight peaks of her hard nipples.

I inhale her scent and hum.

Then she cups my cheeks and analyses me. I turn to stone. I

say nothing. I barely respond, but for my fists that clench and unclench on the rests on either side of her as she studies my eyes.

I blink slowly.

"Triple lidded," she mutters. That is first indicator of Xin De genes besides my obvious monstrous height and girth.

My frown twists to a scowl.

At her manner.

Blatant disrespect.

But then she runs her soft hands down my cheeks, fingers coasting casually, cooling a path down to either side of my neck. "Your skin is so... I don't know the word for it."

"There isn't one," I state, stiff.

"Smooth like suede," she offers, continuing her exploration, finding the divot at the base of my neck. "Yet, harder and heavy. Dense even though I cannot feel the weight of it. And it moves over your muscles with a kind of elasticity more like that of a—"

"Beast," I warn, wanting her to get the fuck off me but unwilling to toss her aside... *Fuck.*

She smiles softly. "Yes."

Unclenching my hands, I bring them forward. I sweep her warm, onyx hair backward over her shoulders, exposing her long, slim neck and the pulse that flutters inside like a captured butterfly.

I make her nervous, but not nervous enough. Not as much as I'd like to, perhaps when I cover her body with mine, sink inside...

"Why weren't you afraid of Odio? He could pick you up and drop you to your death."

I look down at her lips as she speaks.

"I am not frightened of birds." Her hands move down either side of the thick column of my throat, to my shoulders, then fall off as she relaxes backward. "I grew up with birds in the Silk Aviary. Birds of all kinds. People are far more terrifying than birds. Even modified ones like Odio."

"You used a different word."

"What word?"

"I am enhanced, but he is modified. Explain."

"Um." She blinks, thinking. "Enhanced are new traits we didn't previously have, like, erm, the membrane on your eyes, the film in your nose, but modified is, like…" She looks at the ceiling in a way that suggests she is picturing the sky. "Well, Odio could already fly and do all the things he does now, only, he's bigger and better at it than his ancestors."

I place my finger under her chin, lifting to examine the smooth plane of her porcelain skin, from her throat, across her collarbone…

Fuck me, she is pretty.

She is slim—two clavicles like bird wings open up to frame the top of her chest. I want to lick them, lap my tongue the entire length, and worship the delicate structure I could so easily crush. "You look like a Silk Girl, but you're too clever to be one. Where did you learn such exact terminology?"

"I have thought about it." Her eyes flutter under the intensity of my gaze. Unsettled, she shuffles on my lap, her arse slides over my groin, my cock pulses, and I grab her upper arms to hold her still.

"Don't do that. Don't move, or I will rip your skirt off and tear you in two, do you understand?"

Her breath catches, and she nods.

"Continue," I order.

"That's all, my king. I spend a lot of time thinking about the world. I *spent* a lot of time thinking and not much time talking… like, now." She stares up at me dreamily, and it's ridiculous. Silly little girl with a death wish. "This might be the longest conversation I have ever had. I know I am not meant to ask questions, but there are so many, the echoes have become permanent marks in my mind. I am not meant to think too much. It's not a virtue—curiosity." She shakes her head. "But I can't seem to stop it."

I look at her lips again, map them. A subtle lower curve holds the weight of a plump and defined heart-shaped upper lip.

Fuck... She will remain pure. It is a kindness on my part, as I have never been a gentle lover.

She will be a little pet that I play with, that tortures me with questions and her body, but that I do not fuck.

I will choose the redhead— the one with the Xin De genetics. "You should go now, little creature."

I lean backward and ignore the disappointment that flashes in her glossy eyes as she slides from my lap.

Walking toward the double doors, she smooths her hair and then her skirt.

She stills, staring at the pool of blood for a long moment before following the crimson smear painted with a dead body as it was dragged to the doors.

I wait for her to sob or gasp or—

"My king?" She looks back at me.

I stare deadpan at her. "Yes."

"Did they deserve it?"

"Never ask me that again."

"Were you going to shoot me?"

Fuck. This girl. Cairo would have her backside red and raw for such questions... I grit my teeth and force the words past the cage they create. "No more questions."

Her breathing increases as she tiptoes over the bloody mess and reaches for the door handle.

"Little creature."

She turns.

"Go back to your room."

"But you said—"

"You're aroused." My eyes drop to her legs. "You're trying to hide it, but you're pressing your thighs together, rubbing them." I growl my restraint and fist my fingers in tight. "And every Xin De male out there will notice this."

And I can't very well execute them all. *Can I?*

Blood rushes to her cheeks again. She pinches the sides of her skirt, tucking one leg behind the other and bows like the perfect ballerina I know veils something much more interesting. And dangerous to my common sense, it seems.

"Goodnight, my king."

She walks from the room.

No, little creature.

I was aiming at Odio.

CHAPTER SEVEN

ROME

"Rome. Sire? Are you listening?" Medan is losing patience, as he so often does.

Picking my teeth with a skewer and leaning back in my chair, I casually glance across the aged oak table surrounded by my Collective. "I am."

"Then you need to prepare us." He points at the table as he speaks. "What the hell happened with Darwin? Where did you go during the carnival? There will be questions."

"I executed him," I state plainly.

"Y-you, what?" Medan grips the bridge of his nose, shaking his head and breathing. It's a mild panic attack, one that he'll hide beneath concerns for Darwin and The Cradle, when really, he is fucking shit scared that his king is so quick to remove members of his Collective. Darwin isn't the first. "I have known him my entire life…" He trails off, then clears his throat looking at me again.

Turin Two, my half-brother, stares at me, not intimidated as he knows that even I have my limits—executing my brother is one of them. "Why?"

The words "because I can" are on my tongue when Cairo saunters in answering him in the fashion Cairo is best known for, "For the good of The Trade," with irrevocable reasoning.

He grips the edge of his seat and nods to each member of my Collective in acknowledgment. He is very good at pretending he respects them. Perhaps he does, in a way. "He is in coalition with rogues. We had to put a stop to it. Rome actioned it while everyone enjoyed the festivities, and no one is the wiser."

Interesting...

I smirk. "For The Trade."

Bled shakes his head, chuckling softly, as Turin Two continues, "And what of the Half-tower? They won't like this at all. They may come to The Estate."

"They do harbour most of our warships," Bled states, smoothing his hands out on the table, his fingers admiring the grain and organic motions of authentic, ancient wood. Yes, I know this about him. He is a tactile man. "I just acquired a massive Ice Breaker for them to hunt the sharks. They can venture far and attack us directly from the south."

Being The Cradle's Lord of Procurement, with his manners and likability, he was always the right choice for the position, and he knows exactly what tower has what.

And what each need.

I frown at Bled. "And why didn't you acquire an Ice Breaker for me to keep in The Estate?"

His lips lift in one corner because he knows I'm using the casual conversation to further stir my apathy through Medan's concerns. "Are you taking up whale and shark fishing as a pastime, Sire?" Bled asks.

"Not today." I drop the toothpick and lean forward. "I wasn't going to risk the Silk Girls' safety, now, was I?" I say, looking straight at Medan. "Are we really going to let him enter The Circle and have free access to their doors? To our legacies." I lean back again. "I think not."

Bled, who knows all too well what happened and suspects

why, agrees, "A reason is all *I* needed. For The Trade. For the protection of the Silk Girls. Fine. What to do with the Half-tower?"

"You want it?"

"Fuck no."

Cairo looks at Bled. "It will get out of control now that Darwin is missing, and we cannot have his chosen Collective speculating. So, we will have the Shadows enter and finish twenty-one Xin De Trade men and Darwin's Collective. We will kill them in the Common way—with poison from the La Mu root. Xin De will turn on Common, and we will send the Martial Blues in to keep the peace. We will put the entire tower under heavy restrictions and organise a new management team from the ashes of this—"

"Civil unrest," I finish.

"*Yes.*" The Trade Master smiles, but it does not meet his sharp gaze. "And we are their hope for peace and Meaningful Purpose."

Impressive.

I slash a man's throat open for touching a silly, little girl, and Cairo somehow redirects the entire event to suit his damn agenda. Most of the time, I hate the man— No, I *despise* him all of the time. I would reach in and pull out his beating heart most days, but I must admit he is a narcissistic mastermind.

"Do you have a lord in mind for the task, Sire?" Turin Two asks, probing to get to the guts of this topic. He might want it. A tower far away from me, but because he wants it, I desperately do not desire to give it to him.

"Not as yet," I answer.

"All settled then." Bled looks at Medan. "Execute Darwin's Collective. Stoke the civil disputes over who is to blame, then save the day. Happy, Lord Medan?"

Medan nods stiffly.

Cairo clasps his hands on the large oak table, entwining his fingers, his many rings glinting under the lights. "It may seem less than authentic, but it's necessary to keep the peace. For the citizens of The Cradle, we needed to remove Lord Darwin, and I assure you, Lord Medan, we will move in before there are too many casualties."

I rub the rough, hard surface of my jaw. My mind is now tickled with the memory of a little creature gagging on my cock while Darwin choked on blood... And her sweet questions after, her warm thighs and pussy on my lap, her big violet eyes full of arousal, her interest in my genetics and—

"Are you smiling?"

I glare across at Turin Two, cocky fucker. "I was thinking about Darwin's sliced arteries." It's not completely a lie. My eyes narrow on him. "For such a small Xin De, he sure had a lot of blood inside him." I stand, ending the meeting. "I have hunting to do. Bled, join me."

He stands, smooths his leathers down his chest and walks to open the door for me. "Aquilla Cats?"

"Pests. And the beasts used to be extinct." I walk through the door, and he trails me. "But I do enjoy culling the fuckers. To think our ancestors thousands of years before The Cradle used to sit around and watch a screen all day."

Bled hums. "Well, bored people are boring."

CHAPTER EIGHT

ASTER

Silk Girl Vows:

For The Trade, I will share my last breath if The Cradle need me to. Whether it is land, man, or breath, I do not take possession.

I spoon some oatmeal between my lips, humming.

My cheeks radiate heat, so I wave a small parchment hand fan in front of my face, fanning the sweat to a glistening cool mist.

Glancing around the table, I notice the others are rosy-faced, while above us, the air conditioner hums softly so I know this isn't an external heat. *Nope.* We are burning up from the inside out. All of us.

'Ovulating, little creature.'

I suppress a groan as the events from yesterday unfold behind my eyes like turning pages in my memory.

"Lick."

"Concentrate on me, little creature."

"Go to your room."

"You're aroused."

I knew what being a Silk Girl entailed. Adore. Pleasure. I understood the process and the anatomy, but nothing could have prepared me for the... *intensity.* Of bringing a massive man to shuddering pleasure. Of being praised with a silent lap of his lusty eyes.

I press my legs together, heat rolling between my thighs. I'm worried I'll leak through my knickers and leave a patch of moisture on the chair.

"He didn't come last night," Ana mutters, snatching my attention away from the memory.

"Come inside you or to your room?" Blossom asks, and I nearly spit out my meal. So, we do talk about *things.*

"Not at all," she answers, playing with her food.

I sit up, remembering the blood and the body-shaped pattern smeared through it. "Really? Is that strange? Does he usually visit every night?"

I like Ana more than any girl I've ever met, but I suddenly feel two opposing forces. One is regretful that something may have happened to her lord, and one is guilt-mixed with relief that if that is true, the king has not chosen a Silk Girl for his heirs yet.

After yesterday, after the feel of him throbbing down my throat, his growls of ecstasy, his thighs tightening under my palms, and then—I almost sigh aloud—our candid conversations... we *talked.*

The king is my... *friend.*

I don't want him to be that close to anyone else, and that goes against everything we are taught, but I'm not made of stone, carved with a blade. I am made of flesh, with a brain and heart that lives independently of what the world tries to carve into my character.

But having character is not virtuous.

I inhale hard, wishing my mind was at peace.

I chant the vows; I take no possessions! I do not own my own breath should The Cradle need it. I know this. I know, but...

I am helplessly drawn to him.

To his cruel honesty. To his blunt demands. I like the iron boundaries he builds around himself because I *love* that he lets me peer through the cracks every now and then.

It is like seeing inside a mystery.

She pulls me from my thoughts. "He comes to me every night that the lords visit The Estate. Sometimes, he talks to me after the act. About all kinds of secrets. He knows they won't travel far, because who would I tell, and who would even believe me if I did?"

"They are not meant to talk to you. Ever. Not during your Purpose or in the light-hours. What if you recognise his voice?" Iris says. She has finished her studies. She can probably recite the contents word for word. If she'd only share some of it with me, maybe I wouldn't ask any more ignorant questions.

Lord Darwin spoke to me...

Maybe because he never intended on picking me, so voice recognition or not, it would never be a problem.

"Besides Sire's occasional orders, none of the lords have ever spoken to me," Daisy muses, looking at her meal. "I am thankful. I do not wish to know them outside of my Purpose. It would confuse me."

Ana looks at Iris. "You would be surprised how much you rely on sight to give you information. I feel lost in the dark. Anyway, I've never spoken to a lord outside of my room either, so I cannot *recognise* anything... And his touch and voice become one at night." She lowers her voice. "We are in love."

"You're not," Daisy says, lifting her hand to soothe Ana's back, concerned. "Don't talk like that. You'll get hurt."

"Fur talk like that," Iris spits out.

I snap my eyes to her, narrowing her to a tiny target in my vision. *I should warn them about you.*

"Love is not such a bad thing," Blossom offers, placing her spoon in an empty bowl.

"It's not a virtue." Iris darts her gaze around the table, trying to pull in an ally. She doesn't get one. "It's dangerous."

"He will let you go," Daisy says, gentle but firm. "You will leave The Estate when you stop birthing, but he will stay. And he will continue with a new Silk Girl or be pleasured by the House Girls."

Blossom shrugs. "Nothing lasts forever. She can enjoy it while it lasts. That's not unseemly."

I look at her. "What does that mean?"

Blossom glances across at me. "Nothing lasts forever? Well, she is a Silk Girl today and in love. Then she'll be a Sired Mother, and she'll have the love of the babies. She will be fine in both places."

Oh. I see.

"Love is such a Common issue." Iris turns her nose up and takes a sip of juice, as though to swallow the conversation. "It's simply parasitic."

Suddenly, a blur of white catches my eyes.

I glance out the long, sweeping window that exposes the large courtyard surrounded by high limestone walls.

Through the thick glass, a girl drops backward to the lawn as though she passes out. A man thunders over, Kong, I recognise him, and he drops to check on her.

Wow, he got to her side fast...

He reaches for her cheek, but she flinches away. She looks like a tiny fairy, and he is her monstrous Guardian. Kong is a huge Xin De male, easily two feet taller and three times thicker than her. It dawns on me then, that must be what I look like beside the king.

Ana interrupts my thoughts when she addresses Iris with subtle disdain. "I'm in support of The Revive, Iris. So, if by *Common*, you mean *Human*, then yes—"

"Who is that?" I interrupt, protecting Ana from oversharing her thoughts with Iris.

"Who?" Blossom turns around just as the girl waves Kong away, and lays still like a doll on the greenery. Her honey-brown hair arches like wings in the emerald mesh. "Oh, that's the Queen."

No...

Tuscany?

The king's sister?

Can't be.

"How old is she?" My gaze rolls over her petite body, at her chest she clutches a small brown fluffy toy eagle.

Ana says, "She is in her late twenties, I believe. She was ten when she became Queen. So twenty-eight, maybe."

I cannot stop staring. "She looks no older than me."

"It's the Xin De genus," Ana offers, and I return my gaze to her kind face.

I know about this. Kong shows no signs of aging yet must have past his fiftieth year. *Will I die of old age before the king even does?*

Ana lifts one brow. "The treatments also help."

"Treatments?" Iris asks.

"My lord told me," Ana mentions, directly. "Men like to talk after the act, Iris. They don't want a statue. She is given all these treatments to keep her looking youthful. She looks younger than us if you ask me."

Iris straightens. "Treatments? Genetic engineering is completely illegal. You are either born with the genus or you don't have it. That is it!"

Ana frowns. "I didn't say anything about engineering, Iris. I said *treatments.*"

Daisy presses her hand to her chest, clearly unsettled, and whispers, "Can we stop talking about treatments and engineering, please?"

I sway the conversation a little. "She looks sad." My heart aches looking at her, the thin shell of a girl—or woman.

"What could she be sad about?" Blossom asks.

"Why is she holding a doll?" Iris points out, the smallest hint of bitterness punches through her words. The only girl more precious than a pregnant Silk Girl is the queen.

"You cannot judge her because you don't know her or anything she's been through," I point out.

I stand up and walk to the door to the courtyard.

"You cannot go, Aster. Only speak when spoken to. She is the queen!" Daisy shoots up to stop me.

I lift my hand. "But if she is sad and no one is allowed to speak to her, then who will make her feel better?"

"The rules are there for a reason. You're new. I am just trying to look after you," Daisy says again, and Blossom and Ana both share glances.

"I'll be fine." I enter the courtyard and Paisley is immediately a wall in front of me.

"Where are you going? Aster, you can't go into the courtyard today. It is closed."

Wow, this poor girl is guarded like a bomb. I am not going to detonate her, nor detonate around her.

I swerve past Paisley and head toward the queen. Each step along the grass feels like a small achievement, but I ready myself to be tackled to the ground.

I see movement to my side; Kong is on guard, staring at me with his back to a nearby limestone wall.

Isn't he the king's Guardian?

Our eyes meet. Smiling with a silent plea, I keep going until I am standing beside the queen.

"May I lay with you?"

She looks up at me, staring through my existence, as if to determine whether I am real. I understand that look. It is the same one I had when I was in a three-day fever dream.

I look at her toy. "Who is that?" Lying beside her on the grass, I quietly mirror her position, back flat, legs slightly apart, hands resting on my torso.

"Rome," she answers, with a soft, melodic cadence that dances in my ears. "He is always going away." She pulls the teddy to her chest. "He leaves me here, and I miss him so."

Sad. I chew my lip. "I'm Aster."

"I know," she sighs. "I'm supposed to have visited you. All of you. To welcome you to The Estate. But when I go places, smiles crumble, and you all have such lovely smiles."

My heart squeezes.

We lie in silence, and I watch the grey dome above us as it reaches into a dusty red distance, wondering what could have happened to her to make her so strangely unhappy.

I want to understand...

The light breeze sweeps over us, moving our hair in the grass, bringing with it floral notes from the garden and something else. Something from her.

Sweet and citrus... orange.

The queen smells like oranges.

Many moments pass by. And it's truly surreal, but my soul finds an easy companion in hers.

"It was blue once. The sky," I finally say.

"I would have liked to see that."

I exhale with relief. "Tuscany is a lovely name." I shuffle to look at her face, and she drops her cheek to the grass to meet my gaze. "If I were named after a city from the old-world, I would like to be London. If you were a flower, just a flower, what would your name be?"

Her lips make a tiny smile. "In all my life, no one has ever asked me a question like that before."

"I'm odd."

"*Mm.*" Her eyes, glimmering amber orbs, say she agrees. "I am odd, too. I'd be Marigold. It's bright, and the bees love them. I'll pollinate the entire planet until we are overrun with flowers." She looks me over, nodding to herself. "We must look a sight lying on the grass together."

I shrug. "I don't mind, if you don't mind."

Her measured smile softens on me. "I can see you as London. It was supposedly a royal city."

A moment of reluctance pauses her, but then she reaches for my wrist, lifting it up for her perusal. Her touch is lighter than the breeze.

"They mutilated you," she whispers.

She takes in the healing skin graft.

My brows pinch as I trace the sad curve of her lips. She has been through something traumatic, like me. Maybe. Or nothing like me, but something has scratched her soul. I can see the blemishes left in her eyes.

"They were going to eat me," I admit.

She carefully lowers my hand to the soft, green blades. "Silk Girls aren't meant to have any negative experiences. It's better for the cells, no cortisol, no stress, peaceful births and babies."

My throat tightens. I've messed up. It's not like it was a choice, but it is my problem. "I'm sorry, my queen."

"You're not a very good Silk Girl," she mentions, and though the words are harsh, she utters them without malice. As though she were merely recognising the colour of my hair.

"I know."

She sighs long and slow. "I'm not a very good queen."

Wow.

"The fuck are you doing!"

Rome grabs my upper arm, dragging me to my feet, where I barely manage to stand.

It all happens so quickly. He is holding my arm too high. I'm too short. I cry out; the weight of my dangling body on my shoulder hurts. I feel as if I may split in two.

"Boy." Kong is upon us. "Let her go."

Rome drops me to the ground.

"*Rome.*" Tuscany breathes. "Don't."

I fall like a wet cloth, the grass scraping my arm as I land. Shocked, I peer up at him, shrinking into a tiny, insignificant puddle at his huge feet. I scoot backward on my backside.

He points at me. "You're out!"

"*Rome!*" Tuscany yells.

"My king," I plead, shaking hard. "She was sad. I was just talking to Tuscan—"

"What?" He jolts toward me. "Did you just use her name?" If he could burn me to nonexistence with his dark, cruel gaze, he would. "You will never speak her name again! She gave that up for

152

you people! You will never speak again. And that is a damn kindness. No more questions from you. No more special treatment. I don't care who you are. I understand the need for obedience and conditioning right the fuck *now!*" he roars, his body shaking with rage. "There is no place for a girl like you here! You're lucky you have your pretty throat. Get her out of my sight!"

His words are bullets, and they find their target, right in my heart. "My king, please," I beg.

"Sire!" he roars, the sound booting me in the chest, his eyes burning with fury so powerful it sparks through the air.

"Come, girl." Kong grabs my arm and pulls me to my feet, nudging me forward.

Shallow breaths racket through me—words, panic, pleading, apologies, confusion, all bursting up my throat simultaneously.

I stumble but peer back to see Tuscany—my queen— standing, angry, and waving her little finger at his broad chest, but Rome glares at me. She reaches up and, with one finger, she directs his cheek back to her.

My heart hammers.

I spin to face forward.

"Better not to look back," Kong advises smoothly as he ushers me inside, almost protective, but that wouldn't make sense at all.

Shame nests in my stomach.

It finds company with naivety.

Kong directs me like a towering guard to my small significant self, past the wide-eyed Silk Girls and Paisley, who cups her mouth in shock, all the way through the various halls until we stop outside The Circle.

"The first time I saw the effect you had over him, I thought you were a spy," Kong says, "the entire raid a setup. But seeing you feed Odio changed my mind. That bird can see the truth inside everything. You're too naïve to be a spy."

Too naïve to be a Silk Girl.

I look at the door. Blink. "Do I leave now? Who—"

"Stay in your room," Kong states, and I turn to look up at him — basically a wall of muscles in dark leather armour. "Sleep. Tomorrow you will know what is next for you."

I grip my shoulder as a dull throb circles the joint. Kong notices and frowns. He has a distinctive stance, as though the plates in his back are made of pure indestructible metal, never bending.

I feel numb. Everything escalated so quickly to a place I didn't realise was possible.

I have been so wrong, for so long. Daisy was right. Rules are there for a reason. Iris was right. There is something wrong with me.

"Will I be executed?"

"That is unlikely." Kong's voice is the deepest note I have ever heard. "The Trade has invested in your womb."

My eyes burn; I barely ever cry. "You saw me. You let me speak to her." I clear my throat. "To the Queen. You could have stopped me."

"I was thinking about what she would have wanted," he says, roughly. "Not him or you. I was thinking about her."

"I don't understand."

"You don't need to. And if you know what is good for you, you will stop trying to understand."

CHAPTER NINE

ASTER

Silk Girl Vows:
For The Cradle, I will guard my seal of purity.

A voice stirs me.

The Endigo's snarl coils around me. "Your tongue can't be trusted, little girl. Let's take it off for you. It gets you in so much trouble."

I wake up to those words and a rumbling stomach. I cover my face, breathing into my palms.

Panic and anguish coil together in my mind, growing in size with each new thought.

'You will never speak again.' 'No more questions from you.' 'Your tongue can't be trusted.' What about my Meaningful Purpose? What about all I have endured to get here? The nights I convince myself it would be better here, the split toes from ballet training, the hope of being a Sired Mother. The loneliness and optimism and perseverance.

The ball in my head pops.

Jolting upright, I fist my pillow and toss it across the room, knocking a small fertility statue over, the thing falling, shattering across a black boot.

Wait.

My eyes shoot up from the steel-capped boot to see Rome sitting in the dark corner of the room on the large red leather sofa I've yet to sit on.

Radiating confidence, he is leaning back, his thick arm draped over the high rest. His chest is bare—shirtless— and shadows dance across the deep grooves of his abdomen.

I swallow.

He stares at me. "You dream."

Shit.

I'm not ready to see him.

My pulse thumps so hard the thin column of my throat seems to protest.

I have so many things I want to say, 'get out', 'why?', 'you're a monster', 'I trusted you', 'I liked you', but my mouth only peeps open before closing on a thought: 'You will never speak again.'

Never speak again...

The image of my tiny hand scooping that small bird up comes to mind. I seem to always seek meaning from my oldest memory. After all, it must be there for a reason.

Maybe the useless little thing didn't try to escape, wasn't brave or determined to spread its wings. It simply hit the glass because it was ignorant and confused about its situation and place in the world.

I feel ignorant and confused about mine.

Upside-down bird.

Upside-down bird.

"Are you hurt?"

I turn my face from him and roll my shoulder. There is the dullest of aches, but nothing new to me, given I have been bullied and shoved around my entire life.

"Answer me."

All the contradictory messages suddenly pull me in every direction. This way—'you're weak.'

And that way—'I am enamoured with you.'

This way—'get out.'

And that way—'are you hurt?'

I can usually roll with the punches; I always have. Iris. The Endigo. A life of servitude. No questions. No answers. But lately the punches have been soothed and kissed and I don't know how to adapt to kindness after cruelty.

I suddenly let a quick, pathetic little sob break from between my lips. Then, wipe a single defiant tear away.

He rises to his feet.

"Aster. You're in pain."

He walks toward me, and I shuffle backward along the bed, not wanting him to touch me—*melt* me.

"Don't do that, little creature." Darkness barely conceals the regret in his gaze. "I lost my temper. I'm here to make amends, dammit."

He could slide on and stalk me across the mattress, but he doesn't. He circles the post and comes to the side, sitting down, facing away from where I huddle.

Outside of the shadows now, his muscular back is completely visible, a landscape of stories written with angry scars and tattoos.

"Fuck," he mutters, thrusting his hands through his hair and dragging them down his face as if to tear at his thoughts. "You missed dinner, too."

That is what he has to say?

I missed dinner?

I sit in confused silence, and my soul is not as content with him as it was with the queen.

Nope.

It is on fire.

When he finally turns to stare at me, my shoulders fall to behold the regret in his blue gaze.

I don't care.

I will not forgive him.

But... But I want to hold him. My hand twitches with need. The need to run my fingers down his thick neck again. He liked that. He practically purred as if the beast inside him was being stroked and tamed.

"Say something. That is a direct order. Did I hurt you?"

"Yes," I admit, but not the kind of pain he means. "I'm Fur. Did you know that?" I want him to know. So he can send me away to a new catchment, once and for all. I can be a Silk Girl to another lord.

Never see him...

Never see him again.

Stop this whiplash.

For good.

Another small tear slides down my cheek.

"That is why I am unfit to be a Silk Girl." I add. *"Different*. It must be."

"You're not unfit," he says, curt.

He stands up and nods toward my cloak, which hangs on a silver claw by the closet. "Put on your cloak. I'm taking you to get something to eat."

I blink at him. My body is frozen on the mattress. I admitted to him that I am Fur, not just Common but born amongst outlaws, that I wasn't born to be a Silk Girl originally, that my need for Meaningful Purpose didn't start in the womb, and he...

"Did you hear what I said, Sire?" I press.

"I heard. I know what you are. Better than you do. Now, do as you're told. Cloak."

I don't like that answer or its ambiguity.

I stand up in my night dress, the ends skirting the flooring, tickling my toes. "I am awful at my Trade." I square my shoulders at him and peer up, immediately shadowed by his giant frame. "Yes," I press on despite looking like a mouse agitated with a bear. "I ask too many questions. I'm suspicious and pry. I consider the world, now and before, and why it is the way it is. This is true. But you, you started this thing."

I pace in front of him, focused on the floor before each step. "You held my hand and pretended to care. You saved me and carried me to your military vehicle—you could have made someone else do it. You organised oatmeal with honey for me. You cornered me in the banquet room and... Now you're here, in this room while I have no veil on. *You* blur the line of our appropriate interactions. Why? Why do that to me? I could have been well-behaved. I could have if you had kept the line between us."

Breathing hard, I stop my back-and-forth and stand in front of him with my hands gripping my hips.

I peer up at him and... I blink. He is grinning. Not smirking but actually *grinning*. I've never seen him grin. It- it transforms his face.

How patronising.

How annoying.

I smile back.

"You're so tiny." His lips only widen and while my knees buckle under the beauty of his grin, his *words* irritate me.

So tiny...

Drained to the point of mindlessness, I relent and watch him retrieve my cloak, coming up behind me.

A warm caress rolls down my spine as he drapes the cloak on my shoulders and lifts the hood over my black hair.

"You need to keep your head low. Hide your pretty face. Do you have any energy left after that little outburst to do as you're told, little creature?"

Drained, I simply nod. I'm too emotionally exhausted for much else.

My stomach rolls, the movement large enough to speak volumes for the hunger I've been quelling.

Still behind me, he says, "I want you to know that I heard you."

I exhale hard, closing my eyes and holding them like that as he speaks. With his chest, large and hard, so close to my back, he warms me to my bones.

"I blurred the lines because I don't want the lines. I apologise if that confused you. I was thinking of myself, and what I wanted."

His huge hand moves to the side of my neck, sliding down to massage the shoulder he wounded.

"I will make amends for hurting you," he whispers, a deep baritone of dark promises. "Now. Follow me. Chin to your chest. Don't let anyone see your face or I will have to kill them."

That last phrase widens my eyes.

The door opens, and I am walking into The Circle, with his looming body a barricade behind me, before my next thought can surface.

I amble slowly through the holding space.

The cloak cuts across my eyes but I risk looking at the Guard who is passed out on the floor by the entrance. What about the other girls? They aren't secure.

Rome's body presses to my spine, and I realise I have stopped moving forward.

"Move forward, girl," he states, and I continue taking a step at a time down the dark corridors.

Girl? He never calls me that.

His hand grips my neck through the fabric of my cloak, heat wrapping around my throat with his long fingers. Despite my best efforts not to, I hum from the sense of security he brings.

I stumble.

Concentrate.

I'm too busy watching my step from under the seam of the hood that I can only take in the hues of the lamps reflecting on the polished white and gold flooring.

We turn and enter a room with heavy white double doors, the floor decor changes to grey ceramic tiles, the scent of sizzling butter swirls around my nose.

"Out while I eat," Rome suddenly orders, his voice proceeding the sound of pans and other metal items being placed down, and quick, nervous footsteps.

Then silence.

It's unsettling, yet I like the energy his power creates. I only wish he wielded it with more kindness.

I hear my breath in my ears.

Rome lowers my hood. Bright lights make me squint. I peer around to see a large kitchen fit to create banquets, fitted with triple ovens, twin stone tops, a walk-in fridge, and a long, wide shiny steel island bench for preparation. This space is so clean, it sparkles.

When I feel his hands on my shoulders, I inhale quickly. His knuckles caress the skin at my collarbone as he slides my cloak off my shoulders. He lays it to the side.

Vulnerable like this, I hug myself. The material of my white night gown is thin and slightly translucent. It's the same one that every Silk Girl wears to sleep in.

Rome lifts me to sit on the island bench, my legs dangling, toes just free of the hem of my skirting.

Warmth pools in my belly and makes me squirm.

He moves close.

My mind blurs as he stands, an intimidating wall of muscles, only a head taller than me now.

And I'm not sure I like it. I'm scared of being this close to his lips. Lips that snarl and hurt me, but that I want to touch with mine.

I look at him. Study him.

It's bright in here so I can identify the different blues in his gaze and understand his state of mind from his deliciously dishevelled hair and large black irises— he is wearing all his remorse on the outside right now.

I like seeing him.

The real him—Rome.

Concerned eyes move over me, stopping at my shoulder. He lifts my arm, inspecting the entire length, then the other. He brushes his finger over a small grass wound from when he dropped me. "My temper is a problem. My sister..." He sighs roughly, changing the course of his sentence. "This will not happen again."

His stare is paralysing when he lifts his hand to my lips and traces the curves. I part my mouth to let him explore the flesh. His fingers are warm, firm, demanding.

"I like your lips," he states, then sweeps my hair over my shoulders, exposing my bare neck. "And your throat."

"Because you want to strangle it?" I ask, sad, throwing his own nasty threats back at him before he can do it himself. Warn me. How awful he is. I know. I saw.

He drops his hand.

Picks up mine and places them on his bare abdomen.

Shit.

He's like a rock—course and unforgiving.

I stroke the rippling muscles as they respond to my touch as if his inner beast presses back, demanding more gentle attention. He grips the counter on either side of my hips, his knuckles turning white as he leans in. Caging me. It feels intimate in an emotional way—a wholesome way.

Like he just wants to be stroked in privacy with me.

"No," he says, his voice deep. "Not because I want to strangle it." He leans down and presses his lips to my pulse.

And. I. Almost. *Explode.*

The warmth from his mouth currents across my skin, rising hairs and tightening my nipples.

He groans at my response to his soft, barely-there kiss.

I close my eyes.

More.

Touch me.

Touch me.

My body starts to vibrate, burn, and my core pulses.

I rock my hips into the space between us, lifting my chin and inviting more of his mouth.

He accepts. Dragging his lips upward from my throat to my chin, where his teeth trail along my jawline.

I part my knees and shuffle forward to the edge, wanting his body to fill the inches of space between us. Before my backside can slide off, he presses his hips to catch me, his hard length meeting the soft, warm delta between my thighs.

He grinds against me, his abdominals bunching beneath my fingertips as he applies pressure to that spot—that spot. *Yes.*

I drop my head back further as his lips roam around my neck, down to my collarbone.

He nips it.

Drops to my heaving chest.

He skates his lips over my hard nipples, tormenting the aching beads with very little attention. I wonder if that is for him or me— the light touch.

Will he combust if he does more?

I will combust if he doesn't.

"Please, my king." I don't know what I am asking for. I do. And I don't. "Make it stop."

A groan leaves him, his shattering resolve thickening the air. I pant its heavy, dark essence into my lungs as he releases the counter to position my feet on top.

My hands leave his abdomen as I lean backward, placing them behind me to brace my torso on an angle. I don't know what he is doing. *It*—are we going to do it here?

We can't.

It's against the rules.

I thrust my hips in the air and his mouth hovers over my dress as he slides down to my breasts, taking his time. He kisses my nipple. The subtle stimulation reaches inside me and draws out a moan.

He continues leisurely over my stomach, stopping between my legs, where he nuzzles the place that yearns for attention— pressure. He mouths me over my dress, and I shudder from hundreds of tiny electric shocks.

"What are you doing with your mouth?"

This was *not* in my studies.

"My king?"

Between one confused thought and another, Rome has pushed my skirting to bunch at my hips.

Between my 'no, this isn't right,' and my, 'please make the need stop,' he has torn my knickers down the centre and snapped the threads at each leg, stuffing the tatted remains of it into his front pocket.

My brain turns to mush.

With me exposed and weeping with demand, he straightens. Groaning under some kind of restraint, he stares at me open for him. All for him.

I can feel the wetness between my thighs cooling in the air and know that he can see it.

I pant as his hungry gaze penetrates the slit between my thighs, its heat driving in deep. So deep, I almost feel him, what he wants, what he'll do.

"I'm going to keep you," he declares, tracing a thin scar on my inner thigh leftover from Iris's attack months ago.

One of his hands wraps around my upper leg, holding me, while two thick fingers touch the swelling valley between my lips, sliding up and down with ease.

I blush from my ears to my toes.

"You blush really pretty for me, little creature. *Mm.* I have thought about this pussy," he tells me, moving his fingers in the warmth from my entrance, then lower, to a place that should not be touched. Ever. But he explores the outside of every inch between my thighs. "I couldn't have even imagined *this.* And I imagined it a lot. So, so fucking sweet."

He uses his thumb and forefinger to open my lips.

I close my eyes, unable to watch him staring so intensely at me *there.*

"Your hymen is perfect." The warm tip of his finger slides around something strange and sensitive inside me, as though mapping the dimensions. "I don't want to ruin this, but fuck. Fuck. I have to taste you."

He moves. I hear it.

Then his hot mouth is on me, lips open and sucking at my centre while his thick tongue flattens and laps at me.

That does it. I drop to my back on a throaty cry, my legs spasming and shaking.

"Mine," I hear the word rumble through me.

The overwhelming size of Rome, in comparison to me, has my pelvis pinned to the counter under his weight.

And the pressure.

Yes.

The pressure is everywhere I need it.

"Fuck. I've wanted my tongue inside you since that first day in the parlour."

Writhing, I reach for his hair and tug on it, pulling him away and pushing him down. "Is this— Is this normal?"

He reaches up with his other hand and wraps it around my throat, bracketing me to the counter and sending me a message —'Nothing will stop me.'

He uses his thick tongue to part the folds of skin that protect the place I've barely ever touched and never seen.

I open my mouth, moaning, my eyes squeezed shut, veiling the reality of where we are and what he's doing so inappropriately with my body. And how I want more of it. I'm insatiable with need for him.

I don't know how long he licks and mouths me, or what sensation is what, or what my name is, but my ears are burning, and my spine feels like it might snap, and then—

He turns his mouth and sucks on something higher than my opening, a bundle of nerves tightly pressed together.

Over and Over.

It feels like my bones seize-up, agonising and wonderful, like reaching out and touching death's fingers without the pain, on the edge of something, a sensation that eclipses everything else.

165

I moan long and hard, writhing against his face. Shuddering, heart thrashing, feverish— Am I dying?

His tongue thrusts into me as I convulse around it.

Terrified of what is happening inside my body, my moans mix with whimpers as I ride the wonderful sensation despite my fears.

The pulsing, the electricity, the heat and tightness, slowly dwindle.

Bringing me down.

Lowering me.

Unfolding me.

When it's all over, sweat mists my forehead and slides down my temples. My palms meet my face. I pant into them as he hovers over me, the heat from his body rolling along mine.

"You're safe, sweet Aster. *My* sweet Aster with the *sweetest* pussy and the *softest* moans."

"Is that what you felt?" I say, reeling from that otherworldly experience. "When I pleasured you?"

"Let me see you." When he pulls my hands away from my face, his blue eyes dive into mine. "I'm going to do that," he purrs, his tongue lashing out to taste his lips as he talks, "every time I need to make amends. It will be often, little creature. I'm short-tempered, but I'm keeping you. Understand?"

I blink at him, floating. "How?"

"Just obey me. Do as I say. I'll spoil you. You'll always be safe with me."

"Always?"

Questions fire inside my brain all at once: what about when I've finished birthing? What happens then? He must mean, until then. Correct? Until I've fulfilled my Meaningful Purpose. Then I will be a Sired Mother, and...

Blossom's words echo in my hazy mind, 'nothing lasts forever. Enjoy it while it lasts.'

Okay.

I can do that.

Can't I?

He strokes his knuckles down my blushing cheek. "Look at you. Dragged into depravity with me. Embarrassed by how much you enjoy the way I lick your wet pussy."

"My what?"

He taps my nose. "Now that I've eaten. It is your turn, little creature."

Aiding my shaky body, he helps me sit again, my muscles like goo, my brain mush—all my anatomy basically loose and gummy. I like it.

He grabs a muffin from within a glass dome container and holds it out for me, the fluffy pastry looking small in his big hand.

I take it, but notice it's got a dollop of that yellow pudding stuff on the top. My nose creases for a moment but I soften it. I've never been a fan of it. We were served it on apples in the aviary.

His brows furrow. "What is it? You don't like something."

"No. It's fine." I smooth my silken gown down my legs. "I'm dizzy, is all." I lower the muffin to my lap. "What did you just do to me? What was that part of me at the top, a... *button*... or something, that you touched?"

"You know all about my anatomy, but the part of you that is *specifically* for your pleasure, you know nothing about. Interesting." His nose dips into my hair, and he hums. "I will show you very soon. I will take you on a little tour of all the pretty parts that will make you moan for me. But, for now, tell me what is wrong with that muffin."

I try to focus. "It's fine, my king."

He leans back to stare down at me. "Fine is not acceptable. Ever. Tell me what you want, or I'll summon The Trade Cooks in here and have them slave away all night until they create something worthy of more than a *fine* from you."

"Don't do that." I breathe out hard. "I just don't like the yellow pudding stuff on the top."

"Custard."

"Yes."

His lips quirk. "That's lemon butter."

167

I look at the blob. "Oh."

My face feels warm from what he did to me, and when he scoops a dollop of the lemon butter onto his finger, pleasure stirs me to a puddle.

I instantly wrap my mouth around the tip, sucking the sweet, citrus flavours, moaning.

His eyes darken and he steps backward, leaning against the opposite counter, his gaze never leaving me. "Eat."

I look down and see the hard, long length between his legs even through his pants. I know how big that is. How thick and hard. In the Silk House, when I imagined the male anatomy, I always considered it would be... *tender.*

I lick the butter from the top of the muffin, and it pulses in his pants. *Shit.*

When I had the thick head inside my mouth, it throbbed like that heart I fed Odio. I didn't know that they moved on their own.

I thought they were, well, fragile.

Nothing fragile about his...

"Stop looking at me like that, little creature. You don't know what you're asking for with those big, fuck-me eyes."

I snap my gaze back to his, finding an expression, dark and frightening.

Using the muffin to redirect my mind, I eat it. It's good. Tart and sweet and dense, filling.

He watches me enjoy it

Too soon, I take the last bite and lick the doughy residue off each finger, feeling better now that my stomach isn't empty.

"Is it unbearably heavy...?" I ask, glances at *it* again. "When it's like that?"

It unsettles me how still he is at this moment.

"You want to know what my cock feels like while I watch you lick that muffin and then suck your fingers?" His voice strains. "When your little tongue comes out and laps at that butter, my cock throbs like a wound. I can feel my arteries pounding, the pulse is thunder between my ears." He reaches down and palms his large bulge curving up between his hips. "It feels like my blood is literally boiling."

He pushes off the counter and possesses the column of my throat. "Like your throat right now. Thump. Thump."

I whimper, because he's hot and close and threatening, but I'm not afraid. Without meaning to, I relax into the tight collar he makes with his hand. He dips, his lips meeting my ear, heavy breath rushing into my hair. "But the pain I felt inside my cock while I was licking your wet pussy was worse. Much worse. That was the sweetest agony of my life."

The question dances on my tongue; will you come to me later tonight? *I'll stare at my veil and pretend I don't recognise your deep groans, scent, possessive touch.*

I open my mouth to ask when he reaches for my cloak. "Time to go back to your room. The Guard will be awake soon. We can't have him reporting this."

Chapter Ten

ROME

Her scars...

The tiny white rivers of past wounds that snake down her inner thighs. *How did she get them?* I could not be more pleased that I executed that Wardeness in the Lower-tower last week. She was careless and blind. This girl—my Aster—has not lived a gentle life needed to be a Silk Girl.

The last-light dim creeps away in the corridor as I leave The Circle and Aster...

"Aster is out," I state, pushing open the door to Cairo's quarters to find him hunched on the side of the bed, pulling a shirt on, the lashes from his flagellation on display for a slither of a moment. When I was a young man, I used to wonder what thoughts made him want to pursue a path of penance each last-light before he slept.

Now, I do not care.

I continue, "We are a lord down and she is the smallest. I will take the redhead."

"Iris," he confirms, standing and stopping in front of me.

Bowing his head, he says, "Sire." He continues his routine, hovering over a small basin, and begins to wash his hands.

His chambers are as barren as his heart, a wooden bed, desk, basin, and bookcases. The minimalist space reflects his commitment to The Trade as his sole identity and interest. "Aster has two very interested lords. It is a pity."

My back muscles bunch. "Who?"

"You know I cannot say," he states.

"She is out." I widen my stance and remember a time when I was eager to be an emotionless warlord like my father. How very unlike him I am when my thoughts and passions bubble away in my veins like molten lava. "Her thighs are scarred. She has been through too much to be a Silk Girl."

"I'm not going to ask how you know such things."

"I will not repeat myself. She is out."

He smiles wirily and looks up from his hands, meeting my gaze in the small brass-framed mirror. "Shall I leave now to inform the other lords they are required to start immediately? We have missed a night waiting for you to finalise your decision." His brows weave, and I know this is it. "I will ensure there will be no crossovers. You will start with Iris tonight. This is your first time making an heir. Let me explain how it works." He turns to face me. "Usually, a Guard would monitor the comings and goings, to ensure only one lord is inside The Circle at any time, but over the next five nights, I will stand at the door. You will go first. Do her well."

I sneer. "She'll be limping by the time I'm through with her. You'll have an heir this season."

"*We* will have an heir. Make it happen, Sire."

Teeth grinding, I turn to walk back through the door, when his words slice through me, halting my step.

"I shall send Aster to a new placement."

I talk to the open door, my blood roars, ready for what he might say next. Clenching my fists at my sides, I say, "She is mine. I will do whatever I want with her."

I hear his dark chuckle. "You would keep Meaningful Purpose from her? It is all she has known. She will not take this well. Let me reassign her to a lord with less… standards."

"No."

"If you want to fuck that girl, Sire. You need to treat her in the appropriate manner. As a Silk Girl," he states smoothly, reading me too fucking well. I loathe his intuitions, not that I have managed to hide my interest in Aster well. "She is a breeder. She will get pregnant easily. If you want to fuck her at leisure not Purpose, we will need to remove all the parts that may bring you an unauthorised heir... you understand?"

I see black.

I don't intend to fuck her.

I want to keep her pure, safe.

My last piece of humanity.

Perfectly intact.

But his threat digs at the grave of my darkest memory, and my weakness. I want to. There is no doubt that I want to fuck her and if I do…

He will cut her open.

Pull out her womb.

Leave her broken.

Just like my sister.

Hatred and disdain creep into my vision like phantoms finding my humanity and choking it. I do not dare turn around.

I lower my voice, deepen it. "If you touch a hair on her head, I will drag your spine from your torso by your skull."

Without another word, I storm away from his chamber. The Guards I pass flatten themselves to the brick walls as I violently shake, visibly fighting to control my anger.

If he didn't know I cared for her before, he sure as hell knows now.

CHAPTER ELEVEN

ASTER

Silk Girl Vows:

For The Cradle, I will be proud of every pregnancy no less than I am my own.

"Rome," I whisper as I come to, the warmth of his gaze still a tangible memory. He makes me feel as though I can be myself. A Silk Girl and Aster. A flower and a person with my own little differences. I adore what he is, and I adore what I am when he looks at me.

Like he's going to choose me.

I blink my eyes open to the back of the veil. I slide it down to my neck and look around the dim room. Orange light spills from the ornamental fire— a first-light indicator. Yellow is crown-light. Red is last-light. It's how I know what time of day it is in this room. The sun's brilliance is filtered heavily with the haze, it is only direct enough at crown-light for us to truly mark the time of day.

In the Silk House, we also had the colour codes. I've become conditioned to them without knowing.

He didn't come last night.

That's fine.

Pouting my disappointment, I sit up and instantly see something strange floating on the closed door. At first, my breath catches, and I think it's a person. Then I realise it's a black dress hanging on the silvery hook.

Sliding the golden sheet to the side, I rub my eyes until they focus. I walk to the dress and run my fingers down the line of black lace buttons sewn vertically down the centre.

It's for me to wear today. Growing up in the Silk Aviary meant waking to many dresses hung on the backs of doors.

I ready myself, wash and dress in the mournful black outfit, and walk from my room into The Circle.

Instantly, I'm stilled by the sight of the five Watchers, standing in a line with their hands clasped together, their expressions sombre and serious, and their pleated trousers and neat shirts also black.

The other Silk Girls stand quietly opposite their Watcher, so I head to Paisley and stop in front of her.

"What's going on?" I ask, peering down the line.

"We were just waiting for you," Ana's Watcher says.

"We have some terrible news to share," Paisley offers, sadness curling her lips down.

"And such awful timing for you," Blossom's Watcher adds sweetly, shaking her head in slow sorrowful waves.

Iris's Watcher, the tallest of all of us, the broadest, too, steps forward from the others. "I am afraid that Lord Darwin of the Half-tower has passed. He has returned to The Crust. He is at peace. Today we mourn for him in black like our ancestors have done for thousands of years."

Ana covers her gasp.

"I know." Iris's Watcher takes a big breath in. "I want you all to rest assured that even though this is a tragedy we do not wish to take away from the living and what they experience."

The blood in the banquet hall.

"What you girls are doing for The Cradle will remain our priority and yours," she goes on. "So, please remember how important you are. *Especially* now when you have them inside you. You are expected to eat all your breakfast, even though, I know grief can affect hunger, you will need extra nutrients after last night. Please focus on your bodies and help them bloom."

Wait. What did she say?

I feel the blood drain from my cheeks. I whip my eyes up to Paisley, and she looks evasively at the floor between us, avoiding my stare of pure scrutiny and dread.

"Paisley?" I whisper, too quiet for the others to hear.

Daisy's Watcher starts talking. "During breakfast, each girl will be taken to Master Cairo for inspection. Your first night with a lord can leave pain and discomfort and any tenderness needs to be treated immediately.

"After your visit with Master Cairo, we will organise a mineral bath and massage for you should your body ache. Anything we can do to help for tonight."

As my stomach sinks with the weight of envy, the nasty unseemly monster, it hits me— I *presumed* that he chose me. That last night was his way of showing me that he had chosen me to be his Silk Girl, but it was an apology and nothing more.

No. No. It can't be. What about: 'I'm going to keep you.' 'You will be safe.' 'You're mine.'

Blossom's Watcher nods, her voice is smooth like honey, but the words sting me like a bee. "The second and third nights are often the most painful, and we will do anything and everything to make sure you're comfortable so you can take your lord successfully."

"Paisley," I mutter again.

She doesn't look up. She knows. My vows hammer my chest

and heart to pulp: his indifference toward me would be my greatest failure.

"You must relax. That is very important."

"Your lord needs your natural lubricants."

I try to fight the nausea that rises in my throat. I don't know who is speaking anymore. My mind is now a rolling drum, and questions pour out, one after the other.

Why didn't he come?

Did everyone else get visited?

Did I make a mistake?

Is it because I admitted that I am Fur.

The questions clap between my ears, the warmth of his memory and touch turning to ice in my veins.

Did he visit someone else?

After he was with me?

As if to answer me, three young Trade girls, barely ten years old, step into The Circle from inside Blossom, Daisy, and Iris's bedrooms. They carry blood-stained sheets. I peer sideways at Iris, but she is already staring at me, her smirk mocks me.

I lock my jaw.

"In case you have forgotten or have breeding-brain, your lord will visit you every night for the next four, and then it will depend on their schedules as to what happens until your next heat."

My legs get weak.

Wobble.

Give out.

Who am I now?

Filthy Fur Girl.

As the questions and uncertainty assail me, the betrayal in them nests into places deep and visceral.

My body grows weak. In my mind, images rush like a torrent —the Silk Girl from my drawing now bears Iris's face and Rome is thrusting into her.

The floor suddenly seems to draw nearer, and before I can stop myself, I collide with it.

"Aster!"
Girls huddle around me.
But my mind goes blank.

CHAPTER TWELVE

ASTER

As I open my eyes, the blur of an overhead light comes into focus. The scent of sage and sandalwood from a candle or oil burner sails around me.

A shiver rushes down my spine.

I peer down my body, seeing I'm naked and lying on an examination table. The same ones they have at the Silk House for our annual checkups.

Am I at the doctor's?

But why am I naked?

While my breath struggles in and out of my body, instinct takes over. Unmoving at first, I survey the area, seeing a pair of scissors on a far reflective steel desk.

I slide from the high bed, dropping to my bare feet. Without a second of hesitation, I rush to the desk and grab the shiny scissors, holding them out in front of my body.

"Easy, Aster, I won't hurt you."

I spin to see a tall, gorgeous, dark-haired Xin De man in a

purple cloak approaching unhurried and smiling, with the powerful aura and angelic features of a fallen angel.

"Why am I naked?" I ask, fingering the scissors.

"I undressed you."

I step backward. "Why?"

"I was checking you over." He stops a few paces away and drops his gaze down my legs. "You have scars on your thighs. I wanted to see if they were anywhere else. How did you get them?"

I blink at him, biding my time as I consider what to say. "I don't remember." It's all I have.

"My apologies," —he opens his arms, seemingly finding my defensive stance amusing— "what terrible manners. Most people know me. I'm Master—"

"Cairo," I finish, realising. I have seen his picture before, studied him even, but he is different in the flesh in a way I cannot even put my finger on.

"No one came to me," I offer, schooling my expression so he cannot see my disappointment, anger, jealousy. *Shit.* I clear my throat. "I don't need to be here. I am not in pain as no one chose me."

"You fell unconscious," he says, plainly.

"I was shocked by Lord Darwin's passing."

His dark eyes narrow on me, finding a clear target in my throat as I swallow my nerves down. "Very good. I almost believed you."

Exhaling hard, I mutter. "I'm a Silk Girl." I set the scissors down, surrendering, and glance at the fresh skin graft on my wrist, where my tattoo used to be, where my identity was marked in flesh.

Finding my head and ignoring my heart, I say, "My mother was a Silk Girl. I am one. What about my Meaningful Purpose now that no one wants me?"

He studies me. "It will change."

"No." I shake my head over and over. "No, I've been raised my entire life for this. I want it. I'm a Silk Girl."

I can't let them win, can't let Iris win.

I am a Silk Girl.

My palms start to sweat. My jealous yearning sets ablaze to anger, the potent feeling incinerating my silly affections toward him, building ashy disdain around the name Rome. Rome who took this from me. "The king did this! Didn't he?" As the words come out, I know I've crossed a line, revealed myself and Rome, to the one person I should never bare my soul to.

One of his eyebrows lifts. "The king? That's how you address The Cradle's Monarch?"

I rub my palms down my naked thighs. "*Sire.*"

He makes a clicking sound with his tongue before walking toward the high examination table. "I am not one to smack a pet when the owner has clearly allowed it on the bed. So, tell me, Aster, has he touched you already?"

"No," I peep.

"Are you lying to me?"

"No."

He looks at me—*through* me. "On the bed," he orders, the words uncompromising. "I will check your seal. *If* you're intact, I will relocate you. You are lovely, your movements graceful, your eye contact is perfection, and you haven't insisted on dressing so I can presume you're not prideful and understand that your body is The Cradle's, not yours. It would be a great pity if we let what we invested in you go to waste."

His eyes track me as I stroll over to the bed, take the steps up the side, and lie down on it again. "You promise?"

"Promise?"

"That I can leave," I spit out. "And be a Silk Girl somewhere else? Far, far away."

Far away from him. So far away the distance wipes his memory. So far away I forget the warmth of his touch. So, so far, that I forget that he once promised to keep me.

My throat tightens, and a single tear slides down my temple, pooling in my ear. I hate him. I hate him.

Channelling all that loathing, I make it loud and deafening. No other emotions can filter through. Not affection. Not sorrow. Not melancholy or desire.

As I rest my hands on my stomach, I feel Master Cairo push my knees apart. He says, "You're a confident little thing. I knew the girl who birthed you to The Cradle. She spoke with adamance and confidence, also. I hope you don't make the same mistakes she did."

I peer down my naked body to where he sits between my thighs, the sight rising hairs all over my skin. "You knew my mother?"

"Your mother is the queen," he states, his voice smooth and even, dangerously so. "But, yes. I knew the girl who birthed you."

"What happened to her?"

"She ran away."

"Pardon? I thought she was kidnapped."

Fingers part my lips. I drop my head back to the firm cushioning and fight my innate response to whimper.

"She fell in love with a lord, and when he rejected her, she let her emotions in and ran," he talks while touching me, barely, but enough for me to know where his fingers are. "She met a Common man and had two daughters and two sons with him. Perfect babies. Clean births. She was an exceptional breeder, after all, The Trade invested much time and resources in her. Unfortunately her babes were not born for The Cradle but for a Fur community. You were one of those babes.

"We got you back. You will be a *wonderful* breeder, too. *Unlike* her, you understand that love is not a virtue. Which is why you are choosing to leave *him*. You're choosing The Cradle. She lost her life to an Endigo raid. She died without Meaningful Purpose." His hands leave that special place, cool air sweeping over me as he leans backward. "That's not what you want, is it, Aster?"

"No."

"No, what?"

"No, Master."

"Good girl. Sit up."

Chapter Thirteen

Rome

"Where is my Silk Girl?" I roar, backing her Watcher into the brick wall of the corridor, seeing the girl tremble so hard her teeth clatter in her jaw.

"Iris?" she asks.

"Who the fuck is Iris? You fucking imbecile!" I punch my fists into the brick on either side of her head, the clay fracturing inward. "Aster!"

Her gaze flickers from side to side, frantic with confusion. How does she not know? How well has she been 'Watching?'

"She fainted, Sire. Wh- When we told her about Lord Darwin and then—"

"Where. The fuck. Is she?" My words hit her hard, making her flinch again.

I have searched The Circle, her room, the Silk Girl Dining Hall, and the courtyard. She is nowhere to be found. She's fucking gone.

My skin crawls along my muscles like it's desperate to unleash them, grant them freedom to reap hell.

"Master Cair—" she stammers and starts to hiccup her words, laced with fear and panic.

When I snap my head toward his chambers, Aster's Watcher slides down the wall to the floor.

Steeled, my shoulders turn, and my deadly gaze pierces his closed door. I charge down the corridor toward it. Memories of my broken sister—of her bandaged abdomen, trembling thighs, slim, naked body, broken fucking gaze—carve sanity from my mind and plant rage into the bloody slit.

I hear my growl as I kick the door open, splintering it against the inside wall.

My chest heaves as I search the room, finding my sweet Aster sitting on the examination table naked and him— I see red. I don't see anything else.

He holds his palms up like that will slow me as I lung at him, but before I have his head in my hands, two Guards grip my arms, holding me back.

I slide their feet along the floor as I take another step.

"Sire," a Guard behind me calls. "Stop."

Growling, I jolt my shoulders and throw the Guards from my arms. I prowl forward again and, again, two more men grab hold of me from behind.

More hands.

More men.

Four fucking fully-grown Xin De Guards claw at me as I growl and hiss and reach to get my bare hands around The Trade Master's pretty fucking head.

"Easy, boy," I hear Kong's voice behind me. "Take a moment before you do something you'll regret."

"Sire," Cairo says from the other side of the room, seemingly un-fucking-bothered.

I want him, want to feel his head slowly cave in, feel the moment it gives way, the bone compressing his brain, his eyeballs popping from their sockets.

"Tell the king you are okay, Aster," Cairo orders.

"Sire." She slides from the bed, dropping to the ground—so tiny—*and* completely fucking naked.

I growl louder. "Why the fuck are you naked!"

"I was examining her. I did nothing improper. I assure you." He smiles. "I did not touch a single hair on her head."

My lips sneer.

Done with this. I take the fuckers behind me by surprise when I spin around and grab hold of their heads, playing their skulls like cymbals and smashing them together. The other two back away with their hands up—they even close their eyes, because they know they aren't allowed to look at the Silk Girls.

As I turn back to Cairo, hatred in my eyes, he softens his smooth smile and says, "If you kill me, the Shadows in The Estate will be activated, and they will kill your Collective." I don't give a fuck about anyone. I stalk toward him. "The first casualty will be your sister."

I stop midstride.

"Boy," Kong warns.

My blood is volcanic, and my fingers are curled and raised at his head, shaking with fury and ready to tear his fucking skull and spine from his body. My hands vibrate. Just inches away from him. Just right there. *Fuck.*

"Tell the king you are well, Aster," Cairo repeats.

"I'm well." I hear her soft voice, drawing my gaze to her as she pulls her dress over her head, the silky black material falling down her lithe body.

I still.

Stare at her.

What has she done to me?

It hits me like a bullet right in the chest. A bullet I'll keep with the others. I don't want her to be a piece of The Trade. *I* want her. I don't want to share her. It's not simply about preserving her— the manifestation of my last act of human kindness—I want *her*.

I've been bored, playing the same game of chess to bring The Trade and The Cradle a state of compliance. Each piece with its place, with its Purpose, including her, and I dug my fingers into the guts of what that meant.

I adhere to my vows, create an aura of fear around myself, but I do not want her to follow the rules or behave for them! Not for them. *For me.*

Maddening little girl.

Without a second thought, I stride to her as she backs away from me until she hits the brick wall.

I scoop her into my arms, and she bursts into tears, beating her little fists into my chest. She is trying to hurt me. "Little creature, calm down."

"You didn't come! You didn't come!"

The damage is cemented with Cairo. It's irreversible now. He knows. I know. She seems to be the only one with no concept of how much she fucking affects me.

As Cairo smirks, I stride from the room with her punching at me, but her spitting tears and angry brows are what bothers me, not her sweet little fists.

"You deceived me. You made me think that you were choosing me. And then you gave Iris Meaningful Purpose, not me! How could you? Not her!"

I can't follow her chaotic trail of thoughts right now. I don't have the right words, so I keep walking.

She punches me the entire way, down the corridor, past the Guard, into the Medi-deck, The Circle, and then into her room.

I kick her door shut.

I distantly notice her fists have flattened to slaps as she loses strength.

"Fuck. For whatever I have done to make you behave this way, I will make amends!" I finally say, my chest warm and tight and fucking aching all at once.

"No! I can't."

"You will!"

With her protected against my torso, I crawl along the bed, lowering her to the mattress.

Groaning at having her under me, even as she fights, I grab both her bony wrists and pin them above her head.

"I hate you," she spits out.

Hovering over her, I use my other arm to keep my weight from crushing her. She bucks beneath me, such a little thing fighting off a beast. Her squirming makes my cock pulse, fill with blood, ache and demand.

"What do you want from me? I'll give it to you."

"You didn't come for me. Now, it's too late!"

"Like hell it is." I growl, voice savage. "This feeling in my chest, this damn tight, warm agony. That is my response to you. It's been driving me mad. Agitating me. Controlling me. Making me do things that are not in my nature. Dangerous things. And I just can't fight it anymore. I understand it. You are the first thing I've ever really wanted. Now! What do *you* want?"

"I wanted to be your Silk Girl!" she screeches.

At her manner, heat builds in my temples. "I can fuck any girl, any time! I wanted to give you more than that, you silly little thing. You're different. Better. I don't want to share you with The Trade. I want you to be mine! Mine, dammit. Not The Trade's!"

She shakes her head as she says, "That is my Meaningful Purpose. One day"—she sobs— "when you're an old man and I'm dead because I don't have the Xin De genes, you're going to look out over the children *I've* made for you, and *their* children, and *their* children, dozens of them that all originated from *my* body, and you'll understand why being your Silk Girl means everything to me!"

Fuck. I don't want to imagine a room filled with her babies but without her...

Then she licks her dry lips. Bad move. Her tongue, tiny and pink, wetting her perfect bow lips. A groan rumbles deep inside me as though vibrating in a cold, hard cave.

Jealous of her tongue.

I seal my mouth over hers.

I kiss her.

She melts into the mattress, letting go of the anger as I work her soft, wet lips with mine. She sighs, giving in to me, opening her mouth for me to explore.

She tastes good. So sweet. So vulnerable. My little aster flower, little creature. Mine.

Her hips roll upward, begging for pressure, for my body on hers, and my cock strains to her demand. The pain is blinding.

"Fuck, Aster. Stop," I hiss, so close to losing complete control with her.

Needing to still her writhing body, I lower my torso to press on her, and she mindlessly grinds her pussy against my abdomen and fuck... I'm fucked.

So fucked.

As her inexperienced mouth grows in confidence, her tongue meets mine, her lips begin to move, and I can feel the raging beat of her heart against me.

And now I want that, too.

Her heart.

Her womb.

All of her.

She wants to be my Silk Girl, but I want her to be more. I was going to allow her to torture me, torment me with her body, keep her the one thing I won't allow myself... Who is the damn obsessed one here? It is meant to be her!

I tear myself from her lips and press my forehead to hers. "Eat well. Sleep early. I will come to you, little creature."

She pants against me, and I inhale the sweet breath, taking it as my own. "Then I'll make you mine in the way you desperately desire."

The demanding little thing trembles beneath me, sweet, nervous energy even as I offer her what she wants.

"So—" She gathers her thoughts and steadies her breath. "So you'll take two Silk Girls then?"

Why is she asking this? "Two?"

"Iris..." she mutters, the name heavy with emotion. That name again. "Red hair, big breasts, tall, leggy, the nictitating membrane." Agitation pitches her voice. "You were with her last night!"

Her tone pisses me off.

Impertinent.

Improper.

Disrespectful.

I lift my head and glare down at her.

Fuck me, she's pretty.

"I realise you're emotional," I offer, checking my temper. "But the next time you raise your voice to me, little creature, I'll be fucking those sounds from you with my cock down your throat. Do you understand?"

Her breath hitches. "Yes, my king."

I exhale roughly—that's better.

My eyes pin her to the mattress, the effect instant as a shy pink glow gathers on her cheeks.

"You will not ask me this again," I state smoothly. "Do not test my loyalties, make assumptions, or accusations. You have no right to ask me who I fuck or when or why."

Her pretty violet eyes well up.

Dammit.

I touch my forehead to hers again, our breath mingling together. "I did not take another Silk Girl last night. I have never taken a Silk Girl, Aster. You are the first."

Too much sentimentality and possessive rage make the need to taste her insufferable. Time to introduce my Silk Girl to her clit.

She whimpers as I climb down her body and slide my head under her dress. I know she's naked underneath; I saw her scurry to put her clothes on in front of me…

And in front of Cairo.

A territorial growl rumbles low in my guts as I eat at her pussy lips. They are neat and closed, barely touched. I part them with my tongue.

She bucks off the bed, long moans escaping her in an instant.

Her knees rise, presenting more for me to enjoy, but not enough, so I throw her legs over my shoulders.

Her hands fist the sheets by her hips, and my tongue laps from her arsehole to her clit and back. Over and over.

Groaning, I indulge on her as I admit, "Licking your sweet pussy lips makes me so hard."

It takes every fibre of my restraint not to literally chew on her skin, imprint my teeth into her folds. Want more.

I don't just lick her pussy, I claim it, feeding my hands between the mattress and her little arse, holding each cheek completely, controlling her pelvis.

I lap up and down.

"This little bud is your clitoris," I utter, using the tip of my tongue on the tiny hidden knot, flicking it until she is jerking and mewling like a speared animal.

"It's for your pleasure."

I kiss the tiny hood, then push it down and suck the pink, supple bead that rises from it.

Still sucking, I use the tip of my tongue to bear down on the bundle of nerves. They fire. I hear her breathing become jagged, hear her cries of pleasure hint at anguish. At angst. At needing something just on the brim.

Too intense, her sounds tell me.

I lessen the pressure and focus on dipping into her wet, tight hole. She gets wet easily.

My perfect, little Silk Girl with her wet pussy. That will help when I fuck her. The juices filling my mouth are made to help my massive cock stretch her open.

When she ripples on my tongue, I groan into her, knowing her inner walls are clenching around her narrow channel, begging for friction and pressure.

I will comply.

Soon.

I fuck the mattress.

Very, very soon.

Coming back to her clit, I find the perfect pace and suck with gentle authority, wanting something from inside—her nerves to explode.

Her thighs tighten around my face.

Her left leg jerks from my shoulder.

She comes on my tongue.

And like the rest of Aster, her orgasm is sweet with vulnerability and confusion but still curious. As though she is unsure its real, I'm real, or what might be happening to her inexperienced, young body.

I am what is happening to her.

I am what is claiming her.

"Do you enjoy your clit?"

She is whimpering through her climax; her little cheeks jiggle in my cupped palms; her clit vibrates on my tongue. She is too lost to respond. *Lovely.* "Answer me, Aster."

"Yes," she cries.

Pleasing this pussy will undoubtedly become an addiction of mine, the rich flavour and soft scent perfectly balanced is enough to drive a man to thirst for it, beg for it, war for it.

And I am very skilled in the ways of war.

CHAPTER FOURTEEN

ASTER

A Silk Girl Vow—The Act.

For The Cradle, my skin will be smooth like silk, my entrance wet, warm, and welcoming, and I'll draw the weight from my lord with my core.

He will pierce me open, and blood will flow from my delta; a heavy fall is my mark of a pure soul.

I will thrill and quiver in being the vessel that brings him peace. I will massage him inside my heat, clearing his mind and mine to all but Meaningful Purpose. And should I feel pleasure build within me, I will thank him for it, in each thrust, and I will protect what he inserts inside me.

I do as I'm told. I visit the Silk Dining Room while the others are treated for aches. I bathe in hot water and minerals until my body feels loose, and I climb into bed early.

Well before last-light.

With my veil on, I curl on my side, the sheets shuffling over my naked body.

I try to welcome slumber.

But my mind rolls.

I don't understand relationships. Mine have been staged, dutiful, and procedural. I know nothing of human emotions besides the ones I feel inside me. And I definitely don't understand the actions or afflictions of a Xin De king.

But I understand anger.

And he was furious.

He threatened Master Cairo…

For me.

Does he care about me?

I touch my lips below the hem of the veil, feeling his phantom warmth. He kissed me. He kissed me, and I could feel how much he cared, how angry and unsure, possessive and annoyed he was. I felt it all. All those truths.

From one kiss.

I know I assumed—another shameful trait—but bloody sheets left Iris', Blossom's, and Daisy's rooms, so… That leaves Ana. And…

Shit.

Lord Darwin.

Does she carry his heir?

I want to ask her if her lord visited last night, but I'm afraid that if I do, she will start to suspect…

And suspicion is not a virtue.

What becomes of her now?

Or the king is lying.

I just don't think he is.

The kiss didn't lie.

~

Somewhere in the midst of one thought and another, slumber wraps me in a tight, warm hold.

Not until I feel air whispering across my legs do I stir. Sheets glide down my body. The bed rocks me from side to side, and I know he is prowling over me.

I don't move, but I open my eyes, blinking my lashes against the smooth black veil. The seam of the silken material caresses my upper lip, my mouth mostly free and exposed to the air.

My heart races immediately.

"Aster." My name purrs across my ear as he hovers over me. "Are you wet for me, little Silk Girl? Are your smooth, white thighs quivering for me? Are you afraid of what I'm going to do to you?"

My mouth parts, the thick weight of his words pressing on my chest, squeezing air from my lungs. *Shit.* His palm moves up to grip my throat, rolling me to my spine within the cave of his large body.

"Fuck," he utters, strained. His breath blows through my hair and his rough, warm cheek touches mine through the silk veil. "You smell so fucking good."

I start to tremble.

He glides his hand up from my shin, gripping and massaging a shearing path to my knee before pushing my thigh to the mattress. Spreading me.

His touch is firm—authoritarian—yet gentle and reverent. As if he knows how fragile I am in his arms, but he can work the pieces of me so they do not shatter.

A strong, large hand spans out over my core, pressing his palm to my weeping lips. "So wet for me. Your defiant mind may misbehave, but your body is so very obedient to me."

He moves down my torso.

Mouths my throat.

Then, licks across my chest. Treats each nipple to his lips until the aching buds stiffen, forcing whimpers from me. He hums, his exhale gushing heat along my flesh.

199

I gasp and arch into him.

One arm braces him just above me.

The other traces from the back of my knee, over my hip to the side of my breast, and down again, scorching a path of warmth and yearning.

Then he shifts.

And it's time.

My eyes widen behind the silk veil when he positions himself. My senses heighten, touch, sound. Everything—*him.*

With his lips to my forehead, his muscular arm slides up my spine until he cups my head and cradles my torso, controlling me against him.

His hard, long length is a pulsing rod that bruises my core and up my trembling stomach.

"My king," I plea, terrified.

With no room to move, my arms curled between us and my fingers by my chin, I can only flatten my hands to his chest. I am utterly vulnerable to him, more now, in this position than ever before.

"I'm going to get lost in the feel of your tight, wet pussy, little creature. Use your claws on me. If I hurt you, make sure I know what you're feeling. Bring me back to you."

I curl my fingers into the hard, warm plane of his carved muscles to show him that I can, even with his pressure—everywhere. I shudder and try to lift into him, grinding, already desperate for the pleasure I know he can bring.

It dawns on me then, as I become aware of the entire mass of his length, measuring it in my mind in comparison to me... And I swallow. It's too big, but that is why we breed Xin De with Common now. To fix our physical differences.

"Is it possible that you're too big?" I blurt out.

His hips demand mine to open wider. "You are soaking wet for me; you will let me in. And I will restrain myself. Just relax for me, sweet creature."

Fingers touch inside my folds, swept up and down, spreading

my natural lubricant around. With a grunt, he is fisting his length and swirling the swollen head up and down my entrance, stirring me into a frenzy of panic and anguish.

"Need this." The words beat against my forehead as he presses the crown through my folds. "*Easy.*" He isn't talking to me. "*Fuck.*"

My body sinks, swallowed up by the mattress.

When he beats against the sensitive seal inside me, I'm hit with a bolt of warning. A whimper escapes my throat, but he doesn't stop working his way against the resistance inside me.

Not for a second.

The sensation burns and burns. Then he stabs through me, folding me inward like a new rosebud. Agony heats my abdomen. Spasms twist in my thighs. Turns me inside out.

Crying out, I dig my nails into his chest.

"Aster." He whispers apologies and praise while he thrusts deeper, possessing my body entirely. "It'll be over soon, little Silk Girl. You're perfect. Untouched. Let me in."

I let his words overrun my senses. "Yes, my king."

Holding me with dominance, preventing me from recoiling, he stretches me open, one thick inch at a time, until I can no longer fit anymore. No longer breathe, think, or feel anything but the weight and pressure of him absolutely everywhere.

"There you go. You have taken as much of me as you can. I'm so proud of my sweet creature."

He rolls against me, his length sliding but never completely withdrawing, never allowing me a full breath, consuming my every cell with him.

His rhythmic strokes are powerful, painful—overwhelming. Each one wrenches a long, moan through my lips. And I'm lost in them.

"My king," I whimper, needing reassurance.

"Yes, sweet thing. I'm here. I'm going to fuck you, over and over, until you're pregnant." His words spur him on further. "Until my sons and daughters grow inside your womb. Swell your belly. This is my pussy, my womb, my damn body. Fuck." Heat from his growl caresses my forehead. "Remember your claws, little creature."

He speeds up, pumping, his mouth mauling and licking at my forehead. I feel the beast inside him breaking loose, threatening to tear me apart with passion.

I'm wet. So wet for him. It helps. The tightness inside me melts around his thorough penetration, the pain transforming into beautiful agony that I don't want to end.

He feels like pain and desire.

Like danger and grace.

Tears rush down my temples.

He rears up and possesses my throat, pinning me, pumping in and out, my entire body gyrating beneath him. Pain shoots through my abdomen again, too deep, too thick.

Desperate, I reach up, needing my hands on him to feel safe, but he's out of reach.

He catches my swinging wrists and presses my palms to his warm abdomen, where the muscles tighten with each thrust. "I'm here."

My head is spinning, and I think I might blackout when he grabs my thigh and angles my backside, taking me down a path of pleasure.

Then there is no gravity.

No room. No bed. No up. No down.

Just him and me and his length rubbing every nerve that lines my channel.

"Fuck." He groans, his hips moving, methodical and powerful. "That's my good girl. Squeeze my cock. Let me feel you fall apart for your king."

My pleasure blooms, then it quickly erupts, warmth rushing down the inside of my legs and curling my toes. I never want him to stop.

Even with the pain.

A deep, dark groan rumbles from him, and he tense as if he may shed his skin, his abdominals bulking beneath my fingers.

He pumps into me with a rough growl and comes, filling me between the legs until it's pouring out of me, down my thighs. It's violent and intense.

He stills, breathing loud and fierce.

I wish I could see him.

He drops down to his elbows, his body completely covering mine, his lips finding their place against my wet forehead. "My sweet Aster." His breath is heavy. "My little creature. Tell me you're not hurt."

Coming down from that place of intensity, I feel my body. Feel him still inside me, hard and softly pulsing. Feel a tightness in my chest as I inhale a deep breath, perhaps the first since he started. Feel my pussy—that's what he calls it—sore, swollen around him. Feel my thighs ache.

"Aster?"

"I'm okay, my king," I say, my words a butterfly on the breeze, fragile but determined.

Lifting my trembling arms, I cup the back of his thick neck. Stroke him. Subtle. And immediately, his tension lessens, his inner beast shuddering.

A rough sigh cascades across me. "Is this what you wanted, little creature? Are you happy?"

Blinking, my lashes tickling the silk, I smile despite my lethargy. It strikes me—this is why we spent hours in ballet. To keep us nimble, loose and flexible, and to train the body to recover after intensity. It was always sold as a means for grace and posture, but as a familiar muscle fatigue squeezes me, I realise this is the main reason. "To be your Silk Girl, my king. Yes. I've been training to be one, and to be yours, to carry a lord. What more could a girl want?"

"More," he utters, but it's hardly audible.

He moves down to my lips, his length drags from inside me, and I gasp at being emptied, but he swallows my sounds, kissing me hard and confusing my senses.

"Don't move," he orders against my soft, nervous lips. As his mouth moves on mine, he slides a pillow under my backside, hoisting my hips.

My spine pangs with shock as he moves me, trails kisses down my naked body and leaves me panting to the dark, air cooling my sweaty flesh.

I can't see, but I can feel his gaze between my legs. Warm fingertips touch my aching core.

"Is there a lot of blood?" I ask.

"Yes," he hisses, a tight jaw dulling the word.

Something warm and wet laps along the outside of my swollen lips, the stimulation so subtle and so profound.

I blush. "What are you doing?"

"I want to taste your virgin blood."

"Master Cairo will be glad," I offer in response to having a heavy bleed. My seal was strong; it's a sign of purity.

Blood is good.

And I'm fine.

Still unsure how I feel, I try to focus on one emotion, but I feel so many. I almost want to cry, overwhelmed. And I wonder whether Iris felt anything or whether she was a perfect vessel without useless emotions, only focused on her Purpose.

I hear his growl against my pussy. "Don't say his name while we are together, especially while I am licking your blood from your swollen pussy lips. This is what he made me do to you. Break you. Hurt you."

His words tear into me.

It's what *I* wanted.

I'm so confused.

Didn't I do this right?

My vows: I'll thrill and quiver in being the vessel that brings him peace. I'll massage him inside my heat, clearing his mind and mine to all but Meaningful Purpose.

He is meant to be peaceful. I'm meant to have taken his darkness and frustrations. I failed—my throat tightens with tears. "You don't want an heir, my king?"

"It's not that simple."

Yes, it is.

Still blind, I squint as the dark shadows dance around the room. "It is. Didn't I bring you peace? Was I not good?"

"Your life may be simple and peaceful," he states, his voice growing rougher, bearing a dark hatred. "Bat your eyelashes, spread your pretty thighs, and let a lord fuck you bloody, but I'm not so easily conditioned to my so-called-Purpose."

He makes it sound awful.

His cruel utterance delivers a crushing hit, bursting the cracked dam of my resolve. Overcome, overstimulated, I give in—tears spring from my eyes, a sob wrenches from me.

He curses, prowls up the bed, and pulls the veil from my face, demanding I look at him.

"No!" I try to keep it on, to hide from him.

He doesn't let me, his fist holding the silk in the curve of my neck. "I'm sorry." He kisses my eyes as they weep. "Aster. I'm sorry."

"Why are you ruining this for us?" I sob.

"I'm not a kind man! I warned you."

"Yes, you warned me. You warned me well." Glaring up at him through the dim, I see his perfectly virile features through a sheet of tears. "You're not a kind man! You're not a man, not human at all!"

I want to hurt him. Like he just hurt me. Though I doubt he cares. He's probably pleased to be without humanity, without Common romanticisms. Just like Iris is, all my emotions are disorders to their kind.

"Aster." He kisses me once. "Only for you."

"Only for me what?"

He drops his forehead to mine, exhaling hard. "Humanity only clings to me for you, little creature. Don't cry."

"I was meant to bring you peace," I admit.

"Peace." He lifts his head, his dark gaze softening on my face, following the roll of my tears. "Is that what this feeling is?"

I sniffle. "You feel peaceful?"

A small smile wars with his lips. "I feel something… I want to stare at you and your pretty human tears, don't want to move from this moment, and will kill the man who interrupts this— This still. This… *contentment.* Is that peace, little creature?"

"Almost," I answer. "I think you're fighting it."

"I was built to fight."

My chest squeezes for him. "You can stop when you're with me, my king. You can be gentle because I like it. You can be kind because your words matter to me. They *hurt* me. I won't tell anyone what you look like under the thick skin they made you wear in this life."

"*Fuck.*" Groaning, he drops to my side, keeping his body close and his hands on me.

I don't move, my spine flat to the mattress like it advises in my studies. Backside elevated. Breathing even.

My skin tingles beneath his fingers as they slide up, settling on my lower abdomen. "You make me weak, little creature."

I turn to look at him and shuffle slightly without moving my hips from the pillow. "Do you care for me?"

"Did I not just say that?"

"No." I pause, shaking my head. "You didn't."

"I did." His brows pinch together, shadowing the dark message in his gaze. "You weren't listening very well. I won't often repeat myself, little creature. You are my weakness because I care."

I swallow.

He reaches out and taps my nose, bringing a smile to my lips with how tender and wholesome that is. "Sleep. You have a big day tomorrow. As do I."

"Will you be gone when I wake up?"

"Yes," he states, his eyes are warm, with something hidden. My hopeful soul deems it disappointment, but I don't know what else is buried beneath his stoic blue gaze.

I blink a few times, thinking of what I might say to keep him for longer.

We could discuss The Trade and The Cradle.

I could touch his tattoos, follow the scars and wounds, learn each one's dark history.

We could be friends...

But it's not done.

Not between a king and Silk Girl.

And no one can see him leave, at least not the *wrong* people, like the other Silk Girls or Watchers. People who could whisper in the corners of The Estate and put the heir in danger. So he must go.

He pulls me closer, tucking me into the curve of his long, muscular torso. "You have me, Aster. Inside you. Remember that. You are the most precious possession of The Cradle. I know that was never your motivation in this, but it is true. You will eat, rest, and behave. If you need me, I will come."

I bury my face in the crook of his neck, feeling the powerful thumping of his pulse on my cheek. "You'll come?"

His throat moves as he says, "I will."

CHAPTER FIFTEEN

ROME

I hold the sweet creature against my chest, and when she starts to dream, her eyelids flicker, her lips roll together, and a small sound leaves her mouth.

Then she nuzzles me.

What the hell is that?

Do I look huggable?

Am I soft and welcoming?

She needs to stop that.

I pull her in tighter.

Fuck. For over a decade, I have watched Kong gaze at my sister as though she were the blood in his veins.

It seemed unbearable for someone else to be the reason your heart beats.

But as I brush my calloused, tattooed fingertips from her shoulder to her elbow, lifting tiny hairs to attention along smooth skin, I suddenly feel—it.

And I was right. It is fucking unbearable.

I slide her from my arms.

The fire is orange—first-light—so I leave her room and The Circle.

A Guard is stationed outside the Medi-deck door. I stop and look straight at him, but he stares ahead at the brick wall. I follow the roll of his throat, nervous under my scrutiny.

"Cairo?"

"Just left, Sire." His voice shakes.

Yep, I'm not a huggable man.

I stride away.

Down the long, dim corridor in his chamber, I find The Trade Master at his desk, the large screen open, articles in Latin projected on the brick wall.

"Here." I force my body forward, grit my teeth against my pride, and place Aster's personal sheet on his desk. Her blood darkens a patch of the gold fabric. "This" —I stroke the scarlet stain, her body writhing beneath me is still a strong memory— "changes nothing. If you want my co-operation, then you will stay away from Aster. You will not examine her. I will. No one touches her. She is going to carry The Cradle's heirs."

He doesn't look from his screen.

It is not the first time I have threatened to kill him, nor will it be the last, though, is the closest I have come to following through of my threat. I would have.

And even he believed it.

He revealed his masked fear when he threatened me with the Shadows. Should The Trade fall, the Crown falls. Should Cairo lose his life, my Collective lose theirs—we are linked.

And now that includes Aster.

Cairo ensured our coalition, the binding agents: my sweet sister and my little creature.

Balance, it is written, is steadfast when both forces rest with equal importance and power on either end of the scale. What it really means is we all tumble down together.

I look down at the blood under my fingertips, wanting to snatch the fabric and keep it. "What would you have done if I went to the redhead last night?" Returning my eyes to him, I say, "She obviously had others interested, given all the girls have been claimed now. There would have been a clash of interest."

He continues to read, and the silence plays with the power struggle between us. Then he finally says, "She didn't. One of our lords has not chosen. He is unable."

I frown. "Explain."

Mouthing the last few words on his screen, he slowly slides his eyes to meet mine, his expression indifferent. "He enjoys the company of men. So, *I* gave her Meaningful Purpose after you were absent. I knew you wouldn't visit The Circle last night. And when you did not, I allowed it to play out. But the girl deserves Meaningful Purpose. She followed the rules. The women in her line have never lost a child. She deserves her Meaningful Purpose, even if the babe becomes no more than a Trade citizen."

Is that a genuine consideration?

Or another hidden motivation?

The Trade Master is appointed by the lords of The Cradle— Cairo by Turin and his Collective—and holds the title until death, but he has no legacy, no heirs of his own. His title dies with him. So, he would not consider this child an heir, merely another babe for The Trade. I don't bother asking him why he did it. I don't really care.

"And if I had changed my mind? Today? Tomorrow? What if I wanted the redheaded."

"I was rather certain that you would not." He stands, bows and stares straight at me, levelling me. "I've known you for a very long time, Rome. Your entire life." My name on his lips is a double-edged sword. "I know what you want. I will do my best to give it to you. We have had our differences for many years. One thing that is assured, despite us, is the Crown does not exist without The Trade, and The Trade does not exist without the Crown. We are twin pillars that heal The Cradle. Do you believe this?"

Stiff, I nod. "To some degree."

I know that before The Trade birthed The Cradle and

humbled everyone as equals, Xin De and Common alike, the two divisions of human were at war.

Genocide. Prejudice. Slavery.

Now, citizens live for Purpose. With value. And, yes, it's flawed, like most things, but it stays true to its code and assurances—you will be safe in The Trade system.

Outside it, nothing is certain.

"Well, you're still young for a Xin De, but I see that some space between us will be good." As he continues, he pulls a large hide case from under his single bed and places it on the perfectly crease-free sheet. "You'll be glad that I'm taking my leave to visit the Half-tower. The Shadows have completed their task, and the unrest is imminent. They need me now."

Turning to leave, an odd sense of relief loosens my muscles, but then he says,

"Sire. She asked a lot of questions about the woman who birthed her. She is curious. It's quite dangerous for one so young to be so inquisitive in these matters. I would punish her with a firm hand if she were mine."

"But she is not," I state, curt. "So, the pregnant Silk Girl? She is Darwin's, then? What becomes of her?"

"Lantana. Yes. She will join another Trade after the birth. If she has a girl, they will become an excellent Silk Girl, I am sure," he continues, dutifully laying the procedure out for me. "If she has a boy, we will wait to see what kind of babe he is and what Trade he fits."

I leave. Shutting the door, I stride away. He could be in the Half-tower for months, reappointing lords and settling the unrest.

I grin at that.

After I shower and dress, I head outside with my rifle. First-light mist touches my shoulder from the east; it filters the sun, creating an eery glow.

Fortunately, I know the woods surrounding The Estate. Know the edges that cut along the windmill farm and the greenhouses, know the valley where the Aquilla cats stow away chickens stolen from our hutches.

And I have Odio.

Stalking across the gardens to the tree-line, I hear a branch snap in each ear. I scan the area, finding Bled and Turin Two at my left shoulder and Medan and Kong at my right.

Ready to hunt—we share this message in our stance, our weapons braced in front of us.

Behind them, Trade Hunters.

We hunt for leisure.

They hunt for Purpose.

With a nod, we stalk forward, weaving between the trees, woody limbs and leaves becoming mesh walls that filter the sand-burdened winds. As even the foliage in The Cradle has adapted to the gale.

The forest is dense.

Fielding off from me, my Collective disappear from view. The forest reaches all the way to the ocean, the bottom of the world.

We hunt in isolation, the only camaraderie shared is silent approval as short rounds echo, sending birds to the skies, wrenching howls and hisses from the surrounding cats.

Over the following hours, Odio guides me, hovering over warrens, and the forest reverberates with tormented squeals and cries.

The island's native cat was once fucking extinct and now a damn pest.

It is crown-light, the brightest time of day, when I stroll into the forest clearing with three dead beasts hung around my neck, legs dangling down my chest.

Ahead, Turin Two, Medan, Kong, and The Trade Hunters are already regrouping, one by one, with their kill.

"How many did you see?" I ask Turin Two.

He is on his haunches on the grass, stabbing his knife into the thick coat of the cat, carving a seam down the stomach, and opening it up. He is wrist-deep in the guts while he says, "I saw at least a dozen make a break for it before I got this one and the other two in the sack. I shot down another two, but they dropped off the cliff into the ocean."

"Kong?" I ask, looking over at him as he wraps a bite wound on his forearm with a piece of cloth.

"Ten, maybe fourteen," he replies. "They breed as fast as the fucking chickens in summer."

"Good." Bled approaches from the east, dead cats stacked on his shoulders like logs. "I like the taste of cat. Better than chicken, and you know I'm not partial to ocean game."

"Shark is beautiful," Medan says.

Bled lays his beasts on the pile with the others. "Beg to differ. It's the texture for me."

Sitting on a hacked tree trunk, I lean forward, my elbows meeting my knees. I look between them. "Speaking of sharks, we may have a low supply for The Cradle until the Half-tower is settled. Cairo left this first-light. I'm certain, he will have it suitably organised within a few months. Man has a way with fucking words."

"I leave tomorrow as well," Medan states.

"And I," Bled adds. "Back to my Hall."

Turin Two laughs. "Orgies. We know."

"As much as I enjoy dipping my fingers into a bit of vanilla cake," Bled says, "it's the tart that really does it for me."

"The Common House Girl." Turin laughs.

"If I remember correctly." Bled raises a brow. "You quite enjoyed my group activities the last time you visited the Lower-tower."

"I enjoy a great many things," Turin Two muses, emptying the cat's innards onto the grass. His arms are painted with guts as he rubs the bloody organs with poison, kneading the scentless flakes into the meat. He will leave the corpse in the clearing and kill a few more that turn cannibalistic.

Bled looks past me across the open grass. "They like it when you join them. It motivates them."

I gaze over my shoulder to see The Trade Hunters, fifty feet away or so, in a circle, comparing their kills—they'll hit the markets in first-light, fresh steaks for The Estate's residents.

I nod at one; he bows.

Turning back, I stand, adjust the cats on my shoulders, fleshy stomachs warming my neck, and walk away, calling out, "If I don't see you in the first-light, I will welcome you back next month. Congratulations on securing your legacy, my lords."

Medan says, "And you, Sire."

CHAPTER SIXTEEN

Aster

I rub my upper arm; my vitamin shot this first-light seems to ache while between my legs, my pussy throbs. I am swollen there, but it is proof of everything we shared last night.

The pain is sweet.

Smiling, I regard the perfect temperature in the courtyard as a gift while my black hair tickles my neck and sways around my back.

With a book each to enjoy, we sit on the lush grass. Tiny white flowers wiggle up between the blades. Our circle has a bite in the loop where Ana would have been sitting if she were well today. She is nauseated; we are told that resting in bed is best for the pregnancy.

I'm sure that is true.

She is not actually mourning.

This isn't about Lord Darwin.

My heart hurts for her.

"The shot changes. The dose, the ingredients, it can sometimes ache," Daisy offers, her eyes following my hand as I massage my shoulder.

I look to the right, seeing she has put her book down on her lap. "Not just vitamins?" I ask.

"Anything that will support our Meaningful Purpose," Iris states, eyes glaring at me over the butterflied novel covering her face, measuring me up and down as though she can sense the discomfort between my thighs.

I stare back, deadpan. My eyes scream the fiery words: 'I will be birthing an heir. Your worst nightmare has come to fruition— a Fur-born girl with no Xin Den genes is the king's chosen Silk Girl.'

I smile, sigh the words from my mind, and decide to ignore her scrutiny.

So, for the hundredth time today, my gaze veers across the grassed yard to the marble stone building where Paisley converses with the other Watchers. She has not offered me so much as a greeting since I woke.

Blossom leans close to me. "She is afraid of Sire."

"He wouldn't hurt her," I say, still looking across the lush courtyard to where she stands.

"My Watcher told me that he reprimanded her this past day," she explains. "And now your Watcher believes she will end up like your Wardeness did. Hung."

I snap my eyes to Blossom, feeling them wide and giving my shock away. "Pardon? How do you—"

"She was executed," she whispers again. "For being careless with you and Iris."

My heart plunges to my stomach.

At the sound of her name, Iris's ears pluck up, her body inching into the circle to better hear us. "What did you say?"

"It is the law." Daisy sits taller, always ready to remind us of our vows. Her gaze dances between us as we mutter quietly; secrecy never looks polite. "We know nothing of the guidelines of a Wardeness. I'm sure what had to be done was done for the necessary reasons."

"She was not a bad woman," I mutter, swallowing down a lump that forms over more words.

"Good alone is not virtuous. Purposeful is," Daisy offers, a half-smile set on her lips. She bends across and taps my thighs. "Smile. We will all have round bellies soon, just like Ana."

Blossom giggles. "And huge appetites."

"And everyone will adore us," Iris adds, then clears her throat, the five words overly revealing.

"And we will visit the spa every day. Have mineral baths together. The Trade believes in water therapy." Blossom retires her book, closing it completely and setting it down on the lawn. "You will join us this time? Won't you? We go after the Watchers have finished their meeting." She looks at me, eyes smiling. "You have a small bruise on your collarbone."

I place my hand over the delicate area.

"I have a few, too," she adds.

My fingers pan out to hold the marks he left on my skin, and I stare across the distance, losing focus to the memory of his warmth and words. So many hot words, I cannot pick a favourite.

I feel a smile, sense the other girls' eyes on me, and then the misguided word 'love' tickles my brain. Ana—Ana is in love. I look at her empty spot of the grass, the broken loop in our seated Silk Girl circle.

Concern nests in my chest.

With a sigh, I push to stand and walk toward Paisley and the other girls born for parchment. I don't need to hear the gasps behind me to know Daisy and Blossom are holding their breath as I stop in front of the five Watchers.

"May I speak with you?" I ask Ana's Watcher, and Paisley stares at me wide-eyed, a flicker of annoyance revealing itself.

"That is not the way," Paisley states through grit teeth.

"It's fine," Ana's Watcher offers, touching Paisley's arm. "You can ask in front of all of us. We have no secrets, Aster."

"Can I see Ana?" Clutching my hips, I attempt to look older

and more serious than my height and stature could ever really pull off. "She might need a friend. I could read to her."

"She has requested no visitors."

"Well"—I shuffle— "will you please tell her that I would like to. That I'll just sit with her."

The sound of metal groaning draws my eyes to the far side of the courtyard, to a great gate as it opens. My heart leaps into my head and bounces from left to right when he appears. A monster of a man, seven feet at least, carrying a stack of dead animals over his shoulders like a collar.

He stares at me.

The courtyard shrinks.

For a moment, it is only us.

I consider this to be a stolen moment, over too soon, but then he walks toward me, huge, powerful legs taking him faster than I can match my shallow breaths to his predatory stride. His every footfall is a statement, his intent warning the grass beneath his boots.

Breathing nervously, I back up until I hit the courtyard wall. He crowds me against it, uninterested in the others.

The girls are watching.

"My king," I curtsy, unsure what to do, and the corner of his lip twitches with a smile.

"Did you just curtsy? It is a bit late for formalities."

Suddenly, Odio's hovering black shadow captures my attention. As he lands with a thud on the grass behind the king, the weight of nervous gasps rustle even the flowers.

I search behind him, checking the girls, but they are cowering together. The Watchers have the Silk Girls tucked behind them, like I did with Ana the day of the carnival. They would give up their lives for us…

"This isn't the way it's done. They will know," I say, returning my gaze to the king.

"Do you trust your Collective?"

Iris's face crashes into my mind, then a hallucination of the Silk Wardeness hanging by a broken neck.

No. The word halts on my tongue because Iris can be almost bearable to be around at times and she's my oldest companion. I don't want to condemn her this way.

I peer up at him, but our height difference and his close proximity to me make it a hard angle for my neck. My gaze locks on the frozen jowls of a dead beast leaking blood that slides down Rome's leather armours.

My eyes widen, and I mutter, "Yes. I trust them."

"Let them suspect, then." His deep voice draws my gaze up to his heated blue eyes. "I have been thinking about you, little creature."

Odio begins to pull at his feathers, making a spectacle that blocks the king and me from the girls in the courtyard. I wonder if the beautiful, winged god is trained in securing private moments for the king or if he simply caught a whiff of the gamey, dead animals.

Either way, I decide to revel in the stolen time we have in the lighter hours of the day. "You have?"

"Your moans echo in my mind."

The heat from his words fire beneath my cheeks, illuminating them with the glow of arousal.

He runs his knuckles down my blushing cheek. "Is that pretty colour for me?"

"Yes."

Suddenly, he slumps the beasts from his shoulders, dropping them to the floor, and I cannot help but notice the contrast between the lush greenery, white flowers, and the bloodied mass.

Behind Rome, Odio halts his pruning at the soft thudding sound. His keen gaze snaps to the gory heap.

Rome clicks his fingers to the side, snatching Odio's attention. "Not for you. Wait your turn."

Odio almost sulks, narrowing his beady eyes at Rome in angry defeat while he sharpens his beak on the thin bones between his black feathers.

Rome watches me.

Free from the dead animals, he leans on the stone above my head and dips, his mouth pressing to my forehead. Lips caress my skin, the words they expel stirring the warm pool inside me. "And how do you feel between your pretty thighs now that I have opened you?"

I press my palms to the stone by my thighs, flattened to the wall, cloaked by him, fingers flexing on the rough surface. The stone's coarse skin reminds me of his rough abdominals pulsing as he thrust. "Swollen, my king.

"I was gentle."

I know he was.

I could tell in the way he vibrated with restraint as he moved, using energy to control himself, and as his hands pawed at my thighs, idling on the right pressure.

My body is suddenly a furnace.

I reach up and touch the divot at his throat, wiping a crimson smear down the thick column with my thumb. "You're covered in blood."

He lets me touch him, but my arm shakes as I hold it above my head to continue touching the sweat on his neck, feel the bob of his throat, so utterly virile, it's dizzying.

"Not mine," he assures. "Don't worry yourself. The only thing you need to be concerned with is growing my heir. You'll look so pretty swollen and flushed. Pregnancy makes a Silk Girl particularly needy. I imagine you'll spend many hours sitting on my face while I tend to you."

"You'll tend to me?"

His smirk rattles my heart. "I'm as shocked as you are by my choice of wording, but yes. I feel tasting you will become an addiction of mine. I'll start tonight while you're too sore to take my cock. How does that sound?"

I lower my hand and smile. "Lovely."

"Show your king where you want his tongue."

What? My cheeks burn from pink to red.

I lean past him again and deduce that, as I cannot see the others, they cannot see me.

"Do as you're told."

With my heart thumping, my fingers trembling, and my core a warm pool of desire, I lift my dress to cup myself over my knickers. "Here, my king."

His eyes lick over me, darkening in an instant. "You know I need my cum inside you," he states, his deep timbre, bottomless and dangerous, rumbling behind a bar of teeth that cage his needy bite.

I press harder between my thighs; the lovely pressure squeezes a whimper from me. "Yes."

His tongue runs along his lower lip, while his eyes scream his intent. "I'll put it there with my fingers tonight, nice and deep between your swollen folds. That is a kindness. But tomorrow, you will take me again."

"I understand."

He leans down and lifts the beasts from the grass as though they weigh no more than the white flowers they have crushed. "Behave."

As Rome strides from the courtyard, Odio takes to the air, leaving me alone, pressed to the wall while the others huddle together in shock.

CHAPTER SEVENTEEN

ASTER

There is no denying his effect over me. My body wakes way before my mind, warmth flooding my core, my back arching into a greedy mouth, and I'm dreaming, but then…

I'm not.

Batting my lashes open to the back of the veil, a meshed vision greets me at the same time as my consciousness.

He is here.

Between my legs.

I reach down and grip his dark hair, curling my fingers in as his tongue licks up the side of my thigh.

"What happened here," he asks, a tone as rough as the words spoken. "How, rather, when you're kept so safe."

He means the little scars from the branch.

I don't want to think about Iris.

Not while his breath strokes my skin to prickles of attention, not while his lips approach my core, while the incline of his dangerous kiss arouses me to a wet, wanting mess. I don't want to answer, but I do. "I don't remember."

Condemning my Silk Wardeness further for her carelessness with Iris and me. Had she been a Sired Mother, and Iris and I, babes instead of Silk Girls, and they were injured under her watch, would I feel as angry and vengeful as Rome. I don't know.

His hand traces my leg, from ankle to the back of my knee, a strangely erogenous sensation. This, paired with his tongue as it climbs, causes me to squirm underneath his body. I feel so small whenever he is near, not just physically, but his presence is vast and concrete.

His tongue laps at my folds the way I like, and he hums to show his enjoyment matches my own.

"So swollen," he utters—two words dark with delight.

After a few moments of gentle attention, he crawls over me, his tongue painting a trail up my trembling stomach, between my breasts. He settles his forearms on either side of my face. He slides the veil down, our eyes meeting.

I shrink a little.

He is a predator ready to devour willing prey.

I gaze down the long, hard length of him.

He is naked and stunning. The light from the artificial fire illuminates the bulges and darkens the grooves that define each muscle. His chest tattoos are lightly dusted in hair that arrows down to the long length, hard and pulsing between his hips. It curves upward, like a forearm with a pink fist.

There is so much beast in him. All the parts are there hidden in what as a whole looks human and yet... doesn't.

He is too large. Too scarred. Too muscular. Eyes pretty and blue yet set into stark features that express a need to dominate or destroy.

"Aster." His lips meet mine.

We both hum, tongues tangling gently before greed and lust demand more pressure.

"My king."

"I needed to taste these lips." His tongue, much longer and thicker than mine, licks my mouth on the outside.

"Why?" I pant.

"Because, little creature, I seem to breathe better when I can taste you," he offers, his weight lowering to mine, reminding me that he is capable of ending my life without even trying to.

I cup the back of his thick neck, circling the muscles along his rising shoulders with my fingertips. "Did you know that when I do this... your groan rumbles in your muscles like you're purring."

"Does it?" He sounds amused. "And you think you have tamed me, sweet creature?"

"No." I can hardly breathe now as he applies more pressure, as if his kind words are refuted by his own body. "I don't think that will ever happen."

"Keep your eyes open," he says into my mouth. "Watch. Look what your pretty body can do to your king."

I don't understand until he shifts and wraps his large hand around his... cock. That's what he calls it. I think I like the word now; it's not so crass. One syllable. With a punching sound. Cock. Like thrust, thud, fuck, pound. *Cock.*

Between our bodies, he strokes his fist from the root along the throbbing rod, to the crown, and rolls his palm over the slit a few times before dragging his hand back down.

It's incredibly erotic.

Like in the picture.

"You may help me breathe deep, but I own you." He groans. "All the ways I will take you. All the different positions I will bend your body into, all the ways I'll move you, manhandle you. You will never stand a chance if I want you bent or spread, little creature. You're mine."

He pumps himself, squeezes upward toward the flushing tip, and then starts again. His abdomen contracts to the violent friction. Along his forearms, coils of veins lift his tattoos, pulsing his skin like his heartbeat is everywhere.

"Your womb is sacred," he goes on, voice like gravel. "But your little body is mine to enjoy. And I'll move you around wherever I want you, hold you, force you to take me."

227

I can hear his teeth grit together, his heavy panting pummelling me. His arousal is palpable; I feel the tight agony inside him, twisting us both like rubber bands, like the building of a song or pirouette that gains in speed and intensity.

And then peaks.

On a low growl, he moves up the mattress, aligning his cock between my thighs. And I am pressed to his heaving chest, moaning, as the brunt of his fist beats against my core. He wrings his cum up from the base, shooting warm, white fluid over my pelvis, shuddering and groaning as he works every spurt from inside him.

Grabbing my throat, he drags me up the mattress so he can take my lips in a kiss that matches the intensity of this moment. Of seeing him unravel.

Leaning on one arm, holding his weight, he scoops the warm, wet fluid from the inside of my trembling legs. My knees fall open, shameless, needy. After that and the vitamins this first-light, I am almost feverish.

He pulls from our kiss and gazes at me through hooded eyes like spears that hold an animal in place. "Such a good little Silk Girl. Do you want my cum inside you? Want your stomach swollen, like your pussy?"

I moan, pressing my head back into the pillow when he slides a finger carefully between my puffy pussy lips. "There you go. Hmm. Very tight." He continues, sliding out again to scoop more from my thigh before pushing gently back in.

Out.

In.

Out.

In.

The slow, thorough penetration brings me to the edge of something... something only he draws from me. That feeling—my own release. I didn't know I could have one, until he showed me.

My eyes flutter shut against the intensity of his blue stare.

Pushing his cum into me, he plants it deep. He collects more from my pelvis and repeats the action.

When I can no longer bear the slow thrusting, I clench for him to stay deep. To give me my sweet release.

A husky chuckle leaves him—deep and dangerous—and rumbles around the small space between us. "Okay, little creature." He slides in until his knuckle touches my lips and stirs, spinning my nerves and wrapping them around his finger. Just one finger. One thick, rough, long Xin De finger coiled with the fibres of my pleasure.

My hips circle with his motion. "Yes."

"Yes, what?"

"Yes," I stammer again because I actually don't know what I'm answering—he didn't ask me a question. "Yes, to everything. Everything you do to my body."

"I never gave you a choice, sweet creature." He rotates his finger. "Can you feel my cum inside you? You'll always be filled with me, your pussy, your womb, and your mind. You occupy so much of mine I demand the same from you."

Do all males speak such heated words? How can *words* consume me so entirely? How can mere speech turn me around, flip my stomach, and force my core to pulse? I like it.

Moaning as he strokes inside me, I let the raw words seep in as he brings me over the edge, no, throws me over it. I shake and shudder around his unhurried penetration.

"You ripple so beautifully when you come for me. My cock is viciously jealous of my finger right now."

And as the pleasure blooms, unfurling me, and my insides massage his fingers, wanting them to stay there forever, I realise I might love him. That it's okay to admit it to myself. Nothing lasts forever, but right now, I love him.

Nothing lasts forever.

The lovely feeling mellows.

Rome's finger is still deep inside me as I gasp for air and slump further into the mattress.

"I know what you say—" I pant, licking my dry mouth to get the words out. "All the ways you'll take my body, force me, but I see what you do." I open my eyes to his, stunning blue beacons. "And you could have done that tonight, forced me open, even as I am sore, but you didn't. You don't want to hurt me, my king."

His eyes narrow on me, amusement and menace both dwelling within their azure depths. "True," he purrs. "I do not desire to hurt you, sweet creature. The thought of your pain... angers me. I'm not sure what to make of it."

A small smile hits my lips, and I store that sentence away for when... 'nothing lasts forever.' I ask, "But my body is just yours to use? Is that all it is? I feel so much... more."

His hand moves to the side of my face, and his thumb meets my lower lip. "No," he purrs, eyes roaming my face, surprising me with their softness. "Your body is not just for me to use. Inside you is when I feel most human."

Nothing lasts forever.

I'm okay with that.

I have to be okay with that.

"And I bring you peace." I turn my head into his bicep, nuzzle his warm skin, and inhale his scent to store that along with his words. "You're at odds with peace, but I see it."

"I am not at odds with peace." His gaze rolls over me, soft but pained. "I am suspicious of it. If I let it live inside me, even when with you, my humanity will not survive losing it."

"Nothing lasts forever," I whisper, drifting.

I think I might be in love with you, and that is quite fine. I can love you now and wish you farewell when the time comes.

Senseless for him in this moment, high on him and us and everything we are *right now*, that when he moves away from me, I almost lunge for his arm. But I do not.

He stands, then slides the gold sheet over my body, looking down at me, defiance moving in his blue eyes.

What did I do?

I sit, the sheet sliding down again, exposing my nipples to the bite of air. "My king...?"

My hope gutters as he stares at me, eyes empty and cold, his looming figure a brawny, detached silhouette.

"Nothing lasts forever?" He chuckles coldly. "Very well. Tomorrow night, little creature. No need for the veil. I want you gazing into my eyes when I fuck you, when it hurts, so you remember me when I send you away."

CHAPTER EIGHTEEN

ROME

The Missing Moon must be at its highest peak in the sky, though I can't see but a muddied glow of its presence.

I avoid sleep, her, and "nothing lasts forever."

How willing she is to accept this. How brutal her words were after I shared my need for her. Dammit—that 'I breathe better with her.' Fuck.

And she will retire to a Sired Mother, leave this dark, murderous chasm I carry around, and take all my air away, leave me suffocating on her memory...

'Nothing lasts forever' imbeds deeper than a bullet.

Well, that is quite fine, little Silk Girl. The perfect product of The Trade. Not an individual.

Not mine... But theirs.

I snarl. I told her I would kill the man who interrupted us, in turn, it was me. Always me. Self-hate found a home within me the day Tuscany was mutilated, and it's been breeding ever since. I no longer recognise it as hatred, but as a part of me.

She must already see it.

Must already want to be rid of it.

Soft, rhythmic music sails through the piazza, coiling around my entertainers, moving them to its seductive rhythm. They share intimate encounters. Dancers, House Girls, clad in barely-there slips of fabric, touch each other and moan.

I lean forward on the throne, rubbing my jawline, watching them, finding them boring, unattractive, even. Pointless. This entire hedonistic last-moment gathering was my attempt to sabotage whatever feelings I have before it is too late and I am unwilling to let her go.

A memory slams into my mind, further foregrounding everything I expect from her once she sees me for who I am, once she sees the bleak, black chasm of my heart.

My bloodied hands shake with rage and my teeth bare on a growl as I enter Tuscany's quarters with the dripping head of our father.

I scan the room, and, as always, the bed is made and empty. The kitten she was gifted months ago is now taxidermized on her nightstand.

I stomp into the bathroom.

With her back to me, she lays in the glossy ceramic bathtub, her slender arms draped over the lips; the water is as still as her body.

A hysterical scream bounces around the small, tiled bathroom as a member of The Queen's Army gapes at the severed head of their king in the tight fist of their prince.

But Tuscany doesn't even flinch.

So I storm forward, circling the tub, towering at the foot of it, angry at myself for leaving her that night, furious at The Trade.

As lost as her.

I have our revenge.

You can get up now, Tuscany.

I lick the blood gushing down my jaw from a talon-deep wound that carved my lower lip to my chin. The metallic taste stokes my hatred.

So, I hold the head out for my sweet, broken sister and slowly, she lifts her blank regard to meet the lifeless eyes of her father, of her betrayer.

She blinks once. "Rome."

"Not anymore. Now, they will call me Sire."

"He was your father, Rome." Unmoved, she looks down, her gaze disappearing into the bath, swimming in her watery grave.

She gives me nothing for my offering, not standing and shaking off the sorrow, not throwing her arms around me and thanking me for her revenge, not healing, not—

I drop the head into the bathtub.

A long hiss of anger presses through my teeth, hatred becoming a solid form in my very cells. "I did it for you!"

She stares blankly at the bobbing head as the dangling veins move like tentacles in the water between her knees, marbling the clear fluid with their blood-red ink.

Then she peers up at me.

The disappointment in her broken eyes shoves me backward a step. After what I've just done. This is for her. This is her revenge. To lift her up, to bring her back.

To bring her back to me.

Shocked, I empty my humanity.

My soul blackens against her gaze.

"Very well." I lift the head from the bath. "I'll give it to Cairo," I snarl. "He can put it in a glass case, store it next to the vase that holds your womb."

"Sire?"

Slowly, I lean back into my throne and ram the memory down. With a long, rough breath, I turn my chin to acknowledged Aster's Watcher.

"Speak up," I say to her.

She leans into my ear so I can hear her over the hypnotic music that matches the writhing bodies in front of me. "You asked for an update on Aster. Her basal body temperature dropped since yesterday, Sire. It's unlikely she'll be in prime condition to breed tomorrow night. I will repeat the routine again in three weeks after her body runs a natural cycle."

Relief and anger both war to respond to her soft, nervous whispers. "Very well," I state.

"Do you—" She hesitates and then swallows. "Do you wish to know about the other Silk Girls?"

A girl in front of me paws at another young thing's breasts, and I feel nothing. "You know that I do not," I answer, never removing my eyes from the spectacle, challenging the erotic scene to get me hard... like she can. "You don't need to pretend. You know who she is. So shut the gossip down. And if anyone speaks her name in hushed tones, in corners, you come to me."

Her exhale is heavy. "Not Master Cairo?"

"He will not be back for a few months."

"I understand, Sire."

"Good. You can leave."

And so can I. If she is no longer ovulating, I can accompany the CR Guard to the Black Matter Mines, show them my support for their Meaningful Purpose, and gift them some House Girls. I glare at the sleazy creatures ahead of me. Obviously, they are no use to me anymore.

"*Paisley*," Kong calls from his station behind me. "You look exhausted."

"I haven't slept well," she says from a small distance away, and I turn my head to stare at her for the first time this night. Dark bitten-moons cup her hollow eyes.

"Perhaps she should take a break now, Sire," Kong offers. "She's not needed around at all hours to monitor the Silk Girl. Now is the right time."

I shut it down. "She *is* needed at all hours."

With a polite bow, she walks away, and I prepare myself for Kong's imminent insight.

"Everyone needs sleep."

And there it is.

"She can sleep when she is dead."

He sighs roughly, and I feel it's significance even as he stands behind my throne. "You care for that girl. I never thought I'd see the day."

Deliberately obtuse, I ask, "The Watcher?"

He chuckles. "Aster."

"It's unbearable," I grit out, still willing the House Girls, dancing and playful before me, to wake up my cock. They don't. "And I want her, all the time, right now. I want to be around her. She keeps fucking curling into me, and I want to throw her from the bed, but I pull her closer instead. I want to freeze time and hold her. It's like a fucking curse. She is just a Silk Girl, and I am a fucking fool."

"She curls into you? Seeks safety in you. What I would give for..." He clears his throat, and I save him from my warnings about dreaming of my fragile sister. She is no man's. That is her vow. And he knows better.

I consider the moment I fought my father, the night I killed him, when I tore his head from his shoulders.

Did he let me?

It was that or kill me.

I will never know.

He was huge, far bigger than me at the time, but I did it fuelled with rage. Perhaps that was my strength. The emotion he lacked powered me. "Did my father ever have this kind of affection for anyone, for a girl?"

"No. No, he didn't."

"Of course he didn't." He was no one's fool, not soft, nor kind, nor gentle. "He was a king."

"It's not that he couldn't or even wouldn't. Simply, the right someone never crossed his path, boy. Pity, really. Everyone should feel it once."

"She's going to have our heirs. That is all," I confirm, forcing apathy along the length of that statement. That is all. That is all she desires, all she is. To adore, pleasure, provide, fuck right off.

Fine.

"In the dark. In secret," he baits me, trying to decipher how far I am willing to go for her.

To the end...

But she doesn't want that.

He wants to know how many rules I will break. *All of them...* He wants me to. And yet, like him, the woman of my affections belongs to The Trade.

"Will you let her go?" he asks.

"When the time comes," I grit my teeth together, "I will watch her leave."

The energy thickens as he states, "You might *want* to figure out how to freeze time then, boy, and not waste it here with me and these House Girls."

I laugh without mirth. "She softens me," I admit with a growl, both hating it and... No. Just hating it. "I forget what *I* want and do what's best for her. It needs to stop. This is exactly why the old-world concept of marriage failed society. It was self-serving. Pathetic." I am king. She is silly Common Silk Girl. "What I do, what she does, should be for the good of The Cradle and that is all."

"You hate The Trade," Kong reminds me.

"I do not hate *The Cradle*." My words are hollow as I state, "I am its king. A piece. Remember? You taught me that."

"I taught you to watch the player," he corrects. "Not to give in to him. Understand him, that is all. But... when someone comes into your life." His tone, though the deep timbre of a Xin De male, takes on a thoughtful, meaningful edge. "And you start to feel like an individual, like your motivations are not a collective thought but for your very soul, it's as though you just woke up. You might not have known this person for long, but you'd be a fool to go back to sleep. You know that. All of sudden, you take a backseat in your own life. Out of fucking nowhere, they become the main character in your story."

I recite my vows, angry. Cold. Wanting the nothingness and

boredom I have lived with to return, replace her. "To be a king is to suffer alone under the burden of decisions and the weight of necessary evils and truths."

"This is love, Rome."

"Love is for the Common."

"Love is human!" he spits out. "Do you have any humanity left to see this?"

I will not love her only to have her leave!

With that unwelcome admission, I stand, finished. Need perspective away from her torturous sweetness. "We leave when I wake. We take the CR Guard to the Black Matter Tower in the first-light."

"It's a five-day journey."

"I am aware."

Kong stares at me. "You have never been to the Black Matter Tower. Why now? The mines are not safe for you, Sire. The water... it's toxic."

I stride away, calling over my shoulder, "Good thing I have very little *human* left then, isn't it?" I sneer. "I will survive." I halt and turn to face him. "And bring the House Girls for them to fuck. They all work hard on their Purpose mining and recycling matter for our batteries, Kong. I want to show them my gratitude. Nothing expresses thanks like warm, wet pussy."

CHAPTER NINETEEN

ASTER

"Hello, Aster. You slept in."

The night was warm, but something inside me felt cold and empty after he left. He seemed to enter my room as a storm, only to exit as a phantom, and leave me wondering which parts of our shadowed intimacy were real.

Paisley brightens the ornamental fire, bathing the room in orange light. "All the lords have left The Estate except for Lord and Warden Turin Two, but he won't be available." As she busies herself in my room, collecting the old flowers and ensuring my bathroom is stocked, she says, "He'll be rather occupied. Trade Master Cairo and Sire are both on campaigns, so we have this wing to ourselves. It's always nice, I mean, I like it when we can relax, and each day we will have a different activity for you. Puzzles. Reading. Dancing. *But* today is a special day! You have been invited to the aviary."

Still half-asleep, I sit up in bed and rub my dry eyes. "There's an aviary here?"

"Yes, in the queen's wing." Her tone is happier than I have heard in days. I smile at that. "You can visit one at a time. Blossom is there now. We have hatchlings, and the mammas can get protective, so it is best to have a very small audience."

"Wait." My mind levels. "Did you say the king is away? I mean, Sire. I saw him las— day. I mean, I saw him last—yesterday." I fumble on my lie. "In the courtyard."

She stops at the foot of my bed, holding a bundle of used towels and a throw. "Yes, Aster. He has The Cradle to manage, after all. He is not often here. Only for your rite, when the Silk Girls ovulate, which has finished for the month, so you may not see him for a few weeks."

Her matter-of-fact answer chips at my heart. "Oh." I draw my knees up and hold them to my chest in case the tiny fragment falls through my flesh.

Tuscany's words float back to me, along with a sadness I now share. 'He is always going away. He leaves me here, and I miss him so.'

Nothing lasts forever.

She eyes me, uncaring or clueless, though I prefer the latter. "Are you ready to get up?"

"Is Ana awake?" I ask, accepting she might be the only person to understand my misguided and naïve emotions.

As I suspect, she says, "No. She's still unwell." The lie barely makes it to my ears. I don't believe it. "You like birds." Paisley wiggles her brows. "I know you do."

Sighing hard, I concede, "Very much. They are the closest thing to a dinosaur."

"Dinosaur?"

"Yes." I slide from the bed and drop to the floor. "Great animals. Some like giants. Some like crocodiles."

Paisley watches me amble across the room toward my closet, her gaze assessing my naked skin; I know she sees evidence of him painted over my thighs.

"But they were real?" she asks, genuine interest pitching her voice.

"Once." I pull my robe on. "Or so the book said."

"Which book?"

"One I wasn't supposed to read." I walk to the bathroom and pause at the door. Sensing the shower will be my salvation to sit in my sorrow, I anticipate bursting into tears between the cool, tiled walls. A small cry in privacy is not so shameful. "I'll be ready shortly."

I move inside, close the door, and as I wash, cleaning his cum from my thighs and stomach, I let myself *feel.*

Feel anger toward my childish heart, regret for my naïve tongue and wishful utterances under the veil of night when we are alone... And disappointment... Unjustified, unwelcome, disappointment.

Crown-light is nearly over when it is my turn.

Between the queen's wing and the forest edge, there is a large silvery cage housing hundreds of birds. Birds with bright wings and insects on leaves, flowers in mid-bloom and hidden stony pathways, red-brick bird houses, flapping wings, the sound of freedom and excitement, these things make it difficult not to smile.

Tuscany and I walk a few paces ahead of a member of The Queen's Army. A brawny, tall woman capable of lifting both of us and rushing us through fire... probably.

The contentment and ease I feel with the queen is immediate, like our brief interaction on the grass.

"I want to apologise," she offers, "for the other day."

I shake my head. "Please, my queen, there is no need."

"Rome..." She sighs. "Never mind."

I blink a few times, thinking. "I wonder why birds survived

when so many other animals became extinct." I change the subject. "It's the Redwind that makes The Cradle so uninhabitable." I look at her profile, her expression soft and quietly filled with contemplations. "I hear the Horizon is thousands of miles of nothing but Redwind and desert ground."

Gazing ahead, she says, "I have never seen it."

"No one has seen the Horizon."

"The Redwind," she corrects.

"What?" I stop in my tracks, inadvertently touching her shoulder, though one should never touch the queen. I retract my hand instantly. "Sorry. What do you mean?"

The Redwind is everywhere, outside The Estate, outside the towers, the aviaries, it is the atmosphere that cloaks every inch of The Cradle.

She peers over her shoulder, eyes meeting the woman behind us as she says, "You can wait by the entrance. I am in no danger with Aster."

"But my queen—"

"Leave," she orders.

I press my lips together under her tone, a strong, curt cadence that somehow has just as much enchanting melody as her softer-spoken words.

She waits for our privacy.

When she continues to stroll onward, I follow by her side. "I have never left The Estate, Aster."

"Never?"

"Never."

How is that possible?

I frown, gazing at a large brick archway ahead, veined with the lost green fingers of nearby trees. Just like in the Silk Aviary, they appear to be reaching for something, seeking. True beams from the sun, I always presumed.

"What about when you were a babe?"

The curated breeze gently moves her honey-swirled brown hair around her dainty features, carrying her unique scent of sweet oranges. "There is a hidden nursery in The Estate. It is where Rome and I were both raised. All the babes born for his Collective will be raised there."

Under The Estate—the thought comes unbidden. Like in the tunnel with the flickering overhead lights, the one I was never meant to see.

"You are the queen," I say. "You're everyone's mother. You visit the Common—"

"Rome will not allow it." His name and her declaration threaten to awaken the torment I left as salty tears over the shower tiles this first-light.

I swallow. "Do you want to visit them?"

The aviary goes still as she slows her step, the question almost paralysing her and the birds.

"In theory." Her voice is detached for a blink. "He may be right after all." She returns to her steady, graceful pace, and I mirror her. "I may not cope. I may break into tiny pieces and lose my mind... all over again."

I knew she had experienced something awful; I could feel her suffering low inside my stomach. Maybe she will tell me one day, or maybe not, but her sorrow doesn't seem the kind you ask questions about. It is the kind you merely cradle so it is not so lonely.

"Or maybe you heal." I shouldn't have said that. "Through your Purpose," I add quickly.

"Purpose." She breathes.

"I'm a naïve Silk Girl," I dismiss. "I couldn't possibly understand your great Purpose, but... imagine the smiles on everyone's faces when they see you."

"It has been too long," she whispers, stopping to pluck a small flower worming up between two silvery stones. "What if they do not like me?"

Turning to face me, eyes only inches away from mine, she tucks the little, yellow floret behind my ear.

I smile. "What if they do?"

A small pause circles us, and then something pulls her attention over my shoulder. "Look."

Spinning around, I follow her gaze to the split between two branches that cup a wooden platform bedded with tangled leaves and twigs.

"There is a nest with three baby birds inside," she says.

They are all chirping to the sky. They are big... eagles, I think. Where is their mother? Close, I imagine.

Three babes...

Maybe two boys and a girl. It doesn't matter to their mother. They are all beautiful and... hers.

I find myself standing in The Circle, outside of Ana's door, willing myself not to knock. Not to disturb her while she grieves. It's such a strange feeling—loss. I knew what Rome was, what we were and what we would never be, and I fell in love with him anyway. If I feel this sick, yearning for him, then Ana's suffering must be unbearable.

"Ana?" I call softly through the door, rapping my knuckles gently along the wooden grain. With a sigh, I press my forehead to it. I know you're not sick... Let me comfort you. "I have a puzzle," I say it as the idea strikes me. Lifting my head, I decide to put my entire heart into this.

I leave The Circle, go to the activity room, retrieve a two thousand piece floral puzzle, and return in haste.

Knocking again, I say, "I have a small puzzle, and I think we should do it together." I test the knob; it turns with ease.

It's open. Shit.

Of course it is.

Our doors don't lock.

Don't do go in, Aster.

It's none of your business.

She needs her rest.

Holding my breath, I gently push the door open and peer inside, seeing an identical room to the one I sleep in and an unmoving human-shaped lump beneath a gold sheet on the bed.

My throat tightens. "Ana?"

The ornamental fire on the wall emits a glow of deep yellow and warm, cosy waves.

I step inside and close the door, the puzzle clutched in my hand. "Ana?"

"Go away."

I exhale audibly hard. "Oh, my. I was so worried, Ana."

I walk over to her bedside and peer down at her. The golden sheet is pulled up to her chin, her fingers curled over the top, holding it there. There is a little tendril of her dark hair laying over her face, and I want to sweep it aside for her.

"Are you sedated with Opi?" I ask.

She blinks and shakes her head—no.

A long unbearable silence circles the room.

As she stares at the fake yellow flames, I slide down to the floor and press my back to the mattress.

I empty the puzzle on the carpet and begin organising the pieces by colour. "I know we are meant to make the border first," I say quietly. "But I like to make smaller pictures first, and then fit them all together at the end to make a larger image. The Silk Wardeness used to say this was because I wanted immediate satisfaction and was impatient. But that's not true. It is because when I make the border first and simply fill it in, I don't get to appreciate the smaller details as much."

I sigh. The small details of Rome and I and our intimacy don't create a greater picture. *Accept it, Aster.*

Tears sting the back of my eyes as I work on the puzzle in silence on the floor beside her bed until the fire turns a deep red and I know I have to leave her room.

∾

Despite trying to be quiet, the next first-light Ana wakes to the sound of me clearing my throat. Or maybe it's the steaming scent of honey that lifts her lids.

"Your Watcher allowed me to bring you oatmeal in bed," I say, looking at the bowl on her nightstand. "They are worried, too, and I don't think they know what to do."

Thumbing a puzzle piece into place, I slide the second completed flower aside and get to work on the third. Jumbling and sorting the puzzle shapes together.

She groans. "You're not going away."

"You were nice to me," I mumble. That is not something I will forget. *I know you feel awful, Ana.*

"I will never be a Sired Mother."

She means, 'I will never see him again.' Her softly spoken words are choked with sorrow, but I cannot help but feel relief in hearing her voice. I don't know how to respond, to not scare her voice away with the wrong thought. Blossom would give her hope. Daisy would state the facts.

We can work on this together, just like the puzzle. I'm sure she is worried she will never have two boys and a girl. No other lord will take a Silk Girl who has been opened by another man. It just isn't done.

I start to talk with a lie on my tongue, about how she may still be given a chance, but instead stop. "You have Meaningful Purpose, Ana," I offer. *And I will, too.* "You have to appreciate the smaller pieces, like with this puzzle." *And maybe I can, too.* "You have a bowl of oatmeal and honey, a swollen belly, this puzzle, and me. The whole picture comes later."

"That one goes there," she says by my ear, so I peer over my shoulder to see her eyes open and scanning the puzzle. I smile. Her gaze is present, not miles away like it was yesterday.

"This one?" I point.

She nods once. I pick it up and fit it into place with a smile. Then I continue sorting.

Over the next two days, between meals, mineral baths, and

Silk Girl checkups, Ana helps me connect many pieces, and eventually, she joins me on the floor by her bed.

By the first-light on day three, we have connected over one thousand five hundred pieces, Ana has eaten a few small meals, and a spark has returned to her eyes.

Chapter Twenty

ROME

Standing in the depths of a lithium mine, the air dense with an acrid odour, I scan the cavernous abyss.

I know now why I wanted to visit. The five-day journey with my thoughts, distance from all that threatens to tame me, and an emotional void to disappear into.

It is here, that I belong. Not in her arms, not smelling her hair, or deep inside her. In this suffocating blackness, the oppressive silence broken only by the clanks of hammers from men working into the last-light, I am reminded of what my soul must look like.

I continue into the mine. Each descending step is like a demand to fill me with more darkness and press her from my mind. Nothing soft and gentle down here; the walls are jagged, sharp, and lance inward as if on the attack.

I can relate.

"Sire," a man says, his voice muffed behind a mask, his body in a black shroud, entirely covered as he hammers through the rock. "Do you require my mask?"

"I do not," I state, and he continues his Purpose.

All the way through last-light, I spend the time walking the labyrinth until I am alone with only the crunch of rock under my feet that echoes into the void.

I breach the top, greeted by the black sky, harsh winds, and the absence of the Missing Moon. However, I have heard that on rare occasions, a star has been spotted above these mines that skirt the beginning of the Horizon. I have never seen a star, but if I ever did, I'd want to show it to her...

Fuck. She is pretty.

On a rough sigh, I stride through the gale toward the large brick fort, which was once a penitentiary, now transformed into the Black Matter Tower.

Inside, the residence houses thousands of men and women. It is simplistic but safe and clean as is assured by The Trade; all seeking Meaningful Purpose are provided for.

I am strolling down the corridor toward my temporary chamber when the soft whimpering from behind a door piques my interest. The gentle cadence reminds me of... her.

Pushing open the door, I find the Black Matter Lord and a Trade doctor conversing while a young girl lies on a small bed, her complexion that of awaiting death. A yellowing to her clammy face. Breath short and rapid.

"What is happening here?"

"Sire," Lord Coober of the Black Matter Tower bows for me, his short and lean physique perfectly bred for the Mine Trade. "Her mask has been leaking."

"She's poisoned, Sire," the doctor confirms. "Her liver is shutting down; we are in the final days of her life. We are discussing ending her suffering now with the La Mu Root."

"This is the third Silk Girl to come to poisoning here," Coober states, as I measure the girl up: pretty and strong. Far stronger in appearance than my little creature. "Only one managed to birth a son for my legacy but was so frail from toxicity that it broke her apart during delivery. They do not survive here. I feel I need a Silk Girl with the Xin De genus."

I walk to her, my chest pulling as I notice the small swell at her hips. My little creature has softened me beyond repair, it seems. The others in the room part for me as I stare down at her. See more than a silk girl. See...

Her eyes blink on my form. "Sire?"

"Yes." I clasp my hands in front of me, unsmiling. "Do you wish to die today, Silk Girl?"

A shuddering breath escapes her, sucked back in as quickly as it expels. "I will never have Meaningful Purpose."

"No," I state. "But you will return to The Crust. You will be part of The Cradle eternally."

"That is the best I deserve." She wheezes, slowly batting her long lashes as if the weight of each hair is unbearable.

I feel that fucking pull again—consideration, empathy? What the fuck is this?

I have seen enough.

Felt enough.

I turn to leave when she whispers, "I do not want to die without knowing she has Purpose."

Her strange declaration sets steel into my boots, halting me midstride. "Who?"

"Aster."

That name hits me like a bullet, and I lurch around to lean over the girl, hating the use of my little creature's name through another's lips. "The fuck did you just say?"

She swallows, her moment of hesitation hangs in the thick, electrified air.

"Say that name again," I dare.

"My name is Lavender," she finally manages on a choked exhale. "I know, knew, Aster from the Aquilla Silk Aviary."

My blood simmers with possessiveness. "What of her?"

She tries to smile, but it's a distant expression she barely achieves. "Did she get her Meaningful Purpose?"

"She will," I declare, curt, not trusting this girl, her motivations, her intent until—

"That's good," she mumbles, and the tension in my shoulders loosens enough for me to think straight. "Can you tell her I said so," she continues. "That it's good. Can you tell her that I saw her bird? The mutant one. We all did. It chased Iris. It was funny, but we didn't dare laugh at her. Can you please tell her I'm sorry for what we did?"

"Sire is not your messenger, girl!" Coober growls.

I spin around, take a fist full of his silver hair, and slam his face into the wooden bedframe, hard enough that he goes limp. I release him, and he drops to the ground.

"Do you have anything to say!" I thunder at the doctor, who backs away with his hands held in surrender.

"No, Sire."

"Leave!" I order, and he scurries from the room.

I kneel at her bed. "Sorry for what?" She gasps, staring at the body on the floor. "Look at me," I demand. "Sorry for what?"

Her wide eyes lift. "She will know."

"I must know!"

"I cannot." She shakes her head over and over. "And condemn her again. I will not do it."

Anger's burning presence returns to my veins. "You will tell me, or I will—"

"I'm dying, Sire." Her words are softly spoken but I pause under their weight. "There is nothing you can do to me. Silk girls must be without negative experiences. I do not wish to—"

"There are worse fates than death." I grit my teeth, caging the threats that sit inside. Torture. Flaying. Skinning. A slow, bloody death that leaves screams embedded into the atmosphere. I hold the darkness. "Nothing you say will condemn her," I declare. "You have my word."

"The word of Rome of The Strait." She sighs. "I remember when she spoke with you in the parlour. I was viciously jealous of her that day."

Patience waning, I hiss. "What are you sorry for?"

"I was cruel," she admits, a shiver racketing through her body despite her sweats. "Many times in her life. For no reason. It felt good to be stronger than her because she seemed so mentally impenetrable. It bothered me, and then you touched her, so before I left the aviary, we held her down and tried to ruin her seal. There was blood. I've not stopped thinking about it—"

Barely, I hold my temper. "We?"

"Yes. Iris, Ivy and I." She winces. "Forgive me."

"No."

I reach forward and snap her neck in one swift movement, letting a growl of protective energy rumble from within my soul, giving it significance, berthing it into the old penitentiary walls.

I rise to my feet, my scowl stripping skin from her lifeless face, when her arm flops from the bed. It dangles. Sways. And her Silk Girl tattoo becomes a pendulum for my internal conflict over loving... *Aster.*

The scene from my first campaign as heir gutters into me. The dead woman in the van with the Silk Girl tattoo... Her swinging arm. I always suspected she was the birth mother of one of the babes we took. The realisation burns a river through my chest. Now I know.

That was her mother.

And we had her raped and murdered.

I walk from the room.

CHAPTER TWENTY-ONE

ASTER

The white beam scans my body, from crown to toes, as it does every first-light but unlike every other time, when I try to leave, the door doesn't open.

I stand at the blockade, waiting for it to move or click. I push it and stand back, stare at it. Glare. "Paisley?"

Am I in trouble?

Has Master Cairo returned?

I know a Silk Girl's room is sacred, but Ana's Watcher seemed to approve as I made progress. And Ana eventually left her mattress. It is not like I spent the night with her. She still had her privacy. I only moved from reading and accompanying the other Silk Girls to completing a puzzle with Ana.

Has *he* returned?

The door opens, and I step backward a few paces as Paisley rushes into the space.

"Aster!" She locks my arms by my sides in an awkward hug, I think. I think she is hugging me. I don't mind.

I chuckle. "What is it?"

She pushes me out in front of her, holding my shoulders. "You're pregnant, Aster." She nods, joy bouncing around her expression, and I let the words sink in. "Your ovum has implanted. Oh, my,"—her eyes widen— "I need to get the news to Sire. And Master Cairo and—" Her hands slide down my arms, releasing me. She begins to pace. "You need a Guardian. Yes. You need one because everyone knows, Aster. They know who you are. It isn't safe. And the baby will grow fast. Sire outgrew his—"

"His womb at six months," I say, remembering this from my studies. If the Silk Girl is Common, they remove the babes with a higher Xin De genus surgically before seven months to prevent Xin De Maternal deaths, but Sire, he was so big they incubated him in the sixth month.

All of a sudden, my heartbeat is in my ears, and it's all I can hear and feel. The pulse is in my neck, and I wish *his* hand was wrapped protectively around my throat. So he could feel the flutter. Know my emotions. So he could hold me. I miss him, even though he was never mine.

But I do have Meaningful Purpose.

"I have Meaningful Purpose," I whisper, a string of words I have waited my entire life to say. I hear the phrase filter through the drone between my temples, its certainty and meaning lifting my lips at each corner.

I touch my smile. "Paisley," I say and grab her hand, stopping her from pacing. "Stop. You know. Who else knows? Everyone? What does this mean?"

Frazzled, she stills, gaping at me. "I don't know. As far as I'm aware, this has never happened before. You are not even meant to converse with the lords, Aster." She grips her forehead, distress building in her eyes. "I am at fault. I should have... I don't know. Watched better. Informed you better."

I pull her in for another hug. "No. You are not at fault."

"During this term"—she speaks over my shoulder, truths pouring from her— "a Silk Girl has become pregnant outside of The Circle and before Sire even started, a lord has died, and the heir is no longer a secret. I don't know what this means for us, or where to go from here."

"Please," I say into her hair, "Don't panic. I'm pregnant, Paisley." I let her go and find her worried gaze. "I'm pregnant. This is good news."

"I'm sorry." She shakes herself. "This is my first pregnancy, too. Let's get you fed first, and I will go to the Trade Connect Building and get the message to the Black Matter Tower and the Half-tower where Master Cairo is." She inhales and exhales, letting herself relax. "I only want to keep you and the heir safe. I *am* so happy for you, for us—for The Cradle."

PART FOUR
FOR THE CRADLE

Chapter One

Aster

Though it has been four days since the news of my pregnancy, I've kept it a hard secret.

The reasons are many. I want to wait until Ana's grief releases her enough for her to rejoin our regular routine, and for Paisley to announce the next steps, given the babe in my belly lacks anonymity.

'Do you trust your Collective?'

Rome's questioning rolls in my mind. No. I do not. Not Iris, at least. That truth is profound and undeniable, weighing like a stone inside me, unmoving, steadfast.

I am sitting with the Silk Girls on the lush emerald courtyard lawn when I hear a commotion inside the wing. Blossom, Daisy, and I share questioning glances, but Iris does not even look up from the book open on her lap.

We hold our voices and breath as the sound of heavy footsteps grows. More than one set and they rap with unyielding focus. Tension crackles in the air.

Suddenly, I see them. Through the window, four Guards stride into the Silk Dining Hall.

We jump to our feet with a start.

They breach the courtyard, their faces hardened with Purpose. Behind them... My breath catches as Rome turns the corner, his black cloak a phantom behind him, the hood bunched at his neck, his dark hair dishevelled and wild as if he has been thrusting his fingers through it, clawing at the dark thoughts that make his eyes appear thunderous.

He is back.

My heart starts to spark.

I want to nurture the warmth.

But my arousal from seeing him is quickly extinguished when the Guards halt, and Rome paces through the middle, stopping a mere ten feet away from where we stand shoulder to shoulder, seeking reassurances together.

Something is wrong.

Rome doesn't look at me.

He is glaring at Iris.

"Iris of the Aquilla Silk Aviary," one of The Guard booms at Rome's flank.

I pale.

"You are under arrest by order of The Trade and The Crown for crimes against your Collective and for deceiving Rome of The Strait, The Cradle's Monarch and Protector."

I gasp, my stare panning across, landing on Iris. Her chest rises and falls, erratic and shallow, like there is a little bird inside, desperate to get out. A moment from weeks ago, when she was dragged through the van's glass screen, flashes before me. I see her fear—she's not strong, not a survivor at all.

Two Guards move to her and grip her arms; she doesn't struggle, too paralysed to react. Her mouth opens, but no words come out, merely silent shock.

I would struggle.

I would question, but she is... *weak*. She knows it, too. Jealousy became her, because, despite her Xin De genus, she is terrified of the world. Of her failings. Of everything.

"Aster," Iris mutters to me, not with disdain, anger, or accusation, but with a quiet plea for help.

From me...

But what can I do?

My throat tightens, and I'm desperate to go to her, stand by her side, but something has my feet rooted to the lush grass. I set my hand on my lower belly; it's her or you...

Can you trust your Collective?

Rome finally looks at me—studies me—with a piercing blue gaze, eyes dark and intense, spearing through my thoughts.

Do you trust your Collective?

No.

He knows. I do not know how, but his understanding churns the air, building a tangible storm around us.

As the Guards usher her away, the other Silk Girls watch in horror until screeches echo through the skies above.

Only moments later, Odio's wings umbrella me, painting the grass around my body with a black shadow.

The Silk Girls' frightened gasps resonate as they field out and away from the descending giant eagle.

Odio lands hard. Separates me from everyone else. His black and silver feathers are fanned open and ruffled from the Redwind, mirroring Rome's dishevelled appearance.

They have been travelling.

For how long?

Days? Since Paisley sent the message?

"Guard her, Odio," Rome orders, and then turns to follow his men and Iris back into the Silk Girl Wing, leaving only a stirring silence in their wake.

In like a storm.

Away like a phantom.

Rome of The Strait.

I press my palm to my lower belly again, align myself with my

Meaningful Purpose, and stare through the long window to watch the last whisper of Rome's cloak disappear into the corridor.

Did I do this?

Manifest this?

How did he find out?

What did he find out?

Startled, I look at Odio as if for answers, and he stares straight back at me. Cocking his head, his sharp gaze locks on my belly. I touch the place that holds his attention.

"You know," I mutter.

Unwavering from me, his nictitating membrane slides across his eye, presumably wiping the red dust from his glossy cornea.

"*It* isn't leaving," Daisy whispers. "Why isn't it leaving?"

"Aster?" Blossom moves toward me, and Odio jerks his head in her direction, targeting her. "Woah." Freezing her step, she raises her hands. "Aster? What do we do?"

I don't know...

Through a long shuddering breath, I slowly walk toward them, with Odio's eyes tracking my every step. "Easy, handsome boy. They are my friends. Companions. My *Collective*, Odio."

His head tilts, listening.

That's it. "Yes, *Collective*." I nod at Odio, rounding him. I manage to get to the girls, and we embrace, press our heads together and pant heavily into our huddle.

"It's okay." I breathe. "It's okay."

"What happened?" Daisy asks.

"I don't know."

"Where have they taken Iris?" Blossom adds.

"I don't know."

Daisy lifts her head first, her eyes meeting mine. "What did she do, Aster?

Shit.

I've spent weeks with these girls. I've not trusted anyone enough to release the secrets and spill them into the wild. It wasn't just to protect Iris, but... I am ashamed. I feel *shame* over being disliked, over being Fur born, and I wanted them to like me.

But that was selfish.

Guilt now plays with my shame; I didn't warn them about Iris and put them in danger of having her claws sharpened against their confessions.

"She hurt me, but..." I start, wondering how to explain Iris without making her seem like a complete monster. It isn't black and white. Iris is grey, so very grey. "I don't think she can help herself. I think that if she could turn the nasty parts inside her off, she would."

Daisy frowns. "What do you mean?"

"Yeah, I don't understand," Blossom adds.

I sigh, blinking as my mind reaches for an explanation. "Have you heard the story about the *Scorpion and the Frog?*" I ask them, and their brows furrow in unison. "I read it once in an old fairytale book before it was banned. It was raining, or there was a pond in the way, or something like that. I can't remember exactly, but the scorpion needed to cross the water. It asked the frog for help, 'Can I climb on your back?' it said. The frog said, 'No way. You will sting me.' But the scorpion was adamant. 'No, I won't, because then we will both drown. That makes no sense.' The frog thought about this. Then he agreed, and just as they got to the middle of the body of water, the scorpion stung him. As the frog began to die and sink, he called out, 'Why? Now we will both die.' The scorpion started to drown, and with his last breath, he said, 'I'm sorry, it is just in my nature.'"

Daisy and Blossom both share a meaningful glance, their expression sad and tight with confusion.

With what feels like tunnel vision, the horizon of light at the end being me, Odio watches as though he is also listening to my folktale.

"She cannot help herself." I shrug, sad. "She is rotten inside, and I don't know if she'll ever change."

Daisy swallows. "What did she do to you?"

"The thing about betrayal is it never comes from your enemies," I say. "You have to trust first." I take a big breath and exhale the heavy words, "Can I trust you?"

"Of course," Blossom blurts out.

"Yes," Daisy agrees softly. "I swear it."

With shaking fingers, I slide my mauve dress up to my knicker-line and display the long, thin scars snaking down my inner thighs. "It is just in her nature."

Their eyes widen.

I drop the skirting.

I tell them everything that happened. I confide in them; all the secrets and the truth about being Fur Born, Raptor, the dead birds, the pond—the entire private life I lived that I wasn't supposed to. Not as a Silk Girl. I wasn't supposed to feed beasts. I wasn't supposed to swim. I wasn't supposed to suffer.

Daisy grabs my hand, holding it between two of hers. "Does Sire know? How much? We need to know in case conversations move around us."

A breath hitches in my throat. "I don't know."

Blossom nods slowly. "You know that we *know*, right? That Sire chose you, Aster. We saw the way he looked at you. It was as if he wanted everyone to know that you were his. It's okay."

I exhale hard. "Am I safe?"

"With us?" Daisy's shoulders deflate, her pretty eyes glinting with remorse. "Yes, of course you are. I know that I recite protocol and vows, but that is because I am trying to protect you. All of you."

I smile at that. "I know."

The quiet drags through the air as we absorb everything, as we make room inside our consciousness for moving forward with secrets and truths and... Trust that now wraps us together with twine made of silk.

And I am the one they are counting on.

For answers.

For guidance.

That wasn't what I expected or wanted, but I feel responsible for throwing our peaceful, simple lives into disarray. Just by being me, I've messed things up.

Daisy shuffles along the emerald grass when Odio's arrowed glare becomes too hot on us. "Do you think he can understand us?"

The great winged deity stares sideways, beady-eyed but magnificent, at our joined hands.

It makes me wonder how tame he is... Or not. Is he like Rome? Deep down, he is longing to have his feathers stroked. I doubt Rome ever offers him gentle attention.

"I don't think he understands much," I assure them, though I do not know for certain. "And what he does, he cannot exactly repeat, can he? Animals have energy. We do, too. I was never afraid of him. And even less today."

I pull my hand from Daisy and hold it up at Odio's head height, bracing my palm in the air.

He stares at it.

"Come," I say to him. "Pet?"

He cocks his head and suddenly turns his neck as if sensing an itch, digging his beak into his wings and ripping out a mangled black feather the length of my forearm.

I lower my hand. "Next time, then, handsome boy."

Across the courtyard, the breeze rolls steadily, the designed environment we exist in sometimes makes it hard to remember that outside The Estate walls, through the trees, there is a dangerous force of unrelenting power—Redwind. Odio sees it every time he hits the skies. Rome sees it when he leaves...

When he leaves Tuscany and me.

Without saying a word.

Not even a goodbye.

I don't know what he knows.

But I'm going to find out.

"Odio." I point to the courtyard wall, and the handsome beast cocks his head up from pruning his feathers, a coal-coloured blade in his beak. "Sire. Show me where Sire is."

Chapter Two

Aster

I follow Odio's shadow as it soars over the grass like a black mist. The crown-light bakes the atmosphere. This time of day can be stifling, the air thick, but I think I am hotter than the environment. Fired with ambition and—nerves.

Small beads of perspiration collect on my brows, as Odio guides me through The Estate, between renewed Romanesque buildings and down lanes, until his shadow climbs up a stone wall—

I stop, staring ahead at the entrance to a hall.

Right. I look up to the sky, to the cloudy outline of an eagle. "He is in there?"

Odio hovers in the red haze.

Straightening, I take a big breath in. I'm about to walk with my head held high when I hear footfalls and a man yell, "You are not permitted in there."

I spin to see a Guard approaching, and brace myself for what I might say to him or if I am even allowed to speak to him—

Suddenly, Odio lands with a thunderous pulse, and he is not

happy, menacing even—wings outstretched, head arched low, eyes like darts. He blocks the man from me.

He lets out long screech, and the wave of his sound trips the Guard backward with its intent and warning. Puffs his chest. Scrapes his talons along the stone path, flicking loose rocks and dirt. I've never seen him behave like this, which means he's never been aggressive toward me, not once.

"I yield, Odio!" The Guard scurries backward on the floor with one hand raised in surrender.

Blinking at the spectacle, I decide it's now or never. I slowly turn and walk between the twin marble pillars and into a grand foyer with high-painted ceilings and two elaborate wooden doors at the far end.

Voices come from behind one of the doors almost instantly. I peer back at the entrance, seeing Odio steadfast, and other Guards beyond him, trying to soothe the giant beast.

"You're going to trust the eagle to be her Guardian?" I hear a voice say, drawing my chin back to the door.

"I trust his loyalty more than I trust yours," Rome states, his deep, otherworldly timbre resonating in my toes, flooding me with an ocean of tangible memories. The feel of his weight on me, his mouth at my forehead, and that powerful voice spilling praise across my skin.

My nipples bead and my core clutches and kneads together, wanting his pressure.

Shit.

I stifle a moan.

"That is truly hurtful, Sire." The other man says, genuine offence lacing his tone. "I am your brother. We may not see eye to eye on certain political matters, but your heir is mine, too."

"So, it's you."

I walk to the door and press my ear to it.

"What is me?"

"You will not have an heir," Rome confirms.

"Cairo—"

"Said nothing of you."

Leaning away from the door, I wrestle internally with what to do. Stay. Listen. Leave. Mind my own business.

"Correct. I will not have an heir."

Who will have no heir... his brother?

I hold my breath to the beat of my heart, the torturous silence amplifying the frantic organ. It's too quiet, so inadvertently, I lean in again, my ear meeting the wooden grain, stamping it with sweat from my cheek.

"So, Aster will carry our blood into the next generations," the man who must be Turin Two says. He is talking about me. They all know. "Her safety, now that it's no secret, is a matter of great importance to me."

"You are Warden of The Estate," Rome's smooth utterance sails with further meaning. "You know every inch of it. You can ensure it is locked down and secure."

"And the eagle?"

"I trust no man or woman to watch my little Silk Girl and not want to taste what is between her pretty thighs. I know I was unprepared for her affect, and I'm a far stronger being than most."

My affect? On him?

My heart doesn't just race; it gallops.

But then the room falls silent, as if everyone inside dissolved in one of my raging heartbeats.

Pulse pounding, I press my entire body to the door, no breathing, no words, just the lingering echoes of his last sentence to hook me and then dangle me—

The door opens.

I stumble forward into a man's hands. I look up and see Turin Two, a younger, far more Common looking version of Rome, smiling softly.

My mind stalls.

"Hello, little creature." Rome's voice sails from the other side of the room, curling around me effortless with power. "Are your ears extra big today?"

Abruptly, a Guard is at my back.

"Sire, I apologise"—he huffs— "The eagle let her in."

"Did he?"

A ball of nerves and regret expands in my throat.

What the hell was I thinking, barging in on him?

Across the long span of a sweeping wooden desk, Rome sits in his casual black shirt, one arm slung over the back of a wing-back throne, looking every inch the man in charge, domination radiating from his very skin.

I swallow, and he watches the nervous action playing inside the slender column of my neck. His hot gaze roams around my body, indecent, intimidating, and tangible.

The hairs on my arms lift.

"Out now," he orders.

I almost whimper.

Not wanting to leave, hating his reaction to merely order me away like one of his pets, I grit my teeth. Feel shame. Feel sad. With that, I turn on my heels to leave with my head still high, but his dismissal chews on my strength.

I hope he chokes on it.

"Not you."

What?

I spin, quickly stepping aside as Turin Two, Kong, and two Guards leave the room, one after the other, and meet Rome's dark gaze once more.

I missed you.

The Guard behind me shuffles. "Sire?"

"Must I repeat myself..." Rome's eyes penetrate me. "Everyone out while I eat."

The nerves in my throat expand, blocking air. I open my mouth, inhaling hard, before saying, "I should not have been listening, my king. That was..." Rude. Improper. Disrespectful— "Disrespectful."

A slow grin spreads across his lips. "Don't apologise." He pushes back from the table and widens his thighs, taking up so much space it is any surprise he fits at all. The chair is huge. The table, too. This hall is not for Common. "I said if you needed me, you could ask, and I would come to you."

Liar. The thought comes, and I almost say it aloud. What is becoming of me? I feel wild and out of control. "That would have been a bit hard when you were hundreds of miles away for the past two weeks."

Woah.

"You're angry."

Warranted! Since you just left! Stifling the truth, I shake my head stiffly. "No. I have no right to feel anything like that toward you, my king. I told you I wanted to be your Silk Girl, and you gave me Meaningful Purpose. I have no right to be angry with you in the slightest."

He chuckles. "Really?"

Am I amusing to him?

My lips curl in frustration. "Well, yes. I am then. But I'm not here for you or me. I am here because of Iris, so what will you do with her?"

His smile falls, and my eyes widen.

"Does it scare you how apathetically I will execute her?" His tone is anything but amused now. "Do you see the black hole in my chest? Is that why you will happily leave me for a peaceful, pathetic life with the babies?"

I shuffle my feet. "I don't understand."

He stares at me, unsmiling. "Come here."

My hands start to shake. Have I pushed this too far? I am pregnant, which means I am untouchable. Is that why I am so quick to misbehave?

"Now!"

Shit. I force my feet forward, walking slowly around the giant table that seems more like a wall to me. I circle it and stop a foot away from Rome, eye to eye with him as he leans back, authority rippling through his relaxed posture.

His eyes pierce me, and I squirm. An angry sound comes from

the armrest as he squeezes the leather. "Lay your little body over my lap." He rolls up his sleeves, displaying thick forearms larger than my thighs and angry veins that ripple his scars and tattoos. He is a monster, and stunning, and I am completely at his mercy.

I can't breathe. "My king?"

"You walk in here" —he grips my wrist and pulls me to lay, face down, on his lap. "This tiny human with all this attitude. Asking for attention. Here it is." His hand slaps my backside, and I buck into his thigh as a yelp bounces from my lips and a defiant moan builds in my throat.

I don't want to want this.

He is spanking me

I've done the wrong thing.

I moan, long and rough.

"Yes." His voice is liquid silk. "That's what I thought."

Slap.

Moan.

Feeding his fingers up the back of my leg, they dip beneath my skirting and trail up to my thighs. I roll backward into their warm caress. He meets my centre.

"Fuck," he hisses, the pads of his fingers stroking the damp spot, circling it. "You are so mine."

I try to remember why I'm here. "I don't need attention. I need answers, my king."

He rubs my throbbing pussy through my knickers, firm circles that confuse me and that send my hips chasing the motion. "Answers to all the questions you should not have inside your pathetic conditioned mind."

His words find a mark inside my heart, but his fingers draw whimpers of delight through my lips. "What?"

"I can smell your arousal." The fabric between my thighs is soaked as he pushes it aside, dips his finger between my folds, and penetrates me.

I cry out in relief.

My muscles work and ripple along the length of his finger as he slides in and out of me, so deep and full, then empty and wanting. He controls me.

"I want this on my tongue. It's been weeks, and I'm hard as rock for you."

"You left..." The truth falls from me.

"You're just a silly little girl. Why wouldn't I?"

The backs of my eyes burn. "You don't mean that."

"You desire to be a Sired Mother. Nothing more."

Of course. That is what we are taught to want, trained to want, the perfect retirement. A special place. His words don't make sense.

"Every Silk Girl wants to be a Sired Moth—" My sentence is cut short when he pushes a second finger inside me.

"And you do, too," he purrs, dark.

My eyes roll.

I ignore his words; they drown in my racing heartbeat, in the rushing of my blood to the place where his fingers work at a meticulous pace.

"Pathetic, wet, little girl."

"Don't call me pathetic!"

He growls, stands and scoops me up with one arm as he goes. Placing me on all fours on the table, he comes up behind me, grips the back of my dress in both big hands, and rips it down the centre, exposing my spine and backside.

A dark sound rumbles throughout the room, thickening the air I try to breathe: a hiss from his teeth, a groan from his throat. "Is that what *you* really want? What if you could choose? What would you do?"

"I— I don't know. That's a scary question. I only know what is required of me, not what I want."

A huge hand lands on my upper back, covering the plane shoulder to shoulder, and pushes me down until my cheek stamps the cool table.

"Remember to be very still for your king."

That is all he has to say...

My eyes widen on the shiny wooden surface that spans out in front of me, as I listen to him unfastening his belt and lowering his pants.

A hand grips my hip, long fingers reaching to hold my pelvis. "I will feel myself here when I'm inside you." The thick, hot bulb of his cock rubs between my thighs, travelling up and down the slick valley.

I push back into him, wanting the stretch, to be filled. Needing all the nerves that prickle inside me to be touched, stroked, praised. Like he can do. I never knew it before, but now that I know, I want it.

He hums. "Good girl. Arching your back like a wanton, little Silk Girl. It will hurt, sweet thing. I'll see your pussy stretched to its limits."

His grip on me tightens as he pushes through my folds, opening me up in one long, thorough thrust inward. "Oh, fuck, Aster. My sweet Aster."

Sounds of relief, pain, fear, and excitement burst from me as he takes me from full to almost empty, and then full again. Each time he hits the end of me, hard, a spark of fire bursts through my abdomen, moments before warmth rolls the length of my inner walls as he draws out, thoroughly massaging every tender spot inside that secret place. Then he is inside me again.

I gasp for air.

His warm, rough hand on my hip bruises, his fingers holding my pubis, as though he can feel the area expanding with each pump of his hips. "I can't stop. Tell me to stop, little creature. I don't want to hurt you, but... *fuck*." He pants and groans as he continues to use my body. "Use your claws on the table. I am watching. I will stop."

My fear disappears.

Instantly, I lift my hands to either side of my head, but... I don't dig my nails into the wood. I don't need to. It's painful in the most unnatural, pleasurable way and... He gives me the power to stop him, and so I don't *fear* the pain.

I feel it.

Feel all the intensity of each thrust. Feel his heaving weight. The bite of his hand at my hip. The power in his thighs as he tenses.

I feel high—euphoric and crazed.

I feel free from my thoughts.

And when he starts to shudder and growl, the beast in him rears up with three punishing thrusts that buck yelps through my lips, knock reality from my vision, and show me three seconds of how powerful he can be.

He stays deep, his cock filling and pumping, filling and pumping, the pulses so precise, so powerful that pleasure bursts into my ears and seizes my thighs. And I tremble with my own release at the same time.

I mewl, lost, my body sore and heavy.

He holds my backside up with one hand.

"I'll make it easy then." His voice is deep, strained, and deliciously satiated. "I'll erase the decades of conditioning. I will own you, body, mind, spirit. You will stay with me. Let me make myself very clear to you, little creature. You are *mine*. And this"— his hand presses over my womb— "child, is mine. Not The Trade's. Not The Cradle's. Mine!"

If a word could bite, the way he expels 'mine' would draw scarlet ribbons from flesh.

Panting, I lay lax on the table, my backside elevated by his hand.

Earlier, when I saw him again, my heart was hot and frantic for him, and I wanted to nurture that warmth. His words feed and nest in just the right place, and I realise, I want to stay with him, but... We cannot.

Can we?

"Everything we do is for The Cradle," I say, utterly confused, completely spent.

As he slides his cock out, a choked cry burst from me. Being empty of his thick, pulsing pressure throws me into another wave of pleasure, where I'm left spinning and dizzy.

"Oh, *my king...*"

He lowers my backside, and muscles I didn't know I had ache with exhaustion.

"That's a good girl." He brushes his palm down my spine, and I practically vibration with delight. "I will serve The Cradle. *You* serve me. Only me. Rest assured that you're safe. That the men in power, the men you fear, *fear me.* You will never leave my side. You will never be sent away. You belong to me until the last beat of your heart."

A trembling breath squeezes from my lungs.

"Say it, Aster. Who do you belong to?"

A happy tear slides to the table. "You, my king."

"Forever, little creature."

"Forever, my king."

CHAPTER THREE

ROME

Cairo's message from the Half-tower burns a hole in my mind: 'The Silk Girl is known. Protect the heir.'

It is an entire lecture.

My Silk Girl is pregnant and *known*. This has not happened in hundreds of years, but we move forward and take hard measures. Aster won't always like what that means, no more privacy, eyes glued to her, eyes watching the babe grow in her womb... I don't like it.

Up ahead, the Redwind enters through a gap in The Estate fort, a strategic vent to deter Common.

She walks a step before me along the stone path, her hood pulled up, a mask covering her fragile face, even though she is hidden by my larger body from the aggressive wind and the sly gaze of Trade personnel.

We head toward my wing.

I have a wing where I used to fuck the House Girls—though it has been inactive since the night of the carnival when a little five-foot-two Silk Girl climbed into my lap.

I have a wing for business.

And this wing.

As we approach the five-storey stone structure untouched by modern reformations, she slows her step, and I practically stop to accommodate her sweet hesitation.

Her violet eyes sweep upward, gaping at the sheer walls as she enters the dark shadow it casts with thick stone and sturdy piers. I have always liked the Romanesque architecture that characterises the majority of The Estate's older buildings — fortress-like, domineering, defensive, a style for survival.

She removes her mask and sets it on the hallway table. From her shoulders, she slinks her hood, exposing her personalised Silk Girl dress with straight elegant lines down her lithe body. Across her upper chest, I can make out the faint rows of tiny bones beneath her skin while at her breast, the shadow of each nipple teases me. She is delicate and fine. I crack my neck from side to side, releasing some tension.

As we walk through the wing, she observes the space, the servers setting the table for three—her, Tuscany, and myself—the absurd amount of flowers, a floor-to-ceiling synthetic fire that spans the length of a soaring stone wall.

She stares at my personal space, and I...

I stare at her.

She has clawed her way into my mind, completely consuming it.

Aster... flower. A little flower that I plucked from the dirt and refuse to replant.

Nothing can be done now the heir is known, so the Silk Girl must stay by my side for her safety. That is all. Under this condition, she is most secure.

I do not trust her with any man or woman; I do not trust her with her Collective. And I will execute every being that interferes with... *this*. This thing between us which has no title nor law attached.

I will kill the creatures that have hurt her in the past and those who plot to do so in the future, those that glance her way with lust, bother her, force her to move, change her smile—

I growl. The rampage of thoughts thunder within me, but then she catches my eye again...

"Wow." She reaches her tiny hands out to feel the flame hearth, humming when it radiates but doesn't burn.

I sigh, her sweet cadence giving me breath. Her awe forces me to smile, a rarity, and one I'll only allow to exist for her, with her.

I realise that while I relish the crimson slashes of death on my calloused hands, the Redwind carving through the skin of Common—war—sharing quiet moments with her might be equally as pleasurable.

"Your wing, my king." She spins to face me, and I try not to let her see the effect she has, flattening my smile. "It looks just like you. If you were a building."

"What an odd thing to say."

A coy smile bunches her cheeks. "I know."

"I want to hear more."

She blinks. "More of what?"

"Of your mind."

I stride to her and cup her face, holding her tiny Common head in my hands, lifting her chin so her eyes peer through fluttering, black lashes to meet my gaze.

"You will stay here. You will not argue appropriate interactions or draw lines between us in the name of The Trade. Do you understand that everything is different now? Say yes, my king, and I will take you to my room."

She swallows, and my cock stiffens.

"Say it."

"What of my shots?"

"Your question implies you do not trust me to take care of you." I frown, but answer, "Your Watcher will take you to the Medi-deck each first-light for your scan and vitamins."

"Paisley," she informs, as though I should use her name. *Insolent little creature.* "What of my Collective?"

This fucking girl.

Just say, 'Yes, my king.'

I talk through grit teeth. "What of them?"

"I wish to see them—often."

Sighing roughly, I sweep my thumb over her smooth cheek. Why the fuck do I want to give her everything? "You may see them when you wish, but Odio will accompany you outside this wing."

"He scares people."

"That is by design."

She chews on her bottom lip and shows her acceptance in two slow nods. "Yes, my king."

Better.

I walk her down the corridor toward my chamber, allowing her time to study each taxidermized eagle head mounted along the walls. The magnificent beasts increase in size until the skulls are larger than her own.

Odio's lineage.

She muses. "Does this not make you sad?"

My boots rap on the tiles while her feet glide, weightless.

"If my heirs wish to cut off my head and hang it once I am dead," I say, "they are more than welcome to."

I expect a gasp, but she simply hums. "I don't think you'll have that opportunity. No one could rest with you staring at them, my king."

A chuckle breaks from me.

"Was that a laugh that I heard?" Tuscany's voice sails down the corridor, the melodic flow drawing Aster's attention.

"My queen." Aster curtsies.

My sweet sister stops a few feet away from us. I'm surprised she is here... nosy, perhaps. Though, that is not in her nature. Disappearing is.

She enjoys her space and very rarely touches anyone. When she does, it's a fucking butterfly on skin, terrified a small twitch will turn it to dust on broken wings.

She rests her small hands in front of her waist, her hair as straight as her posture. "It has been many years since I heard a laugh in these halls."

My smile thins, her presence reminding me of my failings. "To what do I owe the pleasure of your company?"

"I came to say a few words." She squares her narrow shoulders, pretending to have confidence that does not exist. "I approve, but please do not keep her locked in this wing, *Sire*. She is far too bright."

Not Rome.

Sire.

Her words land a blow to my chest, embedding with the bullets and shrapnel I have claimed over years of war. I don't answer, and she doesn't elaborate. I hear her.

She reaches out to touch me but retracts her hand and slowly turns to leave. Tuscany does not walk as though the floor is a shell she might crack beneath each heel—my sister walks as though she is the shell.

I watch her disappear around a corner, my chest pounding with anger, not at her, not at all. At my own fucking helplessness.

Tearing my eyes away, I am met with the enquiring violet gaze that slows my heart to a steady, powerful beat. My little creature, now mine, somehow levels me.

"You do bring me peace," I declare, staring down at her; though, she is tiny, a power greater than my darkness resides within her.

"Tell me," I ask, guiding her into my room and shutting the door behind us. "Why did you pick gold for your sheet?"

Her brows weave. "My king asks an odd question."

"I learned from the best."

My little creature looks at the floor. Blushes. Her eyes glisten with something akin to what I feel but cannot put into words. "It was a little fever dream, but I didn't pick gold. I picked yellow. Like the missing sun." She spins to take in my room, as elaborate, yet traditional as the rest of my wing.

My eyes track her as she moves around the space, looking like a baby bird in the cage of a monstrous eagle.

"Paisley noted down gold," I state.

"Maybe they are the same colour to her."

That I had not considered. "Perhaps."

"What is your favourite colour, my king?"

"I'm not a child. I do not have a favourite colour."

"You're a being of decisions and actions. What about a favourite number? I am sure you have a favourite number." She looks at the bed. "No steps?"

"No Common."

She beams at that admission. Yes, sweet creature, you're the only one. Tuscany is right, she is bright. "Let me guess your favourite number."

"I don't have one."

My little creature strolls to me, her steps far sultrier, like a dance, than my sister's. Craning her neck, she stares into my eyes, diving in deep, intent on finding a silent answer.

She stares until it hurts. "One."

The corner of my mouth lifts, smirking. *I want her.* Her eyes widen when I pick her up at her waist. Her legs dangle, shoes two feet off the floor, not knowing what to do now.

"Wrap your legs around my waist."

She does, and her warm core presses to my abdomen. With a little hesitance, her hands rest on my shoulders, her gentle fingers feed into my hair, and I fucking groan when she strokes me.

"Purring for me again, my king."

I should hate this—

I do hate this.

I roll my head further against her caress, closing my eyes. Not sure of anything in this moment. *My reality has been changed since I met you, little creature.* I don't even recognise myself, but instead, see what I am through you.

"Am I right? Is that your favourite number?"

I open my eyes to hers inches away and answer—a lie and

truth. "Yes." But I don't have a favourite number because I'm not that man, not a man at all, but— Now I have a favourite number.

And it's one.

Her eyes suddenly well up, and I frown. "What is it." She peers down and squirms to get free, but I don't release her. "No."

"Please, put me down so I can discuss something of great importance with you, my king."

A deep, rough sigh leaves me. I don't want to discuss anything of 'great importance.' I want to fuck her on my bed until the sheets smell like her pussy.

"Please."

Well, fuck.

I walk us to the sunken circular rest area in the centre of the room and sit down with her on my lap.

Her legs stretch wide to accommodate the breadth of my hips, and my cock fills with blood, creating a long thick bulge right at her warm apex.

Her eyes widen.

I thrust my hips upward to show her how hard I am, what I want, what I will have. Growling, I imagine every way I will taste her, places that will feed my depravities.

My eyes home-in on her throat. The fluttering pulse in her thin neck calls to me. I lean in and kiss it. Her sweet nerves feel like a frantic little butterfly beneath my tongue as I lick her.

She moans and tilts her head.

That's a good girl.

"Please, my king," she says to the ceiling, her words contorted with moans and whimpers. I massage both hands up her back, leaving no inch uncovered, from her hips to her neck and back, arching and curving her, consuming her with my attention and pressure.

"Oh, my king. Please. I cannot think."

That is the point.

"Tell me how you feel" —I run my nose along the thin column

of her throat before leaning back to watch her expression—
"inside your pussy right now?"

She chews on her lip and blinks her thoughts. So revealing. So
innocent. "I feel like I'm pulsing from the inside." She takes a big
breath in. "Like my heart is there."

I control my impulses—barely.

"*Where?*" I rasp. "Show your king exactly where your pulse is?"

Uncertain, she lifts her hips to sit on her hand, cradling her
core. I clench my teeth on another groan.

"I will indulge all of your questions as soon you come on my
cock," I say, bucking my hips, spurring her forward.

She removes her hand.

Slowly, with nervous energy, she begins to hump me like a
good girl, already trembling as she dances on my lap. My cock
throbs for more pressure.

Fuck.

I catch her wrist when her shaky hands drop between us and
try to undo my belt. I stare. Hard. "You can take me out, little
creature, and use me on the outside, grind your wet folds along
the full length of me, but you cannot put me inside you in this
position. I will puncture you. Do you understand?"

She blinks; my blinky, uncertain girl.

"I take you," she states, then adds, "don't I?"

A slow grin spreads across my lips. "No, sweet thing. You can
take about half of my length inside this tight body, but that is all."
She looks at her hands, disappointed. I hate it. I brush her long,
blackberry-swirled hair off her shoulders, exposing her neck and
torso. "Take off your little dress and sit back on your king's lap."

She pouts. "Are Xin De girls deeper?"

Adorable. I try not to grin at her jealous tone. "It's
proportionate... So, yes, sometimes." Her folded lips only thicken
my cock further. "Don't sulk, little creature."

"Well, will you"—she mimics my tone—"'indulge my questions
soon,' my king?"

I glare. "*Careful.*"

She swallows.

Taking my narrowed eyes as seriously as they are intended, she climbs to her feet and slowly lifts her dress over her head, exposing slim white legs, white knickers with a clear wet core, a smooth, supple belly that nurtures my heir, and naked sweet, pert tits.

"No brassieres? Why?"

Blush rushes up her neck under my scrutiny, her arms wrapping around her chest, covering the perky mounds. "I know. They are small. I don't always wear one. They will get bigger, my king. In the coming months."

"Are you apologising for something?" I suffocate another growl that lurks in my chest; it will only intimidate her further. *Dammit,* I am in physical pain over how hard I am, yet she's trembling with insecurities.

Glaring at her, unable to mask the disapproval, I unbutton my pants and drag my cock out, fisting it, squeezing it until the head swells and reddens. "Climb onto your king's lap. Now. And slide along my cock. Let me feel your heartbeat between your thighs."

I wrench my shirt over my head, push my pants down and widen my legs, my cock jutting out, bouncing and leaking.

Her mouth parts, her eyes roaming my chest and abdomen. "You're so hard, my king. And... so many scars."

A whisper of sorrow glosses her eyes as if she wants to kiss each one and take the pain away.

You can't, sweet creature.

With her legs wide, she climbs over my thighs and hovers, unsure what to do with me.

I chuckle deep.

Pressing my weight into the backrest, it declines slightly. She is too fucking nervous, so I reach out, possess her throat with a growl and drag her lips to meet mine. I devour her mouth. Eat it. Holding her neck with one hand, I position her backside with the other. Setting her on my long, throbbing cock, I pin it between my abdominals and her delta. I work her along the shaft, feel her pussy lips open and show her what she needs to do all by herself when I let go.

"That's my good girl."

I loosen my hold but leave my palm resting on her fragile spine and my other as a collar around her neck.

Her lips fumble in confusion on mine—whimpers, moans, and cries all mingle together while she tries to return my hard kiss.

Her heart pulses in her heat as she rides me, rocking her hips backward, her pussy lips hugging the root before sliding up to the swelling crown.

I rest my head, stare, and *feel* her.

Let her play on me. Perfect. Her. Vulnerable, sweet, and unknowingly seductive; her tits jiggle, nipples flushing; her mouth hangs open, lips red and pouty, draining the thick air; her hands flex on my chest for control.

But she has none.

None at all.

Watching this tiny naked human working the pleasure from her core, bringing it to the surface, is my new preferred activity.

My balls tighten, ready to explode, but I withhold my insatiable need to come. Instead, I enjoy *this*. I watch her pussy glazing my shaft. Hear her moans building, pitching higher.

When my cock throbs under her, pounding for more weight, her body loses rhythm. She is so close to crumbling, so close I can almost taste it.

She shakes her head over and over. "I can't—" Her chest heaves. "Cannot do it on my own."

I smirk and lean forward to capture her nipple between my teeth. Roll the bead. Suck hard enough to revel in the metallic essence of her bruising skin.

Then I fully band her hips with my hands and get myself off using her body to lather along the entire length of my cock, unrelentingly even as violent whimpers sound from her pouty lips and convulsions whip through her body.

I draw her orgasm out, long, hard, unyielding, keeping the

pace she is unable to master herself. Feeling her orgasm, tasting blood from her plush nipple, I growl from the dark chasm in my chest in unison with her pitched cries, painting cum across my abdomen and hers.

Breathing hard, I praise her.

"That was beautiful."

I feed my hands between her hair and her neck, holding her up as she fights her fatigue. "You can let go now," I say, standing with her and taking her to my bed.

"But what about my questions?" She yawns. "I had questions. Important ones about..." Her lashes flutter as she thinks. "It is only just last-light. I can stay"—yawn— "up."

Fuck me, she is pretty. Her voice, her scent, her sweet body in my arms, so lax, so mine. "I will be here with you in the first-light for all your interrogations," I offer.

She giggles. *"Interrogations."*

I frown at the jumpy soft cadence of her childlike laugh, hating how much I love it. It is one thing to accept humanity and another to welcome castration... I like my balls.

"You'll stay?" It finally dawns on her. "We sleep together all night? Every night?"

"Always."

I hold her to my chest, and she curls her knees to the side. Safe. Safe with me.

Like I promised her sister decades ago.

With a hand covering the back of her head, fingers laced in silky black strands, and another scooped around her hips, I rock my new Purpose to sleep.

Chapter Four

Aster

Feeling a warm presence beneath me, I slowly bat my eyes open, and for a breath, I almost forget where I am. Then his room blinks into place, the conversations from yesterday and how 'everything is different now' soak into me.

His chest rises and falls, and I trace the rippling tattoos with my finger. I absorb the moment, exploring his skin, trailing my fingertip in the valley between thick muscles. Then I poke a scar to find it unyielding like lead.

"Bullets..." he murmurs, his voice sleepy— husky. "Bullet holes. The bullets are inside."

"Pardon?"

With a deep growl that rumbles beneath me, he stretches out, his body tightening with strength and power as he wakes up. "I earned them."

A lump swells in my throat. "That's tragic."

I think about the big scar on his lower lip, the one that easily shapes his resting expression into a snarl.

"And the one on your lip?" I ask.

"Odio."

I blink fast. *"Why?"*

"To punish me."

"For what exactly?"

A dark laugh leaves him, but it's hollow, haunting. "I decapitated his previous master. He needed to show me that it mattered to him in the only way he knew how."

Woah.

I don't know what to say to that, but I am not entirely surprised. After all, Odio is a beast of loyalty. Of defence. Of royalty. The books say that when the eagles all die, it will mean the end of The Cradle as we know it.

"How old is Odio?" I ask.

Rome's arms cover me, a blanket of impossible warmth and shelter. My skin prickles as he explores my naked form curled on top of him.

"He is fifty-five." His answer is mechanical, as though he is no longer interested in the conversation, but keeps his word and allows me to ask my questions.

"How long do they live?"

"His mother lived to eighty-six. Twice the lifespan of the Wedgetailed Eagle from the old-world."

His hands would be roaming and lazy if they weren't so large, warm, and involuntarily firm, handling and consuming every inch of my flesh.

His nose moves into my hair, *"Aster."* He inhales. "Vulnerability. Mine."

He is trying to distract me... The sound of my name rolling along his tongue drags a moan along my tongue, but I need to focus. On... my 'interrogations.'

I want to push off his chest, but his hands are everywhere, and I'm not sure I can.

"My king," I start, worrying my bottom lip, "What did Iris do? What is to become of her?"

His palms freeze on me, the long pause rising the hairs along my skin. "These"—a big hand pushes between my legs and wraps around my upper thigh— "scars. Don't lie to me, little creature. You have already done it once."

How does he know? I fight my lungs for the courage to breathe steady. "I was worried for Iris... You killed my Silk Wardeness, my king."

"I *executed* her," he corrects.

"And Iris?"

"Was examined for implanting yesterday." His voice is dangerously even. "She is not pregnant and so will suffer the same fate."

I don't think as I push up off his chest, the word flying out with a punch. "No!"

He glares down at me through his lashes. "*Yes.*" Breath shakes from me, seeing the endless pits of his darkness shrink the blue in his eyes to thin rings.

"Show her mercy, my king," I plea. "Show her mercy. She is my oldest companion."

"You only need Odio and me."

"I want my Collective, too."

I gasp as his hand launches for my throat, wrapping around the column, dragging me up until I am close to his face. To catch myself, my hands meet the mattress beside his head.

"I have decided," he growls the words through a tight jaw, his savage dominance assaulting me.

My beast...

Instinctively, my body twitches to recoil, but I don't. I am not afraid of him.

I press my forehead to his, squeeze my eyes shut, and exhale hard. "Please, my king. For me."

A long hiss leaves his mouth, and the pressure from his hand lessens around my neck. "I will spare her execution, bu—"

I lift my head. "Honestly?" Hope blazes in my eyes.

His expression remains dark, an internal battle carves across sharp, tense features. "But she will be sent to the Black Matter

Tower to birth a legacy for Lord Coober. Accept this. And be very careful with what you say next. This concept of love is somewhat new to me. Do not make me despise it before I have a chance to adapt to its incessant rule."

But she is broken.

My brows pinch, confused. "But— But she has been opened by another."

"This will not bother him. He will merely appreciate her strong Xin De genus."

"Wait?" My heart swarms with heat as a word he used earlier finds a home in my chest. "Did you use the word, 'love?' You mean…" I hesitate. "That you…"

"Unbearably, yes."

I inhale his response, accepting the answer, however strangled, as if this tiny one-syllable word has the power to wrap my skin in a warm hold and ensure my happiness. I know that's not true, but maybe, love does last forever…

Maybe it is the only thing that truly can.

Chapter Five

Aster

I soon learn that at the conclusion of a Trade campaign, when Rome returns, activity bursts across The Estate like an exploding mosaic. They celebrate his presence.

Gripping the top of the balcony, I lean over and watch another carnival unfold like a living tapestry, spreading colourful tents and lights across the streets.

The citizens move around in waves. The music lifts up to where I stand on the roof of his personal wing, a teasing melody I am not allowed to completely enjoy.

I am not allowed to go.

I place my hand over my womb.

Protect the heir...

From here, I can see the piazza fountains shooting into the sky, and if I lift to my tippy-toes, I can see the stage erected between the ancient city buildings and Rome sitting on his throne with an empty seat to his right and Lord Turin Two, Lord Bled, Lord Medan, and Kong to his left.

Mm, he is so handsome.

I flatten my feet and pout.

"I suspected as much." A soft voice comes from behind me, and when I turn, I see Tuscany strolling onto the balcony. "I could disguise you." She stops a few feet away and smiles, faint but sweet. "We could put you in a pretty mask and hood and have you wander in the shadows to enjoy the festivities."

As if he understood, Odio screeches from the skies above the building. Not approving the plan.

"Oh, Odio. *Really?*" Tuscany half-laughs at the great beast as he lands on the roof above us, leaning over the brink to watch us converse on the platform below. "Well, he misses nothing. He is probably wary of my guests."

I lift a brow. "Your guests?"

Suddenly, a familiar voice soars from inside. "Aster!" I beam. Blossom and Daisy dash through the balcony's open doors, the purple drapes swaying as they fly past.

Daisy grins. "I have news."

"I do, too." Blossom bounces over.

My heart warms as the three of us embrace, our soft squeals and greetings singing in the air.

"I do miss our routines and the courtyard," I admit, "I feel as though I have abandoned you."

"It has only been a few days." Daisy chuckles but pulls me in a little tighter to show how she feels.

My smile reaches every inch of my face, when another voice comes from inside. "What is the intention of the mantled eagles? They are… welcoming?"

My chin turns in time to see a stunning dark-skinned girl with a round belly walking—waddling—toward us.

"Ana!"

She presses into our huddle on the balcony, and I revel in the moment, my yearning to join the distant carnival melting away. "You're feeling well?"

"I am *feeling*," she simply says. "And accepting. I want to appreciate the smaller details before the puzzle is complete and I miss them. Like you. You're a very pretty detail that I do not ever wish to take for granted."

A lump forms in my throat. "*Ana.*"

As sentiment bites at our smiles and glosses our eyes, Ana clears her throat, shaking it away. She bumps Daisy with her hip. "Tell her."

"I am pregnant," Blossom blurts out.

"*Blossom,*" Daisy mock-moans. "We flipped a puzzle piece on who would go first."

Blossom covers her smile. "Sorry!"

"As am I." Daisy's expression takes on a serious, significant manner when she places both of her palms on my lower abdomen. "And I hear you carry a king, Aster."

My heart jets to the skies, and I nod.

"Aster made me realise something," Ana says, and we all look at her. "While I was in my room."

We form a relaxed circle, and the carnival music floats to our platform, creating a private festival just for us.

The Silk Girls.

"Meaningful Purpose is the completed puzzle," she states. "But the journey, the pieces, can be meaningful, too. You and you and you"—she bounces her soft, brown gaze around the circle— "my Collective."

"Aster..." Blossom's eyes fill with hope. "You're still one of us, aren't you? You're not something different now?"

"I am still one of you." I cup the back of her auburn hair. "He has said I can see you as often as I wish, only I must bring..." On a heavy exhale, my gaze hits the roofline.

They follow my line of sight to where Odio is perched on the tiles above us, head tilting as if listening.

Ana shrugs. "It will be nice to have a man around."

I laugh.

Remembering the queen, I spin to thank her for allowing this to happen, but... she is gone. Sadness flickers inside me, but I remember my Collective. I force myself to surrender the simmering need to help her. Sometimes, it is best to accept that not everything can be fixed. Some people are not ready... some are paralysed with fear.

A memory whispers in her absence. Small feathers in my palm. An upside-down bird trapped in a glass house.

If she could only see the Redwind.

See something outside of these walls.

Maybe she would spread her wings.

"What happened to Iris?" Daisy pulls me to the present, her question a chisel hacking for the truth.

Blossom looks ashamed. "We told Ana."

"I thought you would want her to know," Daisy adds, glancing quickly at her hands. "We should trust each other in all things. I hope you're not up—"

"It is fine." I touch her shoulder. "I'm glad." Taking a step back so I can better see all three of them, I answer with all that I know. "She has been banished from The Estate. Sent to another Tower. One on The Mainland. A mining Tower. That is all I know."

Ana frowns. "They are not executing her? For what she did to you? For crimes against her Collective? Against us?"

It is not that simple. I see her grey...

I shake my head as I say, "No. I begged the king to show her mercy."

"*Aster,*" Ana sighs my name, heavy disapproval dropping her tone. "She deserves far worse."

"She is the scorpion," Blossom bids.

Ana's eyes dart around in confusion. "A scorpion? Huh, she is a scorpion, that is for sure."

"The House Girls are at the carnival." Daisy points, and we all follow her finger out toward the stage.

I lift to my tippy-toes again, squinting at where Lord Medan, Lord Bled, and Rome are surrounded by women. Tall and curvaceous women, but any further details are lost to the distance. With that height and thickness, one can only presume they have a high Xin De genus.

Envy embeds its claws in my stomach.

I recall a conversation from last night when Rome said that Xin De girls can take more of him inside them. And I feel it, the most shameful of emotions—jealousy. It traps focus, distracting us from our Purpose. I don't have time for it.

Jealousy makes us lose our path.

"Maybe they are dancing for the lords at the carnival." She hums. "That's a little... provocative, but then, the men need to unwind. It is good for their temperament."

"Dancing." I find myself grinding out the word, hoping to turn the jealousy it carries to dust between my teeth. Jealous inflictions imply I want something that they have... But I don't.

Because he is mine.

My king.

They want what is *mine*. I don't feel jealous; I feel territorial. There is a distinct difference.

We stay on the balcony, enjoying the music and occasional cheer from the carnival below. Crown-light fades into last-light, and fires, torches, and lamps from lanes create blazing dots across The Estate.

Ana, Daisy, Blossom, and I open up to each other. We share stories from books we were never meant to read and discuss the old-world. We consider the ideology of The Crust—a state of peace and endless happiness or just a place to decay. And while we talk, I realise I am not that different. They have the same wandering mind, only they are better at controlling it.

After they leave, the Missing Moon must be hanging high, surrounded by stars that will never filter the haze, as I roll around in his bed, the enormous surface swallowing me.

I dream about a small boy holding a dead baby bird, not knowing what has happened to it. I don't know how I know that, but he is in pain and desperate to stroke the feathers, to soothe it.

The little thing is upside down, its legs curled, feet crimped in tight agony. I follow this boy as he strolls around a grey underground with flickering lights, which does not make sense because how would a bird get down there?

The boy in the dim fades to the words, "Aster..." He slowly drifts away from me, and I feel myself reaching out my fingers, feeling a sadness I cannot comprehend—I don't know him.

"Aster."

I flutter my eyes open to Rome crawling on the mattress, his heavy weight rocking me from side to side as he climbs over me.

"My king," I whisper in my sleepy daze, but the sadness clings to me for a few conscious moments longer.

Then warm lips seal my mouth and flood my heart with love and contentment.

Heat blankets my skin as his kisses deepens, and his hands trail over my body, seeking, searching, worshipping. I should be frightened by how large his palms are, how much surface they cover, how possessive his grip is.

But I'm not.

His fingers slide between my thighs and find my core wet and warm already.

A moan leaks from my sleepy mouth and into his kiss.

He dips between my folds, playing up and down the slick valley but not pushing past the entrance and into me. He stirs me, my eyes rolling to his perfect rhythm.

"The thought of you has been distracting me all night. You have power over me."

More moans roll along my tongue. My hips circle with his skilled fingers, chasing the edging pleasure. "I need to take back some power, little creature," he utters darkly.

With that, he rolls me onto my side and covers my back and legs entirely with his large form.

Between my thighs, two fingers return to their motion, to their mixing of pleasure, to their stoking of need.

His other hand positions his cock. He doesn't wait, rousing me with his warm touch while he takes his power back and pushes through me.

My eyes fly open, and my steady, soft moans spiral into uncertain whimpers and mewls.

I dig my nails into his sheets.

He hooks my leg backward over his and pumps into me. "Fuck, yes. You're so wet."

"My king." My voice trembles.

"I am here. You're safe" He reaches for my hand, brings it back, and sets my fingers on his thick, veined forearm. "Remember your claws, little creature."

The stretch is...

Oh, the stretch.

Warmth.

Tension.

Pressure.

But then... I cannot quell the thought of him with a Xin De girl. Sinking all the way in. I push my backside into him, and immediately, his crown bashes something inside me—the end of me. I cry out, both frustrated and in pain.

"Stop that!" He grunts. "You have a lot of nerves on your cervix, and you're pregnant. If you do that again, I will pull out and fuck your other hole as punishment."

Fuck my?

I blink.

He cannot mean...

My confusion churns to pleasure when his fingers slide down and play with my clit, strumming the bead. My mouth opens, and I whimper my thoughts. "I saw you."

"Saw me what?"

"With the House Girls." The words fall out before I have time to swallow them. Can't swallow. Can barely feel anything as he brings my pleasure up, up, from my toes. Down. Down from my hot ears. Across, across from thighs. Landing a ball of pleasure at the tips of his fingers that leaves me writhing and taking fast thrusts from behind.

His fingers leave me.

"Did you?" A firm hand slides up, roaming along my trembling belly, between my ribs, to my throat, where he grabs the column, possessiveness rearing up.

Groaning, he holds me still to take his thrusts from behind, beating upward into me but still cloaking my spine in his hot body.

I shake when he does.

I swelter when he burns.

"What are you implying," he hisses between heavy pants that match his inward drives. "That I want someone else? That I'll take them over you?"

I answer through choppy whimpers. "It is none of my business who you..." I hesitate, but say it anyway, "fuck."

"That word is beneath you, sweet creature. I fuck you," he says as he does. "I fuck, you do not. You adore, pleasure, love. Don't use words that are beneath you."

He groans, the pumping of his hips gets faster, and I close my eyes, taking the need, feeling his desperation to come in the precision, in the focus of every inward drive.

My pussy ripples and flutters around him, opening only when he pushes in and closing as he pulls out.

I'm mindless with him. "*Oh*, my king."

"Don't disrespect this, little creature. Don't underestimate my obsession for you!" His fingers tighten around my throat. "I am *consumed*. I cannot go a night without this. I cannot concentrate."

Thrust.

"The thought—"

Thrust.

"Of touching—"

Thrust.

"Another and then using the same hands to touch you—" His muscles tighten. He lifts my thigh higher, angling me, holding me like a doll for his hard final thrust.

"Fills me with rage." He comes inside me with a throaty growl that projects through the room, warning every inch of space, every fibre, that he claims me. As he spurts inside me, rumbles of his pleasure vibrate against my spine and blanket me in pride. I can bring this man, this beast, pleasure with my body. I suppose that is powerful... But one should not think such things. Not about a king.

His long exhale beats down on me as he relaxes, lowering my thigh to meet the other, but he does not drop the muscle. Instead, kneads the tension.

"That's my good girl."

I press my head back into his heaving chest, feeling him. Feeling his heart thumping like a well-worked machine. His length still slowly pulsing.

"I mean no disrespect, my king." I breathe. "But monogamy is self-serving. I do not own you, and it would be—"

"You own me."

My breath lodges beneath his palm. "Pardon?"

"I am the king of The Cradle." He relaxes his grip around my throat, resting but not releasing. "I was built to protect and serve the land, but I swear to you that no part of it is more important than the piece beneath your feet."

"My king," I sob, happy.

I love you. I love you.

My heart feels like it may burst through my chest. I want to cry, because this is terrifying. Want to shake the moment, pinch it, because it isn't real. Can't be.

"Say it."

I blink. "Say what?"

"What you are thinking. I demand it."

I snuggle backward into him, and he doesn't tense. He relaxes. His heavy bicep surrenders to his fatigue, becoming a heavy band that pins me down. His palm continues to cradle the pulse in my neck.

The pulse that he owns.

That speeds for him.

Slows for him, flutters.

Beats for him, hard.

"I love you, my king."

The beast inside purrs under the affect of my words, and I feel something shift. Something deep inside him that was black and hard. I feel it soften.

Then he says, *"Rome."*

My eyes fill with tears, but I don't know why. I am a silly, little girl. It's only... I have never said his name. I have heard it, thought it, but never, wouldn't dare, say it.

The word comes from a smile. *"Rome."*

"Say it all again."

"I love you, Rome."

A Silk Girl's
Second Trimester

Aster
of the Aquilla Silk Aviary

CHAPTER SIX

ROME

Breathing heavily, I stride into the courtyard, desperate to see her —just for a moment. Blood paints my leather vest, the crimson guts of cats drying under the crown-light.

Usually, my time in the forest flies by, but these days, away from her, they crawl on all-fours.

It's been long enough. She has had time with her Collective, as requested.

But now, I am wired; tight muscles tremble with endorphins; my mind reels in the death calls of animals, in the silence before a kill, in the climax of the blank stare. It is tangible energy, and it fuels the black parts inside me.

It is hard to snap out of…

Then I see her.

She strolls around the gardens, a cape of dark hair swaying gently down the back of her silky white dress.

I drop my gaze.

Grin.

Fuck me.

From hip to hip, her swelling womb shows beneath the silken fabric, pulling it taut as she leans to pick another flower, feeding the purple bloom into the bunch in her hand.

My attention is literally paralysed.

Her Collective strolls alongside her, gathering flowers of different colours. Aster's side brushes the hip of Darwin's Silk Girl, the round one, mere days shy of birthing. Such a pity Darwin opened her before Bled or Medan had a chance. I look at her large stomach—she has carried the babe with ease. My eyes war to get back to Aster... I look at her as she smiles and converses, unaware of my watchful gaze.

Above me, a winged silhouette hovers in the red haze. Odio maps a grid of sky, every inch of land near her is within a second of his descending razor-sharp talons.

My body vibrates, being too far away, can't smell her, can't feel her heat, but she begged me this first-light for time with them, and I allowed it. I will always grant her... anything.

Despite my approval, the distance meant I needed to kill something. So, I hunt... Something that used to be my preferred pastime, but now. *Fuck.* I can just stare at her.

I lean on the courtyard wall, watching her.

A screech from the depths of the haze alerts me to... In my peripherals, I note one of our Trade doctors approaching me from inside the Silk Girl Wing. An older Common man, intelligent—and castrated. That's important if he is to touch what is mine. Might cut his hands off one day... Maybe. Keep them in a jar beside my father's head.

"She is swelling fast," he advises in a quiet tone, stopping beside me. Not in front. He wouldn't dare block my view; I would cut a window into his flesh.

I'm in a volatile mood.

I smile at his words—she is swelling fast—my attention roaming her swollen abdomen again, my cock thickening inside my pants. I am certain he can see it. Of that, I am glad.

I adjust myself, my bloody hands palming my cock to the

thought of her smooth skin, stretching to grow my heir, matching the smooth, strained pussy that I fuck and lick. I've never felt more ownership. Never felt more possessive greed.

"What I mean, Sire, is that the baby grows fast. A high Xin De genus. I am certain. We should keep the babe in the Silk Girl for as long as possible, even if it means sh—"

Now you have my fucking attention.

My stare snaps to him. "She what?"

His eyes widen on my fist, and I realise I have reached for the gutting knife in my belt, and now I hold it erected in front of me.

"Sire." He swallows and takes a single step backward, as if that distance will aid him. My arm is longer.

"She what?" I repeat.

"Degrades."

"Say that sentence again."

Sweat instantly mists his pasty skin. "We should keep the babe in the Silk Girl for as long as possible, even if it means she— She degrades."

I spin the blade in my hand, using the rhythmic motion to soothe myself. A mild comfort. "You pull the heir out as soon as she feels any discomfort."

His brows weave. "But, Sire, there are other silk gir—"

He doesn't finish his sentence.

Eyes gape at me as I carve a scarlet smile into his throat. Blood rushes from the flapping slit, the crimson fall chasing gravity's inevitable draw.

Thick, hot blood blankets him.

Quick, so my sweet creature doesn't see, I drag him through the courtyard gate, position his swaying body on the outside wall, and watch him slide down the limestone. Stare at his wide, startled eyes. That is the energy... Neck down, he is a blood-dyed mannequin.

He flops to the side. Dead. "And there are other doctors," I hiss.

Odio lands beside him, talons already extended. His keen,

piercing eyes lock on the corpse, his curved, sharp beak slightly open, ready to pull pieces from it.

"I'll watch her," I state, leaving him to pull the old man apart, and walk back inside the courtyard.

What the fuck?

I halt. Really agitated now—Kong and Turin Two, both dishevelled from the hunt, are standing opposite the gathering of tiny girls, speaking words I cannot hear.

The world around me fades, channels, as Aster offers them both a flower from her bunch. Leaving me with only the pulse of my possessiveness, the energy of the kills, of my claim, of my need, of my desire for her, I scowl.

I let her play with her Collective, not pick fucking pointless flowers for them. For other men.

Where are my flowers?

Rational thought drowns in territorial rage as I stride toward the small gathering and stop behind my little creature, a shadow at her back. A warning and an accusation.

The Silk Girls quickly duck away.

From over Aster's head, my eyes target Turin Two and then Kong. "What do you think you're doing?"

Turin chuckles. "Accepting a token."

Fuck him.

I glare at him through my lashes, mirthless.

Aster turns around, a sweet smile on her lips. I don't need to look at her to see her mouth flatten and thin when she sees my scowl.

"Are you unhappy? They are aster, my king," she offers, soothing me with her melodic cadence. The same sweet vocals that moan a lullaby when she climaxes on my face. "The petals are so soft, so open, and smell so sweet." She blushes.

Why are you blushing?

Heat hits my temples.

My Aster. My flower. My sweet, soft, open little... She gave them aster flowers to wear on their armour or put in their chambers? To smell, to look at. Like hell they will!

"Drop the flowers," I order, staring at them.

They both chuckle, but the sound dies on my snarl.

"I said drop them."

Shaking his head, stifling amusement that only he and my brother can get away with, Kong hands back the flowers.

Turin Two laughs, returning the blooms to her. "Good luck with him, Aster."

My little creature takes the flowers, confused, blinking over and over as she sorts her thoughts. "I don't understand. I wasn't trying to soften them, or make them less focused on the hunt, or... I don't understand."

"Give them to me."

I watch as her eyes roam my leather vest, taking in the brutal dashes of red, before stopping on the thick blood drying, akin to cracked paint, on my fingers and knuckles.

She swallows, clearly nervous. "I didn't think you would want... flowers, my king."

I'm insane; I fucking realise this.

I don't want fucking flowers.

I want *her* flowers.

Dropping to my knees, I meet her eye to eye. "If *you* pick the flowers, they are mine. Give me the damn flowers."

The simmering of uncertainty in her gaze blinks away softly. Slowly, a sweet smile slides across her lips, as if she understands me. "You're jealous, my king."

I laugh coldly. "Unbearably, so."

"Don't underestimate my obsession with you." She repeats my words back to me, her playful smile stirring my monstrous soul with her purity, diluting the black, taming the claws and teeth.

Well, fuck.

I drop my forehead on her shoulder, sighing hard. *What the fuck is wrong with me?* I place my palms on either side of her hips. The white silk sliding over her lithe body. I glide my palms forward, low on her pelvis and cradle her beautiful, swollen lower stomach.

She sighs. "There you are." Her fingers feed up my back, my muscles rippling, responding to the gentle, arousing stimulation, as though I am—fucking purring. She's right. And I let it happen. As she drags her nails up my neck and into my hair, I growl approvingly from inside my chest. "You can have all my flowers from now on, my king."

"I want the one between your pretty thighs."

"When?"

"Right the fuck now."

Chapter Seven

Aster

After we bathe, he is true to his demand.

I squeeze my eyes shut as I ride the strong, wet muscle in his mouth. My body hums from overstimulation. I cannot take much more—my skin prickles, stretching around my swollen belly; his mouth and tongue explore my wet, pulsing core; And the pregnancy leaves me feverish beyond reason.

"Rome," I whimper, squeezing the bedframe as I rock on his long, thick tongue. His hands hold me up, supporting my body as I shudder and lose balance. I roll backward, using his rough chin at my opening, retreating from my climax. Still scared of it... I do that. It's *so* much.

"You like sitting on your king's face." His voice is rough like gravel and greedy like a flame licking for oxygen. "Come back here. Don't wriggle this little arse away. Don't shy away." Hot, demanding palms trail to my hips, grab and angle them, steering my hesitant movements.

"Rome..." His name is a moan of anguish on my lips. My

temperature spikes, sweat films my skin, as his devious kiss becomes greedy.

As he flicks my clit with his tongue, he quickly stokes the pleasure inside me. Builds heat.

The room gets small. No thoughts. No shame. He rocks me on the firm, wet plane, throwing me into the pit of stimulation. No way out. No escape. The only way forward is through the heart of it to the other side where bliss awaits me.

My core tightens, my pussy undulates around the thrusting of his demanding tongue, and I burst apart, thrashing my head from side to side as my muscles gyrate and convulse.

Bliss...

"Rome. *Oh*. My king."

He laps me gently, helping me ride the pleasure down. "I've got you, sweet creature."

Sighing peacefully, I loosen my hold on the bedhead and just sit on his tongue for a while.

This seems so indecent. So...unnatural. And perfect. He is right. The pregnancy makes me want this, all the time. I am constantly wet for him.

My body is humming, a mindless vessel of pleasure, when he says, "Now that my Silk Girl is relaxed and wet." His hand presses the centre of my back, arching me so his tongue can dip to a private place between my cheeks.

"Rome!" I fist the wooden frame.

He stops. "You drip everywhere. My soaking, little creature." Lifting me an inch higher, he manages to slide out with me on my knees.

"Keep hold of the bed. Stay like that."

Peering quietly over my shoulder, I watch his magnificent, steel-like physique step from the mattress, a naked, all-muscles Xin De man striding across the room. His backside is so firm, perfectly moulded.

He stops by the small cabinet and pours a drink; the sound of a spoon singing on a glass makes me shuffle with uncertainty.

He turns, and I look back at the wall as he catches me ogling him.

"Like what you see?" he purrs.

A blush creeps up my neck. "Yes, Rome."

"I like my name on your lips."

I hear him groan, but don't peer back to watch what he is doing. I merely listen as his heavy breaths gain in volume and then stop...

Shit.

"Rome?"

At the sound of his menacing steps, I risk another glance to view him, powerful in his gait, long, toned legs, and a heavy, veined cock beating at his abdomen, entirely too big to be human. Glossy, too. With something oily? It looks polished.

Stopping beside me, he cups the back of my head and holds the cool crystal to my lower lip.

"Open," he orders, pouring the liquid into my mouth.

Obediently, I swallow.

"Good girl. That's La Mu Leaf serum. It'll help, sweet creature. Relax you."

I peer up at him, feeling shy and vulnerable, finding his gaze for strength. He leans down and kisses me slowly. My eyes close to the reassurance of his affection.

He pulls from my lips to inhale my hair, humming to the scent. "Vulnerability." He straightens. "Look back at the wall."

I do, and my heart thrashes.

It all happens dream-like. I shiver when he trails his coarse hand up and down my spine, my pulse rushes between my ears when his hot, hard body closes in on me, and I freeze entirely when his fingers touch the place... I blink fast.

"Rome?"

"Are you ready to take your king deep inside your body, little creature? So deep you will struggle to know where I finish, and you begin."

He grips my hip with one hand and uses his cock on my

weeping lips, coating the solid, throbbing length in my slick arousal. "I told you that I would introduce you to all the parts of your pretty body that will make you moan for me."

Controlled and slow, he pushes into my other hole, and my eyes pop open with only the stretch of his crown.

I squeeze the wooden board. "My king?" I beg, scared, nervous —everything. All at once.

"Reach your hand back. Claw my thigh."

I intend to when suddenly warmth gathers low in my belly like a soothing whirlpool. A mesmerising presence that brings something pleasantly *numbing* and...

Am I floating?

"My King..." I wriggle. "I feel strange."

A coarse palm moves around my smooth waist, stilling at my swollen abdomen. "It is safe for the heir, but will help you with your first time taking me in your tight arsehole. Numb the pain and loosen your pretty rim for me."

His fingers descend, dipping to my clit where he massages the bead just as he pushes inside me from behind.

I moan for him—hard. Long.

"That's my girl."

There is no air.

And too much.

No space.

Yet, I'm swollen.

I cannot do anything but *feel* him. There is no sting; he made sure of that. Only the feeling of being full, so utterly full—everywhere. And the stretch, the stretch is... exquisite.

Needing more control, he releases my hip and possesses my throat, his arm supporting the front of my torso as he presses me forward with his hips and sinks his throbbing length in until he is flush with my backside. It is as if stones have been set on the base of my pelvis—the weight is otherworldly.

I could crack open.

In half—down the centre.

"You're doing so good, my sweet creature. No need to ever feel jealous. You have taken all of me. Every inch of my manhood. Every possessive cell in my veins. The dustings of my humanity. All of your king. Yours."

The sounds from my throat are endless. My pussy spasms with longing, working the empty space he usually fills. As if he understands, two fingers feed between my wet folds to satiate the needy clenching.

He lifts me from my pussy, two fingers deep, his palm a cradle for my pelvis, his cock taking my weight.

I am suspended by him.

The primal groans thundering against my spine encourage me to rock my hips forward along his attentive fingers and roll backward to welcome his firm, thick length as it impales me.

He starts to move.

Really, really move.

My moans become short like a punch while his grunts match the pounding of his hips as he sets a brutal pace, hard enough to beat sounds through my panting lips.

"Fuck," he growls, almost a roar, taking me hard with real desperation, with the beast on the surface. "Look how well you take me. So relaxed for my cock."

My frantic palms climb the wall behind the bedhead, being lifted beyond the reach of the wooden frame, but it makes no difference. All I can do is brace myself while he dominates me so entirely. I close my eyes and pleasure my king with my willing body, letting him take what he needs, letting him claim. Thrust.

"I love you, my king," I whimper, my voice breaking, my body plummeting into another bottomless abyss of pleasure just as he loses his pace.

"I need you, little creature." He comes inside me, groaning and working his length in and out. "Don't make me jealous! It is unbearable. It is torture."

Ardent hands paw my body, roaming, exploring as he finds his centre and strength.

Steadily, he pulls out excruciatingly slow, and I moan through the thick of my throat, emptied. Lighter. Exhausted.

I struggle to inhale, exhale—to do anything for a long pause while I regain my thoughts. But my ears tingle. So, I know his eyes are on me.

I finally take a big breath.

"*Yes,*" he gushes, "that's very pretty. You are coated in cum, mine, yours."

I don't see how that is pretty.

"Flowers are pretty," I murmur.

I hear his smile as he says, "This is my favourite flower. Like the ones you pick, this is mine, too. Mine." His fingers slide around. "I do not share, understand? Nothing. Not your body. Your scent. Your flowers. Your smiles. Say it?"

Unreasonable...

I must smile at people.

Too fatigued to argue, I mutter, "I am yours," and slump in his hold, exhaustion clinging to my limbs, pulling me down to the mattress, begging me to relent. Sleep.

He lays on the bed with me on his torso.

Curling to the side, I lift my knees and snuggle into his chest. With my mind satiated, my body heavy under fatigue's weight, I inhale him as my eyes finally close...

CHAPTER EIGHT

ASTER

I sit with my knees tucked to the side on his sofa.

Watching my huge, magnificent king sprawled out naked in bed, thick arm slung over his eyes, round bicep framing his chiselled face, is one of my new favourite things to do.

Shuffling in place, I gaze down to study his long, thick cock, lying heavily over his thigh.

It pulses, fills. Expands.

"I can feel the heat of your pretty eyes *in* my cock, little creature." He doesn't move, only talks through a husky first-light tone as his length thickens and rises to attention. "Why are you awake? The fire is barely orange."

"I have something to ask you," I whisper honestly, sitting higher and squaring my shoulders.

I had the same dream last night. The one with the little boy, but this time it was a girl with honey-coloured hair. She was lost in the tunnel with the flickering lights, cradling my upside-down bird.

And she looked just like Tuscany...

"Anything," he mutters.

I smile. "The queen—"

A disapproving growl rattles the room before I can finish my sentence. "Don't talk about my sister right now—"

"Now is the perfect time, my king. We have both had an excellent sleep." I watch his cock deflate and find the entire appendage wildly interesting. So... autonomous.

"Please?" I add.

He stretches out like a great beast, awakening his muscles in a lazy yet powerful way. "What is it?"

"She wishes to see the Redwind and—"

"Absolutely not!"

Words bunch on my tongue. "Rome. Please. I—" I pause, shaking my head; he is utterly unreasonable. Fur men and women, Common communities, and hundreds of people living outside gated sanctuaries still survive.

I press, "This may be the last time I am able to leave The Estate for quite some time. I am getting bigger. *Please.*"

"It is not safe. For either of you."

I find a small growl in my jaw, letting it loose.

He sits up and stares at me. "Did you just growl at me? That was somewhat of a kitten call, sweet creature."

I huff. "I do not believe in quarrelling with you. So, yes, maybe it is not *entirely* safe. But I do not wish to live in a glass dome. I grew up in one. And Tuscan—" I clear my throat when his brows furrow. "*The queen* will adore the journey. Please. We could see the never-ending Windmill Forest."

"No." He rises from the bed, tension a tangible presence rolling across his muscular back. Walking to the drink cabinet, he manifests his dominance and authority with each heavy step. "You don't know what you are asking of me. What if something happens to you? Or to her?"

I stand up on nervous legs, pleading. "What if something *wonderful* happens to me? Or to her? Imagine her smile when she sees the propellers?"

All his muscles freeze.

He goes quiet with his back to me, and silence cracks through the air as I wait. My hope flitters on the electrical current, encouraging my feet toward him—

"No."

I stop midstride. "Rom—"

"I said"—he barks the word— "NO!"

My pulse leaps into my neck.

He hisses, "Fuck." He spins around and heads straight at me, forcing my feet to shuffle backward as he charges.

He catches my neck and drags me to stand before him, using his thumb to crane my chin. Catch my wide-eyed expression. Stare. "I need your pussy pinned to my tongue until you obey and submit to me. It is not your place to heal wounds you know nothing about, not mine, not Tusc—"

A knock at the door severs his warning.

My throat rolls within his fist, my eyes holding his blue stare. Fearless.

Stepping onto his feet, I reach to touch his rough jaw, not letting his temper scare me. He has never hurt me, never laid a hand on me that wasn't welcome.

I gaze up at him. *I am not afraid of you, Rome. I love you so wildly.* "Please."

"Boy," Kong calls.

Rome stares down his long, dark lashes at me, his eyes searing heat that makes my core clench. His threat to dominate me until I submit swirls in his fractured blue gaze, but the love I radiate for him finds a mark. And digs in.

He softens. *"Aster..."*

"Sire?" Kong tries again. "The Silk Girl is about to give birth. She is in the ward as we speak, and Cairo is less than an hour outside of The Estate. You need to prepare."

My eyes veer to the closed door. *"Ana."*

Rome releases me, heading into the washroom. "Do not leave this room without me, little creature. Wait."

I have every intension of obeying him as I dart around, gathering my clothes, dressing in a hurry, throwing on my favourite mauve silk gown.

Dressed. Ready. Cloaked.

I freeze. I stare at his closed washroom door but feel as if I cannot wait. Or perhaps, I don't want to. Through this long pause, something tugs at me. To make my way to her. To be there for her.

Swallowing, I push through the bedroom door and rush past Kong and a Guard.

"Aster!" I hear Rome roar.

Needing to get to Ana, I sprint from the royal wing, down the paths and around the gardens, Odio coasting above me, his shadow a dark patch below my tread.

Inside, my nerves flutter.

That feeling heightens the moment I enter the Silk Girl Ward and see Daisy, Blossom, their Watchers, and Paisley with their hands pressed to a window, peering in.

I pace over.

Through the glass, Ana is lying awake on a high trundle bed, looking both exposed and brave, while a woman in white stitches a smile-shaped wound in her abdomen. Ana nervously chews on her lip but does not appear to be in any pain as she peers past the woman, desperate to find something.

I whip my gaze around the room. It is full of machines, bright lights, but still unsettlingly stark. A woman in coral colours—a Trade nurse—fusses around Ana, and a man in white holds a bundle of— My mouth drops open. A baby. He holds a lovely, tiny baby swaddled in a purple cloth.

I press my palms to the glass that divides us, feeling the floor under my feet shift. My heart twists, but I am unsure what emotion is causing this tight anguish. Happiness? Am I not utterly happy? What do I feel? There is something else, something I cannot identify. Something with a heavy, haunting presence.

What is it?

"Is she well?" I breathe.

"They both are," Daisy answers.

A tear slides down my cheek as the doctor places the babe in Ana's outstretched arms before moving to approve the stitches in her abdomen.

"Would the Silk Girls like to come inside and say a quick hello to the new baby boy?" A nurse is leaning through the door beside the viewing window, looking at us.

"Oh, yes, please," Daisy answers.

And we waste no time at all, flocking into the room and surrounding Ana and her baby. My skin prickles as the cooler air wraps around me. It smells like fresh skin, blood, and lemons, but somehow, their mingling scent is pleasant.

"Look at *you*," Blossom coos softly, touching the babe's flushing cheeks.

"He is divine," Daisy gushes. "You have Meaningful Purpose, Ana. You did it."

The tight feeling has followed me into this room, a dark phantom with no name. It coils itself around me as I reach out and run my fingertip down the inside of a chubby pink palm.

So soft.

Like a pillow.

"He is everything," Ana says, her eyes flooding with awe, her smile filling with tears.

I want to speak but cannot find the words. *Why don't I have words for you, little one?*

Then I see them.

Then I know why.

My eyes pan across as Rome—my Rome, my king—and Master Cairo enter the room, sending ice through my spine, provoking my hand to cradle the swelling at my abdomen. The phantom at my back hisses in my ear, 'For The Cradle, I shall adore all its children equally and with quiet humility. I have no claim over what I provide for The Cradle.'

Daisy's smile falls.

Blossom's chin trembles.

I find a word. "No."

No. No. Not now.

The baby is scooped from Ana's arms by one of the women in coral and set into Master Cairo's.

I look at Ana's face.

I read in a book that we have over two billion muscle cells in our heart. I didn't think it was possible to see them, but it is, because I just saw all two billion cells in Ana's heart break.

"I know what The Crust is now," Ana mutters as her newborn is taken away, her voice vibrating and hollow. "The Crust is a place with a baby that you can keep."

And I know the name of the haunting emotion... The one twisting me, squeezing my heart and wringing it dry. It is grief.

CHAPTER NINE

ASTER

None of us can talk.

There is nothing to say.

Blossom has no optimism to share, and Daisy has no strength to ground us with rationale. I have no stories, no puzzle metaphors, or folktales.

And Ana…

She has nothing.

We watch with helpless eyes as the room clears, doctors and nurses, Rome and Master Cairo with the baby, leaving us alone with her empty arms and hollow expression.

Without a word, Ana twists her face toward the wall. With all two billion of her heart cells broken, I don't think she has enough pulse left for anything.

I reach out my hand, desperate to comfort her, to touch her dark hair, and tell her it will all be okay, but I stop. It won't. I retract my hand. It's not enough. It is unbearably inadequate.

Unable to stay and remain calm, I walk from the Silk Girl

Wing with my head down, the breeze stirring silence around me until I hear two men talking.

Rome...

How could he?

What did I expect?

I knew it would happen. Was warned. Prepared, even. But nothing could have prepared me for that level of... vulnerability. We cannot object, rally together or even mourn.

How do you mourn something that was never yours?

The ache is profound. And even though we are not meant to feel it, it is bottomless.

I follow the building until I get to the edge, listening to the private conversation as it takes place just around the corner.

"Was that necessary?"

I almost collapse under his rough tone, but my spine finds strength in the limestone wall, needing it to hold me upright as Rome speaks with such deep, dark apathy.

"*Sire.* This is the great problem with removing boundaries. One's place in The Cradle becomes confusing." I hear Master Cairo's sigh. "The girls will move on. I assure you. They will focus on their Purpose."

His voice drops, hinting at anger. "You could have waited until the other Silk Girls left the room."

"And protect them from reality? This is life. The babe needs to bond with the Sired Mother as soon as possible. A young Silk Girl can barely care for itself. They are spoiled and have leisure—luxuries. Fed. Bathed. Dressed. A Sired Mother is a mature, highly skilled caregiver. This is what is best for the child. When the Silk Girls finish producing, they will have matured and be ready to take on the important task of raising the children of The Cradle."

I cannot listen anymore.

Strolling away, I head straight for the garden with the rose fields. The one that holds my first memory here in The Estate. When Meaningful Purpose was all I wanted. How has four months changed my desires so drastically?

I beg for the ignorance back. For the bliss of small pleasures, chocolate, reading, and birds. How I wish for the mysteries of love, not this... Not the reality of love. Love creates falsities—expectations that cannot be met. Love betrays.

It is painful and... unkind.

I sit on a disarrayed patch of grass between barricading rose bushes, long arms twist and creep from the trunks. I nestle between them. Pulling my knees up to my chest, I hold on as tears race down each cheek, leaving tracks of salty residue that cling and tighten the skin.

My eyes sting.

"Aster?" Paisley's voice calls from the distance, but I ignore her. Crouching lower, I hold my breath. "Aster?" Her voice gets further away, and I know I can let go—just a little.

I sob softly.

Then, with a gentle thud, Odio lands to my side. My heavy gaze sweeps across to acknowledge him. Taken aback by how close he is, I should be frightened, but I don't have it in me.

Lazily, I reach out a trembling hand and hold it elevated in the air. "Pet."

Odio's piercing eyes target mine, homing in, somehow pecking at all my shattered pieces. Edging closer, he lowers his head and presses his beak to my palm.

A sad smile touches my lip. I trace the smooth surface. It is like polished stone, but warm from his radiant body temperature.

Dropping my knees to the grass, I shuffle to better feel the contours and ridges, before exploring further. I slide my palm down his neck and stroke the feathers at his puffy crest, causing him to shudder.

He likes it.

He steps one talon closer so that I can explore the distinct tactile surface. Soft and airy, weightless, fragile, yet as a whole, can lift this great beast into the skies and carve a path through the Redwind.

More tears prickle my eyes. "How I wish to be an eagle today, handsome boy." I shake my head as the memory of Ana's broken gaze rattles it. "I cannot feel betrayed." A sob punches from my chest. "None of us can. We knew. We were prepared. We were trained for this. Born for this." I look at the skin graft on my wrist. "Born For Silk."

But I wasn't...

The thought is unwelcome.

I was Fur Born.

"Like you," I whisper to the great deity as I smooth his feathers down his chest.

They are going to take my baby, too. Aren't they?

Abruptly, lusty claims and reverent promises echo between my ears:

'Let me make myself very clear to you, little creature. You are *mine*. And this"—his hand pressed over my womb— 'child, is mine. Not The Trade's. Not The Cradle's. Mine!'

Was it a moment of weakness?

What did he actually mean?

Then, the day I sat on Master Cairo's examination table slices through me like glass. I see myself—a silly, little Silk Girl begging for a lord and Meaningful Purpose. Sulking and jealous.

And then he tells me of my mother. She was in love and when her lord rejected her, she ran away. She had children in a Common Community. A baby she was able to keep—me.

But I am not my mother.

I couldn't run from my Collective.

I would never be so selfish to leave Blossom, Daisy, and Ana— and... *Him.*

He needs someone to be tame with. He chose me. If I run from him... The wonderful, sweet parts inside him will be swallowed by the cruel beast they engineered to rule this chaotic world.

My Rome...

He is so much more than even he knows... And I love him. He is the man who pleasures me and holds me at night in thick arms of protection. Who smiles only for me, who loves and feels, who has humanity only for me...

My lower lip trembles.

I cannot escape my duties to The Crown and The Trade else rip my heart down the centre, leaving one scarlet half for Rome. *No.* I cannot do what my mother did.

And I cannot stay like this either.

Every detail in the puzzle eventually creates the same greater picture. No matter what, it ends the same way

With a billion broken heart cells.

Chapter Ten

Rome

"Odio!" I roar before pinching my thumb and forefinger together, whistling for him to show himself. To guide me to her as is his damn duty. But he does not.

I'll kill him. I'll rip his head off and hang it next to his ancestors for this. She is not his!

I stalk across the gardens.

Her useless Watcher and the Guards field out, searching.

Inhaling the thick air, laced with sadness, I catch a hint of her —vulnerability.

The possessive parts inside me sigh, my muscles rolling, satiated that she is nearby.

Good, I need to calm down.

I scare her.

My temper is a problem.

My chin is dragged to the right, as though her presence can grapple me, draw me to her without a single touch. Effortless. She summons me.

I freeze when I step between rose hedges to find her sitting on a sparse patch of grass, hidden low among crowding wiry limbs. Looking sad, she strokes Odio's feathers gently.

Jealousy stirs inside me.

Fuck me, she's pretty.

My muscles jerk to go to her, but I force my feet backward to watch as a tear squeezes from the inside of her eye, escapes into the valley beside her nose, and drips from her trembling upper lip.

Fuck me.

Hate that fucking tear.

"Little creature."

She shoots into the air in search of the voice, her gaze landing on me from over the top of the hedges.

I step into view. My eyes carve a path from her to Odio, who rises to his full height—almost the same as hers—and puffs his chest in obstinance.

I scowl at him.

I'll deal with you later.

"You ran," I grit out. "You ran in your condition." Growling, I warn her. "*Fuck*, the colour I want to turn your arse for that behaviour."

She steps backward, shaking her head over and over. "You took her baby…" Her words tumble through sad lips like immature fruit from a rattling tree. "You—" She hiccups a sob.

I hate that sound.

"I did not take anything," I correct and claim another step toward her, only to watch her recoil. "Stop that now!"

She stiffens and digs her heels into the dirt. Jutting out her chin, she glares at me, flames of burning hatred targeting my soul.

Not love.

Not love…

I clench my teeth on a growl.

Sighing angrily, I strain to manage the rage building through my veins against the heated lick of her gaze. I have to stay in control.

Don't scare her…

"What would you have me do?" I pose and take another step toward her. "Give me your orders, sweet creature. How would you rule The Cradle? Have infants born to women who cannot care for them, have them starving or worse? Have a lack of infrastructure, minerals, and Marshals because men do not want to work in their Trade anymore, seeking something *brighter*. Women want to stay at home with their children, and now we have starving citizens, laziness, under-nourished children, and men with far too much time on their hands creating havoc, aimless, without Purpose."

Her lashes beat as she thinks; the question throws her and confuses her.

I take another step. "The silk gir—"

"Ana!" she barks.

"*Ana*," I comply, though I want that bark coming from her throat when I fuck her between these rose hedges. "Ana takes no ownership," I continue, slowly edging closer to her. "The babe is the property of The Cradle. We do not operate in the best interest of the individual but of the Collective. Do you dispute that? Are we so unkind, little creature? So unfair."

Another step.

Her eyes burn me.

"Don't look at me like that. I will give *you* anything, everything. You once took a bloody heart from a box. It belonged to a usurper who tried to poison me. You claimed it. You became my personal brand of poison. My weakness. I am weak for you, Aster. Don't do this."

Another step.

I snatch her throat in one long movement, pulling a gasping little creature to my chest where I rock her against me as she struggles and hisses. "Stop fighting me."

Sobbing, kitten-growling, punching, panting, she bashes my chest and kicks her little feet into my boots. "You took her baby!" she cries harder. "*Rome*," she says my name, betrayal laced. "No. Why? *Why?*"

My heart squeezes. "Stop, little creature."

She beats my chest and thrashes in my grip. "You took her baby!"

"Stop."

"Are you going to take mine?" She gasps between words. "Are you going to... going to—"

Her—my weakness—sinks in and nearly cripples me. I replace the pain, the hurt—

With anger.

"Stop that! I will make amends," I grit out, unleashed fury coiling around each syllable. Her sorrow grates strips from my veins, every inch of me that is human turning to bloody ribbons. "I will make amends." It is all I have. A promise.

Desperate, she cries, "Am I yours?"

"Yes, dammit!"

"Not The Trade's?"

"No!"

Then she looks up at me, tears streaming down her cheeks... And her eyes. I never want to see them like this ever again. Broken. Like my sister.

"Then we keep our baby, Rome," she says. "We keep our baby."

A growl wrenches from the base of my shadowed soul, rumbling against her tiny form, demanding and dominant.

"Yes!" That is my declaration; the only word I have, the only certainty in my life is that she is mine. The babies that grow in her womb are mine. I am keeping them all.

Whatever the dark deal, whatever I must sacrifice—*whoever*— I will make it happen through blood or bargain, I will not give them up!

My volatile muscles convulse, wanting her soft caress to tame them, but it doesn't come...

Frowning, I stare down my lashes, cup her wet cheeks in my hands, and guide her chin upward.

A pooling violet gaze loses focus on me, reality sinking in. Her forgiveness drifting.

"That look in your eyes, little creature. Hurts more than I can handle. I can bear the bullets, but not your broken heart."

Her head shakes over and over. "No." She isn't in her eyes as she whispers, "I cannot keep my baby and watch you take away my Collective's... I cannot. I don't... Can't."

She goes limp in my arms, the battle stripped from her, her words as defeated as her body feels against mine.

I want to roar. Feel it stirring. "I will take you to the Windmill Forest, Aster." *I will do anything.* "You and Tuscany. I will make amends."

Detached, she says, "And Ana," but there is no hope, no pulse to her words.

It isn't enough for her.

But she will take it.

Fuck.

CHAPTER ELEVEN

ASTER

It has been two weeks since my whole body crumbled in Rome's arms. I let go of something inside… Something I have been trying to get back with each passing day.

Hope.

Hope that I can dance in my love for Rome like rain coating me in the chill of winter and put aside the certainty of watching Daisy and Blossom lose their babes…

And even me.

I know what he says—I will keep my baby—but I don't know what that looks like. It is as foreign a picture as the ones I've seen of the Missing Moon.

A huge rock in the sky?

Surrounded by twinkling lights?

Sounds like a fairytale.

A baby in my bed? In a cot? In a hammock? Surrounded by strangers and on display?

Also a fairytale.

I have not been present. Not with my heart or my body, and *my Rome* has seen this. Felt it. He hunts until he is bloodied each day and gives me that beautiful feeling between my legs each night in the dark without words, but I am half there and half... Not.

I did find a little hope today; I was able to convince Ana to see the Windmill Forest with me.

∽

Outside, red dirt stirs in the air.

Inside the tank, the machinery surrounding me vibrates, low but strong, sturdy and protective, like the growling that comes from Rome's chest when he thrusts into me each night...

I ignore the longing.

Focus on the tank.

On Ana and Tuscany.

This is not my first time in a military vehicle, but it might as well be. I was dazed and feverish the first time, distracted, too. By Rome...

Feels like forever ago.

Rome sits in the centre of the great fortress, a square portal offering him a view of us. One he takes every chance he can.

I don't return his heavy gaze. Can't. Even as I feel the pain beating from his flesh, the distance I enforce affects him—me, too.

You took her baby.

If I look at him, I will show him the wrong emotions, the angry ones threatening to blast and incinerate. If I open my mouth to him, I will say hurtful things; he will let me cut into him, claw at him because I need someone to blame for this... injustice. This... *painful reality.*

It *is* his fault—

And it isn't.

He didn't create The Trade, nor did Master Cairo. They only

manage what was handed to them, both the product of thousands of years of generational conditioning. Like me.

And he is right—I do not know how to rule or what is best for a baby. It makes sense that a child is raised by a skilled, mature caregiver, but... No one will love my baby as much as I will.

Then again, love is not a virtue.

I cannot decide how to feel. Cannot decide what I want. So, I refuse to look at him.

My emotions are too raw. Like weeping flesh, I need time to self-heal.

Snuggling into Ana's side and she into mine, I wrap my arms around my swollen belly as the tank moves up and down the terrain. We agreed to see today as a detail in the puzzle of our lives and will ourselves to appreciate it.

Appreciate the air which smells like oil and metal. The cramped but tolerable space we share with Tuscany and a member of The Queen's Army.

Appreciate the working art of jumbled textures. Smooth metal surfaces, various viewports, firm, green seats, and woven straps that bind utilities to the walls. Tools. Gear.

It feels like a hidden realm.

We both like tanks.

The queen's attention does not dwell inside the tank; instead, it is captured by the blasting Redwind outside. It howls. Whistles. Builds.

Her eyes are pinned to a viewing window.

"Are you nervous?" I ask her and feel Rome's gaze again, as if the sound of my voice is an arrow, and his attention, the target.

A small smile touches her lip, and her amber eyes flick to the graft on my wrist before returning to my face. "Not with you here. I can be brave, too."

"We are just entering the Aquilla Windmill Forest. Look through your periscopes," a motorised voice says from somewhere further inside the tank.

With a big breath, I look through the scope that has a better viewing capacity to the ports. At first, I see nothing but Redwind, then—

Then I see them.

The Windmills.

One after the other.

Encroaching as if they are inches away from colliding with the tank, but then gone in a blur of grey.

Awe fills my chest.

The first time I jumped into the pond at the Silk Aviary, eager to fish out a broken bird, the weightlessness of being in water that deep threw me into another reality. I remember it distinctly. The shift imprisoned my breath. And in the presence of this vast forest of powerful machines, that is how I feel.

Breath suspended.

Glee shapes my eyes.

I dart my gaze quickly between Tuscany and Ana, their attention fixed to the vision outside. Their expressions, soft and smiling, fill my heart with joy.

Healing—not healed. Merely taking a moment to appreciate a spectacular detail in the greater puzzle of The Cradle.

We watch the sky-scraping Windmills chew through the red haze; I don't know how long we travel, from crown-light to last-light.

Time flies by.

But then—

The tank suddenly slows.

I peer forward through the metal sections to find Rome with fierce brows set above dark eyes locked on me. Taking laps of my body from my hair to the swell at my hips, his stare is mine while his chin is turned. He listens to someone further down the giant machine.

His jaw muscles pulse.

Something is wrong...

Energy sparks. I don't like it, but this could be irrational pregnancy senses, but—

When Rome's expression darkens, I realise I am not wrong. My pulse shudders in my neck. I feel I could cough up a butterfly.

Rome nods stiffly.

"There is a storm coming from due north, my queen," the mechanical voice says, and Tuscany leans closer to the front. "We are unable to make it to the Upper-tower without hitting it head-on, so we will need to seek refuge."

"The Trade-tower? Or follow the east coast to the Upper-Tower Port?" she asks.

My brows rise; shocked. I don't know why I am surprised she knows the landscape. Of course, she does. Just as I know details about Rome, The Estate, the lords, and how to pleasure and provide.

She knows The Cradle.

Rome answers, his tone disturbingly even. "We won't make it across the Red Decline before the storm hits. It is one risk"—he stares at me— "or the other." I cannot read him. "We need to park the tank in a nearby Common community for the night."

My eyes widen.

A Common community?

The Endigo boy's face flashes in my mind, the stench, the meat, the wild unkempt scene.

I startle when a horrible, long scratch on the tank rooftop coils around my spine, near bringing bile up my throat. I stare up, surprised nothing has punctured the metal sheeting.

Another scratch.

And another.

Ana grabs my hand.

I turn to see her expression, eyes wide, dark hair tucked behind each ear. "Aster."

"We will be fine," I assure her.

"A Common community?" she whispers, before gazing at my swollen stomach. "You need to hide your belly."

Another scratch.

Rome lifts from his seat, reaching a large arm up to unlock the hatch and standing until his head disappears through it.

"We know," he growls. "Fly."

Odio.

The tank veers, turning a hard left toward the west, the tracks eating at uneven terrain.

I'm looking out the viewport when a windmill comes out of nowhere— And another, and I realise we are travelling through the core of the Windmill Forest. No longer on a designated road.

Unable to keep my eyes away from him, I peer up to see his awaiting mine. Blue. Fractured blue. Far too turbulent, too menacing, to be peaceful and yet... I breathe deeply. At this moment, I realise Rome of The Strait is my gravity. The thing I seek when I am unsure. Steady ground beneath my feet. The light that guides me through uncertain darkness.

He is where I feel most safe.

If nothing else, that is *hope.*

"*My king...*" I find my voice for him, a breathy cadence, in the midst of my nervousness.

"You're safe, little creature," he states. No— he declares, infallible in tone. I would hate to be the man or woman who challenges it.

I nod and gaze at the space between us with disdain, swiftly hating it as much as he seems to. But there is no room to move. We occupy the cramped metal fortress in its entirety.

A roaring wind engulfs the tank like a monstrous force attacking us.

I cup my ears.

Ana and Tuscany do the same.

Gripping my head, muting the gale, I look through the port. I blink.

It's a dense, red vortex.

Spearing my gaze into the Redwind, I make out the shape of a building, quickly coming into view as we approach at a high speed. At the top of the building is a long barb and, atop it, a symbol...

We get closer.

I squint—

It's a cross.

CHAPTER TWELVE

ROME

I never planned on returning to this place, least of all with her. I should burn it to the ground after we leave, mere embers for the Redwind to swallow and digest.

I *despise* these people.

They gifted her to me. They offered their children in exchange for a windmill and supplies, and she wonders why I cannot fault The Trade entirely. I didn't snatch her from her father's paws. He could have kept her, could have tried, but he did not.

They will have to pry her from my bloody corpse before *I* ever give her up.

So, I despise them for not fighting for her, even though their pathetic lack of protection meant she became *mine*. My responsibility.

My little creature.

Aster... Who loathes me.

She can loath me, scream at me, despise my very existence, as long as her moans crash into my mouth each night, and her body succumbs to sleep in my arms. As long...

I growl; I will make amends!

I climb down the tank, dropping to my heavy feet on the old abbey ground, crimson-coloured dust flying up around me. I rise to my full height, towering over everyone else as the roaring wind prowls the boundary walls.

Kong climbs from the other tank, accompanied by three Guards, rifles ready.

Jaw pulsing to the point of pain, I scan the crowd of twenty or so Common who have braved the growling night to gather before the tank, bowing and nervous—curious.

We could cut them all down in seconds with a single round from one rifle.

But they let us in.

Last-light barely claws through the storming Redwind, and the abbey walls blanket the ground, making it hard to see.

Through the dim, my eyes glow as I search the faces for familiarities— for Colt. It has been nearly two decades, but I would recognise Aster's father if I saw him.

"Colt!" I boom, but the chaotic weather matches my force.

A man dressed in black stands below a wooden cross and signals for me to approach, gesturing toward a door.

We can't talk outside, in this black, in the mouth of the night and storm. *Fuck.*

Checking the Guards are ready, Kong, too, I climb back up the tank to get my precious cargo.

The hatch opens before I get to it, a cloaked head popping up, black hair whispering across a masked face.

Teeth clenching, I hold my hand out for her. "You should have waited. I would have carried you."

But she can't hear me. The growling wind circles the perimeter, hunting for a vulnerability in the brick fortress.

I take her little hand in mine, remembering when I first touched her months ago. Delicate fingers. Dainty wrist.

I watch her step to the top.

Aster's purple cloak is buttoned from knee to neck, barely

concealing the swelling between her hips. Still, she is small, and it's evident by the stretching fabric.

Impatient and protective, I scoop her into my arms and climb down with her.

The Guard takes my place, helping the other Silk Girl and a member of The Queen's Army from the tank. And Kong waits for the queen—my sister. I don't like this, any of it, but we have no choice.

The Common part for me.

Wide eyes tracking. Interested.

Every inch of muscle inside me is on edge—tightening, protective, warm, longing—for Aster's soft body against mine as I carry her toward the man who waits, waving us over.

Ducking beneath the wooden door frame, I follow him into the church.

The wind's fierce presence becomes a drone of white noise when the door closes behind us. An unavoidable sense of history replaces the storm's angry energy. I couldn't give a shit about it, but I am aware of it in the stained-glass windows and the high vaulted ceilings, nonetheless.

This place is old.

Pushing further into the vast space, I set Aster down on a pew. Guard her.

I look the man over. Salt and pepper hair. Fine lines beside his eyes. A casual linen shirt tucked into faded-dark trousers—aged clothing that he admires and cares for. "You open your gates without question," I state smoothly, clasping my hands together and widening my stance. "Did you know who I was?"

"*Sire.*" He bows. "No. I couldn't see the vehicles through the haze, only hear the horn blasting, but anyone outside in this weather would be welcome. Typically, we would offer aid from the boundary walls, but it's life or death out there on days like these."

I sneer; inconceivable. "You would risk your people's lives for the lives of strangers?"

"People are inherently good."

Imbecile.

Abruptly, Kong, my sister, and the others enter, the storm's rage blasting until the door is pushed close again.

White noise.

The Silk Girl rushes to sit beside Aster, quick to fold my little creature's cloak over her swollen abdomen, fussing, and I'm fucking jealous. Of every touch. Of Aster's smile for her.

I haven't had that smile.

Not for weeks.

I would drown in that smile...

Love sick fool.

"Where is Colt?" I ask, directing my attention to the man ahead of me, ignoring my twitching muscles, the ones that yearn for her attention.

"Sadly, we lost him to illness several months ago. I am Han. Did you know him well, Sire?"

I hum, locking my teeth.

Odette? Her name comes unbidden, but I do not utter it aloud. I want to wait out the storm without any further attention.

"We will wait out the storm within your walls," I advise. "Then be on our way."

"The church is welcome to all." Han opens his arms. "You can sleep on the pews, make yourselves comfortable."

"What is this place?" Aster's voice, a soft, breathy cadence, sails from behind me.

Aster...

When I turn, she is on her feet, mask hanging around her neck, purple-dusted eyes filled with awe.

"You have never seen a church before?" Han asks, taking a step closer.

Like hell, you can speak to her.

My eyes cut to him. "You don't speak to—"

"My king." Her tone asks me to hold my temper, and I do. Her fingers slide along my flank, offering me the soothing touch I've been mourning. "Look." She points.

I follow her soft gaze to a door cracked open with three girls peeking through, watching us.

"Hello," Aster says to them. "Come."

"You should be asleep, girls." Han waves them in with a soft chuckle. "Since you're awake, please, come in. Remember your manners. We bow for the King of The Cradle."

"Rome of The Strait, The Cradle's Monarch and Protector," the Guard beside Kong announces.

Slowly, the small, frightened girls step from inside the room, one by one, bowing at me. Awkward. They vary in age. From mere children to Aster's age and older. Moving closer to my little creature with skittish steps, they try to avoid stepping too close to me.

Too close.

Aster nods, encouraging. "We won't hurt you. Come here."

They are entering the clearing between pews, when one gasps, grips the arm of another, and squeezes it. "It's the queen."

Wonder-filled eyes shift to the door where Tuscany has lowered her hood to her shoulders, the fabric bunching around her neck.

The girls freeze when they see the looming presence behind her—Kong—and the Guard, holding rifles the size of their legs.

"Stay by the door," Tuscany orders her two Xin De protectors. "You scare them."

As my sister approaches, graceful and smiling softly, I watch Common girl after Common girl step from inside the door beyond the pews, dressed in nightgowns, holding each other, excitement and nervousness playing across their expressions.

"Oh, you're *all* awake." Han shakes his head, rolling his eyes before looking at me. "The girls like to sleep together in the church when there is a heavy storm, which is often."

"We have seen your picture." A girl gushes and curtsies—clearly for the first time. "You're even more beautiful."

Another flusters. "I made a crochet eagle for you when I was five. I still have it. Do you want me to get it? It is in my room."

And another. "I heard you love chocolate. We have one block that we save for a special occasion. I can get it for you, my queen."

A gush. "Oh, I love your hair."

A swoon. "You're so pretty."

"Can we read to you?"

"Or dance for you?"

Fuck me...

CHAPTER THIRTEEN

ASTER

They adore her.

Their Queen of The Cradle.

While the men and the large woman from The Queen's Army watch from a few benches away, Ana, Tuscany, the girls, and I huddle together, sharing stories and chocolate.

A slumber party, they call it; it should be called a 'trying not to slumber party.'

Rome has his arms folded across his broad chest and his long legs stretch out in front of him, crossed at the ankles, refusing to sleep.

Kong's deep voice vibrates through the room. "Sleep, Sire. We will take shifts."

Rome stares at me and blinks his nictitating membrane once. "No."

I glance back at the women and girls sprawled out, some on the floor, others on the benches. All want to be close to the queen.

The Common girls—Fur Born like me—know the wildest stories. Horrible stories and wonderful ones. Of spirits and devils.

357

Of a man named Jesus who could turn water into wine. I would be beyond endeared by him had he turned water into honey, but it is a fancy story, nonetheless.

Hours pass.

The Missing Moon must be at its topmost perch in the night sky. Most of the girls have returned to the back room, a few others doze on blankets between the benches, close by. Ana is curled on her side, head on my lap, breathing deeply in the pit of sleep.

"I have a story," a young girl with ashy-blonde hair says, leaning into the huddle, words low and careful. "But Han doesn't like these ones. You know Endigos like to tell stories."

The girls nod.

I knew that, too.

The Endigo boy liked hearing mine. As I told him about Odio, his eyes lit up like the lanes of The Estate during a carnival.

She hushes the quiet chatter. "There is an old Endigo legend that the elders tell the young ones. It is about an Endigo boy who ate his baby sister as she was being birthed."

An older girl shuffles, uncomfortably. "We are in church, Colleen."

"I know, Susan, so we must whisper," Colleen says with a wicked, playful grin. "As punishment for feasting on his own, he was lashed back to bones and sent to the Horizon."

Susan pales. "*Stop.* You will give us nightmares."

"Come sit beside me," the queen offers, tapping the spot beside her. "I will protect you."

Susan tries to hide her excitement. "Um, *okay.*" She stands and sits beside Tuscany, her cheeks now full of excitable colourings.

"*So,*" Colleen begins. "He was sent to the Horizon. The Redwind should have killed him, bled him dry, but because he had no flesh left, he lived. A walking a skeleton." They gasp. "The elders say that if you dare venture into the Horizon, you will hear his bones rattling in the wind moments before he tries to pull you in. He wants to wear your skin so he can return to The Mainland once again. So, never, ever walk the Horizon. Unless you have no skin."

Eww.

One of the younger girls curls her nose, cringing. "Why are the stories always about children dying? Why not fully grown men?"

"Because"—Colleen shrugs sad— "We care more for children than fully grown men. We don't worry about them at all."

Another girl nods. "Children are more vulnerable and—

"Fragile," I agree, subtly holding my belly. I look over at Rome who has fatigue clinging to his strong brow and creeping into his gaze.

Our eyes meet.

At some point, he was a child. It makes me wonder... At what point do boys become men? At what point do we stop caring? Do they feel the shift in their hearts? Their outsides get big, intimidating, and strong, but inside— I sigh as he blinks, fighting the night-time pull to keep his gaze on me. *Inside*, he is still that young boy.

His eyelids fan his eyes.

Slowly, I watch him lose his battle, the gravity of sleep dragging him under. Asleep and yet, somehow still scowling, still intimidating.

"I know one."

I am smiling at sleeping Rome when I look back to see a woman approaching from a darkened corner of the church, dressed in dark pants and a dark dress-shirt, red dust on her leather shoes, sweat sparkling on her forehead.

Where has she been?

It's the depths of night.

I blink at her.

My skin prickles. My bully gauge comes out of retirement, warning me of strange intentions.

"And it is about a half man, half eagle," she adds. Sitting down on the bench in front, she twists to look back at me. I cannot quite figure it out, but... I don't feel right. My pulse climbs into my neck; I don't know why. And I don't know why she is staring at me. "The tale goes that this man visits the Endigo and asks them to do horrific things... He is a ruler, you see. He gives the Endigo permission to hunt women, allows them to keep the bodies, the flesh, so he can steal their babies."

"What does he want the babies for?" I find myself asking, quiet, my pulse nesting in my throat.

"For The Trade, of course."

"I think that is enough stories for the night," the queen says, yawning softly. "Aster. Go sit—"

"Your eyes..." The woman's voice is a soft gasp, still staring at me, strange and intense. "Violet. You—" Her eyes veer over my shoulder to sleeping Rome, then return to me. "Are you allergic to anything, Silk Girl?"

I clench my teeth, everything tensing.

How does she...? No. I will not answer. Will not play along.

I lift my chin. "Are you trying to frighten me? Is this a trick?"

"Aster needs to sleep." Tuscany stands. "Aster, please, go sit with Sire. Sit with Rome. I will sit with Ana on my lap."

As I slide Ana from my thighs, my shuddering pulse making it hard to breathe and not bolt away, the girl stands at the same time.

"Wait. I asked him to take her..." Her voice is haunting. "I never knew it was his plan all along."

All the girls are quiet now.

Tuscany tries to find words.

I walk away from her, a sick feeling rushing through my entire body as images and stories whirl through my psyche.

Fur Born girl.

Mother ran away...

'She was an exceptional breeder, after all, The Trade invested much time and resources in her. Unfortunately her babes were not born for The Cradle but for a Fur community. You were one of those babes. We got you back.'

I grip the bench, steady myself.

"Little creature?"

Rome is awake, rising to his feet, but his eyes are no longer on me, for the first time, in weeks, his eyes are not where he promised they would always be. They are on her.

Dark and disturbing.

I glance between the woman and Rome, reading the significant message. The truth attacks me, and not a single one of my billion heart cells avoid the dreadful blow.

They know each other— Rome and the woman. The story is true... Is he the half eagle? Am I one of the babies?

"Is it her?" The woman's chest rises and falls, the air seemingly as heavy as her question. "Is that my baby sister?"

No. No.

My molars saw together.

Stop. Stop.

Rome holds his hand out for me while his eyes plunge hatred into her. "Come here, little creature. Come stand by my side." His deep timbre is like ice, cold and hard, and one punch away from shattering.

The woman swallows. "How many babies have you taken over the years? Hundreds?"

"Odette." Han raises his hands, shock and confusion drawing his brows to his hairline. "What are you doing? Sire"—he looks at Rome— "she means no disrespect—"

Suddenly, two shots of a gun ricochet outside the church walls, the girls drop to the floor between benches, whimpers rush along the ground, and Rome's head snaps to the door.

"Who did you let in?"

The men lurch upright, Kong and the Guard moving to either side of the window, rifles braced and ready. Discreetly, they risk looking outside.

"I didn't approve anything," Han states, his polite smile flattening into a thin line.

My heart races.

A mechanism attached to the Guard's vest crackles with static and then a word. A word that chills the length of my veins.

Endigos.

"How many?" Rome asks.

"Twenty." Kong peaks through the window, then leans back, concealing his location. "Thirty."

Rome shoots his gaze to Han. "Where are the men in your community? Where are they right now? Armed?"

Han swallows over a ball of guilt. "Everyone will be in hiding. The women. Men. They have their own vaults. Secret rooms. We decided as a community to wait out raids. Not to defend. To rebuild. We don't fight, Sire."

"Fuck," Rome bites.

The Guard presses his back to the wall, savouring a moment. "Do you think they followed us from Ruins E? We were careful."

"We cut off the road. They have Snakes all across the desert." Kong frowns with a nod. "Perhaps they saw us."

Suddenly, guns reel off outside the church, one after the other, over and over.

Events throttle faster than my shallow breaths. The girls crawl along the church floor toward the mysterious inside door. Rome has me in his arms, Kong has Tuscany, and the Guard has Ana.

"Let me protect them," Han begs Rome, pointing toward the room where the other women flock. "There is a chamber—a bunker. Full of our old relics, tombs, everything sacred to us. In case the weather wins. They will be protected down there."

"Not out of my sight!" Rome barks.

"She will be safe. As God is my witness."

"Boy,"—Kong warns, using his thick arm to cover the queen's head as more shots roll from rifles outside the walls— *"Listen."*

Han's expression breaks. Desperate. "Believe in the good. In me. Let me protect the Silk Girls and the queen."

Rome looks at me. Stares. "I know you care for all. I know you. But..." His voice breaks in a way that snatches air from my lungs.

"The piece beneath your feet, Aster. The piece beneath your feet. Protect it for me."

With a growl of utter defeat, Rome lowers me to the ground, his hands suddenly everywhere, mapping, remembering.

A frightened Tuscany and Ana are both set down, and we are swept away by Han. The throttle of events stops completely when I get to the door.

Grip it.

Turn back...

"Come with me," I beg.

Now time stalls and everything happens in four heart beats—

One.

Rome's eyes score across me, from the fear in mine, to the black strands tousled down my shoulders and back, to the swell at my hips, and the piece of ground beneath my feet.

Two.

"That piece," he mouths to me.

Tears burn the backs of my eyes.

Three.

And I stare at *him*—memorising—the black armour conceals his bulk, but I know every inch of his muscles, every scar, every hair, all the tension, all the twitches. I know him. My Rome. Mean. Cruel. Unapologetic. A warlord. A ruler.

And mine.

Go to him. Go to him.

Four.

Han closes the door.

Rome disappears outside.

CHAPTER FOURTEEN

ASTER

Tears mist my vision as we scramble through a metal hatch into an underground chamber. The lights flicker once, or maybe, it was my imagination.

I stare at the trapdoor, knowing that in a few moments, an hour, or more or less—I don't know—it will open again.

And someone will be on the other side.

I do not know who...

I cannot change what happens on the other side of that metal door. I have absolutely no impact on those events. I can only control what I will do on this side, on how I will react.

Meltdown?

Fall apart?

Imagine the worst?

Reel in his lies...

I once was told, if I'm ever unsure how I feel, I should toss a puzzle piece in the air and will either be pleased or disappointed by the result.

Colour side up, I forgive him.

Blank side up, I cannot forgive him.

But as I stare at the hatch, deaf to the surrounding commotion from the girls, it is crystal clear without the puzzle piece—half of my heart is out there fighting for our lives.

If somehow, he can feel me down here, I only want him to feel love.

Spinning around, I face the large concrete room. At first, I can barely absorb the details of the enclosure, but I feel it's confinements. The windowless space presses on my chest.

Focus.

I scan the room presented like a small house, with all necessities and cabinets with old books and gold, except... If we need to fight— If the hatch is blown open— Are there any weapons?

"Are there any weapons down here?" I ask Han, my voice uniform and empty.

He opens a closet, displaying a single rifle, and I almost laugh. "We don't believe in murder."

"Right," I mutter, hollow. "Your king will do that for you. How convenient."

The Common girls are climbing onto bunks, staring at me while Ana stays close to my side, seemingly knowing better than to fill the moment with words, or perhaps the glaze in my eyes is frightening them all... What I am willing to do to protect them— to protect him—is frightening me, too.

To my left, Tuscany is with the woman from her Army. That is good. We might need her. She can help me. She is strong and capable. I note that.

But not Tuscany—her complexion is pale, her hands are clasped below her neck, and her fingers are rubbing together. I wonder if she wishes for her toy eagle. I am not one to judge. She has been so brave, but the cracks are showing. This is all my fault; I pushed her to venture outside.

The woman from earlier approaches me while I measure the situation. "I'm Odette. I think I am your sister..."

I glare at her. "And Rome is my king. I need you to leave me alone. I cannot think straight."

She steps within an arm's length of me, but not before Ana slides between us, blocking her. "She said leave her alone. You should listen."

The woman's gaze sweeps past Ana to my belly; my jacket has fallen open, displaying the large swell between my hips.

"Is that my niece or nephew?" Her face lights up, her hands invading my space. "Can I?"

I jerk backward. "Stop. Don't touch me."

Ana shoves her a few steps away. "What do you think you're doing?"

The woman sneers. "I only want to know the baby... You let him touch you?"

"Girls." Han moves to stand beside us, his hands held in the air, ready. "I know nothing of what you speak, but the queen is here. We need to listen to her."

Everyone looks at Tuscany.

"The queen is very tired. And has a small headache." I move to Tuscany's side and guide her to one of the bunks, a girl bouncing from it quickly for her queen. "Lay down." I cover Tuscany with a blanket, protecting her fragile state from their eager eyes.

Feeling anger bubble, I whirl around to confront the woman —*my supposed sister.*

"I let the king touch me, yes. It is my duty and my pleasure. That is my king. Your king! And the man out there fighting to protect your compound and you. What do you think will happen if they find us?"

The woman lifts her chin, proud. "They will kill us. We will go to heaven."

I scoff. "I know nothing of your heaven, but let me tell *you* a story... They won't just *kill* you. They will keep you alive. Live meat. They will rape you, all of you. They will take little pieces from you day by day and rape you without limbs. Then, when you are no more than a head on a torso, they will kill you. It's not just a story. It's a fact. I've seen it. And my..." Tears fill my throat. "*Your king is out there fighting for us. You will respect him!*"

Tension zaps through the air.

"He has brainwashed you." She grips her hips. "I just want to know you. I didn't want to give you away to be a... a concubine."

I grit my teeth. "You're terrified. And angry. I will forgive your disrespectful words, but you will be silent now."

Ana's cheeks glow dark red, furious. "We are Silk Girls, not concubines. Our Trade is highly respected. *We* are highly respected. Things are not what you think. You place no regard on the collective of The Cradle, only on yourselves. We serve The Cradle. Sire serves The Cradle. You serve yourself."

"I serve God. Not myself," she corrects.

"Good for you," I growl, and it does sound like a kitten-call. "Give him a rifle and have him defend us then—have him defend your king!"

She fists her hands at her sides. "Why do you think we even have a bunker? I will tell you. We built it after the first big raid that killed dozens of women and men and our priest! Turin of The Strait organised that raid on our community. An Endigo boy from the desert told me. He killed my mother—*our* mother!"

"And Rome killed Turin." Tuscany's voice soars from the far bunk, wrapping around my rage-fuelled body, squeezing me into coils of anguish.

My gaze softens when I find her sitting up, her words quiet, melodic, and *pained*.

"For all his crimes against humanity," she says. "*Sire* avenged us all. Now, you will sit down and be silent. I order this of you."

There is no outward sound, but I swear I still hear every girl in the room gasp before accepting complete silence.

"You can see them." Han's uncertain utterance kicks me right in the chest, demanding my attention.

I blink at him. "Pardon?"

"I would usually watch, but I feel I am out of my depths. Perhaps, uninformed. Naïve, even. You can prepare us." He clears his throat, regret and humility sinking into his gaze. "You seem to be experienced. Mature beyond your appearance. If you think we need to prepare for a loss, you can watch the compound square so we can be ready when the hatch opens."

My eyes widen.

With slow steps, he walks to a pipe. He swizzles it. It's a periscope, similar to the one in the tank. My heart leaps into my throat, and I race to the cylindrical contraption fixed to the ceiling.

Pressing my eye to the blurry eyelet, it takes a moment for me to align my vision.

I finally focus and recognise the square, and every wisp of air expels from my lungs when I see the litter of Endigo bodies and Rome's tank on fire...

Chapter Fifteen

ROME

Don't kill the Common.

Don't kill the Common.

It will hurt her...

It is hard to know the difference between the few Common residents ducking for cover under the riotous thunders of war and the unruly Endigo sprawling from their trucks in the dozens.

They raid.

They loot.

We hover in the shadows.

Pick them off one by one.

Kong and the small amount of Guard we have are worth ten Endigo with their corroded rifles, rattling off bullets from untrained hands.

Still, odds are one bullet will find a mark.

But she is safe...

That is what matters.

I duck behind the blazing tank, crouching with my rifle to my chest. Men are dying, their death groans and shots ride the howling wind.

The flaming military vehicle illuminates the wind-swept night, casting shadows on the walls, on the ground, distracting and confusing the Endigo. Embers spark into the air, flying and whipping in an almost ethereal wave.

I survey the area.

A man ahead of me.

In the crook of an arch.

Not Common.

To not give my position away, I come up behind him and knock him unconscious with the butt of my rifle. He drops. I step on his cranium as I stride forward, braced and ready for more.

At my left shoulder, rounds rattle off.

At my right, glass smashes.

Her...

She is safe.

Shifty figures gather in pockets of the shadowed compound, the lick of fire from the tank highlighting them every so often. Enough for me to count. One. Two. Three. Four.

Rounds run to my side, prefacing a screech from the sky and then deep, hysterical shouts—"Help me! Help me!"—that battle the wind.

Behind a brick pillar, I scout. I watch the terrified Endigo as he is lifted from the ashy abbey grounds by talons skewed through his neck. Odio hovers in the Redwind and jerks the body around, the heavy weight of it tearing along talon-made incisions, like popping stitches open at a seam.

Gory. Perfection.

The body drops.

Then the head.

Odio swoops for another.

That's my good boy.

Pained whimpers hurtle from my left, triggering me in an

unusual way; I wouldn't usually risk my position to save one—one individual being too fucking noisy.

But *for her*, I snap my gaze to chase the sound, finding a woman scurrying backward on her arse as an Endigo looms over her, foaming at the mouth, knife spinning in one hand, his belt buckle unfastening in the other.

I dart through the shadows and approach him from the rear, using the muzzle of my rifle to skewer him through his fleshy centre. Blood sprays the woman's face, and she howls in terror, drawing attention to herself.

And me.

Rounds rattle at my side. Kong is suddenly there, unloading bullets into an assembly of shady forms, but not before something hits the back of my leg, the side of my arm, somewhere in my shoulder.

I let loose a bellowing growl of anger—not pain. Too much adrenaline to feel pain. I whirl around with my body bulked to my full size and charge the remaining two. The advancing Endigo freeze under the sight of me. Upon them with a roar, I punch my fist into a dirty face, cave a skull inward, before lashing to the other, grabbing a throat and squeezing until a tongue and an eye pop outward.

Blood raves between my temples.

But she is safe.

While Kong roars from somewhere in the abbey, I step over the body of one of our Guards, half his entrails hanging from his middle.

Cracking my neck from side to side, tension carving up my veins like a blade, I stalk toward another huddled figure, unfazed by the rapid staccato of another rifle being unloaded.

Again, I hear Odio screech as he darts for the ground, but this time, the sound bends and contorts into something guttural and pained. The noise seizes me. My eyes hit the sky, where I watch Odio falling, upside down, his body tumbling out of control until he hits the dirt, lifting a mist of red.

Fuck.

No!

Rushing toward the mound of dark ruffled feathers, I take another bullet in my side. Outnumbered. We. Are. Outnumbered.

The abbey, the tank, and the fire begin to blur as I stride. Suddenly, my feet seem to shuffle, not lift. My upper body charges forward, but the weight of my injuries fills my shoes with cement, and I drop to my knees. I go to stand but can't. I reach out my hand toward him. He is not moving. I growl at myself, at my feet, at my knees, not working.

Dammit!

The weight is an unyielding force, and with each passing moment, it builds more depth and adds more concrete to my body.

Focus.

Odio.

I am closing my eyes and shaking my head, demanding the blurry visions dissolve… when the gates to the community open and a light fills the void, making me squint, and then tank tracks roll past me… A Trade tank.

My spine gives way.

My torso hits the dirt.

CHAPTER SIXTEEN

ASTER

My hands shake violently as I lower them from the scope.

Blink.

I know what I just witnessed. My eyes took in the dense, shadowy scene. The fire and wind combined created waves of flickering lights that helped me see, however, intermittently.

I saw. Odio dropped to a heap, and Rome took bullets, so many bullets, trying to get to him right before the Trade arrived with reinforcements and blocked my view with a giant tyre track.

I saw it... But while I *saw* it, my heart and soul are not tearing, not shredding, my subconscious denies my eyes. He isn't dead. I would know.

"Aster? What did you see?" I hear Han, but his voice is far away, or maybe I am drifting.

I answer his true question—he is not asking about Odio or Rome. He asks whether it is safe.

"It's safe," I mutter before spinning, singularly focused, to find the other person who shares my concerns.

Tuscany is walking toward me, the ghost of worry in her

amber gaze. I see my emotions reflected in her glassy pools of love and fear.

Hollow, I mutter, "He was shot."

She covers her gasp. "Where?"

My head shakes over and over, remembering all the bullets. So many. In his back. Side. Leg.

"Everywhere," I say, my throat tightening. *No. No. Not now. Do not break in half now.*

I refuse to believe it.

I am breathing, and so he must be, too. He must be breathing, existing. I cannot have a mind, a consciousness if he does not.

I swallow over the ball of hot, angry tears. Absently, I lift my gaze to the hatch as it opens. To release us. Free us.

Detached.

The girls climb out.

Detached.

The room empties.

Detached.

I am suddenly on the surface.

Detached.

I am walking outside through the grave of the storm, the wind quieter, surrounded by activity, lights from vehicles, Trade personnel, Endigo's being arrested, doctors tending to wounds, and—

Beyond a gathering of people, within a protective circle, I see *his* boots on the ground.

I lurch toward him.

"Odio." I hear his guttural word, twisted with longing and grief, the sound wrapping around my throat, choking the tears from me.

They rush down my cheeks.

Distraught, I watch as Kong carries the great deity toward Rome, setting the lifeless bouquet of silvery feathers beside him on the red dirt.

They lay side by side.

The king and his eagle.

On his back, while a doctor removes his bloodied leather armour, Rome reaches out his hand, but it looks hard, as though his bones strain under the weight of his muscles.

A rough sigh leaves his mouth as he touches Odio's crest and begins to stroke the feathers, soothe his friend and shadow who isn't moving at all.

"Good boy. I never thanked you."

As I slowly approach him, tears stream down my cheeks, twin tracks that drip over my trembling upper lip.

"Aster."

"I'm so sorry." I begin, the words crumbling through my lips. "It was my idea to visit the windmills. If I had—"

"*Shh.*"

While the Trade doctor works on Rome's bullet wounds, digging in, removing, stitching, and sealing, I drop to my knees at his other side. My mauve dress fans out across the red sand.

Beside Odio.

Odio, who is upside-down.

Talons curled in tight, frozen.

His usually piercing eyes are lost in the presence of death, a depthless nothing that I wish to never see again. Tears blur the world. "He is upside-down, Rome." I bawl. Upside down.

"Come closer," he orders, "touch me."

Stay strong.

With a trembling hand, I reach out and touch Rome's face. His cheek is cold, so I press my palm to warm the cool surface.

"I never stroked him," he says to me. "But you did. You make everything, everyone, happier."

Pain fills my throat. "H-he lov-loved you, Rome," I squeak. "He was such a loyal boy."

Rome lifts his hand to cup my cheek, his thumb tracing my wet lips, and I lean into his clammy touch. "Don't cry, sweet Aster."

"*Rome.*"

"*Aster.*" He almost smiles, but it is too peaceful, too lethargic. I hate it. "Aster. My Aster. *Fuck me*, you're pretty."

"Stop. You're going to be fine. A few bullets cannot kill Rome of The Strait."

He inhales hard.

My wide eyes slide over him, to the blood on his throat and splashed across his chest, to the dark pool creeping out from under him, conquering the red dirt—

Shaking my head, my eyes refuse to accept the vision. My giant king. My beast. My Rome.

"Did I make amends?" Blue eyes stare through me. "Do you forgive me, little creature?"

Yes. I nod over and over and over. "Yes. Yes. Yes, but only if you get up now. You have to get up. I need my king."

His gaze rolls to my swollen belly, his hand slips from my cheek to the mound, and he presses his palm to it, cradling his unborn child. "He is going to do great things."

"And you're going to watch him do them."

"*Rome...*" Tuscany's voice spills from behind me moments before she kneels on the old abbey grounds, her shoulder touching mine.

His glassy, fractured blue eyes pan to her. "My sweet sister." He rasps as the doctor stabs a tube into his upper ribcage. A hiss escapes the puncture hole. "Do you forgive me?"

"Please, please." I sob, choking on my tears. "Stop talking like this."

"I never blamed you, Rome." Her voice cracks down the centre. I look at her as sorrowful streams course down her smooth, tanned cheeks. "Not for a second. Please just keep breathing. You were made for this world, remember? Indestructible."

My eyes sting, pools clouding my vision of him as he reaches for my face again. I help him, holding his big, cool palm to my wet cheek.

He isn't warm.

But he is *always* warm...

"I got to love you and be loved by you." His eyes are glossy and dazed as if he is staring into a brilliant fire when he is merely staring at me. "If The Crust is a place, little creature. It is where I spend my days making you smile."

My heart breaks, and I crumble to his chest. Not just hearing his words— But feeling them.

"Ready." The doctor's voice is directed over my head. "We need to get him into the tank now and to the Trade-tower. No one else. Just Sire. We need all the space for medical personnel. You understand, my queen?"

No. A bit more time.

When three men slide Rome onto a stretcher, his hand slides from me, its absence mournful. I stumble to my feet to catch his expression, but his eyes… His eyes.

They are closed.

They carry him to the tank, and my entire body trembles. My eyes believe the scene now, finally caught up with my brutal reality.

And I wonder if this is some kind of message from The Cradle. For breaking my vows. For wanting more than is offered. For jealousy and trying to change the order of things. For asking questions, loving and being loved. And for envisioning first-lights with a baby in a cot beside our bed.

Is this punishment…

Then Tuscany puts her arm around me, and Ana stops on my other side. We stand as a Collective, watching the tank drive away with our king inside.

CHAPTER SEVENTEEN

ROME

Closing my eyes in the square of the old-world abbey, only to open them in the highest tech laboratory in The Cradle, is quite the fucking contrast.

Access to this underground centre beneath the Trade-tower requires a biometric scan, but doctors continue to crowd inside to view their king's latest additions. No—*enhancements*. Aster called them enhancements, so that is what they are.

As I stare at my reflection, bare chest and dark pants, it dawns on me that I appear more like my father, Turin of The Strait, than ever before. Huge. Broad across the chest, carved and marred; long arms and massive hands that have felt death. Titanium plate in my left shoulder. Magnesium alloy in my shin.

Bullets as trophies.

This is what a king looks like.

At least, that is what I always believed.

Eyes scale my form. Watch each large breath. My new lung has the doctors nodding approvingly. The success of it is mainly due to its biocompatibility—Xin De genus approved.

This laboratory is spacious yet utilitarian. The walls leading to the centre are painted dark grey, and the corridor lights are dim— a warren of ambiguity. However, inside the research areas, the overhead beams spot even the dust.

My monstrous size casts a shadow. I peer down at it, grief striking, sinking its essence into my cells like a poisoned blade. *Odio.* My shadow for nearly two decades. Dead. Gone.

Shutting my eyes, I breathe through the anguish in my chest. The restricting pressure. I fight the urge to clutch at it.

I remind myself that Aster is safe. Imagine her face, her smile, her lips, her soft body writhing beneath mine, visions that will ease this tight, painful mourning.

She is safe...

Aster and Tuscany have been escorted back to The Estate under Kong's watchful guard... I don't like it, but if I trust any man, it is him.

I fucking love her.

I stare at myself, frowning.

So, while I appear more like Turin in this moment, I am nothing like him. I *feel* deep affection, deep jealousy, and deep rage. My temper has always been a problem; I was never apathetic.

Rome of The Strait.

The Volatile King.

"We require some privacy." Cairo approaches, dressed in his purple robe, strolling smoothly, unhurried, circling me like a noose as the doctors leave the room.

"You look like a king, Sire." He muses. "I always know where you are. When I heard of the storm, I sent tanks out after you."

"Very considerate."

He laughs and stops in front of me. "I will keep you alive, Sire. It is my duty to The Cradle. And you happen to have a pregnant Silk Girl and the queen with you. Traveling with very precious possessions. I am surprised, given your affection for them both."

The knowing words slide through me, weigh me down, heavy with meaning. "Say it, Cairo."

His brows lift to his hairline. "Have I ever lied to you, Rome?"

"I have never caught you."

He laughs again. "You are lying to me."

"Aster and I—"

His lip quirks. "Aster and I?"

Turning to face him, I widen my stance, expanding my shadow until it creeps toward his shoes. "Will keep our heirs in The Estate," I continue, staunch. "We will raise them. They will each be given an eagle and a Guardian. This is the way I want it. And the Silk Girls from her Collective will have access to their babies."

He stares at me, a smile sliding into place. Fit for a Trade Master. "I've been waiting for you to say that. I told you I know you, and it is true. Part of my Trade is to understand you, your motivations and your needs." He clasps his hands at his waist. "If we put babes in citizen's arms, the people are weak. If we allow Silk Girls to nurse, we lose them as breeders. Girls cannot focus on a man when a babe is present. History shows this."

I deadpan, give nothing away.

For once.

"But put all that aside," he adds, standing with seamless confidence despite my towering physique. "We are also still healing the land. The ruins have communities in the thousands. Tens of thousands in Ruins E. And across The Mainland, the Half-tower regresses, and pockets of land are overrun with Endigo, unmonitored and uncharted. We do not have the resources to warden them all, so as long as they remain peaceful, we leave them to their own devices. Correct? Use them when we need, but The Cradle is dangerous. You have just experienced this—what happens when a Silk Girl and a queen play outside the pretty walls we built for them."

A heavy sigh leaves me.

He continues, "The babies must be kept safe at all costs. No one can know where they are kept. We cannot allow visitors in the nurseries."

His monotone lecture causes my upper lip to curl and a depthless growl to slip through my teeth. With blood or bargain, I will have this. "I am not asking. I am demanding."

"A king demands." Cairo takes me in. "A king claims. Rome, you want to change hundreds of years of law. This is not an easy task."

Volatility prowls inside me. "It won't be the first time a king changes the rules to suit his own interests."

"No." He shakes his head and smiles. "It won't. I saw this conversation. I have been finding it hard to convince myself that the reasons we keep the babes safe apply to you..."

I lift my chin.

"The Estate is the safest place in The Cradle," he states matter-of-factly. "So... For the babes born in The Estate, I do not see why we cannot run a test. See if it is feasible and does not interrupt the flow of production and procedures. We can alter some protocols, add extra measures, extra Guards, and allow the Silk Girls from your Collective visitation rights once a day to spend with the babies."

That will make her smile.

"And in *your* case." He eyes me. "As the heir is known, the safest place is by his father's side. I cannot disagree. This is what I can offer you. What I will approve, no, *support...*"

But then, his pause thickens the air.

"In exchange for something for myself."

Of course.

"I want a succession."

And there it is. His motivation. For fucking the redheaded Silk Girl in The Circle. For his leniency with Aster.

He premeditated this.

Fucker.

Kong's sarcastic inference thunders in my mind. *"What a*

successful campaign, then? It couldn't have gone any better if Cairo had planned it himself."

Cairo must have seen Aster and me in the Parlour the day we met. Paid the Endigo to flip the van, take her, and hold her...

Knowing full well that I was at Breaker Ledge—that I would want to continue my bloodshed from the war, because... He. Knows. Me.

Fuck.

And when I didn't want to breed with her, when I spoke of keeping her as a plaything, he pushed me, fuelling me with jealousy by threatening to give her to another, and made me claim her...

He left The Estate.

Left me to fall in love.

I shake my head, fisting my hands at my sides, reeling in this knowledge.

As always, I do not know whether to be impressed, angry, or thrust my fucking fist through his chest cavity and draw out his pumping heart.

As if reading my thoughts, he says, "You have Aster. Without me, you would not. So when I die, I want my heirs to inherit my Trade."

Never in the history of The Cradle has a Trade Master been granted this; it is incomprehensible. Dangerous. The most powerful person in the game of chess is the player. In The Cradle's present state, The Trade Master is appointed by the lords, keeping us all connected and valued. He is then bestowed phenomenal control—all The Cradle's secrets and the protection of the Shadows.

Luckily, the player changes.

Fortunately, a new Trade Master can be appointed after a natural death. This keeps order in the land. Balance. It keeps us all in check.

He isn't asking for an heir.

He isn't asking for a legacy.

He is asking for *The Cradle.*

I stare at him, my hand twitching to pull that beating organ through his ribcage and watch the blood spurt to the pulse of his dying heart.

"We are twin pillars," he says, pressing. "The Crown and The Trade. That does not change, Sire."

With blood or bargain…

I grit my teeth. "I will speak with the lords. Bled, Medan, Turin Two. I will support your right to a legacy, and they will agree."

"If they do not?"

My brows tighten. "They will."

Cairo nods and turns, walking through the spacious laboratory toward the exit. He pauses with his hand on the sensor. A green light on the wall glows, prefacing a click from inside the security door.

He looks back at me, a smooth smile on his lips. The kind that offers no sentiment, merely confidence. "Did they tell you, Sire? I saved the eagle for you. Odio. He had a wisp of life left, enough for us…" His pause is heavy. "I authorised stem cell rehabilitation, as we did with your lung. We gifted him a titanium metatarsus and ulna and put him in an incubator. When your lung has been properly observed and approved, you will be ready to return to The Estate, and he will be ready to fly above you."

Chapter Eighteen

Aster

Rome is alive.

He is recovering.

But it has been two weeks, and it feels like the days churn, and churn, and churn. Like I am waiting at a closed door, watching it for decades.

I believe the reports we are sent each day from the Trade-tower—he is breathing, he is awake, he will return soon—but my heart won't settle until I see him with my own adoring eyes, until my fingers feel his muscles shudder, until his skin covers mine and radiates warmth...

I roll to the side of his bed, my silky robe sliding over my skin but tight around my swollen belly, and tuck my new book into the drawer.

Han gave it to me.

It is old. The text is small, and it reads like a poem. Odd. Lyrical. Some of the stories are fantastical, others meaningful or completely nonsensical.

Han told me that if I ever wanted to talk about the book, that I could 'come home.'

To the abbey.

I look around Rome's room.

But I am home.

There is a part in the book that reads, 'Even though our outward man is perishing, yet the inward man is being renewed day by day—'

I don't know why, but that snippet reminds me of Rome. Of how he is healing. Day by day. Though, everything I read or see, reminds me of my king. Today, I saw his powerful body striding toward me when I glanced at the courtyard gate during the hour Daisy, Blossom, Ana, and I were given to play with Ana's baby, Cardiff.

I hear his possessive growls each night when I touch myself, failing miserably to reach the pleasure he offers me.

And I sense him inside my womb.

In the Medi-deck, this first-light Paisley told me that the baby is big and strong and as I curl on my side, pulling my knees up, the heir rolls, a limb or shoulder poking out. I poke it back.

It doesn't hurt, *much.*

My back spasms.

But I like the feeling of company, knowing a little piece of my king is here, but it is getting harder to sleep. Harder to relax. I'm hotter. Tighter. The skin around my belly itches and aches.

It does hurt—a little.

I toss and turn, the heir's weight inside me dictating every position and all discomfort. Somewhere between awake and sleep, I hear the door open, feel the bed rock from side to side, and sense... *him.*

"Aster." His nose trails up my throat moments before firm,

warm lips press to mine, demanding I turn my head and accept them.

I moan in my half-conscious state, opening my lips to accept his long, thick tongue.

He tastes good.

So good.

My nipples tighten beneath the silk of my gown, arousal building between my legs as he massages my lips with his.

Wait.

"Rome!" I sit up, cupping my abdomen as the large baby inside me moves like a solid stone pendulum. It is dark in his room, but the maroon-coloured fire casts a glowing light around us, an aura of lusty red.

I blink at him—at Rome—registering the scar on his lower lip, the fragmented blue eyes, and his bare chest carved to angry perfection. It's him. His mouth curves against my startled awe.

My tongue flaps with words; millions of them have been stalking my mind for the past two weeks.

"I thought you died," I manage to say. Happiness floods with old emotions, and tears spit from my eyes. "I thought you died!" My voice pitches higher. "Don't do that. Don't do that again."

"Don't die again?" he asks, amused.

"Don't you laugh at me, Rome of The Strait! I have been all alone! You..." I grab his thick forearm, needing the unyielding pillar to hold myself up. I am so heavy. "You will never do that again. I forbid it. Swear it to me."

He sighs, eyes reverently roaming my face for each detail. "I swear I will never die again, little creature." He humours me.

I beam at him. Hot sweat slides down my forehead. I breathe deep. Dizzy. My body wants to drop backward, tired; my heart wants to leap into his chest, to be with his; my eyes want to take in every new scar, memorise them; my nipples and core want pressure, so much pressure.

Pregnancy.

It's strange.

Demanding.

A potent condition.

Rome's brows pinch, his eyes darting to my swollen stomach. His hands come up, cup either side, covering the entire surface, and cradle the weight. Lift it. Fingers pan out, touching and caressing my tight skin. The baby rolls around, kneading into their father's giant hands.

"Incredible." He grins. "Need me to make amends, sweet creature? Make it all better with my tongue?"

I nod, my lower lip trembling with emotion. "Yes, please, my king."

His eyes darken, menacing intent creeping into the depth of them. "Oh, it's 'my king,' now?"

He leans forward, reaches behind me, forcing me back with his encroaching wall of muscles. The weight of his heir pulls me to my spine, but not before he grabs a pillow and slides it to support my back.

My belly protrudes.

I feel like a blob of custard.

Horrible and vulnerable.

But then his lips meet mine quick, and I forget... "What did you just call me?" The heated words rush along my trembling mouth.

I hesitate. "Rome of The Strait...?"

"You want attention. What happens to your sweet body when you demand attention?"

I swallow as his hot mouth slides down to my chin, sucking and mouthing a trail to my breasts. His tongue flicks my nipple, then treats each sensitive bud through the silk of my gown, wetting the fabric and heating the fibres.

His kiss moves to my stomach.

Moaning, I slide my fingers through his dark hair, the strands parting as my nails drag up and down, up and down.

He shudders and groans. Muscles tremble, vibrating the bed. His chest rumbles—purrs.

My beast.

My king.

Closing my eyes, I simply enjoy the heat of his hands as they travel my skin, exploring and journeying leisurely. Ankle. Leg. Hip.

Between my thighs.

He dips his finger into my core. I immediately arch with a whimper of delirious pleasure. Want it.

Want more.

Deeper.

My body lifts and writhes, missing the depth and thickness of his all-consuming touch.

Hips chasing his finger, I lick my lips and focus on breathing. My lungs are tight.

"Mine," he rasps, crawling between my legs. I spread my thighs. "Wider." His mouth meets the top of my pussy, sucking and licking the coil of nerves while his clever finger slides in and out of me. "Be very cautious with your tone, little creature," he warns, dark and delicious.

My toes curl as he licks and sucks me between his deep utterances. "I may be Rome of The Strait, but you will submit to me. Submit and spread." A second finger slides in. "Adore. Pleasure. Provide. That does not change."

Gasping for air, losing reality to his greedy kiss, I paw the back of his head and lift my pelvis, grinding on him. Grip him. Grind. Not submitting. Demanding. More.

"Oh, you really want attention, huh?"

He rears up to his knees and my heart races, beating so hard inside my heaving chest, as his heated, daring eyes lick up and down my body, hovering over my swollen belly. "You are *so* mine."

Groaning, he undoes his belt and pants.

Rome strips down and fists the heavy, dripping length of his cock, jerking until the crown flushes. "Submitting does not make you inferior to me. It means you respect me. You respect your king. Show me. Show me your respect."

I spread my thighs wider in offering but try to quell my tiny slithers of fear. Having this formidable Xin De King looming over me, stroking the monstrous thing that will be pulsing inside me soon, still intimidates me.

I know he could break me.

He grips the bedframe, and I throw my legs around the back of his thighs. Without any further words, he pushes inside me, stretches me, unfolding me and adding girth that touches and kneads every inch of my channel.

Sobbing with utter relief, I clutch his flanks, holding the powerful muscles as he works his cock in and out of me. Lips graze my forehead. His arm above my head takes his weight, his body rolling against me, brushing the swell of my stomach.

"Is this what you want?" He fills me and empties me, methodical and rhythmic, sending my mind into a haze of bliss and uncertainty.

So deep.

Empty.

So full.

Empty.

"You feel *so* good," he purrs. "You like your king stretching your tight, little pussy open. Don't you, sweet creature?"

Abruptly, he pins me to the pillow by my throat, fingers circling the thin column with ease.

He growls with each thrust.

"Remember your claws, *Aster...*"

When he reminds me of my claws, reinforcing my safety. That he will stop. Listen. I unravel and relax, my insides gripping and grabbing at his hard length.

Then he starts to really move.

Pleasure builds at a relentless pace until I am drowning in its embrace, my entire body awash with it.

"Rome," I cry out.

His cock lengthens within my pulsing core. And he curses, pulls out, throws his head back, and pumps his cum across my stomach, claiming the swollen mound, using his hand. "Aster... I love you. *Fuck me*, Aster, I love you."

I watch the erotic scene, his veined forearms contracting, his fist working every spurt out. "I love you, too, my king."

He drops to his hands on either side of me, creating a frame of muscles around my body. Firm, authoritarian lips move to mine, needing wholesome affection. A kiss.

A kiss from my lover.

From my king.

We both pant into each other's mouths while pleasure lingers and plays a soft encore.

Too soon, he breaks our kiss. Presses his forehead to mine. "Have you been well?" A warm hand touches the mound at my hips. "Is it getting too hard? We can incubate soon."

"I can keep going. A little longer."

"That's my good little Silk Girl." He kisses me once. "You can try, but I will make the call. My heir will survive perfectly fine in the coming months outside your body. You have done such a good job, Aster. And you will respect my decision when it comes. Understand, little creature?"

I nod. "It is only... I am not sleeping well."

He hums, a menacing and depthless sound. "You're working so hard for me. So tired. Let me help my sweet creature get some sleep."

Scooping me up as if I weigh nothing, he lays me on my side, with my pillow, crown to the foot of the bed.

He lies the opposite way.

I squirm. "What are yo—"

My words halt on a moan when he drags my pelvis to his mouth, one thigh to the mattress, one leg slung over his face. In a long, slow stroke, his tongue slides between my folds.

And again.

My skin tingles. He isn't trying to build that wonderful bliss; he is gentle and tender, teasing me with small dips and licks.

He's simply making me feel... *nice.*

I smile and take a big breath.

Rome of The Strait. In like a storm... No longer slipping away like a phantom.

Staying.

CHAPTER NINETEEN

ASTER

"You look like a fertility goddess," Tuscany says, stopping a few paces away from me.

Even after everything we have been through—at the abbey, waiting for Rome to return, mourning Odio—she still keeps space around herself. She seems to draw away from physical touch, whereas I seek it out.

"Thank you." I smile, my cheeks flushing. I disagree, but I refrain from admitting that. A goddess is graceful, airy, and enchanting.

I wobble and pant, even sweat.

I can see why my studies left out this part of the pregnancy journey.

But I am lucky.

I have Meaningful Purpose.

And love.

A perfect gust of wind moves my mauve dress around my body, cooling me and awakening playful bumps along my skin.

Rome comes up behind me; his height lords over me. He

circles a thick arm around my waist, slides his palm beneath my belly, and takes the weight of his heir in one large hand.

I swear my spine literally sighs.

"Better, sweet creature?" His otherworldly stature presses to my back, and I slump against him, my head resting just below his chest.

"I love the roses, my king." I smile softly at the blooming garden, petals unfurling, their posy scent lifting. "But why are we out here?"

"I have someone to show you." His voice slides to the side as he says, "Both of you. I wanted to wait until he was back to his usual self."

Through the gentle rustling of trees, I hear a screech, the thrilling sound creating tangible waves in the atmosphere. They reach inside me and snatch air straight from my lungs, leaving me gasping.

"It can't be…"

My pulse kicks into a rhythm that's anything but regular when massive black wings rise from behind the limestone building ahead like waves bursting from a steady blue sea.

The majestic eagle soars toward me. Happiness and confusion cripple me to the point where I am speechless.

"What? How?" I shake my head, remembering that detached absence in his gaze. "But I saw his eyes. They were open and lifeless, and his legs were curled… He was dead. Upside-down."

"It might have appeared that his eyes were open, but that's his nictitating membrane, little creature." Rome steps in front of me, casting me in his shadow. "His eyes were closed. At least one of his eyelids was." He feeds his hand between the curtain of my hair and neck, gripping me, reassuring me. "I couldn't feel his breath." The memory darkens his gaze. "I could hardly feel my own."

Showing off for me, Odio soars above my head, twirling and screeching through the haze, the fierce waves of his voice deafening. Disappearing into the red distance, only to reappear, opening up the sky like a black lightning bolt.

Yes, handsome boy, you're very scary.

I know what I saw… "But—"

"The Trade still use Gene Therapies, Aster," Tuscany says, capturing my attention with that terrifying declaration.

Therapies?

She means engineering.

Suddenly Ana's use of the word *treatments* echoes in my ears. "Bu- But engineering is illegal. It has been for…" I don't know why I bother questioning it. Am I that naïve? The knowledge is there in text and the technology is available and centralised by The Trade. Of course they use it to save lives…

Hopefully, that's its only Purpose.

Tuscany turns to face me. "Its use is strictly controlled." Lovely, straight, honey-coloured hair dances across her eyes as she looks up at her brother. "Rome, I want to go on a campaign to visit The Cradle. I want to visit the Trades and thank them for their service. To meet the children in the nurseries and listen to stories. To be a queen and mother, as I was born for. Born For Marble."

Her demand dissects the conversation.

And I am quite pleased it does.

"You waited until Aster was here to ask me this?" Rome's brows tighten above his blue gaze. "I thought you would retire thi—"

"Please." She lifts her hand. "I do not wish to argue. I have never fulfilled my Purpose. I would like to try. I did not break apart at the compound. I did not disappear. I was not entirely brave, but I would like the opportunity to try again. Will you allow me to try again?"

I look between them, watching Rome stare at her; his angry rebuttals and fears for her safety are dark phantoms pulsing beneath his tight jaw.

Then he finally says, "You will take Kong."

She closes her eyes on a heavy sigh, relief gushing from her lips. "I have my Army, Sire."

Clasping his hands in front of him, his face smooths to

infallible severity. "You will take Kong. We will not discuss this further. He knows The Cradle. The ruins. And he will die for you."

"Kong is *your* Guardian."

Rome laughs, husky and deep. "He has never been my Guardian, sweet sister. Not since I was young. He has always been yours."

While they talk, Odio lands at my side like a puff of black smoke, demanding my attention.

"So you will allow it then?" she says. "If I agree to have Kong accompany me?"

Odio approaches me, a long step at a time. I ignore their discussions, captivated by a black angel.

"Hello, handsome boy." Tears pool in my eyes. "I mourned you. That was very rude of you. Do not do that again." When I reach out my hand, hesitantly, slowly, he steps straight into my palm.

"I will," Rome says to Tuscany.

My fingers ruffle Odio's crest; his feathers clap like trees in the wind, and inside his chest, he purrs with enjoyment.

Extending a long, fluffy leg, he steps even closer, until he can practically wrap his wings around my body. Dropping his line of sight to my belly, he uses his beak to tap the mound, then draws patterns along the swollen surface. Almost as though he is searching for—

Then the baby in my belly pushes against his beak, halting Odio's meandering. A limb or foot warps my belly, shoving it outward.

"They are not yours, Odio!" Rome states, his attention now on Odio and me, his voice a velvety growl of authority.

My handsome boy cranes his neck, growing to nearly my height. His eyes narrow in defiance, locked on his king, seconds before he digs his beak into his wing and prunes his feathers. One at a time. As if he is sharpening knives in warning.

Rome grits out, "Attitude. Nice to see you're back to your usual obstinance."

A deep rumble vibrates through the air as my king presses his front to my back again, just as Odio takes to the skies. The hairs on my arms rise, the breeze is perfect—conditioned—just like all of us.

Tuscany steps to leave, saying, "I will see you both at mealtime," but stops. "Oh, Aster, I almost forgot—"

I look at her.

"Ana is going to join my Army of lovely ladies. She can visit any time you like, but I very much wish to take her with me when I travel The Cradle in the coming months. If she accepts; I would never force her. I know Ana will miss playing with her baby, but she was very loyal to you in the abbey. I believe she will be excellent at this new Trade."

I nod quickly because I agree. "Thank you."

She smiles, but it doesn't meet her eyes. A smile rarely creeps that far into Tuscany's soul. "No, thank you."

She peels away from us.

"If we have a girl." I arch my neck, gazing directly up to see Rome's possessive stare already on me. As if the top of my crown is far prettier than the roses ahead of us. "Can I name her London? Like the old-world city?"

He smiles; it is a soft one just for me. "As long as that name makes you smile while you greet her each first-light and beckon her to bed each last-light. You will be using that name daily."

That makes me beam.

He means she—or he—will always be with me. Every day. Another reassurance that our children will be raised around these gardens, picking the roses as Odio maps a grid of protection above them.

As we look out over the manicured hill, birds take flight from the unwelcoming forest trees, only to hover just below the threatening Redwind, and I consider *my* upside-down bird. The lost girl with the honey hair, the boy with the bird he wanted to stroke, and Odio.

My mind dives into the reverie of the baby bird at every chance. It is a hazy memory now but somehow crystal clear.

Finding something more vulnerable than myself, in a perfectly conditioned environment, flicked a switch inside me, even at that young age. It made me realise how insignificant we all are. In The Cradle. The Crust.

I have been looking for meaning in this recurring memory for as long as I can remember, but what if there is no meaning.

Just random events.

And my reactions to them.

My upside-down bird is my first question. Maybe I was never meant to have any? My first, what happened and why? And despite my conditioning, this hiccup in my world began an indefinite reel of curiosity.

Curiosity is not a virtue.

Neither is love…

But I feel them anyway.

THE END

A Silk Girl's
Third Trimester

EPILOGUE

In the courtyard, I pace outside the Silk Girl Wing, where the finest doctor in The Cradle prepares Aster for her caesarean.

The grass below my feet is already burnt-umber from the friction of my powerful gait.

Back and forth.

Back and forth.

Glaring at the door.

"Hurry. Open up. Sire is going to kill someone, and I am the only one out here." Turin Two stands by the locked door, watching me, amused by my utter dishevelment.

Fucker.

It happened so fast; I was playing with her sweet body, and she started screaming in pain, clutching her back as it spasmed, and that was that.

I needed the heir out.

I wasn't prepared, so I'm bare-chested, pants barely clinging to my hips without underwear. I thrust my hands through my hair, muscles bubbling with discomfort. The blood on my forearms catches my eye, gripping at my flesh, drying to a shell of crimson.

Odio...

Growling, I glare up at him. It is his fucking fault I am not inside with her as I should be.

Above me, Odio has carved a line through the Redwind, leaving a streak in the wake of his darting form.

Left to right.

His head is angled downwards and his keen eyes are like arrows searching for a target. And I am ready to catch him before he dives for the person who opens that fucking door.

He wouldn't let the Trade doctors touch her. I had to stay outside and wrestle with his talons; my forearms snaked in blood from the altercation. I tried to sedate him, but he dodged all my tranquilliser darts.

Fucker.

His distress floods the atmosphere above me, and nothing is more dangerous than the fear of losing someone you love.

I should know.

I feel feral.

"She will be fine, Sire," Turin Two consoles, and my sharp stare hits him as if his words are unwelcome. They are not. I only have one feeling—volatile—and that cannot be calmed, soothed, or—

A click comes from the door.

Turin Two inhales hard and pushes it open, lunging into the building, but not before Odio descends like a giant shadow, the sound of his sudden decline a riotous clap of feathers.

I reach the door just as the winged giant does, turn around, and bulk to my full size, blocking the entrance. "Not yours, Odio!"

A screech punishes me and the air, and I swear I hear profanity in it. When I don't move, he takes off shrieking, the sound assaulting the atmosphere, and returns to cut a red line in the sky above her wing.

I walk inside and close the back door.

EPILOGUE

ASTER

I have only ever seen him like this once.

And that was at the abbey.

There is something incredibly stirring about my Xin De King —a being so huge, hard and sharp, skin sliced and stitched, arms threaded with veins so prominent they could have their own angry intent— appearing fearful and anxious.

He strides across the surgical chamber where the doctor is already opening my abdomen, a storm brewing behind his blue gaze, and I reach out my hand to him.

"My king." I breathe, smiling softly.

"Pain?" He punches the word out as if it took every ounce of strength to get it through his teeth.

"None. The doctor used La Mu before the spinal needle. I feel floaty."

La Mu isn't something available to the general citizens of The Cradle. The wrong dose or part of the plant, can shrivel veins like a flaming bloom. The right part, in the correct dosage, can make you float and hum. Rome and I use it a lot when he takes me from behind, and I enjoy it so much more than I thought I would.

He presses my hand to his bare chest. Warm muscular skin shifts beneath my touch. I span my finger out, using the tips to stroke him, to calm him. Feeling the heavy beat of his heart, I smile because it is about to double in size.

He often says, 'It only beats for you'. *For me.* That I am a single strand woven through every cell of his humanity, but that is about to change.

I won't be the only strand.

I gaze across to the internal viewing glass where Tuscany, Paisley, and my Collective—Daisy, Ana, and Blossom— await, eyes wide with excitement mixed with concern.

A soft smile meets my lips. I mouth, "You're next," sharing the silent message between Blossom and Daisy.

Standing behind them, Lord Turin Two offers me privacy, but his furrowed brows reveal his anticipation.

This is his heir, too.

The quiet room is punctured by the sound of medical equipment and soft conversation between the Trade doctor and nurse.

My lower half feels heavy, warm, and numb, but for the occasional tugging and pulling. It isn't a natural sensation. It feels as if someone is controlling my body.

A tear forms in the corner of my eye, adrenaline spiking despite the La Mu.

"Pain?" The word threatens the room, his gaze tracking the tear as it slides down my cheek.

"No." I flex my hand on his chest reassuringly. "Emotional, my king. That is all."

The silence that follows could cut the room in two. His eyes seem unable to split from mine while we wait. I study his expression. It is not simply fear but helplessness. To see this titan of a man showing glimpses of helplessness makes me squirm...

Then...

A cry pierces the room.

And his fixed gaze darts toward his heir. His blue eyes become so wide I can practically see the immediate surge of affection flooding them.

Smiling through a heavy exhale, I peer down in time to see the doctor swaddling our baby in a purple cloth.

He presents the babe to Rome, and I smile, but Rome says, "No. Give the baby to Aster."

A slither of sadness courses through me, but I ignore it. I understand. He will get there. He will be ready when he is ready.

I bundle the babe to my chest, my vision overwhelmed by a face made of ivory and cherries. And dark, open eyes, gazing up at me, reflecting the same wonder I feel inside all two billion of my heart cells.

"Hello…" I pause. "What's the gender?"

"A boy." The doctor announces. "The heir of The Cradle."

His declaration raises hairs along my arms, sending skitters of significance through me.

I have Meaningful Purpose.

And you, sweet babe, are to reign.

Studying the flawless being, I shrug a little with an apology. "You're not London. I don't have a name for you yet, little babe."

"Athens."

I like it. I gaze at Rome, drawn to his choked tone, but a gasp fills my throat when I see glistening blue eyes, undeniably full of emotion. And I thought my king had no tear ducts.

Suddenly, my chest is so full it is hard to breathe. "Are you sure you don't want to hold him, my king? He smells divine."

He straightens, eyes lapping us. "No."

"*Please*, Rome."

"Are you done?"

I smile at Athens. "Never."

"Then, no. I will wait."

Uncertainty nests inside my mind, so I blink up at Rome again. Why is he being so withdrawn? His body is stiff, like a statue, one twitch and a crack will race through his stony centre.

But his eyes...

His eyes glisten with truth.

"Why?" I press. "Why won't you hold him?"

And then he says, "I doubt I'll want to let him go once he is in my arms, sweet creature. It is unbearable each first-light to let you go."

Sighing, I couldn't feel more... More *anything*. I barely recognise his voice. It's deep and *gushing*, and I swallow, trying to force the happy tears down, blinking my blurring vision away. I want to see his face. Want to see him hold our son.

"All done," the doctor says—I'd almost forgotten he was in the room, too enraptured by Athens. And Rome.

The room empties.

"Here." I edge the bundle toward Rome with my elbow. "I want you to hold him."

Clearing his throat, he taps my nose and tries to quell all the heavy emotions I see sinking into his azure gaze. Handing Athens to Rome, I watch as the bundle fits entirely in his two palms.

"Incredible," he mutters, eyeing Athens, awe-struck, and Athens equally as engrossed. "You are going to do great things, my boy."

I almost feel Rome's heart expand as the most vulnerable of things is literally held in the palms of his giant hands. In the warm, possessive hold of a man more beast than human, built to reign, to rule The Cradle, through fear and intimidation. Surely, holding a baby isn't nearly as significant as his great Purpose.

THE END

Aster and Rome have a Happily Ever After, but what about our

Queen of The Cradle? All the books in this series are age-gap and size-difference and can be read as standalones.

Up next:

Born For Lace

A grumpy Xin Den named Lagos The Rogue, and a sweet Lace Girl from the Half-tower named Dahlia. **PreOrder**

Born For Marble

A love-sick Xin De Guardian named Kong The Unbreakable, and a broken Queen named Tuscany Of The Strait. **PreOrder**

CRADLED COMMON NEXT UP! YOU MIGHT RECOGNISE A NAME HERE...

Don't like Facebook?
Join my newsletter

An Urban Legend From The Cradle

Endigos like to tell stories around the fire...

Here one goes:

As no one living has ever seen the Missing Moon or the stars, many do not believe that there is a giant rock in the sky surrounded by twinkling lights.

Legend has it, that the moon is actually the face of an evil spirit that watches all. And if you ever see the face, even for a second while the Redwind parts, it will see you, too, and enter your body.

It will use your body to kill children and scoop out their eyes. As children's eyes glow and sparkle. The Missing Moon will then take the eyes back to the sky. But soon, the sparkle in the children's eyes will go out and so the Moon will watch again, until someone looks back, so it can collect more eyes.

Don't look for the Missing Moon.

ACKNOWLEDGEMENTS & EXTRAS

The Cradled Common is a **ROMANCE series**, first and foremost. It is spicy, romantic, and wild.

But…

Here are some thanks and extras and ramblings on The Cradle.

Firstly, I want to thank my husband, **Ed Napoleao**, for spending hours and hours… and hours researching past empires, historical events, and genetic engineering, to help create this dystopian world with me.

And for offering his own personal experiences…

My husband is the first generation born from refugees escaping a war with decades of genocide and guerilla warfare that went nearly undocumented.

They are still picking up the pieces.

You have probably never even heard of his country.

<u>This happened in our life time.</u>

His perspective on creating and building The Cradle is invaluable. And we have so much more to unravel the further we enter The Cradle with each book.

It is rooted in science, and explores technologies, most of which exists today in rudimentary forms, but are not legal.

It also plays with mythology. The Cradle holds on to real world physics—mostly—and delves into our need as a species for a spiritual connection.

For...

Purpose.

Religion.

Love.

Power.

It is not meant to confirm or deny any spiritual or religious ideologies.

The Cradled Common series is mankind at the end and the beginning of humanity.

It is **completely fictional** but draws inspiration from past empires, world wars, guerilla warfare, and civil unrests.

The things I learnt... **WOW.**

Mankind has a very corrupt history.

I want to thank **Margot Swan** for putting up with all my crazy. I could not have done this without you!

I really mean that.

And **Nat Dune**, you wave a Nicci flag high for all to see. You are always available, and one of the only people I trust with my unpolished manuscript.

Thank you, buddy.

Nicci Who?

Nicci is an Amazon number 1 best-selling author in Women's Crime Fiction, Organised Crime, Romantic Er0tica, and Romantic Suspense.

Nicci is from Perth, Western Australia. She has lived many lives. Vet Nurse. Journalist. Barista. Corporate Sales Consultant. Mother.

Now she is a fulltime author, and she lives even more lives. Mafia Don. Ballerina. Doctor. Biker. CEO. Concert Pianist, to name a few.

She considers herself an independent woman... BUT all that womanly power goes out the window when her red flag-waving, morally grey heroes appear on page...

She writes about men who kill, who control, who take their women like it's their last breath, pinning them down and whispering "good girl" and "mine" and "you belong to me" and all the red flag utterances that would have most independent women rolling their eyes so hard they see their brains.

So... if you don't like that... if you don't like reading about controlling, over the top possessive men... then don't read her books. You won't like them. But Nicci wants both. She wants her cake and to have a six-foot-five, tattooed, alphamale to eat it with her.

facebook.com/authornicciharris

amazon.com/author/nicciharris

bookbub.com/authors/nicci-harris

goodreads.com/nicciharris

instagram.com/author.nicciharris

STALK ME...

Stalk me.

Meet other fans on Facebook.
Join Harris's Harem of Dark Romance Lovers
Stalk us.

Don't like Facebook?
Join my newsletter

facebook.com/authornicciharris
amazon.com/author/nicciharris
bookbub.com/authors/nicci-harris
goodreads.com/nicciharris
instagram.com/author.nicciharris

Made in the USA
Middletown, DE
12 September 2024

60872898R00265